# The Sunflower Experience

## RHONDA MUMBY

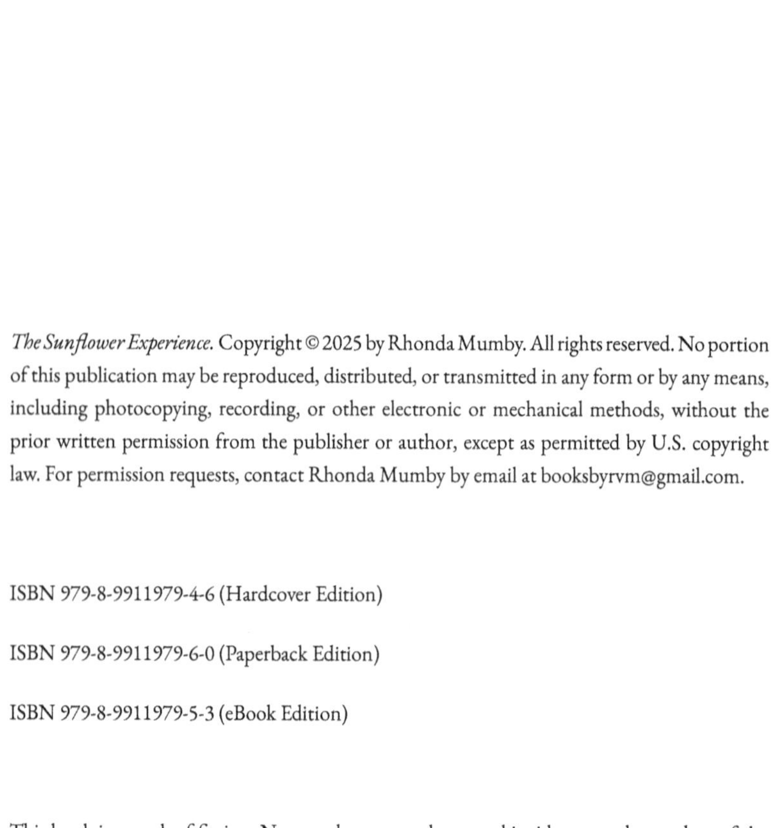



ISBN 979-8-9911979-4-6 (Hardcover Edition)

ISBN 979-8-9911979-6-0 (Paperback Edition)

ISBN 979-8-9911979-5-3 (eBook Edition)

This book is a work of fiction. Names, characters, places, and incidents are the product of the author's imagination or are used fictitiously. Any resemblance to actual events, locales, persons (living or deceased), or products is coincidental.

Book cover by 100 Covers.

First edition 2025

*Scan the code for The
Sunflower Experience
Spotify Playlist*

Trigger warnings:

If you are a reader who feels trigger warnings are akin to spoiler alerts, feel free to skip this section.

If you are a reader who lives and dies by trigger warnings, please read carefully:

This book contains themes of recovering from alcohol addiction, including revisiting past incidents, detailed descriptions of a car accident and near drowning, detailed descriptions of sexual activities, mention of a side characters' cheating spouse, traumas dealing with anaphylactic shock, emergency care for an injured child with detailed injury description, and themes of a side character child with a life-threatening condition.

There is also unfair cookie abuse.

To all those who find a little magic in the majesty of sunsets and seas of
vibrant flowers.
May you find your own special moments of connection with another
soul.

# Contents

# Chapter 1
# Shoplifters, Half-Naked Men, and Other Disasters

**Everleigh**

"Girl, you know I look good."[1] Crestin struck a pose in front of the three-panel mirror beside the fitting rooms as he ran his fingertips along the brim of a bright pink cowboy hat. He threw an equally bright pink chiffon scarf across his right shoulder and shifted his pose, pushing one shoulder forward and resting his chin on it.

Everleigh couldn't keep a laugh from escaping. *This* was why she loved him. Aside from being the first person in school who'd actually struck up a conversation with her when she moved here two years ago, Crestin was all attitude and vibrant energy that could not be contained. You could say she was jealous of her best friend and his ability to talk to anyone, to make anyone smile, to put anyone in their place if the situation called for it. And his ability to make it seem like being yourself was the easiest thing in the world? That's what she envied the most. For example, he was currently clad in a loud Hawaiian shirt, a pair of army green cargo pants, and white flip-flops—an outfit now accentuated with the pink cowboy hat, pink scarf, and two large turquoise rings he'd placed on his right hand for good measure. One would think with his tall, burly frame

---

1. Chappell Roan, "Good Luck, Babe!"

such a fashion statement would look ridiculous. But he was completely pulling it off.

Everleigh glanced from her bestie to the group of older women milling about the clearance rack, looking up from time to time at Crestin's antics. She knew if she were in his flip-flops at this particular moment, all she would be thinking about—worrying about, really—was the judgy thoughts those ladies might be voicing about her to one another.

"Come on. Admit it." Crestin strutted over to her and folded his arms on the glass countertop, tilting his head to give her what he claimed was his best side and forming his full lips into a pout. "I look amazing in this hat."

She loosed another laugh as she looked down on him from the raised platform behind the counter. His thick, dark hair curled out around the bottom of the hat, framing his light brown skin. "You really do. You should buy it."

A tortured sigh expanded in the air around them. "But I don't have any money."

Everleigh gave him a long, sympathetic shrug before she looked toward the front of the store to check on the group of ladies once more.

"Could you hide it under the counter for me until I can buy it?" At her hesitation, he clasped his hands on her forearms and begged, "Pleeeeease?"

"I'm really not supposed to. You know that, Crestin."

"But it's the only one left!"

"I'm sure Marla can order another one when you have the money."

Crestin dragged the hat from his head and held it in both hands. His thick, dark brows furrowed over intense brown eyes, channeling all his drama class training as he pleaded, "But I absolutely *cannot* go see Chappell Roan without this hat! It's too unfair to my Pink Pony Midwest Princess for me to show up without this tribute to her artistry."

*This* was why he'd earned a scholarship to acting school in New York. One more thing for Everleigh to be jealous of: his ability to make you feel whatever it was he wanted you to feel. Which was currently a great despair at the thought of Crestin going to a Chappell Roan concert sans the outfit of his dreams. She chewed on the inside of her mouth for a second before she snapped out of it.

"I'm sorry, Crestin," she said gently as she lifted the hat from his hands. "Maybe you should get a J-O-B?"

"I *do* have a J-O-B," he responded petulantly.

"Since when?" Everleigh was certain if he had a job, she would have been the first one to know.

"Well, not until August, you know."

She squinted her eyes.

"The Sunflower Experience." Her best friend said it like she should have known all along.

"But that's, like, for two weeks two months from now."

"Yes, it's ten or so days, weather permitting. And it's less than a month and a half from now."

Amusement laced her voice. "Well, come back then, and I'm sure the hat will still be here." Everleigh set the cowboy hat on the counter to her right for restocking when she had a free moment. "I've got to go check on our real customers."

Despite Crestin's loud scoff and dramatic flourish at her departure from their conversation, she knew she hadn't truly affected him.

"Maybe I'll just borrow it until then," he muttered as he reached around the counter for the hat.

"Crestin Rafael Domingo, I know your mother!" rang out, just as Everleigh was spinning around to ask him what he thought he was doing. Her boss, Marla Youngbear, had entered from the back office, finger waggling at him. "And you, Everleigh Dawn Wilson, aiding and abetting."

Everleigh's heart constricted. She never got into trouble. And now her friend was getting her into trouble. In truth, he was the main reason any time she almost got into trouble. But that was always *almost*.

Marla stepped up, one hand pushing her long black hair behind her shoulder while the other stretched, palm up, in front of him. Although she stood a good head and a half shorter than Crestin, she was a formidable presence. A no-nonsense kind of woman who ran a tight ship knowing she had to be a shrewd businesswoman to maintain the long-term success of her dream boutique, Fashionably Rustic, in such a small community. Kind and well-liked by many in and around the town, Marla was stern when it came to her operations. Crestin obediently placed the hat in her hand.

"You can go ahead," she looked at Everleigh as she nodded toward the women watching them from their station at the clearance rack.

Worrying the corner of her lip between her teeth again, Everleigh felt the dread of the conversation to come later with her boss. She tried to shove the unease aside and focus on the ladies in front of her. "Can I get anyone a dressing room?"

But anxiety flared as she glanced over to see Marla marching Crestin back to her office, him flourishing the pink scarf and his turquoise-ringed hands as he protested every step of the way.

⚘ ⚘

Could her day get any worse? First, her best friend was caught attempting to shoplift, and all she could think about was how Marla probably called the cops on him. And what punishment was waiting to be doled out to her? Everleigh hadn't seen Marla in the hour since the incident, so of course she feared the worst. Which kept her mind so preoccupied she rang up a clearance sweater for full price, causing the customer to be understandably angry with her. Then she dropped four denim jackets on another customer while using the clothes hook pole to get one from a high rack, and now . . .

Now, just as she knocked over a jewelry display in the middle of the store, sending accessories skittering about the tile floor, a group of boys not much older than her entered Fashionably Rustic.

"Shit!" A rare curse flew out under her breath. She scrambled to set the display back on the table and gather up the scattered bracelets and earrings.

To her surprise, one of the boys knelt beside her. Noah Koeppen. She recognized him from the hardware store across the square.

"Let me help," he offered.

Embarrassment eclipsed any gratitude she had for his assistance, and she remained mute, trying ineffectively to scoop as many earrings as possible into her shaking hands. Thankful she'd worn her hair down today, she dipped her head so the curtain of brunette waves helped hide her flushed cheeks. A shadow fell over them, and Everleigh glanced up to see Noah's friend watching them with a smirk on his face.

But not just any face, she realized while a pit formed in her stomach. No, that face belonged to Ryker Martin. The strong jaw, the angular nose and chiseled cheekbones, the dark brown hair falling across his forehead. Her gaze met his gleaming amber eyes for the briefest moment before the smirk fell from his mouth and he walked away.

"I think that's all of them," Noah said as he placed the last pieces of jewelry up on the table. "Here, let me take some of those," he offered, holding his hands out for Everleigh to drop some of the pieces from her overflowing hands into his.

Still trying to understand what that look on Ryker's face had meant, Everleigh didn't realize she was staring blankly at Noah until he bumped his cupped hands into hers.

"Uh, yeah. Thanks," she managed as she shook her hands over his until her load was much more manageable.

They stood at the same time, knocking shoulders, which caused Everleigh to lose her balance. Noah dropped his handful on the table in a clatter just in time and reached out, steadying her on her feet.

"Oh, sorry. I'm so sorry," he rushed out. He guided her hands over the table to safely deposit the remaining jewelry on top.

Nervous laughter escaped her throat at the pure embarrassment of this whole debacle. "It's fine. No worries. Thanks for your help." She wiped her hand across her brow and brushed her long hair behind her ear.

"Do you need me to help . . . put it all back on the display?"

"Oh, no. I've got it from here. But thank you. For the offer."

Noah flashed a relieved smile. "Okay, good. Because I wouldn't know the first thing about . . ." He waved his hands in front of the display. ". . . arranging jewelry."

She softly laughed again, this time at how he'd put her at ease, using a little self-deprecating humor to lighten the situation. Noah was only a year older than her and had graduated last year. She'd never moved in his circle in school, but he was well known as a nice guy. Rather than attending college, he chose to work in his family's hardware store, a staple on the downtown square in the small town of Rustic.

"No worries," she reiterated.

"Okay." [2] He lingered, his jade green eyes alternating between her and the mess of jewelry on the table. Everleigh couldn't help but notice Ryker over Noah's shoulder, standing next to his other friends. They were actively searching through the rack of branded alcohol T-shirts, but his gaze appeared to be trained on her and Noah, an unreadable expression on his handsome face. Weird.

Noah pulled her attention back when he said something she didn't catch.

"Hmm?"

---

2. Dayglow, "Close to You"

Suddenly, he was the one appearing embarrassed. "Ah, never mind. Never mind," he responded quickly, dragging a hand through his dark hair.

Not knowing what else to do in this utterly awkward moment, Everleigh cleared her throat and turned her attention to replacing the earrings on the display case. When Noah continued to loiter, she glanced up and said a hasty, "Thanks again," then refocused on the task at hand. Out of the corner of her eye, however, she saw him nod and give a little smile before returning to his friends.

Pushing away any thoughts about what that entire exchange meant, Everleigh thought only about getting the bracelets and earrings back in their proper locations. The cleanup was completed in mere minutes. She placed the last bracelet on the display just as one of the boys came up to her with a stack of jeans and shirts in his arms.

"Can I try these on?"

"Sure. Follow me."

Everleigh led Johnny (she thought that was his name) back to the fitting room. There shouldn't have been anybody back there because the store had been empty before their group came in, but she knocked on the first door as a safety precaution before unlocking it. Pausing for a beat, she inserted the key in the lock and opened the door wide.

And this bad day just got worse.

To her horror, there *was* someone already in the dressing room. She gasped in surprise. And then . . . she stared. Because the initial shock of finding someone in a room you thought was empty could be quickly replaced with fascination when faced with the broad-shouldered, muscular perfection of Ryker Martin. In his form-fitting boxer briefs and his miles of abs from just below his firm pecs all the way down to his—

"Excuse me?" Ryker said, holding a pair of jeans in his hand as he turned fully toward Everleigh.

Johnny's belly laugh rang out behind her. "Bro! Put some clothes on!"

"That's kind of what I'm trying to do." Ryker directed a pointed look at Everleigh.

"I'm *so, so* sorry! I knocked."

"And I said, 'Occupied'."

"You did?" Everleigh certainly didn't think she'd heard anything when she knocked. Ryker looked over her shoulder for confirmation from Johnny, who simply held his armful of clothes and cackled.

Ryker must have realized she was highly distracted by his mostly nakedness because he hugged the waist of the jeans to his chest, effectively obscuring her view. Except for those flexing shoulders and bulging biceps folded across his chest. Everleigh noticed the tattoo ink stretching across the taut muscles of his left upper arm before her wandering eyes were pulled back to his face.

"So, can I have the room?" he asked, perfectly sculpted, dark eyebrows raised.

Jarred back to reality, a giant wave of embarrassment crashed over Everleigh when she noticed the look of disdain plastered on Ryker's face. "Sorry. Of course." Quickly pulling the door closed, she took a breath to reset then led Johnny two doors down and knocked twice this time, waiting extra long for a response before she slowly opened the door.

As she rounded the corner to the main floor, her stomach dropped at the sight of Marla behind the register. Marla had to have been the one who assigned Ryker a dressing room. And Everleigh again wondered if Crestin had been carted off to jail. No police had entered the store, but Marla likely would have had them come through the back to avoid alarming the customers or causing unnecessary gossip in their small town. The boutique had suddenly gotten busy, so Everleigh would have to wait until traffic died down to find out his fate. And likely, she'd find out her fate as well. Unless her boss made her work the whole shift before firing her at the end.

Marla was busy arranging new belt buckles and tie tacks in the display beneath the glass countertop as Everleigh passed. She decided to check the jewelry display once more just to make sure she'd put everything back correctly. Marla didn't know about that debacle and hopefully wouldn't find out.

"Girl, you opened the dressing room door on Ryker?"

Everleigh jumped at the sound of Crestin's voice in her ear. She finished untangling two bracelets on the display before she turned her full attention to him. Wearing that pink cowboy hat. "Crestin! What the—"

"I know, right?" He lifted his hands and placed the heels of his palms together under his face. The picture of angelic innocence.

"Well, I'm relieved to know you haven't been arrested for shoplifting or banned from the store. Do tell, how is that?"

"You think Miss Marla Youngbear would have yours truly arrested? She knows I would never steal anything. She merely presented me with an opportunity to earn the hat."

Everleigh choked on air. So loudly Noah cast a glance over at her.

"Good *God*. Not like that. You do know who I am," Crestin scoffed in reproach, giving her a look.

She waited patiently for him to continue.

"All those stacks of overstock clothes and clearance that didn't sell in the back? She had me sort it all into seasons and box it up. Then, we loaded the boxes in her truck and hauled it all over to the Community Closet. Rather than pay me for my labor, she paid me in this fabulous cowboy merch. Pretty sweet deal, if you ask me. You know how I love sorting and organizing, so it really wasn't work." He threw in, like an afterthought, "And I love community service."

"To be fair, it's community service if you volunteer, not earn something for your labor. And I'm pretty sure Marla gets the credit as it's *her* merchandise that was donated."

"Would you like to take my tiara as well? Jeez," Crestin grumbled but immediately returned to his bubbly self. "Back to the Ryker thing. Dish."

"There's nothing to dish. I accidentally opened the door to an occupied dressing room."

Crestin waited, folding his arms across his chest.

"And he was literally almost naked."

Crestin swooned and fanned himself.

"What? Stop it. It was totally embarrassing." She turned her attention to the display once more, verifying for the last time that every piece was in its place. "And it happened right after I spilled this display all over the floor. God, this day cannot get any worse." Everleigh's eyes snapped to Crestin's. "Wait. How did you hear about it?"

"Oh, I overheard him and Johnny talking about it over in the rooms as I was headed up from the back." At her horror-stricken face, he rushed on, "I mean, no, honey. Not like that. It was nothing, really. Johnny was just razzing Ryker about flexing his muscles for you and whatnot."

Her blush deepened. She stood corrected—this day had just gotten worse.

"Girl." Crestin jumped into bestie mode and nearly hugged her. "It's not a big deal. Don't even worry about it, Evs."

She allowed him to rub her back for all of two seconds before Marla called for help at the register. A line was forming. Everleigh joined her behind the counter and bagged the merchandise so her boss could continue the current transaction.

When Johnny stepped up to the counter with his stack of clothes, Everleigh's stomach twisted.

"Did anyone help you today?" Marla asked the standard question.

Johnny burst into laughter as he pointed. Marla appeared stunned at his response then shifted her gaze to Everleigh, who quickly shrugged her shoulder and focused on finding a bag large enough for all the clothes.

Thankfully, Marla chose to ignore his behavior, no doubt chalking it up to his youth, and rang up his purchase.

The next customer was Noah, who carried the awkward vibe from earlier into this interaction as well. Except he seemed to be studying Everleigh more intently than before. She dropped her eyes and focused on folding and bagging clothes until the end, when she allowed a smile as she handed over his bag. He could have grabbed it without touching her hand, so when he grazed his fingers along hers, it seemed very purposeful. And he directed his smile at her rather than Marla when the latter handed him back his debit card. Everleigh's gaze shifted over Noah's shoulder to where Crestin was chatting with Ryker near the fitting rooms entrance. Worry about their conversation immediately blossomed in her chest.

Granted, Crestin had two years of high school with Ryker, having been a freshman when Ryker was a junior. And he'd worked at The Sunflower Experience, which was on the Martin family farm, for three years now. He knew Ryker in a way Everleigh didn't. By the summer she'd moved here—when her dad's job with the railroad was transferred to Rustic, Iowa—Ryker had already graduated high school. And she knew he attended college somewhere. So, the only time she saw him was during school breaks when he came to town or at a party here and there. And although Crestin always made a point to say hi to him, Everleigh always remained stuck in her self-conscious, self-doubting thoughts, never contributing to the conversation. Until today, she'd never said one word to him. Even though she was certain he'd greeted her either with a head nod or a "hi" whenever she tagged along with Crestin. Why couldn't she just bring herself to talk to him?

Oh, that's right: Because he was broody and gorgeous and twenty and a college athlete. And she was certain she was nothing compared to what he'd seen out in the world.

"If you've got this, I'm going to grab us some salads for lunch." Marla pulled Everleigh from her consuming thoughts with a general wave of her hand over the store.

Everleigh nodded. "Thanks." She recognized the weight that had been lifted off her shoulders once her best friend had reappeared safe and sound. And Marla clearly held no lingering concern over the near-shoplifting incident.

The shop had mostly emptied. Johnny and their other friend—Tyson, maybe?—were waiting on the sidewalk outside. Noah still hovered in the boutique, near the door, occasionally glancing her way. She thought he might want her to come over and talk, but since Marla had left and Ryker still had those clothes in his hands, she had a reason to stay near the register. She busied herself by tidying the bags and putting empty hangers on the hanger rack behind her.

His presence prickled the hairs on the back of her neck before she heard him.

"So, I changed my mind."

Everleigh spun around, her expectant eyes staring. Changed his mind . . . ?

"I'm not getting these after all." With an exceptionally broody look in his amber eyes and a tense jaw, Ryker set the two pairs of jeans and three shirts on the counter.

"Oh. Okay."

He paused a beat, looking like he wanted to say something, but turned his attention to Noah, who had suddenly appeared beside him. Not wanting to let Ryker out of her orbit just yet, Everleigh spoke up.

"I'm sorry. About earlier. I can't apologize enough for invading your privacy like that. I'm a terrible person."

*Why did she just say that last bit?*

Ryker's expression softened, and he offered a slight, close-lipped smile. She thought he might say something else when Noah slung his long arm around Ryker's shoulders and joked, "Just don't let it happen again. My boy here likes his privacy."

Just then, Johnny whipped open the front door so fast the bell clattered obnoxiously against it, making Everleigh jump.

"You ready? I'm starved," Johnny called.

"Coming," Noah called back. He locked his gaze on hers once more. "See ya around, Everleigh."

Recovering from the jump-scare, she smiled at them then watched as they walked away, still longing for more interaction with Ryker.

"Tea for two," Crestin said conspiratorially as he leaned on the counter. He motioned for her to come closer even though the store was now empty. "I think I just called out our buddy Ryker."

Who was not *our* buddy. But Everleigh waited with curiosity to find out about their conversation from moments ago.

"We were just talking, Ryker and me. And something struck me. It's late June, right? And he's back in town."

She shrugged with a crinkled brow.

"He plays baseball. He's never home this early. And he's been back for at least a week, maybe more."

Her brows lifted slightly as she waited for the point.

"So I made what I thought was a joke and asked if the team had gotten sick of him already and sent him packing. And his face blanched. Literally *blanched*. So I said, what, did you get kicked off the team? Get into some trouble?"

"What did he say?"

"Nothing. He just stalked away. That's when he came up to the counter."

Everleigh frowned. Was *that* why he'd changed his mind about the clothes purchase? Not because of her barging in on him in the dressing room? "Well, what do you think?"

"You know me. This mind is conjuring all kinds of *American Horror Story* plotlines." Crestin waved his hand around his head. "But I'm definitely gonna find out."

# Chapter 2
# And Ryker Was Annoyed

**Ryker**

"Why don't you ask her out already?"

"What?"

"You heard me."

Noah turned red at Tyson's prodding.

And Ryker was annoyed.

"Actually, I kind of did."

"What? When?" Johnny joined the conversation as they walked along the sidewalk of the square.

"We kind of had a moment. When I helped her clean up the jewelry. And I asked if she wanted to hang out later."

"What did she say?" Tyson asked.

"'Hmm?'"

"What. Did. She. Say?" Tyson repeated.

"That's what she said. 'Hmm?' Like she didn't even hear me."

An obnoxious laugh burst from Johnny, and he slapped Noah on the back. "Oh, man. That's rough. She pretended not to hear you?"

Noah, good-natured guy that he was, shrugged it off. "I mean, there was a lot going on at the moment. And maybe I didn't actually speak above a whisper."

"You got it bad," Tyson declared. "But you miss a hundred percent of the shots you don't take."

Tyson Brantley, a year older than Ryker, was always the sports enthusiast in school and always captain of whatever team he was on. So, of course, much of his advice came from the sports world. Tyson and Ryker were so similar, cut from the same cloth, that they became fast friends in elementary school. Their mutual love for sports had kept them close over the years as they moved together through season after season on one team or another. It was disappointing when Tyson had committed to play baseball and football at a DIII school rather than applying to the same college Ryker had planned on attending. But Tyson was never big on academics, and the Division III school he chose had plenty of resources available to keep its student-athletes eligible. And his success made Ryker second-guess his own decision.

"But it's *Everleigh*," Noah groaned. "She's just so pretty and smart and amazing. Why would she like a guy like me?"

"Why wouldn't she, bro? That's what you should be asking." Tyson, the ever-optimist.

"Your already receding hairline, for one. You're never on time. Ever. Your feet stink like death. Shall I continue?" Johnny chided.

"Come on now, help a brother out. Don't clip his wings before he gets a chance to fly."

"Thanks, Tyson," Noah said as he rubbed his fingers along his forehead. "You really think my hairline is receding already?" He aimed this question at Ryker, knowing that of the three of them, there was only one source of honest truth.

Ryker understood this: Johnny Downing had something broken in him that didn't allow him to give real compliments to anyone, so most of what he said should be taken with a grain of salt. And Tyson, with his ever-optimistic outlook, often told white lies to bolster someone's confidence. Not wanting to be mean but always striving to be truthful—when he wasn't lying to himself that was—Ryker responded, "Nah man, just a bit. *Tiny* bit. You used to have more hair at the front here. But you still look good."

Unfortunately, that seemed to send Noah in a spiral of self-doubt, and he pulled out his phone, opened the camera app, and proceeded to inspect his thick black hair.

"There is one thing you don't have that Everleigh got an eyeful of today," Johnny commented, drawing Noah's attention away from his hairline. "Ryker's twenty-four-pack abs!"

"Ah, man, that's cold," Tyson reproved Johnny and rested a hand on Noah's shoulder.

"But it's true," Johnny continued. "And she got a looooong, *hard* look." He slapped the back of his hand against Ryker's abs.

And Ryker was annoyed.

"Like she was staring? What did she see?" Noah was spiraling again.

"She didn't really see anything."

"She saw *every*thing," Johnny countered.

"She didn't really see anything," Ryker repeated evenly.

*Everything*, Johnny mouthed, dragging his hands down his cheeks as he tried to pull the obnoxious grin away.

Ryker shot a glare in his direction, and Johnny quickly turned somber, folding his arms across his chest. He'd never hit someone, but Johnny made him second-guess that rule quite often, regardless of his friend's short stature.

"Noah, if you want to ask her out, you should do it. You'll never know if you don't ask. She seems like a nice girl," Ryker said.

And he was being honest. Everleigh Wilson *did* seem like a nice girl. Although today was the most Ryker had ever heard her speak. He was a bit surprised at the gentleness in her voice, even as she was apologizing for barging in on him. As pissed as he was initially, his anger had quickly dissipated when he saw the sheer embarrassment on her face. She'd been mortified. And then it was like she was mesmerized. Which was a ridiculous thought, but that was what pressed him to have a little fun with the situation and goad her a bit, covering himself with the jeans like he was trying to protect his modesty.

In truth, Ryker had zero body self-consciousness. He'd gotten used to being partially clothed and fully naked in locker rooms a long time ago, so he didn't feel as if his privacy had been invaded today. And it was almost as if Everleigh had never seen a half-naked man before. It made him want to stand in front of her and let her inspect every inch of his body with her eyes. Or her—

*Stop it. Noah likes her*, he reminded himself. And he didn't have time to mess around with a girl, even just for the summer. He needed to focus on getting his shit together before returning to college this fall. Distractions from any girl would not be conducive to cleaning up his headspace. He had a lot to prove when he returned to his school and his team, and it was a matter of moral importance that he showed them the growth he knew he was capable of. That he made up for all he'd fucked up lately. It was no one's fault but his own, the situation he'd gotten himself into, and it was no one's responsibility but his to fix it.

Ryker thought back to his freshman year, how confident he'd been in his choice of school. Confident he'd be able to manage academics and baseball and college life. But college was harder than he'd anticipated. Much harder than high school had prepared him for. He hadn't been smart enough to seek out the help of academic tutors, although he was pretty certain they were available. And no one made him, either. His coaches cared about him; they cared about all the student-athletes. But Ryker learned early on that every one of them on that team was replaceable. It was a university after all, large enough to have a pool of talented athletes who tried out every year, hoping to be a walk-on player. Any one of them would readily step in to take his place if he failed out of school. He'd seen it happen to three other teammates.

While Ryker struggled with his classes, he poured his efforts into workouts and off-season practices, trying to control the one part of his life that came easy to him. That left little time for homework and studying. He'd finished freshman year with a C+ average. Barely. He'd been pretty sure he was going to fail Intro to Psychology, but the professor was a baseball alum himself, and somehow Ryker ended the semester with a D. The only thing that saved his GPA? The couple of easier Gen Ed classes required of all students and the fact that he could take an elective class each semester. He chose Personal Fitness for the first semester and (ironically) Alcohol and You the second semester.

But that was only the half of it. His assigned dorm was reserved for student-athletes. Meant to provide a positive and healthy environment away from the lure of parties and drinking, in reality it provided a ready group of cronies to go out clubbing with or to attend house parties with. Because they were athletes, people wanted them around, wanted the inevitable following of female groupies to flock to their parties.

Ryker had tried to keep his head focused on his academics and his sport, because he knew how easy it would be to lose it all. At first, he only drank water or soda when they went out, offering to be the sober driver. Ontario Henry—Tari as his friends called him, the shortstop on the team—had thought it was because Ryker didn't have a fake ID, so the third week of school, he'd offered up a Minnesota license with a picture that was an eerie match. Ryker didn't tell him he already had a fake that he'd gotten his junior year of high school. Graciously accepting the ID seemed to be the tipping point, the action that made it feel okay to begin partaking in the drinking at parties. Tari wanted Ryker to be a part of the camaraderie. They all did. A collective cheer rang out amongst his teammates the first time he took a drink of beer at a party. He was officially one of them.

Before Ryker knew it, he was no longer the sober driver, sometimes going as far as getting blackout drunk. He didn't know why he did it.

He felt like shit the next day, often waking up in a strange girl's room, always hoping he'd not done something stupid like have sex without a condom. Or worse, have sex with a girl who was as blackout drunk as he'd been. As difficult as it was for him to articulate, he'd always made sure to ask whichever "her" it was the next morning if he'd done anything . . . ungentlemanly. Sometimes, he was met with a snicker or an outright laugh and a coy, "Were you ever," followed by a "When can we do it again?" But thankfully, never a response that he had gone against anyone's wishes.

Every time it happened, he swore he'd never drink that much again. But more often than not, he would. It was like he couldn't stop once he took that first sip. He drank until he could drink no more.

Ontario had taught him a trick: drink a bottle of water between each alcoholic beverage. And it helped. For the most part. Until they were day drinking on a weekend. There wasn't enough water in the world to keep him from over-imbibing then. He just had to pee a lot more often. Sometimes, he'd wake up in wet sheets, having pissed himself at some point in the night. Or morning, if the day drinking lasted through the night into the early dawn hours.

When he'd noticed his practice results suffering in January, right before the official start of baseball season, Ryker feared he'd lose his spot on the team. He'd stopped cold turkey, swearing off alcohol during the season. It had been easy to do. They were busier than ever during the season with practice and traveling state to state for games. There was little downtime for anything, let alone partying. Thankfully, the season lasted through late June if they made it far through the playoffs. And the team historically made it to the championship rounds.

There was also less time for keeping up with coursework. He once again struggled to get the minimum 2.3 GPA required to maintain his athlete status. But he'd done it. And he used the few remaining weeks of his summer working on his family's farm and resetting his mental focus.

The one bane of that time was his required stint helping at The Sunflower Experience. He'd do anything his parents asked of him on that farm because he took as much pride in the legacy they'd built as his parents did. The land gave back to you what you put into it. Darren and Rita Martin put their souls into their land, and they were rewarded with a thriving organic vegetable business, cattle lot, and the highly successful sunflower patch. People flocked to their annual sunflower event from as far as two states away, claiming nothing compared to the size and beauty of the paths that wound in, around, and through the tall sunflowers. There were several elevated platforms throughout the field to give visitors a spectacular view of vibrant yellow flowers covering the carpet of deep green. Over the years, they'd expanded, adding a corn pit, jumping pillow, and playground for kids. A few years later came the food truck, serving cold lemonade and iced tea as well as snacks and sandwiches, creating a more fulfilling experience and more revenue. Two years ago, they added a professional photographer, which Ryker found kind of creepy. The old guy lurked around the patch with a big camera around his neck, popping up and taking random pictures of people. But those people could then visit The Rustic Sunflower Experience website to see and purchase their photos.

But that wasn't what really bothered Ryker about it. No, the real rub for him was the fact that local teenagers vied to work the event. And he became a babysitter. Because it wasn't like any of them really *wanted* a job. They just wanted to hang out in a "fun" place all day and take photos and videos for their social media to gain more followers. It was annoying as hell. He was run ragged trying to ensure they did their jobs, picking up the slack when they flaked. The only capable employees over the past few years had been Crestin and Marissa, who'd taken the importance of their jobs seriously. He appreciated them coming back as supervisors, helping to keep the newbies in line.

The Sunflower Experience was only maybe fourteen days each summer, depending on the weather, but he'd hoped to be able to opt out of this year's season with Crestin and Marissa returning, knowing they would run a tight ship. But his parents had quickly squelched that idea when he'd returned home, ashamed and defeated. They'd added insult to injury by requiring his presence as part of his punishment. True, he was an adult—half a year from being twenty-one, in fact. He could refuse. But he accepted the discipline right along with the other rules they'd laid out as a condition of being able to stay at home this summer.

Yes, he knew they would kick him out of the house and off the farm if he didn't get his shit together. And he loved them for it. It was discipline he needed—the threat of losing all the things most important to him—to keep him motivated and staying on the straight and narrow.

Ryker had tried it last summer—the reset of home, the grounding of his soul and fortifying of his mental sharpness.[1] Throwing hay every morning in the barn, running every evening in town at the high school track, eating three square meals a day of his mother's amazing cooking. It had carried him safely through the first three months back at school.

But then came Helena. At first, she'd seemed like the breath of fresh air he'd been searching for. Fun, clever, and oh-so-beautiful, he'd fallen quickly. Her raven-black hair and ice-blue irises gave her an exotic look, lending to her aura of intrigue. It took him too long to realize she was an Always Searcher. Always searching for the next fun thing, the next high, the next love.

Within a couple weeks, she'd coaxed him out to a house party, then a few weekends clubbing, and then a party at a house full of strangers in a neighborhood he'd never been in before, pulling him further and further away from his safe zone. When the white lines came out at that party, he was shocked at how quickly she wanted to get in on it. As he watched

---

1. Matt Maeson, "Blood Runs Red"

her snort the line of white powder, he felt everything wrong with their relationship expand in his chest until he could no longer breathe. When she turned and handed him the rolled-up bill, wiping her nose as she beckoned him to join her, he recognized how unattractive she'd suddenly become. He couldn't reconcile the beautiful girl he'd met weeks before with this version staring up at him. Her eyes were already glassy, her eye makeup smeared. He'd waved off her offer and escaped to the bathroom, noting the torn carpeting everywhere, the dirty walls, the people he could only describe as junkies curled around one another in corners and on filthy mattresses behind the bedroom doors he opened as he tried to find the bathroom. She'd brought them to a drug house. If he was caught here, he would lose everything. His spot on the team, his scholarship. Who knows what else.

He'd hoped to splash cold water on his face in the bathroom, but the faucet didn't work. He needed something to wash away this nightmare from his skin, so he tried the tub faucet. Still nothing. There was no running water in this house. Ryker noticed a five-gallon bucket of water next to the toilet, but he didn't dare. Instead, he marched out of the bathroom, planning to grab Helena and get the hell out of there.

But she wasn't where he'd left her. His eyes searched the crowded living room. He ducked into the kitchen, the front room. Where had she gone? On instinct, he stepped out onto the back porch, where he'd watched couples disappear all night, and his stomach fell to the floor. He'd found her. Wrapped around some filthy dude on the ratty couch, making out like they'd come to this party together.

"Helena?" he'd said.

Then, "Helena!" when she didn't respond.

He grabbed her by the shoulder and forced her to look at him. She was high as fuck.

"Come on. We're going."

"What?" She'd feebly batted at his hand. "We're having fun."

"No, we're not."

"We're not?"

"Nope. Let's go."

"You heard her, man. We're having fun." The filthy dude was actually disgusting, missing teeth with food—or vomit—or something in his long hair. The forest of curly, dark chest hair Ryker's girlfriend was clutching was hard to distinguish from the leather biker vest.

Ryker had to get her out of there, and he didn't know any other way than to throw her over his shoulder and carry her out, no matter her screaming protests and ineffective punches on his back.

He heard the disgusting couch gremlin get up before he saw him, and Ryker turned in time to throw his hand out. His palm connected with the gremlin's furry chest, the force sending the man stumbling back onto the couch. As Ryker turned to make their exit, Helena suddenly cried out, "Oh, my handsome hero!" And she then allowed Ryker to carry her over his shoulder through the house and out to his car, calling out to everyone they passed, "Thank you, friends! So nice to meet you. Thank you, you beautiful people!"

He'd managed to get her buckled in. And get her less rambunctious with a detour through a Taco Bell drive-through. By the time he helped her into her apartment and placed her on her side in her bed, informing her roommates to watch her through the night, he was thoroughly exhausted. Helena was not only not the girl he'd thought she was, but she was also not the girl for him.

But the life of partying she'd drawn him back into pulled at him, lulled him into complacency, especially as he wondered what he'd done wrong in their relationship. Ryker had felt something deep for her that he'd never felt before. *She'd* started to become his world. And she'd broken his heart. And now what was there for him?

The weekends partying turned into daily drinking, even when the official baseball season started. He began carrying an insulated water bottle with him to class. Of course, everyone thought it contained water. Only he knew how many parts water to parts vodka it actually held.

His practices started to suffer. His playing time was reduced. He fell from starting first baseman to third-string right field, sitting on the bench. His grades mirrored his baseball performance. And one night, everything came to a screeching halt.

It had to.

That was the night Ryker knew he could no longer sustain the life he was living.

And he wanted to end it all.

# Chapter 3
# Lost in the Woods

**Everleigh**

"Hurry up, Evie! We're gonna be late!"

Everleigh sighed as she finished plaiting her brunette hair into a fishtail braid. "I'll be there in a minute, Saralynn. Calm down!"

Her nine-year-old sister was in the July Fourth parade this year with her softball team, and the little girl was acting like it was the Rose Bowl Parade. Everleigh wanted to tell Saralynn she'd been in several July Fourth parades over the years, and it really was not a big deal . . . but she also kind of delighted in the joy her younger sister exuded in feeling so important. So she took one last glance in the mirror, added her SPF lip balm to her full lips, and headed downstairs to meet up with her family.

After they dropped Saralynn off at the softball float, Everleigh and her mom made their way to Main Street to find a place to watch the parade. It was eighty-eight degrees already at 10:30 in the morning. And don't even talk about the humidity. She was glad she'd worn a light-colored tank top and skort. And thrilled when they found a rare shaded spot under a storefront canopy.

Until she glimpsed Noah sitting three seats away from where they had set up their lawn chairs on the sidewalk. Trying to pretend she didn't see him, she felt his gaze burning into her hotter than the July sun. It had been a week since she'd last seen him, and she'd almost forgotten about his weirdness in Fashionably Rustic. But, boy, was he bringing it back in full force today. After stealing a glance over her shoulder and noticing him still watching her, she looked over at her mom to engage in conversation.

"Are we going to the park after the parade?"

"Of course. Saralynn wants to try and win a goldfish again this year. And I want to buy Cow Chip Bingo tickets," Rosalynn responded.

"Hey, Everleigh."

*Crap.* Her mom had already started talking to someone sitting to her left, so Everleigh couldn't even pretend to be in a conversation with her. She turned slowly to her right and looked up to find Noah, tall and broad-shouldered, looming over her.

"Oh, hi, Noah. Happy Independence Day."

"Yeah. Happy Independence Day."

She waited for him to say something, but he just stood there. Green eyes dancing with what appeared to be entirely too much excitement for her liking. It was quite unsettling.

"So," Everleigh finally said, "what's new?"

She cringed internally. What else was there to say?

"Oh. Um. There's gonna be a fire tonight. At Ryker's farm. If you want to come, I guess. I mean, I'm inviting you to come."

"Oh." Surprise colored her voice. Not what she was expecting.

"Yeah . . . Do you need a ride?"

"Uh . . . I mean, couldn't I ride with Crestin?" She had no idea if Crestin had been invited, but she would be inviting him as her plus one based on this invite if she had to.

"I mean. Yeah. That would be fine. So you're coming?"

The look of relief on Noah's face made her immediately regret what she was about to say, but she *was* heading off to college soon, so it was high time she practiced living outside her comfort zone.

"Yes. I'll be there."

"Why did I let you talk me into this?"

"Girl. What?" Crestin stopped and threw a look at her. "*You* invited *me* here, remember?"

Everleigh pursed her lips as she tried to gather her confidence. She'd been invited by Noah, which meant she'd be accepted by him at least. But who else would be here? This was Ryker's farm. And he was at least two years older than her and Crestin. So most of the people here could be older than the both of them.

At least Crestin was a lifelong resident of Rustic, so he should know most everyone here. She'd just stick very close to him. As if she ever behaved any differently at any party she attended. But she remembered that *she* was the one invited to this party. And Crestin was the plus one. Oh, God. Was she going to have to spend all night talking to Noah? Noah was nice and all, but he was no—

"Heeeey, friends!" Marissa screeched across the bonfire at them as they neared the group of people. She ran over and hugged them both at once.

Everleigh loved Marissa Frey. She did. And she was relieved to see someone else she knew here. But Marissa had been Crestin's best friend since first grade, so it kind of felt like a competition for his favor whenever the three of them were together. And Everleigh thought he secretly reveled in it.

"Hey, Marissa," she said.

"Hey, girl, hey!" Crestin cooed. "The party has officially arrived!"

"I know, right? Come over here." Their friend grabbed their hands and dragged them around to the other side of the fire. She reached into a cooler and handed each of them a can of something.

"Oh, no, I don't—" Everleigh started.

"Tonight, you do!" Marissa cut her off. "Besides, Ben's the sober driver if you need him. It's so okay."

Everleigh noticed Marissa wobbling on her feet—her curly red hair escaping her ponytail in several places and her mascara smudged at the corners of her eyes—and wondered how much she'd already consumed. Marissa was eighteen, like them, but her boyfriend, Ben, was twenty-one, so she'd potentially had access to alcohol all day today. Everleigh looked at Crestin, who gave her a nonchalant shrug before he cracked open his can. *Okay,* she thought and cracked open her can as well.

"Everleigh. Hey."

She'd barely had a sip of her drink and Noah was already at her side. "Noah. Hey."

"I feel like I haven't seen you in forever," he said as he wrapped his large frame around her in a hug.

"Oh, um. Yeah. Clear back this morning. So long ago," she teased as she tried to subtly extract herself from his embrace. He'd clearly been drinking for a minute.

"Yeah," he said as he straightened next to her. His tipsy smile was a little endearing, though. "Hey, you know what?"

"What?"

"There's gonna be some fireworks set off soon."

"Oh, can we see the city fireworks from here?" Everleigh asked as she squinted toward town.

"No, no. Well. I don't think so." Noah narrowed his eyes in the same direction. "No. I mean, Johnny's gonna set off some fireworks. Over the pond by the tree line." He pointed.

"Cool," Everleigh said, her gaze following the direction of his finger to the large grove of trees.

"Yeah. And I want you to sit by me," Noah stated, that smile returning.

"Oh. Um . . ."

"I mean, she came with me, so she'll be sitting by me," Crestin butted in much to her relief. She shrugged as if it was something she had no control over.

Noah looked crestfallen but nodded anyway. He didn't appear to have a response to that.

"Okay, so we'll catch up with you later," Marissa said firmly as she guided them away from Noah.

"Thank you," Everleigh said on a breath.

"No worries. But you know he's got it bad for you, right?" Marissa gave her a knowing look.

"He does?" Everleigh once again regretted her decision to attend this fire. How had Noah, a guy she barely knew, already conjured such strong feelings about her?

"Girl, you have to know," Crestin insisted.

Before her last couple years of high school, it had been such a foreign idea for a boy to be so into her. She was relatively okay with her looks now, but Everleigh had had some severe ugly duckling issues in middle school that haunted her through sophomore year in high school, when her braces finally came off, she grew into her nose and ears, and she learned how to tame her thick brunette tresses with hair products until they became one of her best features. Even though she'd dated a couple of guys over the last two years, she still couldn't get used to the idea of a boy coming on so strong because he *liked her* without really knowing her yet.

"Can I have another drink?" She handed her empty can to Marissa.

⚜

"So, yeah, I think I'm gonna take classes at Kirkwood to get my business degree, so when I take over the hardware store, I'll really know what I'm doing."

Noah had been talking Everleigh's ear off for the past thirty minutes, ever since he'd pulled a chair up beside her. He'd recently repeated that the fireworks were going to start soon, and it had been dark for at least fifteen minutes, so surely, they'd start booming any minute. And she really had to pee now that she'd had three seltzers from Marissa's cooler. But there was no bathroom nearby. And things were starting to get blurry. Maybe she'd drunk a little too quickly. She couldn't decide if she wanted to puke or find something to eat.

"Is there anything to eat?" she asked.

"To eat? Yeah, come with me."

Noah's large hand curled around hers as he pulled Everleigh up from her chair near the fire. His hand was sweaty, but it felt nice around her cold fingers. The temperature had dropped as soon as the sun set, and she wasn't prepared for it. She'd forgotten to bring a sweatshirt with her tonight. Noah seemed to notice her shiver and wrapped his arm around her shoulder as he guided her toward the large deck attached to the back of the Martins' split-level, walk-out basement house. They went up the stairs to the top of the deck, where a buffet of crock-pots and cold salads awaited. *Hallelujah*, she thought. Everleigh hadn't eaten since the funnel cake at the park right after the parade.

Noah grabbed Styrofoam plates and placed one in her hands, followed by plastic silverware and a napkin. Moving along the table, he asked, "Hot dog or pulled pork?"

"Pulled pork," she responded automatically.

"Barbecue sauce?"

"Of course."

"Pickles?"

"Duh."

"Anything else?"

"Is that potato salad?" She pointed at a nearby container.

"Um . . . yes."

"Oooh. Does it have egg slices in it?"

"Um . . ." He glanced into the container. "Yes."

"Then yes! Load me up!"

"You sure?" Noah chuckled as he put a large scoop on her plate.

"Yes! More! More!" she commanded until he'd placed three large scoops on her plate.

"You good?" he said, amusement lacing his voice.

She nodded as she took in the contents on her plate. "This looks amazing."

"Yeah, well, Rita's an amazing cook."

"Rita?"

"Ryker's mom."

Everleigh shoveled a spoonful of potato salad into her mouth. "Mmmm. I agree."

They made a pit stop at the picnic table in the corner of the deck so they could eat. Everleigh mused how Noah wasn't so bad now that she'd spent some real time with him. He was funny. He was polite. He was cute. He gave her lots of potato salad.

"You know, tonight might be the most I've ever heard you talk."

Which was kind of weird, because she'd been doing more listening than anything. "Well, Noah . . . I don't really like to talk about myself."

"What? Why not? I love to hear you talk."

A blush crept up her cheeks, and she was thankful the only light shining on the deck came from clear over by the sliding doors. "Thank you. I'm usually told that I'm a very good listener."

"You are."

She smiled again at his compliment. Noah was an easy guy to hang around with. Her anxiety meter hovered at a pretty low setting in his presence. Which was why she felt comfortable saying, "I have to pee," as she licked her spoon clean of potato salad.

"You can go in the house." He motioned to the sliding doors.

"Are you sure it's okay?"

Noah nodded. "Give me your plate. I'll throw this stuff away and meet you back at the fire. But hurry. The fireworks will be starting soon."

"You keep saying that. Are you sure there's even going to be fireworks?" She narrowed her eyes.

"Yes, I'm sure," he laughed. "You just do your business and meet me at the fire."

Everleigh stumbled through the sliding glass door and caught herself on a small table in the utility room directly to her left. She slipped her shoes off and headed in the direction of the light streaming through the doorway, thinking she should have asked Noah where the bathroom was.

The lights in the large kitchen and dining room combo illuminated the space well enough for her to see into the adjoining living room. It looked like a hallway was to the left of that room, which might be her best chance of finding a bathroom. As she entered the living room, her gaze was drawn to the family portraits on the wall to her right. Without thinking, she detoured to that wall.

Everleigh giggled at how cute wide-eyed Ryker was as a toddler, a young boy, and even as a preteen. And then maybe as a high schooler? He was quite handsome with a square jaw and intense, amber-colored eyes. A slight mullet. It must have been high school. The final family photo most closely resembled the boy he was now. Or the man, she should say. His muscular frame, broad shoulders, the maturity in his eyes, made him seem much older than he was. His mother, Rita, was beautiful, with dark brown curls that cascaded over her shoulders. She had the same intense amber eyes as Ryker. His dad was the spitting image of him, except for the eyes. His light blue irises were a sharp contrast to the other two.

Suddenly realizing how badly she had to use the bathroom, Everleigh hurried down the dark hallway. But when she grabbed the door handle, it was locked. She knocked quietly on the door, thinking maybe Ryker's parents were sleeping nearby.

"Occupied," came through the door.

Occupied? But she really had to pee *now*! Looking around with no idea if there was a second bathroom in this house, she decided to go back outside. This was a farm. There were a ton of trees to the east. Surely, she could find a place to cop a squat. As she reentered the kitchen, she grabbed a few tissues from the box on the island and tucked them into her pocket. She slipped on her shoes before heading outside and making a beeline for the trees.

Everleigh walked several trees in and squatted near a large oak. There were no words for how wonderful it felt to finally relieve her bladder; she sighed and shuddered as she finished.

Marching out of the woods with a renewed purpose, she was ready to find her friends and crack open another seltzer.[1] But her arm was caught in a vice grip, and she nearly fell backward.

"What are you doing here?" The deep voice was full of accusation.

"What? Um . . ." She blinked, trying to focus on the person holding her hostage. His large grip bit into her bare skin. She tripped over her feet and toppled backward into a tree trunk, but he didn't loosen his handle on her. The bark scratched at her back through her tank top as she tried to stand upright. But he wouldn't allow it. Inches from her face, she struggled to focus on him. Why did she drink so much so quickly?

Everleigh said the only thing she could think of: "Noah invited me."

"What? No . . . I mean . . . What are you doing *right* here? We're about to set off fireworks. It's very dangerous."

Everleigh blinked hard once more, and Ryker's face came into focus. Suddenly, she was completely embarrassed. She'd just peed probably right in front of him. At the very least, she had to tell him she'd peed in his trees, right?

"I got lost," she blurted instead, shrugging.

---

1. Cannons, "Fire for You"

"You got lost?"

"Yep," she confirmed as she pushed up from the tree and stood on her own two feet. She would not embarrass herself any further in Ryker's presence.

"Are you drunk?" he asked as she tripped over a tree root, his strong hand the only thing keeping her upright.

So much for not embarrassing herself any further. "No."

"Well, you need to head back to the fire. As I said, we're about to set off fireworks here."

"Okay. Yes, okay," she slurred, but he didn't release her arm. Ryker was unbearably close to her face. If it were Noah, she knew she'd be leaning away from him at this moment. But she found herself leaning forward. Pressing her chest into Ryker's, gazing up at his face. That perfect jawline, those deep-set eyes. The evening wrapped darkness around them, but she could still make out his handsome features in the dim light cast by the electrical pole over in the barnyard. She thought maybe she could feel his heartbeat through his shirt. And it made her dizzy.

Or was that the alcohol affecting her?

Everleigh thought he dipped his head down next to hers, about to place his mouth on her neck, and she inhaled sharply with anticipation. She imagined Ryker touching her all over, what that would feel like, just based on his strong hand wrapped around her upper arm and his heartbeat pounding against her own chest. Imagined his hand snaking around her back, pulling her close. Imagined kissing his neck in the way she felt him kissing hers.

And the next thing she knew, Ryker was sitting her down in the chair between Noah and Crestin by the fire.

"She got lost in the woods by the fireworks," Ryker said, sounding annoyed.

"She what?" Noah asked, concerned. He turned his attention from Ryker to her. "I thought you went in for the bathroom?"

"It was occupied," was all she could say.

Everleigh's heart sank as the long-awaited fireworks exploded up into the night sky near the tree line.

# Chapter 4
# Crumbled Cookies

## Ryker

Everleigh had just kissed him. She'd really just kissed him.

Well, she'd kissed his neck. In a way that drew desire through his body. And he'd almost pressed her up against that tree and shoved his tongue down her throat. Ryker had wanted to, so badly. He'd been seconds away from doing it. His body had ached to do it, even as his mind screamed at him not to. But she'd been so close, smelling of campfire and vanilla, her breasts rubbing against his chest as she breathed so heavily.

At first, he'd attributed it to her being surprised at someone standing right there as she came out of the trees, but it was a delayed response. Moments after he'd found her in a very unsafe area as they were about to set off fireworks, Everleigh had seemed to fall into him rather than struggle away as he'd anticipated she would. That's why Ryker had held her so tightly. He was afraid she'd get scared in the dark and try to run away, and then he'd have to chase her through the trees, trying to keep her safe from the freaking fireworks. That was it. Honestly.

He'd started to pull her close to steady her on her feet, the smell of vanilla intoxicating him, but then she'd gasped. Ryker was about to release her, worried that he'd really scared her, and that's when Everleigh had seemed to move even closer to him, wrapping around his body, his mind. Rubbing up against him, her mouth on his neck, inching up toward the sensitive area behind his ear. And he might have pulled her closer. But he didn't kiss her back. His mouth had never touched her.

Had it?

Ryker looked at her now, watching the glow of the fireworks reflect on her upturned face. She was so young. So innocent. She hadn't experienced any of the troubling things he had in his brief years as an adult. Nor would he ever wish her to. No one should ever experience what he had gone through. But there was something about Everleigh that drew him in. He couldn't explain it. The wonder in her expression as she watched each firework explode in the sky. The way she reached for Crestin to share her joy with the clasp of her hand.

A sudden ache to feel her soft fingers curled around his own gripped Ryker. To feel her warm lips dance on the skin of his neck just as she'd done moments before. To lay her down and worship her body. Maybe she could save him from himself. Maybe someone like her could be the sun he so desperately needed to guide his growth.

As Noah reached over and wrapped his fingers around her other free hand, Ryker remembered Everleigh wasn't his to covet. No, his friend had already expressed his interest in a relationship with her. And it was Ryker's duty as a friend to step away and know what would be would be. He bit the inside of his mouth hard before heading over to see how he could help Johnny with the rest of the fireworks display.

❧ ❧

Everyone had gone.[1] Had been gone for maybe an hour now. The dewy night air clung to Ryker like the thoughts he couldn't rid from his troubled mind, and he knew it was time to head inside. But here he sat. Watching the last glowing embers slowly dying in the fire pit. The lawn

---

1. Breaking Benjamin, "Failure"

was littered with cans and chairs that he'd have to clean up yet tonight. His parents had been gracious enough to let him still have his annual Independence Day party, given the circumstances. At the very least, he needed to make sure all signs of the party were cleared away before they arose for daily chores. Which was probably about three hours from now.

Yes, he needed to clean up and get a couple hours of sleep himself. His father had always told him a man could never play harder than he worked. The land would withhold its rewards from a man who did not follow that tenant. Ryker absently rubbed his finger across his mouth as he pondered his father's words. He'd made a mistake in not heeding the warning. He'd thought with all the time he was logging in the weight room and in the gym, on the practice field, that he was working harder than he was playing. He'd certainly spent more time on his sport and in the classroom than he had partying. But what he'd never realized was the time he spent putting all that bad shit into his body didn't just steal the actual minutes and hours he spent actively engaging in it—it also began to steal his sleep, the valuable recovery time his body needed to be at its best for the next practice, the next game . . . the next course exam. It began to steal his health, his mental toughness, his focus. And when the time spent drinking coincided with the time in the classroom, in the library, in the gym, that's when he really lost control. And his land—his life—withheld its rewards.

He'd done it all to himself.

His gaze drifted toward the can of beer in his right hand. Unopened and warm, it rested in his palm. Ryker did that. Often. Held a beer just to prove he wouldn't crack it open, wouldn't take that first sip that would lead to another beer that would lead to another twelve pack that would lead to unconsciousness. He didn't know why he couldn't control his drinking. He should have learned all about that in his Alcohol and You class. He'd done the coursework, earned a B+ as a final grade. Maybe he didn't want to admit he had a problem. It wasn't genetic. It wasn't learned. It was just something he'd let take over his life. And now he was strong enough to refuse even the first sip.

He only wished he'd been that strong months ago. Wished he'd never let Helena draw him back down that dark path. Wished he hadn't let the heartbreak she'd caused be an excuse for him to lose control of himself. He hungered to find a way to believe his life was worth living, that he was worth the rewards he could get out of this life. He longed to go back in time to last summer and get a do-over.

God, he'd really burned it all down. Turned his life into a fucking dumpster fire.

Ryker sat up in his chair, set his jaw, and cracked open the beer. He stood, holding the can out in front of him. He didn't even know what brand it was, having pulled it out of Tyson's cooler before he left. Even though he'd been holding it for an hour, he just now focused on the can. Michelob Ultra.

He stepped up to the crackling embers in the fire pit and poured the beer over the coals, sending a surge of smoke into the humid night air.

⁂

"Good morning, baby," his mother said as she tousled his hair and planted a kiss on the top of his head. "I'm surprised to see you up so early."

Ryker sat at his usual spot at the dining table and shrugged as she poured coffee into his mug.

"How was the party last night?" His dad glanced up from the farm report on his phone screen. "Nobody got out of hand, I trust."

Ryker tried to stifle a yawn. "Everybody had a good time. I hope nobody woke you up."

"Just the fireworks," his dad replied wryly.

"Sorry about that." Ryker fought the tug of a smile.

"It's once a year, right?" his mom offered, sending a look her husband's way. She set a plate with scrambled eggs, sausage, and toast in front of her son. "I just happened out to the kitchen for a glass of water, oh, about midnight and came upon a couple of hungry girls."

Ryker paused shoveling eggs into his mouth and waited for her to continue.

"It was just Marissa and some other pretty girl. I think her name was Emily?"

"Everleigh?" he offered with a crease in his brow.

His mom snapped her fingers. "That's it. A pretty name for a pretty girl. I haven't seen her out here before. Do you know her?"

Scenes from the night before flooded his thoughts. The smell of vanilla. Her lips on his neck. His hand pressed against the small of her back, pulling her closer into his body. He choked on the last bite of egg. Coughed and took a drink of his coffee. "Ah, she's friends with Marissa and Crestin, I think."

"Then she must be good people," his dad piped up, lifting his mug. "Is she new to the area?"

"She's lived here a couple years maybe. Crestin said she graduated with him."

"Well, she seems darling. And she couldn't get enough of my potato salad. They were sharing a plateful when I came in. She was gushing about how delicious it was, so I sent the leftovers home with her," his mom said.

Ryker nodded as he stabbed at his sausage link. He wished his mom would stop talking already. He didn't want Everleigh on his mind at five o'clock in the morning. The risk of her staying there all damn day was just too great.

"Does she have a boyfriend?"

*Good God.* "No, Mom," he said louder than he intended. Then more evenly, "I think maybe Noah?"

"Oh." The disappointment rang clear in her voice. She patted the back of her head, where her long curls were pulled into a ponytail, then wrapped both hands around her coffee mug and brightened her expression. "Well, Noah's a nice boy."

"I'm going to head out." Ryker pushed up from the table, stabbed the last sausage link and shoved it in his mouth while walking over to the kitchen sink. He rinsed his plate and fork and placed them and his mug in the dishwasher.

"See you in a few," his dad called after him as Ryker stepped into the utility room.

"Darren, do you think he . . . you know . . . last night?" A low question floated in to him. His mother didn't realize he was still in the house, putting on his muck boots.

"I'd like to think he didn't, Rita, but it's not something we can control. Only he can control it."

"I know. You're right . . . but I just want to protect him. He's been through so much this year."

"We need to give him some space to fix what he's broken," his dad said firmly.

"But not too much space," she quickly added.

Ryker opened the sliding door and exited the house as quietly as possible. It killed him that his mother had lost trust in him. And his dad didn't sound very confident either, although it seemed he was trying to be positive for his mom's sake.

He trudged over to the cattle lot and began the morning chore routine. Throwing hay, filling the water trough. He walked past the chicken coop, leaving the egg gathering for his mother. For some odd reason, it was her favorite chore. Fine with him. He hated dealing with those damn territorial roosters.

As he headed toward the barn to check on the horses, his eyes rested on the tree line near the pond, fifty yards away. Thoughts of holding Everleigh in his arms in that exact spot last night bombarded his mind.

And Ryker was annoyed.

"Come on, man. It's just a weekend. It's the biggest country music festival in the tristate area. So many big artists are going to be there."

"I've got chores on the weekend, same as I do every other day," Ryker explained. Johnny had been trying to get him to go to this music festival for a month now. To Johnny, it was the best thing to happen this side of the Mississippi River all year. To Ryker, it seemed like a drunk fest he didn't want any part of, sober or not. "You can't get Noah or Tyson to go with?"

"You know Tyson hates country music, and Noah says he has to work that weekend."

Ryker shrugged in answer.

Johnny finally gave up and focused on finishing his chocolate shake. They sat in silence under the shade of an umbrella at the one outdoor table in front of the Cool Moo Cool Hut. Ryker shoved his spoon into his sundae, suddenly no longer in the mood for ice cream. It had sounded good when Johnny mentioned it half an hour ago. But today was unseasonably cool for July in Iowa. Ryker stood and took his half-eaten sundae over to the trash. Returning to the table he said, "You ready? Noah should be off work by now."

Johnny nodded. He stood, obnoxiously slurped the last of his shake through the straw, and tossed the empty cup in the trash on the way to the truck.

They jumped into Ryker's dad's truck, and as he started the engine, he noted one more thing on his list of to-dos: Buy another vehicle. He'd need to get it done before school started, or he'd be relying on his parents' schedule for dropping him off on campus and picking him up whenever he wanted to come home for a visit. A thought snaked into his mind. He wondered if his Malibu had ever been pulled from the bottom of the Iowa River. Wondered if the authorities had ever found out about that night. Wondered if one day there would be a knock on his parents' door.

Pulling into a parking space near the entrance of Koeppen's Hardware Store, Ryker set the gear to park and idly listened to Johnny yammering about something. A minute later, Noah catapulted through the store door, ripping off his blue uniform vest as he hurried to the passenger side of the truck. He shoved the vest under the seat before he jumped in, appearing ready to burst at the seams.

"What's up there, little guy?" Johnny teased. An ironic phrase coming from Johnny's mouth, since Noah stood a good six inches taller than Johnny.

"Can we stop at Fashionably Rustic for a minute?"

"What for?" Johnny demanded before realization dawned. "Ohh. *She's* working."

Ryker didn't respond—he just made two left turns until they were on the other side of the square. He brought the truck to a stop in front of Marla's shop.

Noah hopped out and spun around when he didn't hear the engine cut out. "You guys coming in?"

"Hadn't planned on it." Ryker kept his eyes fixed on the mannequin in the window display wearing a floral-print blouse and oddly colored orange skirt. He didn't know much about fashion, but how could that combination be considered fashion?

"How long you gonna be?" Johnny asked.

"I mean, not long . . . but I was kinda hoping for some moral support."

"For what? Deciding on white or black underwear? Go with black," Johnny advised sagely.

"No. For—I just—come on, guys. Please."

Reluctantly, Ryker killed the engine. It had been almost two weeks since his party, and he'd managed not to run into Everleigh at all during that time. He'd shied away from plans with his friends that included Noah, which thankfully weren't many now that Noah was busy talking with this girl. He'd stayed off the town square and away from anywhere he thought he might bump into her. It had been good to cleanse her from his system.

So maybe it wouldn't be a big deal seeing her now for a few minutes. It wasn't like Ryker would be alone with her. And it wasn't like she wouldn't be solely focused on Noah.

*It'll be no big deal,* he told himself and followed the guys into the store. The metal bell clanged obnoxiously against the door over and over again as they filed in, which drew Everleigh out from the fitting rooms, arms overflowing with clothes. Ryker's first thought was to rush over, take the burden, and place it on the counter for her.

But Noah was already headed that way. "Let me take those for you," he said as he pulled the tangle of clothes from her arms.

"Oh—I've got it—okay. Um, okay. Thanks. Just there." Everleigh gave up trying to maintain control of the clothes and pointed Noah toward the open space on the counter. "Really? It's my job, but thanks."

Ryker noted the look of annoyance that crossed her face as she scratched the back of her head. Stepping up around the back side of the counter, she reset her expression, offering a smile. "What brings you troublemakers in today?"

He also noted that she seemed much more relaxed now in their presence, likely due to hanging out with Noah so much lately. But one emotion was noticeably lacking from her air, and he felt a tinge disappointed at its absence. He couldn't really put a name to it. What was he feeling that he expected her to display as well? Discomfort? Awkwardness? Embarrassment?

It was as if she was completely unaffected by their interaction on the Fourth.

"Hey, Everleigh," Johnny said.

"Hey." Her gaze slid from Johnny to Ryker, but then quickly returned to Noah. "Hey."

"Hey," Noah replied, a sheepish grin pulling at his cheeks.

*Are we all thirteen?* Ryker cleared his throat, hoping Noah would take the hint and get to the point. Then he feigned interest in the belt buckles in the counter display case so he didn't have to watch Noah bumble through whatever it was he was about to say.

"How's your day been?" Noah started.

"Fine. Yours?"

"Good. Fine. Had to unload the supply truck today, so that kept me busy."

"I see." She bobbed her head as she started folding the clothes and stacking them on the counter. "Was the store busy otherwise?"

"Fairly. You?"

"Pretty dead today."

"Nice."

"Kind of boring, actually. I like to keep busy."

"Oh yeah. Me too," Noah quipped, a touch of nervousness coloring his tone.

Good God, was this how all their conversations went? Ryker clenched his jaw and cleared his throat more loudly this time.

"So, ah. The real reason I stopped by?" Noah leaned forward, folding his hands over the edge of the counter.

Everleigh paused and gave him her full attention. Ryker stared at a large silver buckle with a bald eagle holding an American flag in its talons.

"I was wondering if you, ah, wanted to maybe go to the movies with me tomorrow night? To Cedar Rapids? The new *Sidekick Heroes* movie is out, you know."

"I did know. I've been dying to see it."

"So, is that a yes?"

Ryker glanced at Everleigh from the corner of his eye only to find her already looking in his direction. Chewing on the inside of her mouth. He promptly dropped his stare to the eagle buckle.

"Yeah. Sure."

"Excellent." Elation dripped from Noah's response.

And Ryker was annoyed.

"Will you be picking me up?" she asked sweetly.

"Of course. Six o'clock?"

Ryker refused to look up from the buckle design he now had committed to memory, so he could only assume she was nodding her head in the deafening silence that filled the store.

"I'll call you later," Noah said cheerily as he patted his hand on the countertop.

Thankfully, that meant they could leave.

Ryker started to lead the way out of the shop when her voice stopped him dead in his tracks.

"Hey, Ryker?" Everleigh asked in that same sweet tone.

He turned, stepping to the side so Johnny and Noah could walk past. To his dismay, they both stopped beside him. What could she possibly have to say to him?

She leaned under the counter and straightened with a glass container in her hand. Full of cookies. Ryker squinted in confusion as she slid the container across the countertop toward him.

"I was going to drive out to your house after work to return this to your mom, but since you're here . . . would you mind?"

His confusion mounted until he remembered the potato salad leftovers his mom had said she sent home with Everleigh. Of course. But why the cookies?

She answered his unspoken question. "I made a fresh batch of cookies as a thank-you for that amazing potato salad."

"Cookies!" Johnny hooted his approval.

Just as Ryker reached out to grab the container, she placed her hands protectively over both sides, and he wanted to jerk his hand back at the unexpected warmth of her touch on his skin. But he could also lift a couple of his fingers and effectively intertwine them with hers.

"Now, no." His head jerked up at Everleigh once again reading his mind, but he realized she was talking to Johnny. Her gaze shifted to Ryker, an intensity behind those hazel eyes that burned into his soul. Why had he never noticed those dark rings around her irises before? Never seen how they framed the kaleidoscope of green, blue, brown, and gold and made her stare absolutely arresting? "You make sure your mother gets *all* of these cookies. I made them for her."

Ryker had to swallow to speak around the lump in his throat. "Uh, yeah. Yes."

She lifted the hand that was on his to point a finger at each of them in turn. "I mean it."

The sudden absence of her soft, warm touch left him with an emptiness he was unprepared for. God, what was she doing to him? He slid the container out from under the grip of her other hand as quickly as he could and headed for the door, not caring whether the guys were following him or not.

Jumping into the truck, he shoved the container of cookies on the dash and started the engine. As soon as Johnny and Noah were in the truck, Ryker backed out of the parking space, barely waiting for the latter to shut the door. Johnny said something about the cookies, he thought, but he was too far inside his head to really know. He pulled up to Noah's house first.

"What's up, man? I thought we were going fishing?"

"Sorry—uh . . . I forgot I've got to help my dad with something."

"Oh. Okay. Well, Johnny, do you still wanna go?"

Ryker didn't hear their exchange, but Johnny exited the vehicle along with Noah. Good. He threw the truck in gear before the passenger side door was even closed. He dropped the windows and let the wind whip through the cab. Maybe it would help clear the incessant thoughts of Everleigh from his mind. Two miles out of town. Three. He pressed his foot into the pedal.

Seventy. Eighty. Ninety.

Four miles. Five.

The container of cookies still perched on the dash caught his eye, and he glanced in the rearview mirror as he hit the brakes and brought the truck to a halt on the highway five and a half miles outside of town. Ryker grabbed the container, ripped off the silicone lid, and stared at the neatly stacked cookies. Two rows of three cookies, two high. A dozen. He regretted breathing when he inhaled the delicious smell of chocolate chips. But not just chocolate chips—chocolate *chunks* too. So much chocolate in each cookie. His mouth watered. He grabbed a cookie and took a large bite.

And had an orgasm in his mouth. What. The. *Fuck*. How was it so damn good? Ryker shoved the rest of the cookie into his mouth, closed his eyes, and imagined Everleigh's dark-ringed hazel eyes as he nearly creamed in his shorts. Savoring the sweet, salty, delicious perfection of that one cookie, he cradled the glass container against his chest. When he finally opened his eyes, he checked the rearview mirror. No one else on the road. He reached for the lid on the seat beside him, but then changed his mind. Instead, he set the container in his lap and moved his foot from the brake to the gas.

Accelerating to legal highway speed, Ryker picked up a cookie, closed his fist tightly around it, held his hand out the window, and crumbled it to bits. He crumbled four more cookies over mile six, four cookies over mile seven. And the final two cookies on the gravel road that led to his house.

# Chapter 5
# Not Noah

**Everleigh**

EVERLEIGH PATTED HER FACE dry with a towel as she entered her bedroom. She reached back to flick off the bathroom light, then tossed the towel in her laundry hamper. Sitting on her bed, she pulled the scrunchie from her hair, rubbed her fingers against her scalp, and smoothed out her thick tresses. When she set the scrunchie on her nightstand, she noticed his text.

*Can't wait to see you tomorrow.*

A smile pulled at her lips and she typed, *Same.*

Then a SnapChat notification appeared. Noah again, telling her the same thing he just texted over video. She sent a thumbs up reaction.

Then came a *Good night* text.

She rolled her eyes and typed, *I'm already sleeping.* He sent back a laughing emoji. Smiling, she set her phone beside her on the bed and relaxed onto her pillows. It was weird thinking how just a couple weeks ago, Everleigh had fully expected to finish her summer single and focused on prepping for the move to college. She'd even planned her last day at Marla's for the end of July so she could make sure she had everything lined up for her dorm room and for setting up the optimal study area. For spending a couple full days with Crestin before he moved to New

York City, as she worried the distance meant she might never see him again.

*Is this karma? Or kismet?* If she hadn't made a mess of that jewelry display, if Noah hadn't entered the store right at that moment, if he'd chosen to turn away rather than help, would he have ever gathered the courage to talk to her? Would he have invited her to Ryker's party the following week?

Ryker's party . . .

Where she'd really started to get to know Noah.

Where she'd put her mouth all over the neck of a boy who was *not* Noah.

Where she'd imagined doing things that made her heart race with Not Noah. Who basically told her to sit down and then literally physically made her sit down back in her chair at the fire. To be honest, the rejection had stung pretty badly. Especially since she'd thought he was into her. In reality, she'd been intoxicated and fooled herself into thinking Ryker had felt something for her as he held her so close, so tight to his chiseled body.

So, when Noah had moved his chair right next to her during the fireworks show and slipped his hand around hers, she hadn't minded. It'd bumped her self confidence back up a notch to know at least someone found her attractive.

And it turned out to be the best thing for her. Talking with Noah, hanging out, had been the highlight of her summer so far. They began texting, messaging over Snapchat, talking every day after that party. Then multiple times a day. Taking a couple of evening walks around town, where he provided his life's history all the way from his first preschool memories to why it had taken him a week to work up the courage to talk to Everleigh after that day in the store. Nearly two decades of information on Noah Koeppen. But she enjoyed hearing all about him and not having to think of things to tell him about herself.

He'd come over to her house several times so they could binge watch the most recent season of *Stranger Things*. He'd sat and talked with her and her mom for nearly half an hour the other night before he finally headed home, making them laugh over and over with his stories.

Noah truly seemed like the perfect Nice Guy. Add to that picture thick, dark hair, bright, jade green eyes, a smattering of freckles across his nose and cheeks. Tall. Cute. Real boyfriend material. Mother-approved.

So why was the smell of Ryker's cedarwood cologne and the sight of his tan, half-naked body always sneaking into her mind?

Everleigh sighed and pressed her hands to her forehead, trying to push away the most recent, terribly dirty thought of Ryker Martin that had wormed its way inside her brain.

She picked up her phone and opened the messaging app, selected Crestin's name from her favorites, and started typing a very long text: *Please help. I'm obsessing over a boy who wants nothing to do with me, which is getting in the way of my current quasi-relationship with his friend. The blank spaces in my mind fill with thoughts of all the things I want to do with said boy. My insides burn in his presence. My fingers still tingle where I inadvertently touched his hand earlier today. Please, please, PLEASE tell me how to get him out of my head!!!*

Everleigh chewed on the inside of her mouth then touched the back button until every last guilt-inducing word was deleted from sight. She tried again: *I have a date tomorrow. Want to come help me get ready?*

She didn't know why she allowed herself to feel torn up. Having a real relationship with either boy was not in the cards. Because one—Ryker didn't want her in that way. And two—she'd be leaving for college in a few weeks, and any connection she formed with Noah would surely fizzle as the weeks and months apart rolled along.

"You're going on an actual date with him," Crestin said.

"Yes. We're going to see *Sidekick Heroes: The Next Chapter.* I'm excited."

"Excited for *Sidekick Heroes,* or . . . excited to go on a date with Noah?"

"Both." Right? Yes. "He's really sweet. And he's very cute. And if it doesn't work out, it won't really be that big of a deal, right?" She shrugged. "He knows I'm leaving for school next month."

Crestin's eyes narrowed. "But does he?"

"What do you mean by that?" Everleigh paused with her favorite purple V-neck blouse and long black skirt held up to her body and shifted her eyes in the mirror to Crestin lounging on her bed in the background. He rolled onto his stomach to address her, and she felt like this was an eye contact kind of conversation, so she dropped the clothes onto the chair and turned around to face him.

"Listen," he began as he laced his fingers together under his chin, friendship bracelets adorning both wrists. "This boy is a full-fledged adult still living in Rustic, working at his family's hardware store, planning on taking over management of said store someday."

She stared at him with one eyebrow raised, trying to understand his point.

"My point being," he said with a sassy glare, "that he has already settled into—and accepted—his long-term future as an upstanding, normal, plain-and-boring citizen of this great little town. Have you?"

Everleigh was taken aback by his statement.

"Evs . . ." Crestin turned earnest as he sat up abruptly on her floral-print bedspread and dropped his long legs over the side of her bed, flattening his palms on either side of him. "Are you ready to be a standard fixture in this town for the next sixty or seventy years? Because Noah is.

And I can guarantee you that he thinks you are. He's already picturing you coming back to visit every break, every summer. He's imagining the wedding in the park. The double stroller you'll be pushing around the square on Sunday afternoons. The fact that you will give up your dreams to become his housewife, mother of his minis, and probably even the bookkeeper for the hardware store."

She blinked rapidly as she felt his words sink into her bones.

"And do you think the sex he can lay on your sweet body is worth all that?" Crestin asked as he flourished an outstretched hand in the air between them, gesturing from her head to her toes.

She'd never thought of it in that context. Everleigh had just assumed Noah knew she was available for a brief relationship—a summer fling, if you will. There was no way she was willing to give up the future she saw for herself to become a housewife. To lose her identity and remain in tiny Rustic for the rest of her life? No way.

And she hadn't even thought of having sex with him. She would be going to college next month, focusing on obtaining her degree in political science, setting her sights on a prosperous legal career somewhere like Chicago. Big city connections offered the best opportunities for building the life she dreamt of away from this small, dead-end town. She didn't fault anyone for choosing Rustic as their hometown. She simply knew it wasn't the place she would spend the rest of her life. Even her own father, who was transferred here by his job, had left this town in his dust shortly after forcing their relocation.

It would be unfair of her to lead Noah along knowing Rustic would never be her final destination.

"You get it," Crestin confirmed gently for her.

Everleigh inhaled a deep breath, picked up the blouse and skirt, replaced them on the rod in her closet, and reached for her most comfortable sweatshirt. She pulled it on over her T-shirt and fluffed her hair, then spun around. "How do I look?"

"Like perfection," he cooed as he winked at her. As if suddenly remembering something, he jumped up and grabbed hold of her hands. "I almost forgot! Are you ready to mop up this tea I'm about to spill?"

Crestin pulled her back onto the bed, folding one of his legs under the other. She mirrored his pose. He was breathless, as if struggling to keep the gossip in for just a few more seconds was a workout in and of itself.

"Spit it out already!" she laughed.

He waved an impatient hand at her and said, "Remember when I told you Ryker had a secret?"

The mention of that name sent a shockwave through her body. "Um . . . not really."

"That day in the store, when you saw his goody bag?"

"I did *not* see his goody bag!" she interrupted.

Crestin placed his hand over hers. "Girl, close enough. Anywaaay, I told you I upset him when I asked if he'd been kicked off the baseball team. Remember?"

Everleigh nodded as she recalled that conversation.

"Right. So. Marissa and I went out to grab our work shirts for The Sunflower Experience this season from Rita. And chatted her up for a bit. You know, Mama Rita's really quite funny in general. I just love having a nice chat with her. She adores me and Marissa—"

"I'm sorry, is this the tea?"

"Evs, please! I'm getting there. Hold your Pink Ponies!"

"Sorry."

"It's okay. So—I asked how Ryker's team had done in the championships this year, all innocent and such. And she drew her lips into a line like this—" he demonstrated "—and she sighed. And then she was quiet for a moment, like she was trying to decide how to put it. Then she said Ryker came home early this year. And in my mind, I'm like, *Duh, tell me why!* But of course, I didn't say that. Instead, I acted all concerned and said how I hoped everything was okay and he didn't get into trouble, did he?"

When Crestin finally paused to take a breath, Everleigh processed what he'd said, making sure she understood.

"And Rita said that Ryker's had a tough go this year, but he was working on himself, and she was confident he'd be back on track soon enough."

"That makes me feel bad for him. What does she mean 'a tough go'?"

"Well, let me tell you this: She immediately changed the subject and started talking about the sunflower patch again. But I was clever," Crestin said as he tapped his finger on his temple. "I circled back around at the end, asking if Ryker had sold his Malibu. Said I hadn't seen him driving it this summer, and I'd always told him I'd buy it from him if he ever wanted to sell it. I asked if it was in the shop or if he was trying to sell it. And she said he wrecked it, unfortunately. I could tell right after she'd said it, she knew she shouldn't have said anything. She asked me to please not bring it up around Ryker. He was trying to move past it."

"What else did she say?" Everleigh asked when Crestin appeared to be distracted by his hair in the reflection of her full-length mirror.

"That was it. Her phone rang and she had to go, so Marissa and I left."

"But she didn't say what happened to cause the accident?"

"No, she did not. There's more to the story, I'm certain of it. Drunk driving, drug running, bank robbery gone bad—I'll figure it out."

"Crestin, you do have some imagination."

"That has only served me well in my life. One must be able to imagine all possible scenarios to be prepared for anything life can throw at you," he commented archly.

"I can't argue with you there." Everleigh shrugged a shoulder. As they wasted away the last half hour before Noah was slated to pick her up, she really tried to pay attention to Crestin's chattering. But her mind was stuck on Ryker and what caused him to wreck his car and have to come home early from a collegiate sport. This new information was doing nothing to help her keep Ryker out of her thoughts. It only cemented his place right there in the front corner of her mind, easily accessible.

The movie was nearly over. Noah had laced his fingers through her left hand, and she'd allowed it. At some point, he'd withdrawn his fingers and placed his arm around her shoulders, pulling her a fraction closer to him. By the last action sequence, she noticed his face was mere inches from her, his right arm hugging her close, his left hand clasped on her forearm. He was definitely looking to make some kind of move.

Earlier, before her conversation with her wise friend, Crestin, she would have easily allowed it. She'd probably already be making out with Noah. But Crestin's words reverberated in her mind, and she knew it would be very wrong for her to lead Noah on. No, she needed to stop this before it had a chance to take root, to potentially really hurt him. She knew what he wanted. And she knew what she wanted. And the two didn't match. It wasn't fair to let him think differently.

So, when the movie was nearly over and she felt him dip his face toward hers, she pushed herself forward in her seat. "I've got to use the restroom," she whispered apologetically. Then she hurried from the auditorium. Which really sucked, because the climax of the movie was unfolding at that very moment. Fight sequences and heroism comedically timed and all that jazz. But she rushed out to the hallway and into the restroom.

Everleigh splashed water on her face. Wiped it with a paper towel. Stared hard at her reflection in the mirror. What was wrong with her? Why had she put herself in such an awkward position? She was going to have to let Noah know she wasn't into having a relationship with him, to explain why it was her and not him. She was going to have to figure out how not to break his sensitive little heart.

When she emerged from the restroom, the movie was over, and he stood in the corridor waiting for her. "I'm sorry," she offered. "What did I miss?"

"Only the best part of the movie."

Her shoulders lifted as her mouth twisted to the side.

"But we can come back and watch it again, if you want."

"Oh, no. No," she said quickly as she waved her hand in front of her. "It's okay. Really."

"You sure? Because I don't mind. If you want . . ."

She swallowed hard. Looking up into his waiting green eyes, Everleigh felt like the worst person in the world. She had totally led Noah on. She had no romantic feelings for him. She couldn't.

"I think I'm just ready to go home," she said as she tried to convey her apology through her eyes.

The twenty-minute ride home was virtually silent. Noah tried to keep conversation going by bringing up his favorite parts of the movie, and Everleigh shared her thoughts, but nothing beyond that. She sensed he was slowly realizing the vibe. It just wasn't going to happen between the two of them. So, when he pulled into her driveway, before she exited the car, she wrapped her hands around his right one.

"Noah, you're so great. Really."

"But . . ." he hedged with an ironic smile.

She let out an empathetic breath. "But. I am going away to college next month. And I'm not planning on coming back to Rustic. I'm not planning to settle down here."

"Not even for the right person?"

The hopeful expression on his face stabbed at her heart. She shook her head. "I just don't think it's in the cards."

Noah turned his head and looked out his window for a minute, and she thought he might be biting his lower lip. When he turned back, although she saw the moisture brimming in his eyes, she said nothing. He gave her hand a squeeze and said, "Thanks for giving me a chance."

She patted his hand and nodded, swallowing around the lump in her throat.

"If you change your mind, you know where to find me."

Everleigh released a breathy laugh and placed her hand on his left cheek. She gave him a light kiss on his right. "I do," she confirmed. "Thank you for taking me to the movie."

"Anytime," he said with a smile that didn't reach his eyes.

Deep regret crept up on her as she ascended the porch steps to her home. Mostly because she'd allowed herself to think it wasn't a big deal she didn't like him as much as he liked her. That it wouldn't hurt to have a little summer fling before she went off to college. But it had hurt him. And in turn, that hurt her. She vowed then and there to always listen to her instincts, to listen to her heart. If it didn't feel right, she wouldn't pursue it.

And when she laid her head on her pillow that night to sleep, she took comfort in the fact that she never gave up any part of herself to Noah that she wasn't comfortable giving.

# Chapter 6
# A Double-Dog Challenge

## Ryker

"Hey, hon."[1]

Ryker grunted as he pushed the weight-loaded barbell up from his chest. Not breaking the rhythm of his reps, he waited for his mother to say what it was she'd come downstairs to say.

"You've been down here a while."

"Yeah," he grunted again while pushing up the bar. His parents had converted the basement family room into a workout space once Ryker had convinced them just how serious he was about baseball while still a freshman in high school. He couldn't say how many hours he'd logged down here over the years—likely more than he'd spent in his actual bedroom upstairs.

"I'm making supper. Should be ready in twenty minutes or so."

He lifted the last rep in the set and placed the bar on the cradle with a loud clang. Pulling at the collar of his shirt, he wiped the sweat from his face, then sat up on the bench and said, "I'm almost done."

"How are the workouts going?"

"Fine."

"Have you talked to Coach lately?"

---

1. Breaking Benjamin, "I Will Not Bow"

"No."

"Did you go to your therapy session today?"

His brows raised in anticipation of her response to this one. "No."

"Honey, why not?"

"I just didn't make it." He stood and moved over to the hand weights. He'd rather not have to look his mother's disappointment square in the face yet again.

"Ryker, you need to meet with someone. You need to face your vices and learn how to successfully cope with them. We've talked about this."

He lifted each hand weight in turn, offering nothing in response.

"I know you think you can do it all on your own, but you shouldn't have to."

Dropping the weights onto the rack, he turned to face his mom. "You mean you don't think I can do it on my own. You don't think I've got this, and I'm telling you I do."

"No, that's not it." Frustration crept into her expression. "Your father and I only want what's best for you, you know that. But the help you need is beyond our expertise. Please let a professional help you."

Ryker scratched the back of his neck and stared at the floor. The biggest problem for him was vocalizing his thoughts and his feelings so a professional could actually help. Right now, he had everything under control, locked up tight inside, and it wasn't coming out. He wouldn't let it.

Aside from his parents and Coach Sandoval, the only other person he'd said anything to was Tyson—the only other person he trusted with that truth. Tyson had always been his ride or die, and Ryker knew he'd go to his grave before betraying Ryker's confidence.

As much as it had killed him to tell his best friend about all he'd wrecked in the space of a few months, and to see the same disappointment on Tyson's face he'd seen with his parents and his coach, he really thought it might have saved his life. Because Tyson believed in

Ryker, believed he could overcome all the bad. Believed he could get his life back on course, when it seemed nobody else did.

"Ryker, I'm not kidding. I want to know that when I send you back out into the world, you're going to be able to handle it."

"God, Mom, I'm not a child!"

"Well, then stop acting like one!" Her raised voice startled him into silence.

"You're right, you're not a child," she continued in a strained tone. "But you are certainly not acting like an adult. I get it. Life sucks. It does for us all sometime or other. It's overwhelming. Anxiety-inducing. Hard as hell. But part of being an adult is understanding when you are not capable of managing the load yourself and seeking out help to keep you steady on your feet. To keep you mentally healthy."

Ryker swallowed. He knew she was right, but he was still upset that she had so little faith in his ability to maintain his mental health. He'd been doing it for over a month now. All on his own. He wiped his face with his shirt again. "I'm going to head out."

"What? I just told you supper is almost ready."

"I forgot I'm going with Tyson to the track. I'll eat when I get back," he said as he killed the music on his speaker then stepped past his mom. His friend's text message signaling he was out in the front drive couldn't have come at a better moment.

"Ryker," she tried one more time.

"Thanks for the talk," he called over his shoulder as he jogged up the stairs.

❧ ❧

A nice, brisk three-mile run was exactly what the doctor ordered. And that sprint there at the end, when Tyson kicked it in and challenged him the last quarter mile? Cathartic. Even though Tyson pulled ahead and beat him by a yard at the finish.

"Goddamn, boy," Tyson gasped between breaths as he slapped Ryker on the shoulder. "I need to run against you all the time."

"Against?" he huffed. "I thought we were running *together*."

"Always a competition, buddy. That's how you stay at the top of your game. Never not competing." Tyson placed two fingers on the pulse at his neck while he walked over to the grassy infield of the track and started his cooldown routine. Ryker took a drink from his water jug, swished it around his mouth, spit it out, took another drink that he swallowed down, then followed suit.

"I was starting to wonder about you, man. You doing okay?"

Ryker shrugged before leaning forward and wrapping his hands around his foot, giving his hamstring and calf a nice stretch. "Why wouldn't I be?"

"Don't know. Just checking, I guess. We haven't seen you around much lately."

He couldn't deny that. "There's been a lot to do on the farm. Prepping for the sunflower season. In addition to all the other farm shit. Mowing hay, baling hay, stacking hay. All the best parts of summer."

Tyson smiled, his white teeth brilliant against his dark brown skin. "I hear ya."

Ryker knew that tone. Tyson's *I-know-that's-not-the-full-story* voice. His friend was really going to make a great coach someday. With a sigh, Ryker relented, "I've just needed to keep some distance lately."

"Oh, man, I hope it's nothing I've done."

"No, no. It's hard to explain . . ."

"I've got time." Tyson moved his legs straight out in front of him and leaned forward, wrapping his fingers around the bottoms of his feet as he stretched.

A smile lifted the corner of Ryker's mouth. What had he done to deserve such a good friend? "You know how bad I am at talking about feelings and shit."

"Again, I've got time." Tyson's brown eyes always held a calmness that Ryker envied.

He picked a clover flower in the grass beside him and tossed it into the wind. "I'm trying, very hard, to stay in a good headspace right now. To focus on fixing me. And . . . I find myself . . . losing focus when I'm around certain people."

Tyson nodded with a knowing expression. "Who is she?"

Ryker choked out a laugh. "Ahh, someone I shouldn't be messing with anyway."

"One of those, huh?" Tyson squinted at him.

"Definitely one of those." Ryker leaned back, resting his palms on the thick, prickly blanket of infield grass.

"Well, I'm here if you need to talk about it."

Ryker let those words sit for a moment before he said, "I appreciate you."

After taking a long drink from his water jug, Tyson said, "Let's go. I need to stop and get some groceries before I take you home." He stood, holding his hand out to help Ryker to his feet.

"Your mom makes you buy groceries?"

"No, she does not, my friend. I choose to make the life of the woman who poured her soul into raising my obnoxious ass easier whenever I can. It's the little things you do that can be the most meaningful."

"Wow. Insightful. Maybe I should get some groceries for my mom too."

Five minutes later, Tyson pulled into the parking lot of the dollar-store-slash-grocery-store. As they headed inside, Ryker's reflection caught his eye in the glass doors. Sweat stains covered the front of his sleeveless shirt, and his dark brown hair was a windblown mess. He combed his hands through it to tame it down at least a little bit. Tyson grabbed a basket with handles and seemed to know exactly where he was headed, so Ryker followed behind, lifting his shirt to wipe the sweat beads he still felt on his forehead and temples.

"Oh! Hey, girrrrls."

*That voice definitely belongs to Crestin*, Ryker thought as he pulled his shirt back down and straightened the shoulders. As he came up alongside Tyson, he saw Crestin wasn't alone.

"Hey," Tyson responded. "Umm . . . what's with the ponies?"

"These?" Crestin asked as he held up a fuzzy pink pony head on a stick. A child's toy. "For Chappell Roan."

"I'm sorry?" Tyson inquired around a chuckle.

"We're going to a Chappell Roan concert."

"And you need toy ponies for it?" Ryker asked. His eyes slid from Crestin and the pink pony with a feathery mane and shiny streamers hanging from the base of its neck to Everleigh and her white pony with a rainbow mane and identical shiny streamers. Immediately, he wanted to look away, but he hadn't seen her in over a week, and his eyes thirsted to take in everything about her. From the white, patterned ribbon tying her hair back from her face to the light reflecting the gold flecks in her eyes to the chipped purple paint on her fingernails to the miles of long, tan legs leading down to the same purple paint on her toes peeking out of her sandals.

"As a matter of fact, we do," she replied in that sweet voice with that sweet smile.

"This is one of those concerts you do *not* attend unprepared. If you know, you know," Crestin schooled them.

"I see," Tyson responded.

"We'll leave you to it." Ryker pulled on Tyson's elbow so he could get out of Everleigh's presence before she wormed her way into his every thought and made him feel like an even worse friend to Noah for imagining all the things Ryker wanted to do to his girlfriend.

To his annoyance, after a few steps, Tyson stopped and turned back to the two, forcing Ryker to act normal and do the same. Forcing him to look at Everleigh once more.

"Say, a bunch of us are tubing down the river this Saturday. Wanna join?" Tyson asked.

Ryker's insides solidified. Why was he inviting them? Noah wouldn't be there; his family had their annual reunion this weekend.

"Saturday? I mean, I'm free," Crestin said and looked at Everleigh. "You?"

"Yeah, sounds like fun." There was that smile again.

"Great. Ryker can text you the details," Tyson told Crestin. "See you around."

As they walked out of the store with their bags of groceries, Ryker had to ask. "Why did you invite them?"

"Why not?"

He raked his hand through his hair. "I mean, Noah won't be there."

"And that's why I felt it was safe to invite them." At Ryker's mask of confusion, Tyson furrowed his brow. "You don't know?"

"Know what?"

"Noah and Everleigh didn't work out."

The lightning strike of those words shot through his chest. Ryker wanted to feel bad for his friend, but he only felt . . . troubled. He cleared his throat and said, "I didn't know."

"Yeah, poor kid. She broke up with him after he took her to the movie. Said he never even got to kiss her."

"Hm," was all Ryker could say.

And his thoughts spiraled into how this was a very, very bad thing for him.

Ryker had prepared himself to spend all day with his friends on the river, knowing most everyone would be drinking.[2] He was prepared to stay sober. He'd prepared himself to spend all day around Everleigh. Worked himself into a mental space of indifference.

But nothing could have prepared him for the sight of Everleigh in a black bikini with droplets of water glistening on her tan skin. The way her neck curved into her shoulders, the way the mass of brown hair tied into a messy bun at the base of her neck drew his attention right there. The way his eyes could travel along the fabric of the bikini strap, from the back of her neck, over her collarbone, and right along the curve of her breast to the dip in the center of her chest. Everleigh, Crestin, and Marissa were already in the shallows by the river access, splashing water at one another.

"Here you go." Tyson handed an inner tube out of the back of the truck, followed by another one. Ryker forced himself to focus on the task at hand and tied their tubes together. Tied the cooler float to them. Inspected its contents to make sure they had everything. He reset his mind while he worked and averted his eyes from Everleigh's direction as they headed for the water.

And the first half an hour on the river was peaceful and enjoyable. He and Tyson talked about preseason football starting soon. Johnny, who chose to kayak rather than tube, alternated rowing circles around them and floating backward so he could face them and be involved in the conversation.

But then somehow Crestin, Marissa, and Everleigh caught up to them. Their tubes tied together, they came up along Tyson's side, so Everleigh

---

2. Ethel Cain, "American Teenager"

was farthest away from Ryker. He adjusted his ball cap lower on his forehead and focused his eyes on the groups ahead of them on the river. Ignored the conversations happening among them and instead homed in on the music coming from the speaker in Johnny's kayak.

Until he couldn't.

Crestin had grabbed onto Johnny's kayak and commanded him to row them around to Ryker's side, and suddenly Crestin was clamping a hand onto his tube and jabbering at him about something. "Ryker, tell her I used to play football."

"I'm sorry, I don't believe you, Crestin!" Everleigh was nonplussed. "If there's an elevator, you take it over the stairs. You ride the motorized scooter around Target rather than walk. I cannot picture you in football pads and cleats running up and down the field and tackling other boys."

"Oh, the tackling of other boys was the best part," Crestin said wickedly as he pushed away from Ryker's inner tube and the group of three shifted positions in the water.

"Crestin!" Marissa laughed. "You didn't even know you were gay until sophomore year."

"Maybe it was football that turned me gay! Ever think of that?"

"Ryker?" Everleigh said as her inner tube came up alongside his. She hooked her foot over to keep them floating close, and he couldn't look away from her purple toenails. "Did Crestin really play football?"

"Ah." He cleared his throat. "Yeah. I remember he was on our middle school team. And then you were on JV, right? Freshman year?" he asked Crestin.

"That's right. *Boom*." Crestin stuck his tongue out at Everleigh. "I played from sixth grade to ninth grade. I used to really like football. Until I decided I hated physical exertion."

"Did you like football?"

Ryker forgot he was trying to avoid Everleigh. "What's that?"

"Did you like playing football?" she repeated.

"Oh, yeah. Tyson and I were in literally every sport growing up. Every season. Football, basketball, track, baseball. Soccer when we were little. I loved playing football, but I love baseball the most."

"Do you still love baseball?" If he wasn't mistaken, her head tilted as if she was inspecting the tattoo on his upper arm. But he could be imagining it since her sunglasses camouflaged her eyes.

"Of course," he said, his voice catching unexpectedly. He looked away for a moment, and when he looked back, she seemed to be waiting for him to tell her more. And Ryker couldn't help himself. "Baseball is in my blood. I could never fall out of love with it."

"Would you ever play professionally?"

"That would be a dream come true."

"Are you going to try?"

"I might have, before . . ."

When he didn't continue, Everleigh asked, "Before what?"

Why was he spilling his guts to her? He was trying to keep her out of his mind, but she was climbing in and finding a nice, cozy spot. Ryker rubbed his hand over his jaw as he tried to hold it in, but he just couldn't. Sighing, he admitted, "Before I fucked it all up."

Maybe she sensed he didn't want to talk about it. Maybe she didn't want to know the rest. Whichever it was, she simply replied, "I'm sorry, Ryker."

And she just set up camp and built a fire for two in that nice, cozy spot.

"There it is!" Tyson pointed.

"What is?" Everleigh asked as she looked in that direction.

"The bluff. There's a little cove tucked in behind it. That's where we're taking a break."

"Good, because I have to pee," Marissa volunteered.

"Why not just pee in the river? That's what the hole in the tube is for," Johnny said as he floated in front of them.

"I'm pretty sure that's *not* what the hole in the tube is for!" Marissa exclaimed. Then she turned to Ryker and Tyson and asked, "Is it?"

They laughed in response.

When Tyson recovered, he changed the subject. "You know, the Underground Railroad used to come right along here. Hid people in an old shack tucked along the shore in the cove. It's a collapsed pile of rotting wood now."

"Really?" Everleigh asked.

"That's what my great-granny always told me. And she was good friends with *the* Dr. Martin Luther King, Jr., so she knows a thing or two."

"Wow, that's so cool! Is your great-granny still alive?"

"Ninety-four and still kicking."

"I'll bet she has all kinds of amazing stories. Do you see her often?"

"Not as often as I used to, or as often as I'd like to, but I still call her every other Sunday."

"Oh, Tyson, that is wonderful! I'll bet she's so proud of you."

Ryker found himself watching Everleigh as she continued her conversation with Tyson. He'd never realized how easy a conversationalist she could be, had never had an opportunity to be involved in a real one with her. It was amazing how she pulled information out of people. Like she was truly curious about them, like she really wanted to hear what they had to say.

She'd moved more in front of Ryker now to get a better line of sight with Tyson as they talked, and instead of her foot wrapped around his, her hand was now wrapped over his instep, her fingertips burning into his arch in four distinct heat patterns. Ryker's gaze traveled from the chipped purple polish on her thumbnail up her arm, over her shoulder. He watched her chest dance up and down as she laughed at something Tyson said. Followed the soft, bare skin of her stomach until it disappeared below view in the inner tube, skipped over to where her tan thigh reappeared and led to her perfectly shaped knee. His eyes focused on that spot at the back of her knee. And he imagined lifting that leg in his arm so he could place a kiss on that very spot.

"All right, everyone!" Tyson ripped him from his reverie. "Paddle to the cove!"

Ryker's foot went cold when the warmth of Everleigh's hand disappeared. And it was as if a spell had been lifted. As she moved swiftly out of his line of sight, he forced all thoughts of her to follow. He couldn't get wrapped up in her now. He needed to focus on himself. He knew this. And she was a distraction he couldn't afford.

The cove had a shallow edge along the eastern shore, so that was where everyone headed to exit the water. With the tubes stacked to the side of the small beach, the group spread out to feast on food from their coolers. Some of the girls walked around, offering to share meats and cheeses from their stashes. Someone had brought pickle wraps for all.

Ryker finished his sandwich and pulled a T-shirt from his waterproof bag. He spread it out on the sand and laid his head on it, removed his ball cap, and set it over his face, stacking his hands behind his head. As a chorus of cans cracked open around him, he knew this break would last a while. Might as well take the opportunity for a little nap in the shade.

Too soon, he felt his foot being tugged on. He lifted the ball cap and cracked his eyes open: Johnny.[3] "Come on, man. We're gonna go up on the bluff."

Ryker rubbed his face with his hands and propped himself up on his elbows. He watched Johnny and Tyson follow a group of guys to the rear of the cove, where a path snaked up to the top of the bluff. His gaze rested on the group of girls (and Crestin) doing some kind of dance to music blaring from a speaker. "H-O-T-T-O-G-O! Snap and clap and touch your toes!" His eyes widened, then he blinked as he focused

---

3. Chappell Roan, "HOT TO GO!"

on Everleigh specifically. Because she'd just touched her toes with her bikini-clad ass facing him. He wanted to look away, but she moved on to safer choreography, making letters or something with her arms in the air, so he continued to watch. She looked like she was having so much fun, laughing and dancing with her friends, and he wondered how he'd never seen this carefree side of her before.

Honestly, there were several sides of her he'd seen for the first time today. What a shame he never took the time to get to know her. He suddenly felt like he'd missed out on something he didn't know he wanted. Until now. Until just a few short weeks ago. When it was too late. He looked away toward the guys appearing at the top of the bluff as the chorus started again and he knew she was about to touch her toes.

Ryker stood, shook the sand from his swim shorts, wiped it from his legs, ran a hand through his hair, and walked past the dancing crew to the trail that headed to the bluff. Immediately, he was annoyed with himself when he let his gaze drift to Everleigh's hips swaying to the music as he passed. He forced his eyes to the trail ahead of him.

"Where are you going?"

He nearly jumped out of his skin when Everleigh of all people popped up beside him, grabbing his arm. He couldn't deny the charge of electricity that shot through his body at her touch. Pushing the feeling away, he pointed to the trail. "Up on the bluff."

"Is that where the guys went?"

He nodded.

"Can I come too?"

"I mean, it's not my bluff."

She giggled.

He noticed she was a little unsteady on her feet and wondered what number of seltzer was in her hand now. "Are you sure? It gets pretty steep," he cautioned.

"Well, what's it like up there? Why is everybody going?"

"Not *everybody* is going," he corrected. "Just those of us who want to cliff dive."

Everleigh pushed her sunglasses up on her head in a swift motion, her hazel eyes alight. "I want to cliff dive!"

He looked at her from the corner of his eye. "Are you sure about that?"

She nodded emphatically, "Absolutely!"

Ryker doubted she'd feel the same way once she got up there and saw how far down the water was, but he decided if she changed her mind, he'd make sure she got back down the path safely. He turned to lead the way when she grabbed his arm again.

"Wait a sec." She downed the last of her drink in three large gulps, and a dangerous thought crept into his mind.

He wondered if he kissed Everleigh right now, would her lips taste like blackberry? And would he keep kissing her to taste her lips or to taste the alcohol?

Ryker closed his eyes and blanked his mind, scooped up her hand, then led her along the path to the bluff. She was chattering about something, but he refused to let her voice beyond his ears. He was on one mission now: To get her safely to the top of the bluff and back down if she was too scared to jump. That was it.

When they reached the top, she was breathless and clinging to his hand with both of hers. He may have climbed at too fast of a clip for her, but he couldn't spend any more time in her presence than absolutely necessary. His whole plan to keep his mental toughness in place? It was crumbling. Fast. And he didn't want to blame Everleigh. It wasn't her fault. But he blamed her just the same.

"Ryker! You made it!" Johnny called. "And you brought a little friend!"

"Hey, guys!" She waved and took off to the edge where they were gathered.

"We got a newbie!" Ben exclaimed. "You ever cliff dived before?"

She shook her head.

"Oh, you're in for a treat," Ben replied. "Just don't look over the edge before you jump."

"What? Why?" Everleigh looked at Tyson.

"You'll be fine. Just follow me. Jump where I jump," Tyson explained.

"Oh, okay." She nodded a lot, then almost tripped on a large rock by her foot. Ryker reached out to catch her, but thankfully, she steadied herself. He started to think this really wasn't a good idea. Maybe she'd had too much to drink. God forbid she got hurt. He'd one hundred percent blame himself for letting her come up here.

"Whoo hoo!" Ben hollered as he ran to the edge of the cliff and jumped off. The echo of his voice cut into a second of silence before the sound of him breaking the water's surface with a loud splash traveled up to them.

Everleigh's hand flew to her chest. "Oh my gosh!" She grabbed Johnny's arm. "How deep is it? I wanna see."

"Plenty deep if you stay on the western half here. You sure you want to look?" She nodded and continued to hold on to his arm as he walked her over to where the rock abruptly transitioned to wind and air.

"Oh my *gosh*!" she exclaimed again and spun away from the edge. She swayed and Ryker nearly called out to Johnny to *catch her*, but she regained control of her body and marched back to him.

Ryker couldn't handle the stress she was inflicting on him right now.

They heard another splash, followed by another. They watched as Cameron dove over the edge rather than take a running jump like the rest. And then it was just Tyson, Johnny, Ryker, and Everleigh.

"It's okay if you don't want to," Ryker spoke up, thinking he might be more nervous than she was. "I'll take you back down."

"No, I want to."

"You sure?" Johnny teased. "It's a long way down. And watch out for the rock that juts out halfway down. And make sure you go out far enough but not too far."

"Ummm . . ." Her brows lifted. "Okay?"

"Seriously," Ryker tried again. "It's fine if you don't want to. None of the girls have done it before."

"Whoa. Is that a challenge?" A weird timbre entered her voice, and she looked at Johnny and Tyson. "That sounded like a challenge."

"Like a double-dog challenge," Johnny confirmed. "See you on the other side!" They watched as he raced off the cliff, kicking his legs in the air before he disappeared from view.

"Your turn," she told Tyson.

"I'm here for it!" He moved closer to the edge than where Johnny started from. "Let's go!" he yelled as he ran three steps and propelled himself outward.

Everleigh clapped her hands together and spun around to face Ryker. "You next or me?"

"You go. I want to be here in case you change your mind."

"Ryker." She made a face. "You challenged me. I can't change my mind."

"I didn't challenge you," he argued.

"Pretty sure you did," she rebutted as she marched to the edge.

And his heart jumped into his throat. He couldn't let her do this. She'd kill herself. She'd had too much to drink, and she was going to hurt herself.

"No, I didn't. Now quit playing around. Let's go." He motioned toward the safety of the path behind them.

"I'm not playing, Ryker. I'm doing this."

His stomach lurched. How could he get her away from that ledge? The encouraging hoots and yells from the group below only seemed to excite her more. He inched forward. Maybe he could pull her back without them both falling over the edge.

"I'm ready." She winked at him. *Winked.* And before he could get to her, she disappeared.

"Everleigh, no!" Panic squeezed his heart as he rushed to the edge of the cliff, prepared to dive in to her rescue. Ryker couldn't believe his eyes as she twisted and somersaulted through the air, entering the water below in near perfect form, with barely a sound.

Everyone cheered, but he focused on the water, waiting for her to reemerge.

Five seconds.

Ten.

Ryker didn't wait for fifteen. He dove in after her.

# Chapter 7
# Never Would Be Too Soon

**Everleigh**

SHE EMERGED FROM THE water a little closer to the river than she wanted and felt the current starting to pull her along. Everleigh inhaled a breath, pushed herself back under the surface, and swam until the calm waters of the cove replaced the pressure of the current. As she neared the surface to take another breath, something grabbed her.

Not something. Someone. She was being dragged. She attempted to fight off whoever it was so she could swim to the shore, but they were not letting go. More water than air made it into her lungs, and she started coughing. She wanted to say, "Let me go!" Wanted to wrestle free, but his grip was too strong. Everleigh could tell by the muscular arm around her that it was a him. And he was crushing her chest.

Thankfully, moments later, they entered water shallow enough that her heels slid across the muddy sludge below. She planted her feet and spun out of his grip, balancing for a brief second before falling back into the water with a splash. She pushed herself upright again, one last cough escaping her throat as she caught her breath.

Ryker returned to her side, concern etched on his features. "Are you okay? Are you hurt?"

Everleigh batted his hands away. Other than her ribs hurting where he'd crushed her under his arm? She wiped the water from her eyes and slid her hands up her face to clear her forehead of wet strands of hair.

"Where are my sunglasses?" She felt for them on top of her head, but they were no longer there.

"What?" he asked, an odd look on his face.

"Crap. I must have lost them in the dive."

"*What?*" Ryker repeated, seemingly agitated.

"It's okay." She shrugged. "I've got another pair at home." She made for the shore, a little tired from swimming against the current and almost being drowned by Ryker.

"What the fuck?" he demanded as he caught up to her where the murky water lapped at the sandy beach.

"I'm sorry?"

"What the *actual* fuck?" His voice rose in timbre.

Ryker was angry. But why?

Everleigh stopped and turned her body fully toward him, angling her head even farther to give him a side-eye. "*Why* are you cursing at me?"

And then he lost it. Absolutely lost it. Stomped his feet and flailed his arms and said something about thinking she was dead.

She held up a hand. "*Why* did you jump to the conclusion I was dead?"

"Because you weren't resurfacing. Because no one knew where you were!"

"I knew where I was."

Ryker's amber eyes went wide, glowing in the summer sun, and he blinked one long, slow blink. She could laugh at how ridiculous he was acting, but it was kind of making her *mad*.

"Well, I did. I ended up too close to the current, and I changed course and came back into the cove," she explained.

"But I thought you were dead."

"Again, why?"

"I don't know! Fuck! Because I couldn't find you!"

Everleigh dragged her hands down her face. She'd had too much to drink to be in a conversation like this right now. "Well, thanks for saving me. I guess."

She turned to walk over to Crestin and Marissa but noticed they were already on the edge of the shore. Everyone was. Gathered around them, watching the drama. She shot Crestin a look, which he immediately understood and returned with a hand flourish.

"Show's over folks. Everleigh's been saved," Everleigh announced as she held her hands up in Ryker's direction to credit him as her savior. She continued over to her bag and pulled out a towel to wipe her face.

Why had she ever liked this boy? He was clearly self-absorbed. Hero-complex. Narcissistic in general. She turned around and toweled off her back. Then stopped as she noticed Ryker standing in front of her.

"What?" she snapped as she wrapped the towel around her torso and tucked the corner under her arm. Thankfully, most everyone had moved along to whatever it was they were doing before this awkward scene unfolded, so there was no longer a big audience.

When he didn't say anything, Everleigh offered, "Did you not hear me telling Tyson earlier on the float that I was on the diving team until I moved here my junior year? I know how to dive from heights. I know how to swim. Pretty well."

"I mean . . . I guess not."

"You *guess* not?"

He shook his head, his brow furrowed.

How could she fault him for not knowing? Other than the fact that she'd talked about it right in front of him. Did Ryker really think that little of her that he would tune her out when she was holding a conversation right in front of him?

"Never mind," she muttered, no longer wanting to be anywhere near him. She headed over to Crestin and Marissa, who both told her that her dive was a ten out of ten, and she loved them for it.

Everleigh glanced at Ryker only once more after that as they put their inner tubes back in the water. And she vowed to ignore him the rest of the float down the river.

"Listen to me," Crestin demanded. "I neeeeeed you."

"But I planned on using these last couple of weeks to get everything organized for my move. You *know* I'm done at Marla's on the thirty-first."

"But I *neeeeeed* you! Marissa came down with mono, so there's an opening at The Sunflower Experience. I've already talked you up to Mama Rita, and she remembers you're the girl who loves her potato salad, and she said she'd love to have you as part of the team. The pay is good, and employees get free food from the food truck! *Pleeeease* don't make me do this alone!" he lamented.

"I feel so bad for Marissa! But I can't take her place. I *can't*. I have responsibilities here."

"Girl! You can match your socks and pack your lady garments after work each day. Honestly. Stop being so selfish."

"Crestin!"

"I'm sorry. I love you. But please, love *me* for once."

"You're the worst."

"But you love me!" he sang.

"I don't know . . ."

Everleigh knocked on Marissa's front door and wondered if she should have worn a facemask. She hadn't been around her since last weekend, so hopefully the cooties had been contained.

The door creaked open, and she was a little relieved to be greeted by Marissa's mom. "Hey, hon. Here's her shirts. I washed them all last night, even though she hasn't worn them. Just in case."

"Thank you," Everleigh said. "Tell Marissa I hope she feels better soon!"

"I will, dear. And if I don't see you again before you go, have a great first semester! Remember, you are always welcome here, so stop by any time you're back in town."

Everleigh smiled as she tucked the shirts under her arm. "Thanks again."

Sliding into the driver's seat of her car, she tossed the shirts onto the passenger side, thinking how cool they were this year. Yellow, green, and blue tie-dye with a white The Sunflower Experience logo on the upper left on the front. She lifted a T-shirt and peeked at the back. It read STAFF across the top in white. There were three shirts, so depending on the weather, she might have to call dibs on the washing machine four times. But she had some clothes she'd pulled out of her seasonal totes to wash before college packing, so she could always throw them in with those loads. As she folded the garment and replaced it on the stack, a nagging thought returned. Followed by an ache in her stomach.

She hadn't thought through the implications of agreeing to take Marissa's spot when Crestin had begged and guilt-tripped her into it. He'd pulled the *I'm-going-to-New-York* card and reminded her that he wouldn't see her again until next summer. And how great would it be if they could spend the last couple of weeks together in the magical sunflower patch, soaking up the sun and scoping out cute single boys? Everleigh had told him she didn't think very many cute single boys were drawn to the sunflower patch out of their own desire to see it, but then her thoughts landed on the one cute single boy who was sure to be there: Ryker.

She thought she'd be happier after not seeing or talking to Ryker since the river float last weekend. He'd been nothing but a thorn in her side the few times she'd been around him this summer. She'd been more than glad to see the last of him as they exited the water at the end of that day. And then he'd dragged his heavy cooler over her foot. True, he'd muttered an apology, but she could have sworn he meant to do it.

She still didn't know why he disliked her so much. He'd been chill that morning. They'd talked more than they ever had before. He'd seemed interested in what she had to say. Well, at first he had. But he'd completely tuned her out while she talked with Tyson and therefore had no idea she was a very capable swimmer. Had Ryker just paid a little bit of attention, he'd have known she was not going to drown after diving off that bluff, and he wouldn't have gotten mad at her for "almost dying." And why would someone ever be mad at someone else they barely knew for almost drowning? Who does that?

Maybe there *was* something wrong with Ryker. Like mentally. Crestin had found out from Ryker's mom that he had wrecked his car and was trying to move past the incident, and it seemed like she was trying to keep the details under wraps. What if Ryker had anger issues and a road rage incident caused that accident? Everleigh could imagine that with the way he'd freaked out on her. What if he'd hurt others in that accident?

But if that had happened, surely it would have made the local news. Car accidents almost always made the news here due to the lack of crime and newsworthy incidents. So maybe not. Maybe he was bipolar and not taking his meds? That would explain the mood swings.

Well, whatever it was, she'd just have to try and stay out of his way. That shouldn't be terribly hard on a forty-acre plot of sunflowers. And it was only ten days, fourteen at the most. It was entirely dependent upon Mother Nature and the life cycle of the sunflowers in this season's climate.

Then she would be off to college, and she could forget all about Ryker Martin.

⚜

"Are you kidding me?" Everleigh seethed at Crestin through gritted teeth, folding her arms over her tie-dyed staff shirt as she glowered.

"It's just for the day. You'll get reassigned tomorrow. We all rotate through the jobs," he said lightly as he slid on his favorite purple visor and fluffed his thick, dark hair out over top.

"Are you sure?"

"Yes. Every year is the same. They want everyone to learn each position in case someone is sick and they need a fill-in."

"If you're wrong, you're trading spots with me tomorrow."

"Girl, you know I'm never wrong," Crestin stated as he lifted his eyebrow and gave her his *check-yourself-girl* look.

Everleigh sighed in defeat. She'd been riding on a high since she hopped out of Crestin's El Camino this morning, met with a sea of tall, blossoming yellow sunflowers stretching out as far as her eyes could see. The warm August day promised to stay just under the level of humidity that would torture her hair. The idea of spending the entire day outside in this glorious utopia with her best friend had made her happy she'd accepted Marissa's vacant spot. The half-hour orientation had them reviewing their hand-held maps, so they could easily point visitors in the direction of the viewing platforms, the flower-cutting garden, the sunflower maze, the jumping pillow for kids, the corn pit, and the various photo opportunities with tractors, trellises, benches, and stacked straw bales. A brief lesson on using the walkie talkies had followed. Then they'd learned about the areas they could be assigned: admissions, food truck, cutting garden, kids' area, or general floater, which meant you would wander around the acreage and be available for any questions or assistance. Each position required a team of two to ensure proper work break coverage (other than the general floaters, who did not need to be paired up). Since Everleigh was the only new member on the team this year, Rita had said she wanted to make sure she got a thorough training experience on her first day. So, she'd sent Beth, the person who would have been Everleigh's partner, along with the other floaters for the day.

Instead, Everleigh would be paired up with an expert on The Sunflower Experience who could fill her in on the basics of each area as they were waiting for visitors to come along and cut their personal sunflower souvenirs in the cutting garden.

Rita had lifted her walkie talkie to her mouth and said, "Ryker, you are in the cutting garden today."

And Everleigh's day had been promptly ruined.

---

# Ryker

*What in the actual hell was* she *doing here?* Ryker stopped in his tracks when he saw the last person he'd ever expected to see again. Standing under the canopy at the edge of the cutting garden. With her hair tied up in a ribbon, shirt tucked into her fancy-looking black skort, and perfectly white shoes. Looking like she was about to pull out her phone and start taking selfies at all angles. Her back was to him, so she couldn't see the annoyance plastered all over his face, unfortunately. He wouldn't mind if she *did* see just how much she irritated him. Maybe it would keep her quiet all day and focused on her work. As he strode up to her, he watched her sorting something on the table.

"What are you doing here?" was the first thing out of his mouth.

Everleigh spun around, and her look of surprise was immediately replaced by a raised eyebrow and drawn mouth. She faced her palms up and called attention to her shirt, lifting her hands up and down until he rolled his eyes.

"And what are you doing *here*?" He gestured to the rows of cutting shears on the table.

"I'm uh . . . organizing them. Smaller shears in the front, larger ones in back."

He nodded like it was a good idea, then said, "That's dumb."

"Wha—?" Her mouth fell agape. "I don't think it is. I like to be organized. This way we'll know which shears to give the people with littler hands and the ones to give people with bigger hands."

"And what happens when people drop the shears on the table when they're done with no regard for your little system? Are you gonna spend the whole day rearranging them?"

"I mean . . . I could . . . I guess." As Everleigh stared at her perfectly spaced rows, Ryker wondered what her room looked like at home.

"Dumb." He turned away and jumped onto the UTV to the right of the canopy. He thought he heard her calling something after him as he drove off but kept his eyes on the path before him.

Driving up to the shed on the edge of the patch, Ryker pulled out two five-gallon buckets and filled them with water at the pump beside the shed. He lifted the full buckets into the small bed of the UTV and headed back to the cutting garden, wondering what the hell he'd done to deserve to be tortured by Everleigh Wilson for an entire day. Hadn't karma had enough fun with him this year?

Ryker had literally thought he would never see her again. And never still would have been too soon. After that day on the river, he never wanted to even *think* about Everleigh again. Joke was on him. Thoughts of her crept into his mind, into his dreams, on a daily basis. Two nights ago, he'd finally had some relief on the dream front. Which was a godsend, because his dreams were becoming way too vivid.

At first, Ryker dreamt of the cliff-diving scenario, but with different endings. Each time, Everleigh would disappear over the bluff, even as he begged her to step away from the edge. Sometimes, she would taunt him and then dive off. Sometimes, she would realize he was right and she didn't want to jump, but as she reached out for him, she would lose her balance and fall. And each time, he would dive in after her, would search and search for her underwater. Sometimes, the water around him turned blood-red, but he couldn't find her body. He exhausted himself pushing beneath the surface to search again and again, believing he could find her. Other times, she would resurface too close to the river, the current carrying her swiftly downstream. No matter how hard he kicked and swam, he could never reach her. She'd call his name over and over, and he felt helpless, useless, as she was carried farther away. But in the worst dream—or rather nightmare—he found her floundering in the deepest part of the cove, and he wrapped his arms around her and pulled her to shore, which seemed miles away. He dragged her onto the sandy beach, tried CPR, tried anything he could think of to bring color back to her pale face. But she remained unresponsive. After so long trying to resuscitate her, he collapsed over her body, sobbing. When he raised his face to gaze upon her beauty one last time, her eyes flew open, and he coughed out a laugh, overjoyed she was still alive. That joy fell quickly away to despair as he noticed there was no movement behind those dark-ringed hazel eyes. The sparkling, dancing kaleidoscopes of colors that had mesmerized him were now flat, dead. He'd awakened choking on a sob, his sheets soaked with sweat.

As a solution, he'd thrown himself into his workouts and farmwork. He'd mended eight fences his dad had been "going to get around to." He'd mowed hay, raked it, baled it into square bales, and stacked those bales onto the trailer as his dad drove the tractor. Then he'd thrown them from the elevator into stacks in the barn as his dad fed them up from the trailer below. He'd even started gathering the eggs from the chicken coop, spraying water at the damn roosters when they raced angrily at him. He'd been running on the gravel roads rather than taking the chance of bumping into Everleigh in town. There was a less-than-slight possibility Ryker would see her while at the track, but still. He went to the indoor batting cages and took his frustrations out on the ninety-miles-per-hour fastballs that the machine shot out at him. He'd splintered two wooden bats.

It had dawned on Ryker that he might have a compulsive nature that caused him to fixate on things. Workouts. Alcohol. Everleigh. But he still believed it was something he could overcome. Now that he knew what the problem was, he could fix it. He could find a way to release the fixation from his mind. Couldn't he? He didn't need a professional whatever to show him how to do that. He could do it on his own.

He'd tested the theory two days ago, and it seemed to be working. Whenever he felt himself focusing on something too much—too much time on his workout, for example—he would purposefully blank his mind. Reset. Take several deep breaths and force himself to think about something else, move on to another task.

It had kind of worked for Everleigh. Whenever Ryker realized he was thinking about her, he would shift his thoughts to baseball, or the move back to campus, or what chores still had to be done. But somehow his thoughts would seek her out again. What was she doing now? What was she wearing? Did she ever think about him?

He had gotten better, though, at redirecting his mind. Started filling the blank space in his brain that allowed thoughts of her to creep in with baseball strategies. How bunting with two bases loaded could turn into a run scored. How a low pitch could get a runner to steal so the catcher could throw him out at third. Each of the scenarios relied upon the human element, of course. The players would have to react in the way he figured they would. And in case they didn't, he came up with other strategies. He had filled half a notebook over the course of the week with sketches of these ideas. A playbook, if you will.

And just when Ryker thought he had Everleigh extinguished from his mind, she landed in his lap.

He pulled up beside the canopy and cut the engine. Lifting the five-gallon buckets out of the back of the UTV, he placed one on the ground at each end of the table. Without looking at her, he rattled off, "Give each person a pair of shears to cut a sunflower. They should cut it at an angle, about a foot down the stalk. Remove the extra leaves, then have them hold the stem in the bucket for a bit to soak up some water. Take one of these plastic baggies and wrap it around the stem, wrap it tight. Helps keep it healthy in transit."

He glanced over to see her hazel eyes widen as she took it all in. Ryker had to swiftly look away. "Each person gets only one sunflower with the price of admission, so don't let them talk you into any more than that. And they can only cut in this section here. See the ropes around the sides?"

Out of the corner of his eye, he watched Everleigh nod. And the smell of vanilla floated up to his nose. Ryker turned his head away.

"Okay. Here come our first visitors."

# Everleigh

She'd thought this would be fun, she really did. But Ryker had made that impossible. From the start, his disdain for her had been palpable. He'd criticized everything she did, rolled his eyes, told her she was dumb. The only good thing about all this? He was making it very easy to hate him. Taking any tiny shred of attraction Everleigh had ever had for him and making it disappear like a puff of smoke. Poof. Gone.

Adding insult to injury, when the first visitors arrived to cut their sunflowers, Ryker gestured for her to help them as he stood back and watched. She tried to remember everything he'd just word-vomited all over her. She handed them the shears and instructed them to cut the stalks at an angle, about a foot down. They returned moments later with their chosen sunflowers and she pulled two plastic baggies from the roll and started to wrap them around the stems.

"Nope! No." Ryker stepped up and shot her a look. "Sorry about that," he said in a much nicer tone to the two guests standing with their outstretched flowers. "You'll want to place the stems in the water buckets for a few seconds. Let 'em soak up some water before we wrap them."

Everleigh glared at Ryker for the entire ten seconds they soaked their stems in the buckets. He, of course, was oblivious. She then wrapped each stem in a baggie and made sure she told the guests thank you for visiting today.

When the two visitors were out of earshot, she turned to Ryker and said, "I quit."

# Chapter 8
## That Wizard Is An Asshole

**Everleigh**

SHE DIDN'T QUIT. SHE wasn't a quitter. But Everleigh did kind of enjoy the look of shock on Ryker's face when she said the words. And even more so when she held the walkie talkie up to her mouth and said, "Miss Rita? I quit."

Everleigh had paid attention during the training, so she knew she had to press the button on the side of the walkie to actually communicate with the others. And she didn't do that. But she loved that Ryker *thought* she did. And that when she marched away from him, he hurried after her.

"Wait. You're not serious. You can't quit. It's your first day," he argued as she kept right on walking.

"Yes, I can."

"Everleigh, listen . . ."

She continued on her path.

"Everleigh."

Suddenly, her forward momentum halted, and she stumbled backward. Ryker's hand was wrapped around her wrist. She looked up to see pleading amber eyes boring into her. Everleigh's jaw set. She didn't know why he thought it was okay to act so childishly, but she was going to school him today. "You, sir, need to learn how to work well with others."

He didn't argue.

"You need to learn how to properly communicate, how to act appropriately in a manager position, and how to provide constructive feedback."

Ryker nodded quickly. And as Everleigh stared him down, something in his expression changed.

"I'm sorry. I just . . . I take a lot of pride in this farm, and I've dealt with way too many girls who think they're going to spend the entire time snapping photos for their social media pages. We pride ourselves on the customer experience. People come from two states away because of what they've heard about this place. I want to make sure it lives up to their expectations. I apologize for being too harsh."

"I accept your apology," she said simply and glanced down at his fingers still curled around her wrist.

"So, you won't quit?"

She appeared thoughtful for a moment. Why not let Ryker suffer his punishment just a bit longer?

"Everleigh?"

She sighed. "Fine! Whatever." Rolling her eyes to give him a taste of his own medicine, she cautioned, "I'm doing this for Marissa, you know. And that's it."

"Thank you."

Everleigh shot daggers into his eyes, then dropped her gaze to her wrist. "Can you let go of me now?"

"Oh, sorry. Sorry. Yes." Ryker released his grip and took a step back. As she returned to the canopy, he called, "Will you tell my mom you don't quit?" He motioned to the walkie talkie on her hip.

"Who's quitting?"

Everleigh turned to see Rita emerging from one of the paths to the left. She feigned innocence, shrugging her shoulders as if she had no idea. Rita glanced from Ryker to Everleigh. "I just had a nice conversation with Crestin."

"He is quite the conversationalist," Everleigh confirmed with a little laugh. She reached over and straightened the two shears that had been returned to the table.

Rita nodded. "Found out the funniest thing." She made sure she had the attention of both Everleigh and Ryker before she continued. "Crestin said Everleigh here made some of her famous chocolate-chocolate cookies and put them in the container she returned to me as a thank-you."

Everleigh beamed. She hoped Rita had liked her cookies. But confusion stifled that smile when Rita settled a look on Ryker. His expression shifted to one of discomfort.

"Ryker! You let them eat all the cookies!" Everleigh accused. She'd told them not to touch those cookies. They were for his mom.

"No . . ."

"Well, what happened to them Ryker? I am so disappointed I didn't get to try even *one* of these famous cookies." Rita placed her hand on her son's shoulder.

The discomfort remained on his face as he shrugged. And there was something else there Everleigh couldn't place her finger on as he mumbled, "I was hungry."

"I believe that." Rita frowned. "What I can't believe is how selfishly you acted. That's not like you."

Ryker's jaw flexed, and he focused on the ground rather than either of them.

"I can make more, no worries," Everleigh offered to lighten the awkward tension. It was kind of embarrassing to watch Ryker Martin being scolded by his mother.

"I think you should make Ryker here make them. I'll have to send him over sometime to serve his penance." Rita shifted her disappointed expression into a smile as she turned her attention to Everleigh.

Just as Everleigh was about to argue that that wasn't necessary (leaving out the part that she refused to spend any more time with Ryker than she had to), another group of visitors appeared from one of the paths heading toward them.

"I'll leave you to it," Rita said, then leaned in to say something to Ryker before leaving down a different path. His eyes flickered to Everleigh as he returned to the table, something defeated resonating in his gait.

He barely spoke to her the rest of the morning. When she told him she was going on her lunch break, he only gave a terse nod in acknowledgement, refusing to look up from the pile of sunflower stalks he was stacking in the back of the UTV.

Anger billowed inside as Everleigh marched along the paths to the front of the patch where the food truck was stationed. How could such a gorgeous man be so ugly on the inside? She'd sensed his personality was narcissistic after the way he'd acted last weekend. Like she'd ruined his river float. Ryker was acting that way again, like her presence was wrecking his day. What had she ever done to him to deserve to be treated this way?

Relief expanded in her chest when she spied Crestin waiting for her by the food truck.

"Baby girl! I have parm fries!"

"With ranch?" she asked hopefully as she took the food boat overflowing with fries from him.

"Right there on the side." He pointed. They sat down at a picnic table and feasted on the crispy fries coated with parmesan cheese and seasonings.

"These are amazing," she moaned as she paused stuffing her face long enough to take a drink of water from her metal jug.

"So, how is your first day going?" He leaned forward on folded arms.

The anger that had dissipated came flooding back. "Crestin, I don't know why I let you talk me into this."

"Wha—hold up." He lifted his palm. "What is going on, Evs? There can be no anger amongst the sunflowers. This is sacred, happy space." He circled his splayed fingers around in the air.

Rubbing her forehead with her fingertips, she let out a sigh. "*I* get that. Tell it to your buddy, Ryker."

"Girl, you'd better dish."

"I had no idea he was generally an absolute asshole. I mean, the way he acted last weekend was kind of a clue, but I didn't think he would be that way *all* the time. He's just a jerk. For no reason."

Crestin gave her a sidelong look. "You did say Ryker, right? Ryker Martin?"

"Yes, Ryker Martin. That's who we're talking about."

"I mean, I know the boy can be a little broody sometimes, but that lends to the mystique, does it not?"

"There is no longer any mystique about him. The curtain has been pulled back, and that wizard is an asshole," she declared. Then as an afterthought, "And he ate all my cookies!"

A laugh burst from Crestin. "Is that code for something? New slang you picked up from TikTok?"

"Literal. Rita said she found out from you that I had made cookies for her, but she never got them. Ryker admitted to eating all of them! Asshole! To his own mother!"

He drew in a dramatic breath. "That asshole!" Then he hedged, "Well, maybe he's going through something."

Everleigh stared at Crestin through narrowed eyes. He shrugged, then continued, "I don't know, with what I've been hearing so far, he's going through *something*. Tyson alluded to him trying to turn his life around, but when I tried to dig deeper, he changed the subject. I'm telling you, something happened earlier this summer. I must find out what it is."

"Maybe," she conceded. "But it shouldn't give him license to treat the rest of the world like garbage."

The corner of Crestin's mouth twisted upward as he looked at her.

"What?"

"Nothing."

"No, really."

"Well . . . maybe he just doesn't like you. Ever think of that? You're not for everyone, you know."

"I'm. A. Delight," Everleigh argued before realizing her friend was joking. She laughed and swatted a hand at the bill of his purple visor. "You're such a jerk!"

"But you love me."

"I'm going to miss your obnoxious ass, that's for sure."

⚶⚶⚶⚶

Everleigh returned to her station at the cutting garden, tummy full of parmesan fries and a renewed sense of purpose for her day. She made up her mind on the walk back that she would not let Ryker's foul mood get to her. Maybe he *was* going through something. Maybe she shouldn't judge him for that. She could only control her own actions and her own reactions. If she tried her best the rest of the day, that was the best she could do. She wouldn't assume Ryker's bluntness or sour disposition had anything to do with her job performance, and therefore he wouldn't get to her.

As she neared the table, she heard him interacting with two young girls, their mother standing beside them. He was kneeling at their level as they held sunflower stems in the water bucket. Looking every bit adorable in his cowboy-cut jeans and side-cutout staff shirt, locks of dark brown hair falling across his forehead.

"They have to take a nice, long drink of water. It goes in down here at the bottom and fills all the way up to the top here, just below the flower." Ryker pointed his finger from the stem in the water up to the blossom. A teasing—no—an *amused* look on his face.

"Really?" the taller girl asked, incredulous.

"Really."

"Mine's very thirsty," the younger girl stated. "I can see how fast it drinks the water."

The mother laughed at that, and Ryker did too. He seemed genuinely engaged, like he really cared about them having a good experience. He gingerly wrapped the plastic around each flower stem in turn and gently handed them back to the girls. "Now hold them very carefully all the way home, and they will share their beauty with you for a long time. Give them plenty of water to drink. Can you do that?" Two little heads bobbed in answer. "Okay. See you next year," he said.

As they walked away, the younger girl turned to wave goodbye and Ryker lifted his hand, returning the gesture.

And a tiny voice in the back of Everleigh's mind jabbed, *Maybe he just doesn't like you.*

She shook it off. It shouldn't matter anyway. She just needed to get through the rest of this day, and hopefully she wouldn't have to work with Ryker again for the duration.

# Ryker

While Everleigh was gone, he realized he was being an absolute asshole.[1] For no reason. It wasn't her fault he couldn't get her out of his mind, although he'd love to blame her. Being mad at her made it easier to be around her. But it wasn't fair, and he wanted her experience working here to be good, just as he wanted their guests' experiences to be good. He meant what he'd said to her earlier. He took a lot of pride in this place, in his family's farm.

So, he decided he was going to make every effort to be polite and behave in the way his mother raised him. Ryker wasn't this person Everleigh drew out of him. And he still couldn't understand why she affected him this way. He barely knew her. And what he *did* know of her was that she was a nice girl, kind to others, fun to be around. She was beautiful. Her irises reflected more colors than he'd ever seen in a pair of eyes. The little dimple by the corner of her smile made him want to press his fingertip into it.

Ryker had been around many beautiful girls in college. Girls who made him nervous, girls who made him uncomfortable in his skin with their sexual prowess. Girls who made his heart race with their smiles and the words they whispered into his ear. Girls who formed memories he revisited from time to time with fondness. But none of them had ever seized his mind the way this particular girl did. Not even Helena.

This was a good test of his strength. Of his ability to focus on his goals and how he was going to reach them without distraction. If Ryker could learn to interact with Everleigh in a normal fashion and tame his errant thoughts, he could do anything. It would help with his mental growth and his path back to the ball diamond.

---

1. Noah Kahan, "Sink"

Now, after he returned the wave of a cute little girl clutching her cut sunflower, he noticed Everleigh stepping up to the table. Time to put his theory into practice. As Ryker opened his mouth to apologize, she spoke first.

"Ryker Martin does have a heart somewhere in there." Her arms folded across her chest as she raised a brow. "Color me surprised."

Something in the tone of her voice cut him deeper than he expected. And rendered him speechless. Had he made her hate him so much already?

"You can take your break now. I'll be fine," Everleigh said and turned away from him, proceeding to straighten the shears on the table.

Ryker cleared his throat, trying to regroup and decide how to show her he really was sorry for behaving badly. But he wasn't sure how.

"Are you sure?" he asked, wanting to be certain that if she had any questions, he answered them before he left.

"I. Am. Positive."

When she continued to keep her eyes on her task, he took the hint. She didn't want him around. He jumped in the UTV and drove to the edge of the farm to the compost pile, throwing the sunflower stalks on it before heading to the house to make a sandwich.

As he sat at the breakfast bar, shoveling his turkey on sourdough into his mouth, he thought about how to approach Everleigh when he returned. Would she be receptive to a straight-out apology? Or would she cut him with her words again, doling out punishment he totally deserved?

He wondered if she'd change her mind about him if he slid his arm around her waist, placed his hand on her cheek, and kissed her breathless.

*Dammit!* Ryker was staring down an insurmountable problem. And if he couldn't gain control of his thoughts about her, how could he trust himself to stay in control of the other pieces of his life he'd locked down so tightly?

# Chapter 9
# A Lemonade Bath

**Everleigh**

FOOD TRUCK DUTY. SHE could handle food truck duty. Especially since she was with Crestin today. He had the amazing gift of making anything fun. As long as she didn't have to be around Ryker at all, life would be grand.

True, when Ryker had returned from his lunch break yesterday, he'd had a very different demeanor. Subdued, but not in the way he'd been standoffish in the morning. Surprisingly, when there was a lull in foot traffic midafternoon, he'd asked if she had any questions about the place, about the various jobs. Everleigh didn't really want to have a conversation with him, but she did want to make sure she understood everything that was expected of her at each station. So, she'd asked several questions. And Ryker had answered them all very politely. And then he'd told her to get out her map and he'd quizzed her about what was where. It was almost . . . an enjoyable interaction.

And it left her wondering once again if it was her that he disliked or if there was something in his own life he was dealing with. Everleigh always tried to offer grace to others. You never knew what someone was going through privately and how that affected their ability to be in public.

Although they didn't speak much the rest of the day, the heavy cloud of tension felt just a little bit lighter. By the end of the shift, she didn't think Ryker was a narcissist; she didn't really think he was an asshole, either. But she *was* convinced there was something weighing on him that caused him to act erratically. He continued to be pleasant to all the visitors. He was helpful when Everleigh needed his assistance. And he was generally polite. Until he wasn't.

She didn't even know what had triggered it, but as they packed up the area for the day, something caused him to revert to irritation and clipped responses. They had each dumped their buckets of water at the base of the sunflowers. He'd taken the bucket from her, placed it in his, and put them in the little shed by the canopy. Then he'd helped her gather the shears from the table and put them in the plastic storage tote. Of course, there was that moment when her hand had brushed his, and he pulled away as if she'd burnt him with her touch. (Maybe she'd imagined that. A little Crestin-like overexaggeration.) But then he'd seemed to purposely avoid putting his hands anywhere near hers, even waiting until she had placed all her pairs of shears in the tote before putting his handfuls in. Then, when she'd reached for the tote, Ryker had forcefully said, "I got it."

He'd walked a wide arc around her as he placed his chair in the shed. She'd followed behind with her own chair, unintentionally scaring him when he turned around to see her standing there, handing him her chair. Apparently, he hadn't expected her to follow him. He'd made Everleigh feel like she was doing something she shouldn't be as he grabbed the chair from her grasp and glared at her. She'd apologized, but that seemed to irritate Ryker even more.

"Just—let's get the table in, and we can get out of here," he'd said and pointed out of the shed without looking at her.

She followed directions and helped fold the plastic table. She intended to carry it to the shed with him, but he took it from her hands and left her standing there, wondering yet again what she had done wrong.

"Help me lower this canopy?"

She did.

"I'll give you a ride," Ryker said as he gestured to the UTV.

Everleigh climbed into the passenger seat. He drove them to the front of the sunflower patch, and she thought about how he hadn't looked at her—not once—since that glare in the shed.

And just like that he'd made her feel dumb and insignificant all over again.

"Here's where the food boats are, and here's where the cups and lids are, and here's where the plastic utensils are." Crestin twirled around the small food truck, pointing here and there. "Napkins, wrappers for the sandwiches, condiments. Actually, let's set these out now." He handed her a ketchup bottle and a mustard bottle and pointed to the little shelf on the outside of the right window. She obediently placed them on the ledge, and he placed two on the ledge outside his window as well. He handed her one of the bottles of pickle relish and they repeated their steps.

"Is any of this stuff hard to make?" she asked as she scanned the laminated menu taped to the shelf. Cheese curds, fries, onion rings, maid-rites, cheeseburgers, popcorn. All standard food truck fare.

"Oh, no. It can just get a little hot in here when all the appliances are running. These fans do not keep up," Crestin complained as he fanned his face with a paper food boat. A light sheen of sweat already glistened on his forehead.

Everleigh's gaze traveled around the back of the food truck: two microwaves, four air fryers, a popcorn machine, a pretzel warmer, a roaster for the ground beef, another for the burgers and dogs.

"I don't have to know how to grill, do I?" She crinkled her brow and pointed to the cheeseburger line on the menu.

"Oh, no, baby girl. Don't worry about that. Darren comes over at about 10:30 and starts grilling. He'll put the meat in the roaster to stay warm. We just need to check on it every so often. Anything that starts to burn or looks dried out gets pitched."

She breathed a sigh of relief. "What about the popcorn? I've never used one of these before."

Crestin proceeded to show her how to make a batch of popcorn in the machine. It wasn't hard by any means. He went over when they needed to start cooking the loose meat in the roaster, how many minutes to air fry the appetizers, how long to microwave a twisted pretzel. And then they spent the next half hour discussing episodes of *The Vampire Diaries* and *Grey's Anatomy*.

The morning dragged a little, as few visitors wanted to snack so early in the day. About half past ten, traffic picked up and became a steady stream. The stress of trying to remember multiple items in one order and how long to cook what began working Everleigh's anxiety. Thankfully, Crestin was patient with her and didn't mind repeating things he'd already told her. Darren called her over once to pull out a couple of burnt hot dogs at the bottom of the roaster and pointed out some dried-out burgers that needed to go in the garbage. She was thankful for the coaching on what constituted a dried-out burger and made a mental note for future reference. She cleared those items out and onto a plate beside the roaster and moved the remaining meat over to make room for the fresh items from the grill.

"Crestin, the ones to the left are the ones to serve first," Darren said over his shoulder.

"Left side, got it!"

"You're doing great, kiddo," Darren told Everleigh, and he gave her a wink before exiting the truck.

"Thank you," she replied. As she headed to the window to take the next order, she wondered why Ryker hadn't inherited his dad's positive supervisory skills. Her smile fell flat. Speaking of.

Ryker looked up at her from the other side of the food truck window. His mouth was open, about to place his order. It snapped closed, and she watched his eyes flit over to the other window, as if looking for a better alternative to her.

"What can I get you?" She mustered her sweetest voice with her biggest fake smile. She'd kill him with kindness.

"Ah . . ." His hand rubbed the back of his neck before he decided her assistance was acceptable. "Just a hot dog and a lemonade."

It was all she could do to keep that smile plastered on her face. "One hot dog and one lemonade, coming right up." Everleigh moved to the back of the food truck and grabbed a bun from the bag and a hot dog from the plate, placing them in a food boat. She handed it out the window to Ryker and spun around to get his lemonade.

"Wait a sec."

She froze at the irritation in his voice. As she turned to face him, she wondered what she could possibly have done wrong now.

"This is burnt. You aren't serving burnt food, are you?" he accused.

"Oh! I'm so sorry! No, I—"

"You can't be serving burnt food," Ryker said sternly.

"I'm not—"

He thrust the hot dog forward as proof.

"I grabbed from the wrong plate. Again, I'm sorry. I *literally* just pulled the burnt dogs out of the roaster. I hadn't thrown them away yet."

"Rookie mistake," Crestin said with a shrug, trying to help diffuse Ryker's anger as he counted change to a customer.

"Everleigh, you have to pay better attention." Ryker tossed the food boat onto the inside counter, and it skittered to the edge and toppled onto the floor.

Embarrassment flushed her cheeks scarlet. She bent down to pick up the scattered bun, hot dog, and food boat, chewing on her bottom lip. She could not cry. She *would not* cry.

Drawing a deep breath, she stood and threw it all in the trash. Everleigh snagged the plate of burnt dogs and dried out burgers and dumped it into the trash as well to keep from making the same mistake again. She probably should have known better. She'd been careless. But did he have to call her out so publicly and in such a mean way?

She handed out a fresh hot dog without looking him in the face but caught him exaggeratedly inspecting the food as she turned to get the lemonade.

"That's more like it. Maybe you need to do a better job of training, Crestin," Ryker called over to the other window.

"*Excuse me?*" Crestin said as he shot Ryker his *check-yourself-girl* look.

*What an ass. What a smug ass*, Everleigh thought as she filled a cup with ice and lemonade. She snapped a plastic lid on it and spun around to pass it off to Ryker and get him out of her sight. But Crestin backed up at that exact moment, her foot catching on his heel, and she tripped. Time slowed as gravity took ownership of her body. Throwing her left hand out to catch herself on the inside counter, her momentum propelled her upper body forward. Everleigh's right forearm slammed hard on top of the counter, and the cup of lemonade crushed in her hand, sending the plastic lid flying and lemonade splashing.

All. Over. Ryker.

"Oh, my God!" she exclaimed, eyes wide with shock.

An involuntary choked sound bubbled up her throat as she righted herself and realized what she had done. And then she started laughing. *Hard*. "I'm—so—sor-ry!" she gasped out between peals of laughter. "I'll—get you—another one."

Crestin rushed over to her window with a handful of napkins and leaned out, dramatically dabbing at Ryker's face and chest. "Baby, you okay?" he asked as he tried to keep a straight face.

Ryker snatched the napkins from Crestin's hand with a glare still aimed at Everleigh and wiped his face. She could see the anger boiling in those deep-set amber eyes. "You did that on purpose," he accused.

"I really didn't," she said, trying to control her giggling as she turned away from the utterly ridiculous scene of Ryker bathed in sticky lemonade, his brown hair dripping down his forehead with it. His shirt doused in it.

"I'm sorry." She tried to sound sincere as she returned with a fresh cup of lemonade.

"Just set it there." Ryker pointed to the inside counter. She did. He reached in and picked up the cup, giving her the stinkiest stink eye there ever was before stalking away.

Everleigh and Crestin dissolved into another fit of laughter.

⚜

# Ryker

God, she was infuriating.[1] With her overly sweet façade, she was really a little devil in disguise. And she'd almost had him fooled. There had been glimpses of it yesterday, her headstrong obstinance. Her need to always have the upper hand. She was punishing Ryker for being so harsh on her. Plain and simple. There was no accident about it. Everleigh had seen an opening to gain that precious upper hand once again and she'd taken it.

Ryker stared at his reflection in his bathroom mirror. Wiped his face one last time and tossed the washcloth on the countertop. He pulled at the sticky shirt now plastered to his chest and decided to take a quick shower.

---

1. Eliza & the Delusionals, "Just Exist"

Under the hammering stream of hot water, the sound of her laughter rang in his head, louder than the water squealing from the showerhead. He couldn't get the sight of Everleigh laughing at him out of his thoughts, the way that dimple on the right side of her mouth mocked him. He thought about barging into that food truck and caging his fingers on either side of her mouth, effectively stopping that laugh. About the way her hazel eyes would stare into his, recognizing how childish she'd been acting these past two days—threatening to quit, mocking him when he interacted with little kids, getting upset when he called her out for serving burnt food.

Never mind the fact that he'd acted childishly as well, throwing the hot dog back in at her. But did he deserve a lemonade bath? Did he deserve her condescending laughter? Her sardonic smile? Which brought Ryker back to his fingers holding Everleigh's mouth hostage, containing that dimple in a cage. And how he still wanted to part her lips with his tongue, to see if she tasted like vanilla too. How he wanted to walk her backward into the wall of that food truck until there was no space between their bodies. How he would revel as her sarcastic gaze was overtaken by desire, as she pressed her hips up into him, her hands sliding up his chest and snaking around him, tangling in the hair at the nape of his neck, pulling him closer, closer. How he wanted to feel her lips trace up the side of his neck again.

Shaking himself back to his senses, Ryker shut off the shower and reached for his towel, unable to ignore the fact that his cock was now rock-hard thinking about what he would do to Everleigh in that food truck if she would let him.

# Chapter 10
# Dad and Not-Mom

## Ryker

HONESTLY, RELIEF WAS THE feeling that washed over Ryker when his mother asked if he would run to Cedar Rapids to grab items for the sunflower patch and the farm. It would take him all morning to gather everything on her list. He'd have to go to at least two farm supply stores and a big box store. And maybe grab some fast food on the way out of town. He could smash some fries today. He'd eaten breakfast this morning, but hunger was gnawing at his insides already.

Ryker had been burning more calories than he'd been taking in over the last two days as his plan to control his obsessive thoughts went out the window and he overexerted himself in his weightroom and overexercised at the track. He'd gone to the track rather than running the gravel roads because he needed support from Tyson, needed to confide in someone he trusted that he might not have everything under control. And Tyson coached him as he always did, doling out sage advice and strategies to get his mind right.

Although, Ryker never mentioned anything about the mind-fuck Everleigh was inflicting upon him. He'd wanted to, wanted to see if Tyson had any wisdom on how to exorcise a girl from the brain. But at the same time, he didn't want to let the words escape his mouth. As if speaking them aloud would make it all real and not just something he was battling within his mind.

Because if it really *was* real, then he was really fucked. He could imagine his world crumbling again because of a girl. The distraction of her, breaking his focus on getting back on the team, on getting his GPA up where it needed to be.

In a separate thought pattern, he recognized that Everleigh probably hated him based on their few short interactions. Which would admittedly be a good thing. If she hated him, she'd steer clear of him. She'd avoid being in situations where she might have to spend any time with him. Therefore, any physical contact between the two of them would be impossible.

Yes, impossible. So Ryker needed to stop imagining it happening. He focused on baseball strategies for the rest of the drive to Cedar Rapids and effectively choked out the fuel that fed any thoughts of Everleigh Wilson.

## Everleigh

Day three had Everleigh manning the admissions table at the entrance of The Sunflower Experience. It was a Saturday, and Darren warned her it might be busy. They were short-staffed too, so he encouraged her to call on the walkie talkie if she needed any assistance. He or Rita would be over right away to help, he assured her. After giving a quick tutorial on the digital payment kiosk and showing Everleigh how to enter the code into the cashbox, Darren drove off on a UTV. She idly wondered how many of those they owned. Wondered how many acres of farmland they actually had.

Not that she was jealous of what they had. It was just such a different lifestyle from the one she grew up in. She'd never set foot on a farm until they moved to Rustic and her friend, Amanda, invited her to a birthday sleepover at her house. That was the first time she'd ever ridden a horse. And it had terrified her as much as thrilled her. Everleigh balked at the fact that chickens could run around freely and not run away. She learned that she really did not like the smell of sheep. She learned that she loved the quiet of land so far away from neighbors and honking horns and sirens. She loved seeing the sunset without buildings and homes blocking those perfect moments before the sun dipped below the horizon.

Before her father was transferred to Rustic, they'd lived in Chicago. She'd grown up there. And while she loved all the city had to offer—the art, the entertainment, schools with diving teams—she was surprised how much she enjoyed the quaint feeling of the small town. The way she could walk around the square and feel completely safe, no matter the time of day or night. But as the months rolled along, she'd started to miss the activity of the city. And while Everleigh knew she would never settle permanently in a place as remote as Rustic, she wouldn't mind a town with a similar feel closer to somewhere like Chicago or Minneapolis.

Her phone began vibrating in her pocket, and since it was still fifteen minutes until opening time and no visitors had yet arrived, she took it out and checked the screen. Her stomach immediately constricted. It was as if the briefest thought of him had conjured his spirit. She set the phone face down on the table in front of her, a frown pulling at the corners of her mouth. Tapping her finger on the case nervously, she hoped he wouldn't call a second time, as he so often did. That was his pattern. He'd call, probably hoping she'd pick up and talk to him, and then when she didn't, he'd hang up without leaving a message. Seconds later, maybe a minute, he'd call again, this time leaving a short message, something like: *"Hey, kiddo. Just your dad again. Call me when you get a chance. Love ya."*

The phone started vibrating again. Everleigh picked it up and slipped it into her pocket. She never called him back. She only listened to his messages, maybe three out of ten calls. Maybe two. Today would be no different.

A car pulled into the grass parking area and she reset her mind, preparing to sell them admission to The Sunflower Experience.

⁂

"How's it going up there, Everleigh?" Rita's voice crackled across the walkie.

She finished counting change back to an older gentleman and his wife and wished them a grand adventure inside, then scooped up the walkie before the next group made it from the parking lot to the table. "Fine. I'm managing."

"Okay, good. Let us know if you need a break, all right?"

Actually, Everleigh wouldn't mind a bathroom break. But before she could say anything, the new group lined up at the table, and she noticed another group joining the line as well.

"Someone will be there to relieve you for lunch within the half hour," Rita continued.

Half an hour. She could handle that. She focused on processing card payments and counting change for the steady stream of visitors. It was as if everyone was out eating lunch, and they'd all decided to come to The Sunflower Experience at the same time. Make an afternoon of it.

The sun was high above—radiating August heat and humidity down upon the land—when the heavenly rumble of an approaching UTV reached her ears. Finally, she could use the bathroom and refill her water bottle. She counted change back to a father with his family of five and wished them an amazing experience.

"I'm so happy to see you," Everleigh remarked as she turned to Rita.

Except it wasn't Rita.

"You are?"

*Shit.* Ryker stood before her wearing an annoyingly sexy smirk, in his typical uniform of tie-dyed staff shirt with the sleeves and sides cut out, cowboy-cut jeans, and peek-a-boo abs. Today, he sported a well-worn ball cap pulled low on his forehead, framing those thick, dark brows annoyingly well.

"Nope. Just kidding."

"Can't take it back once you've said it."

"Yes, you can. And I totally take it back." She side-stepped him, careful not to invade his space or touch any part of him that would cause another irrational freakout. "I'll be back shortly."

"Bring me back a lemonade, would you?" Ryker called after her.

Everleigh bit her lip to keep the unexpected smile from surfacing and refused to acknowledge him as she walked away.

⚘ ⚘

When she exited the portable restroom, she stopped at the handwashing station. Everleigh had texted Crestin, who'd said he'd meet her. On floater duty today, he could spare a couple of minutes to hang with her on her lunch break. Shaking the water from her hands, she started walking toward the food truck. By the time Beth handed out her order of parm fries, Crestin was marching up to her.

"Girl, you will *not* believe . . . what I am going to tell you," he said in a huff as he pulled her by the elbow to a nearby table.

"I'm dying to know," she replied casually.

"As you should be," he urged. "I heard from Shelly, who's here with Jana and Tiffany, who heard from Mikey that Noah is telling people *he* broke up with *you*."

A laugh escaped Everleigh, and she couldn't fight the upturn of her mouth. "Okay."

"Oh-kay? What do you mean, *okay*? Are you not *bothered* by that?"

"Not really." She shrugged as she fed another fry dipped in ranch between her teeth.

"Girl, this is your reputation. You need to get ahead of this." Crestin tapped his finger on the picnic table to emphasize his words.

"I'm leaving for school in two weeks and will probably rarely ever be back here. I'm really not worried about what small-town gossips think of my five-minute relationship with Noah."

"But—"

Everleigh held up her hand. "Crestin, I truly appreciate you looking out for me. I love that I have a friend who only wants the best for me all the time. But . . . a little gossip and scandal is nothing I haven't had to endure before. I think this one will be easier to handle than the last. Time and maturity have helped me put even that situation into some perspective. I can't let rumors threaten my peace."

Crestin gave her an empathetic look and stole one of her fries. "Did you ever know that you're my hero?"

❧❧❧❧❧ ❦❦❦❦❦

## Ryker

Everleigh returned within twenty minutes. He knew because he'd checked the time on his smart watch every few minutes. He didn't know why. The steady line of people entering The Sunflower Experience had kept him occupied. Maybe he was just trying to prepare himself for when she returned and he had to deal with every cell of his body vibrating toward her.

Ryker felt her before he saw her. The vibrating cells and all. She appeared on his left side, reached around, and set a cup on the table in front of him before taking a seat to his right.

"What's this?" he asked.

"Your lemonade, Sir Ryker," Everleigh drawled in a British accent.

The corners of his mouth turned up. "I was only kidding."

"You weren't *commanding*?" Again, in a fake accent.

He shook his head, fighting a full smile all the while. "You really are something."

"What does that mean?" she demanded in her regular voice.

Luckily, the admissions table had gotten busy again, a line forming several people deep, and Ryker didn't have to answer her.

Because he didn't know exactly what he meant.

❦

Almost 4:30. There was a lull, so Ryker had told Everleigh to take another break a few minutes ago.

A buzzing sound drew his attention to her phone sitting near the lip of the plastic table. As the phone danced around, he worried it might work its way to the edge and tumble to the ground, so he reached out and slid it more toward the middle. *Dad*, it read. The vibrating stopped but started again within a minute. *Dad*. Ryker wondered if something might be wrong at home. Why would her dad be calling twice in a row? He glanced over his shoulder. She was heading back this way.

After Everleigh settled into her chair, he tried to sound casual as he said, "I think somebody's trying to get ahold of you."

"Hmm?" As if she didn't catch what he'd said.

"Your phone was buzzing. A couple times."

She leaned forward, and a delicate finger tapped the screen to see her notifications. A look of annoyance flashed across her features, and she quickly flipped over the phone. Ryker wanted to ask why she didn't want to talk to her dad, but he sensed that was too personal of a question. Also, he didn't want to let on that he'd noticed who was calling. Knowing Everleigh, she'd be angry with him for invading her privacy or some such nonsense. So, he let it drop.

Silence blossomed between them for a few minutes before she murmured kind of randomly, "I bet the sunsets are spectacular out here."

They were facing west, and Ryker glanced over to see the wistful expression on her face as she gazed at the horizon. "They can be. Depending on the cloud cover."

"Hmmm," Everleigh hummed with something of a sigh. Which made him look more closely at her. It was like she was imagining a sunset at that very moment.

"You like a good sunset?"

"I do. I feel like I've been cheated out of sunsets, since I only discovered their beauty when we moved here."

"To Rustic?"

She nodded, her stare still focused west. When she didn't continue, Ryker asked half-seriously, "Did you live underground before?"

A smile broke across her face. "No, silly. I lived in Chicago."

"Ah, I see. No sun in Chicago."

That elicited a laugh from her.

"There is sun in Chicago. It's just hard to find a place to see the sunset when you live deep in the city. All the tall buildings and air pollution and whatnot."

"Whatnot," he repeated, nodding, still watching her profile.

Everleigh sat upright, an excited expression brightening her features as she turned those hazel eyes toward him once again. "Ryker, do you think I could watch the sunset out here? After hours?"

The question caught him off guard. "I mean, I guess . . . you could ask Rita or Darren. They'd probably say yes."

"You call your parents by their first names?" she asked, her eyes narrowed.

"Habit. People here won't know who I'm talking about if I say Mom or Dad, so I call them by their first names. They have their names embroidered on their shirts, you know."

Everleigh appeared thoughtful for a moment, then nodded her head in agreement. She sat back in her chair. "Maybe I'll ask them."

Another rush of people interrupted their lazy conversation, and they remained busy until after six o'clock. Ryker thought about asking Everleigh if she minded if he took a break.

"Shit," suddenly slipped from her mouth, and he looked over to see what had happened. Her eyes were trained on the parking lot. Following her gaze, he saw a man and a woman walking hand in hand through the grassy lot. The woman held a small child—well, really a large baby—on her hip. "Shit, shit, shit."

"What is it?"

"Um . . . I have to . . . go to the bathroom. Really badly. I'll be back."

Everleigh rushed off before he could ask any questions.

Less than a minute later, the man and woman stepped up to the table.

"Three please," the man said.

"Children under five are free," Ryker responded.

"Oh!" The man looked at the woman and smiled. "Isn't that great?"

"That is great," she agreed as she booped the baby's nose with her finger.

"Sixteen dollars, please." When the man pulled out his card, Ryker touched the screen on the kiosk and then spun it around for the man to complete the transaction. Ryker asked the woman as he bobbed his chin in the kid's direction, "How old?"

"Kyleigh here is almost twenty months." She straightened the sunflower-patterned sunhat on the little girl that matched her own.

"Say?" the man asked as he slid his card back into his wallet. "Does Everleigh Wilson work here?"

Without thinking, Ryker responded, "She does."

"I thought so. Do you know where we can find her by chance?"

Suddenly, Ryker put two and two together. He understood why Everleigh had taken off. The familiar hazel eyes, the same nose. This must be *Dad*. But the woman next to him was *not* Mom. She was way too young to be Everleigh's mom. "I'm not sure actually. She's in there somewhere, though."

"Okay, thank you," the man said, and he reached over to take the woman's hand again.

"Have an amazing experience," Ryker called after them, watching as they headed to the entrance of the sunflower patch. And his mind burned with curiosity. He was dying to ask Everleigh about her dad and her not-mom with a twenty-month-old baby, considering she'd only lived in Rustic for maybe two years.

## Everleigh

"No way!" Crestin demanded as he clasped his hands around hers.

"Yes! They are *here*! And I can't let him see me. What do I do?" Her eyes scanned around frantically. Should she hide in the sunflower maze? What if they went in there, and she ran into them, and she couldn't escape because she got lost in there with them? Her anxiety skyrocketed.

As if her friend recognized this, Crestin put a comforting arm around her and pulled his walkie off his hip. "Rita? Darren?"

"Come back," Rita said.

"Everleigh isn't feeling well. Maybe the heat's gotten to her? Would you mind if I go ahead and take her home for the day? It's starting to slow down out here."

"You go right ahead, Crestin. Don't worry about it. And tell her we hope she feels better soon. Tell her to take a cool bath and drink some electrolytes."

"I will. Thank you, Mama Rita."

"See you tomorrow."

"Ten-four."

He turned to Everleigh and wrapped a hand around hers. "Now, let's get you the hell outta here!"

# Chapter 11
# Safe Spaces

## Everleigh

SHE TIED HER FAVORITE ribbon—white, with a purple, orange, green, and pink alternating chevron design and shiny silver borders—into her hair just behind her ears, critiquing her appearance one last time. Everleigh had decided to leave her hair down today, which might be a big mistake if the air got too humid, but she was tired of wearing it up every day. She slid a scrunchie around her wrist in case her hair got out of control and she had to throw it up at some point. She pulled apart a couple of eyelashes that had stuck together and wiped the mascara off her fingers onto a tissue.

Her dad had called again last night. Twice. She'd deleted all three of his messages without listening to them. Everleigh decided she was not going to worry about him today. It was going to be a glorious Sunday. Probably another busy day at the sunflower patch. And she was only going to think positive thoughts. She applied her SPF lip balm before heading downstairs to wait for Crestin to pick her up.

His text pinged almost as soon as her feet hit the landing, and Everleigh called goodbye to her mom in the kitchen as she rushed outside . . . neglecting to tell her mom about her dad stalker-calling and showing up at the sunflower patch. She'd rather forget the whole thing ever happened. And by the time she slid into the passenger seat of Crestin's El Camino, she had.

"Are you really not taking this beauty to New York when you go?" She ran her hands along the dash.

"Nowhere to park it, baby girl. And besides . . ." He patted the dash with his right hand. "I want to have something to look forward to seeing when I come back to visit."

Everleigh scoffed. "Crestin, you won't look forward to seeing *me*?"

"I shan't hardly know you when I return, I fear. You will be so full of your collegiate knowledge, your learned texts, you won't have time for a lowly thespian such as myself."

"Oh, my God. You are too dramatic, my friend."

"You don't understand. It is a real fear for me—my best friend casting me off for her new world in the Politics of Science."

"It's political science. And I will never allow there to be any world in which there is not a place for my Crestin. You're too important to me."

Crestin let out a happy cry as he pressed his hand to his chest. He reached over and ran that hand through Everleigh's brown tresses. "You are my favorite human."

"And you mine."

❧ ☙

Crestin was assigned to the jumping pillow in the kids' area today, which he lamented. Everleigh was a floater.

"Those horrible, crusty-nosed brats are going to ruin my day!" he exclaimed as they walked toward the middle of the sunflower patch.

"I'm sure it won't be as bad as all that."

"You won't understand until you've served a shift here." He plopped down in a chair under a canopy near the jumping pillow. "You just wait."

"You sound like it's serving a jail sentence rather than a shift."

"It *is*," he hissed. "You just wait."

"My poor Crestin. I'll be sure to check on you several times today. But call me, if the mutants overtake you and lock you in the dungeon." Index finger pointed at her walkie, she backed away.

"You just wait!" he repeated after her.

Everleigh didn't make it very far when Darren came up alongside on a UTV. "How are you feeling today, kiddo?"

"Much better, thank you. Well rested, well hydrated, and ready for the day." Technically, she *had* been ill yesterday afternoon. Sick to her stomach.

"Good. Well, you're looking well, and that's what we like to see. Just holler at us if you need anything."

"I will," she affirmed before he took off. Rita and Darren really were great people. Great bosses. Everleigh wondered if she could maybe work here again next season. Other than the Ryker business, it had been a good time. And speaking of . . .

"Hey." Ryker stepped out from a path to her left. "You a floater too?" She nodded.

He acted like he wanted to say something, but he didn't. Realization dawned on her that he'd seen her freak out when her dad showed up yesterday. Immediately, Everleigh felt her cheeks burn. Why did all the most embarrassing things happen to her in his presence?

An amazingly long, awkward silence passed between the two of them as she struggled with how to explain herself, but she didn't want to explain herself. And Ryker just stood there, waiting for her to say something.

Finally, she did. "Okay, then. See you around."

"Yep." He nodded, and they walked in opposite directions.

## Ryker

That was awkward. Ryker continued down a path in a direction that took him farther and farther from Everleigh. Why couldn't he be normal around her? He'd wanted to ask if she was okay, considering the conversation he'd heard over the walkie talkie yesterday while her dad was here. She had bolted. She'd had to get out of here. And he was dying to know why. But he didn't want to ask. Because he didn't want to open a wound she might be trying to keep closed. He knew what it was like when that happened. All too well.

So he'd stood there like an idiot, waiting for her to say something. Thankfully, she finally did and released them from that purgatory.

But Ryker couldn't keep his mind from circling back, from wondering what he didn't know about her. Feeling like he wanted to know everything about Everleigh Wilson.

***

The day dragged on for some reason. Ryker knew why: He hated being a floater because you literally roamed around forty acres and waited for people to come up to you with questions or to ask for your help. He went through the sunflower maze twice just to kill time. It was a good thing he did the second time, because he found some young kids who had gotten lost, separated from their parents. He walked them out and stood with them until their parents emerged, frantic but immensely grateful to find their children safe and sound.

He walked past Everleigh six separate times. He didn't know why he was counting. But he was. And each time, he nodded a greeting at her, and she tipped her chin up in response. They never stopped and conversed. Ryker noted that she'd worn her hair down today. It fell in brown waves over her shoulders, the sun highlighting golden strands here and there. And she had that ribbon she always wore tied in a way that kept her hair back, but several tendrils had escaped throughout the day and framed her face in such a way that he wanted to go over and tuck her hair behind her shoulders, place his hands on either side of her face, and draw her mouth to his.

The six o'clock hour finally arrived. The place had been packed all day, but it was finally starting to slow. Ryker turned the corner and entered the kids' area with the large jumping pillow anchored to the ground. There was also a corn pit, where kids could play in a large sandbox of dried kernels, and a playset with swings, slides, and various other apparatuses for climbing.

His attention jerked to a commotion on the other side of the jumping pillow, where Crestin was hollering for help. Ryker ran over.

"What is it?" he asked Crestin. His stomach dropped to his feet when he noticed a young boy lying on the ground, gasping for air, his tongue swelling out of his mouth, eyes rolling back in his head. Ryker's mind raced as he tried to think of what to do to help this boy. A teenage girl was kneeling next to the child, sobbing, freaking out. Crestin was frantically babbling into the walkie talkie as he hovered over the kid.

Suddenly, Ryker lost his balance, catching himself as he was shoved aside.

By Everleigh. She rushed forward and knelt beside the boy and proceeded to examine him. Put her fingers on his wrist to feel his pulse. Barked a command at Crestin. Darted her eyes to the teenage girl and asked, "Are you his sister?"

When the girl shook her head, Everleigh asked, "His babysitter?"

The girl nodded, and Everleigh said evenly, "Okay, does he have a backpack that you brought with you?"

The girl lifted a trembling finger to a Buzz Lightyear backpack ten feet away. Everleigh bolted to the backpack, rummaged through it, and hurried back to the boy. There was something in her hand; she pushed up the kid's shorts and jabbed it into his outer thigh.

The minutes stretched out forever, and both Darren and Rita pulled up in their UTVs, rushing over to the boy.

"Ambulance is on the way!" Rita cried.

But the boy was already breathing easier, his tongue returning to a normal size. Everleigh still cradled him in her arms, though. Her left hand held the babysitter's hand, trying to comfort her at the same time.

"I found his EpiPen," Everleigh said, pointing to a raised red mark on his arm. "I think he was stung by a bee. I didn't see a stinger left behind, though."

"Fast thinking," Darren said. "Good work."

Soon enough, the whining sound of the ambulance siren overwhelmed the humid air, growing louder as it neared, cutting off abruptly as it pulled in along an outside path and made its way into the clearing. Paramedics leapt from the rig and jumped into action. Everleigh handed the EpiPen to one of the paramedics and told them what she saw, what she did, how the kid reacted. The paramedic gave her shoulder a squeeze, telling her she did well. They loaded up the boy on a stretcher, helping his babysitter into the rig as well.

As the ambulance drove away, lights flashing but no siren, Ryker realized he hadn't moved during that whole ordeal. He'd just watched Everleigh in action. And she was amazing. He watched his parents tell her how great she did, watched Crestin praise her for being a hero. He observed several onlookers approach, telling her she should be proud of her swift action. She downplayed her role to everyone. And when the flurry of activity settled down, he noticed her walk over to a side path in the sunflowers. He was drawn after her.

Ryker expected to see her walking away, expected to jog to catch up to her, but he was surprised by what he saw instead. Everleigh was folded over, hands on her knees, her back rising and falling furiously. As he neared, he heard her quiet sobs. Unable to help himself, he reached out and placed a gentle hand on her back. She stiffened and stood, and when she turned around, she almost seemed relieved to see him. She fell into his chest, wrapping her arms around his waist. And he held her as she cried.

## Everleigh

She wanted to stop crying. But she couldn't as her mind was assaulted by thoughts of her little sister. Everleigh had been here before. And it never got less frightening.

She vaguely realized she was clutching the back of Ryker's shirt in her fists. Soaking his shirt in her tears, embarrassing herself once again in front of this boy. She forced herself to calm down, to breathe four counts in and four counts out. Eventually, her breathing evened, her tears waned. Everleigh stepped away from him and turned to compose herself, swiping her cheeks with her hands.

"Are you okay?" Ryker asked in a voice so soft that if she hadn't known it was him standing behind her, she wouldn't have believed it was him talking.

Shaking her head to push away the tears that threatened with his kindness, she inhaled a ragged breath. After a moment, she turned to face him.

"It's just a lot."

"I get it."

"I don't think you can. Not unless you've lived it."

"Tell me."

Everleigh stared at Ryker with a new curiosity. Did he really want to know? The intensity of his gaze told her he did.

"My sister, Saralynn," she began. "She's allergic to bee stings as well. Deathly allergic. It's called anaphylaxis. What that boy went through? I've seen it before. Twice. And it's frightening every time. Because you won't know for sure if the EpiPen will work until it starts working. And you hold your breath for every agonizing second until it does."

She inhaled another ragged breath, trying to force control over her emotions.

"Have you had to inject Saralynn before?"

Everleigh nodded. "Once. I took her to the park one summer. My parents were working. I was babysitting. Mom had drilled into me, 'Always take this backpack with you. Everywhere.' She'd shown me where the EpiPen was kept. Told me when to use it. Told me how to use it. Told me it was a matter of life or death, so did I understand? At the time, I told her I did . . . but I didn't really understand. Not how important it was.

"The way that babysitter reacted out there?" She gestured toward the clearing. "I reacted that same way. We were at a city park. In Chicago. So many people around. And when Saralynn fell to the ground, unable to breathe, no one came to help. No one stepped forward to take control of the situation. And as I sat there, helpless, staring at her bluing face—" A choked sob broke free. "I thought I was watching my little sister die. I didn't know what was happening. Didn't know *why* it was happening. And then, suddenly, I thought back to what my mother had told me. I scanned her arms, her legs, her face, her neck, looking for a bee sting. I finally found it, on her tummy under her shirt, and I remembered the EpiPen in the backpack. So I used it." Everleigh shrugged, letting the weight lift from her shoulders. Wiping a tear as it escaped down her cheek. "But the minutes passed, and she only got worse. I realized there was something wrong with the pen. Thank God there was a second one in there, but I'd never prayed so hard in my life until she finally started breathing easier."

"I can't imagine," Ryker said.

Everleigh shook her head. Brushed her hands over her eyes. Blew out a cleansing breath. "I'll be okay."

Was she trying to convince him or herself?

After a long moment, she realized she was staring at the ground in a daze, still trying to pull herself completely together, to settle her anxiety from the fresh trauma. She looked up at Ryker.

"Do you want to watch the sunset?" he asked with squinted eyes, a hand pulling down the back of his neck.

"That would be amazing," Everleigh said on a breath, feeling exhausted. Wanting to sit and watch something simple and magical happen before her eyes.

***

# Ryker

If it were possible, he desired Everleigh now more than ever. She'd been a lifesaver today. A clear head among the frantic lot of them. That little boy could have died if it hadn't been for her. And she'd just swept in and saved him.

Ryker glanced over at her now as they sat upon one of the viewing platforms near the middle of the sunflower patch and wondered what it would take for someone like Everleigh to want to be with someone like him. She was the full package: brains, beauty, superhero. She was the kind of girl, when you found her, you didn't let her go.

And she was sitting up here with him now. They'd been lounging in silence for at least fifteen minutes, but he'd been letting her process the stress of the afternoon, waiting for her to tell him when she was ready to talk.

"Ryker," her voice cut through the quiet. And he loved the way his name sounded in her mouth. She turned toward him. "Why do you hate me?"

His chest constricted. He nearly choked as he rushed to correct her. "I don't hate you." When she didn't respond, he asked, "Why do you think I hate you?"

Everleigh leveled a look at him, and he couldn't help but chuckle. Ryker reiterated, "I *don't* hate you. Can I ask you something?" A question to feel her out. When her expression shifted open, he continued, "Why didn't you want to see your dad and not-mom yesterday?"

A laugh tripped up her throat. "My 'not-mom'? How do you know she wasn't my mom?"

It was his turn to level a look at her.

"Okay, you're right. She's not my mom. And he's not my dad. Not anymore."

"Can I ask what happened?"

"I'd rather you didn't."

"You don't want to talk about it? You know the platforms at The Sunflower Experience are safe spaces, right?"

"I did not know that. Noted." And that smile with that dimple Ryker craved appeared.

He remained silent, letting her decide if she could trust him with her secrets. After a long moment, he was rewarded.

Everleigh sighed, keeping her eyes on the western sky. "I'm a terrible person."

"No, you're not," he blurted. How could she think that?

Her head swung in his direction, and her hazel eyes were pained, self-loathing. "But I am. Ryker, I shut my father out of my life. I won't talk to him. I won't see him. And I kinda hate him."

After meeting her father and plus-two, he got it. "Do you want to talk about it?"

She shook her head.

"But you want to talk about it."

"I do," she said on a loud exhale. Everleigh seemed to be studying Ryker, worrying the inside of her mouth between her teeth. Then a miraculous thing happened, and she opened all the way up.

"My *dad* moved us here. From Chicago. He uprooted our lives, moved us hundreds of miles away to this remote Iowa community. *For his job.* And then he left us."

When she paused, he waited for her to continue.

"It was . . . September, I think. I'd just started school. And I hated it here. Only one person really acted like he even wanted to be my friend. And I knew something wasn't right between my parents, hadn't been for a while. But I didn't know what I could do about it, so I buried my head in the sand. Pretended nothing was wrong.

"I remember the shattered look on my mom's face as my dad told us he was moving out. Saralynn freaked out. She screamed and cried and said it was so unfair—he couldn't leave us alone in this terrible new place that was nothing like Chicago. And although I completely agreed with her, I remember just trying to calm her down, to shut her up. Because I wanted to hear what else he had to say. What he had to say about *why* he didn't want to be with us anymore.

"And the next day, he was gone. Then when he showed up at parents' night for volleyball three weeks later with her—with a very *pregnant* her—that's when I really started to hate him.

"Because we had always been told we moved to Rustic for his job. But at that moment I knew that wasn't true. And I heard my mother crying every night in her room. Shortly after that, I heard through the rumor mill in town that they'd had the baby. And everyone felt so bad for my mom, and for us, and it was just *tragic*. But in my mind, it wasn't tragic. It was freeing. I could openly hate him and not feel guilty. Everyone around us would condone it.

"I stopped talking to him. I shut him out of my life." Everleigh turned to face Ryker. "I told myself he didn't deserve my love. He betrayed us, he made a fool of us in this community, and he ran away from us. I don't think I can ever forgive that."

Ryker's heart ached for the pain she'd been through. He wanted to hug her again, but she was sitting stoically, legs pulled up to her chest, arms wrapped around them. Her expression set. So he remained sitting beside her, watching.

"Just look at it," Everleigh said on a breath, a faraway look on her face.

And he knew she was talking about the sunset. He was certain it was beautiful. The way the clouds had set up in layers earlier in the western sky promised a good one this evening. Ryker could imagine the golden-ringed, bluish clouds, the orange sky, the way the wisps of clouds subtly changed from bluish to purplish, to pink and fire red. But his gaze remained on her profile.

## Everleigh

It'd been a terrible, horrible day.[1] Treacherous, draining. Her worst fears come to life. And yet she'd survived it. She'd survived it and somehow felt stronger on the other side. Everleigh couldn't help but wonder if it

---

1. Taylor Swift, "Guilty as Sin?"

wasn't thanks to this boy sitting beside her now. The one person who had shown up to comfort her in her time of need, despite their conflicts over the past few days.

That meant something.

Ryker had let her release her fears earlier after the ambulance took that poor little boy and his babysitter away. He'd let her cry on him, held her as she'd sobbed. Asked her to watch the sunset. He'd *remembered* that she wanted to watch the *sunset*.

As she glanced over at him now, she worried that he thought she was an absolute mess. After what she'd just told him? Who wouldn't think she was a total basket case?

Everleigh realized he was already looking at her. And she suddenly felt very warm. Was he thinking about all the ways she'd embarrassed herself in front of him lately? Because she was.

"Ryker," she said. And although he'd been looking at her, she felt like she'd pulled him from a trance when she said his name.

"Yes?"

And she stopped breathing. Because the full force of his intense stare met her now. "The sun has set," was all she could say. Her gaze settled upon his full pink lips, shadowed in the waning evening light.

"Has it?"

"Mmmhmm."

The longest moment passed between them. There was a pull in Everleigh's chest, toward him. She wondered if Ryker felt the same. She thought he shifted his body toward her, and she could already feel the pressure of his lips on her own, the tingle of his fingertips drawing lines up the sensitive skin under her shirt. She shuddered as she imagined it.

"Are you cold?" he asked, his brow furrowing.

She shook her head in earnest.

"No? Well . . . I should get you home."

Ryker pulled into her driveway. Cleared his throat. "I'll see you tomorrow."

"Yes," she replied. The world expanded inside the cab of that Dodge Ram. Everleigh saw an infinite future as she caught his gaze and held it steady. She waited for Ryker to move toward her, to confirm the feelings she felt blossoming inside.

But he shifted his eyes away, staring out the windshield. "Okay. Good night."

The desire within her flared as her gaze traced down his perfect profile. His chiseled cheekbone, the straight line of his nose, his square jawline. She debated moving over to the driver's side and straddling Ryker. Imagined kissing his neck, suckling and teasing up behind his ear, nibbling on his earlobe, working her mouth over to his waiting lips. She felt drunk with desire and out of control. And she hated it . . . and she loved it all at once.

"So, this is when you exit the truck and go inside," he said, still not looking at her.

Everleigh blinked several times, digesting his words. And once again, she was the fool. She swallowed, licked her upper lip, gathered herself.

"Yeah—yes," she responded. Although her body screamed to remain in this truck, to see what might happen next, she wrapped her fingers around the door handle, gripped it tightly, and monitored his profile as she slowly opened the door and slid out the passenger side.

He never glanced at her. Not once.

As Everleigh buried herself in bed that night, pulling the covers up around her head, her thoughts traveled back to Ryker and his amber eyes and his thick, brown mess of hair and his strong jaw and his broad, muscular shoulders. To what it would've been like if he'd allowed her to do all the things she wanted to do to his body in that truck in front of her house.

Ryker

What the fuck had he been thinking? Why had he asked her to watch the sunset?

Well, he'd felt bad for her, of course. She'd just been through an extremely traumatic experience. On top of the shit with her dad the day before. So Ryker had blurted it out, *Do you want to watch the sunset?*

And that was the beginning of the end. He'd known it, even as he sat next to Everleigh on the platform overlooking acres of bright yellow and deep green sunflowers, watching her just as their blossoms watched her. Listening to her, falling for her. He still couldn't get over how amazing she was. He'd never known anyone like her.

And that's why she was so dangerous. She'd drawn him in, wrapped her arms around him on that side path, made him feel like she needed him. Like she'd been waiting for him.

Everleigh had opened up to him as they waited for the sunset, telling him things he was certain she'd never told anyone else. She trusted him enough to tell him her secrets. And it felt amazing. They'd created a connection tonight that Ryker hadn't thought possible. It calmed his chaos inside rather than exacerbating it. All he wanted was to sit beside Everleigh and stare into her hazel eyes for eternity.

It was a terrible idea. He could feel his desire for everything else—*anything* else besides her—falling away. School? Who cared. Baseball? Forget about it. The farm? He'd run away with her tomorrow if she asked. As much as Ryker had burned to pull her to him and kiss her on that platform, he'd known one touch would ruin him for anything other than Everleigh.

He'd had to shut it down. Fast. Once and for all. So, Ryker had blanked his mind, reset. Said it was time to take her home. Everleigh hadn't argued; she'd followed him down the stairs of the platform, ridden silently beside him on the UTV over to the farm, where they'd hopped in his dad's truck. She'd been quiet on the ride to town, only asking if she could change the station and messing with the buttons on the radio until she found Alt Nation. She'd relaxed in the passenger seat to a Glass Animals song, gazing out the side window. When Ryker found himself wondering what she was thinking, felt himself almost asking aloud, he'd forced his mind blank again.

After he'd put the truck in park in her driveway, it'd taken everything in him not to drag her over onto his lap. Because Everleigh had looked at him with such intensity, as if begging him with her eyes to *do something*. He'd had to look away, because he'd been about to do just that. The seconds had dragged on forever as she remained in the truck. A fear grew within him that she might actually make a move on him, and if she did, there would be no way he could stop. He'd be lost. He'd tried to appear as disinterested as possible to shut down any thoughts she might have that there could be something between them.

It had worked. Everleigh slowly exited the truck. And as she did, Ryker felt all his hope sliding off the seat and into the night with her.

# Chapter 12
# Like There Ever Could Be

**Everleigh**

THE MIRROR CONFIRMED SOMETHING she'd assumed: Everleigh had bags under her eyes. Rubbing her fingertips around her puffy skin, she sighed. Sleep had eluded her much of the night, and when she had drifted, she'd had weird dreams. Mostly involving the sunflower patch. Like getting lost in that stupid sunflower maze and calling for Crestin, for Rita, for Ryker, even for her *dad*. But no one came to her rescue.

In one dream, she was stuck on the tallest platform. The steps had been removed, and a bee had stung her. Everleigh wasn't worried at first, just annoyed—it hurt. But suddenly, her throat started swelling, and then she couldn't breathe. By the time she realized she was going into anaphylactic shock, she'd collapsed onto the platform, clutching at her throat. She could see Ryker below, staring up at her, curiosity in his eyes. She tried calling out to him, reaching out for his help. Surely, he knew what was happening, knew what to do. They'd just talked about this. Everleigh tried to telepathically will him to find her EpiPen. Then another realization hit—she didn't have an EpiPen. She was going to die. And Ryker would stand there and watch, curious. But then he turned his back to her and walked away.

Shaking the unsettling feeling away, Everleigh tried to find that calm and comforted emotion she'd had yesterday evening. After she'd confided in Ryker. After she'd released some of her trauma from the place it had been locked up inside. He'd done that for her—lifted a weight from her chest she hadn't realized she'd been carrying. But then he'd built a wall up between them again. And she didn't understand why.

Should she care why? It was probably better this way. She would be leaving for college soon. He'd be leaving for college soon. They'd likely never see each other again.

Everleigh shoved the thoughts aside and pulled her ponytail through the back of her favorite Rustic High ball cap. She was too tired to try very hard on her appearance today, doubting anyone would care if she didn't put on any mascara and hid her face under the shadow of the rounded bill. Besides, Crestin would be here soon to pick her up, and she didn't want to make him wait. Pulling a couple of tendrils of wavy hair loose from under the sides of the cap, she framed her face. Applied her SPF lip balm. Stuck her tongue out at her undereye bags in her reflection, then headed downstairs.

"I heard you had quite the ordeal yesterday," her mom said, concern laced in her voice as Everleigh entered the kitchen.

"How did you hear?" Everleigh grabbed a granola bar from the cupboard and peeled away the wrapper. She walked over to the chair beside her mother and sat.

"Marla. I stopped in the store to look for a new blouse. She heard it from Crestin's mom."

"What time did you go to the store? It closes at seven."

"I popped in just before seven, yeah."

Everleigh thought about what time of day the bee-sting incident had happened. It was definitely after six.

Her mom read her mind. "I know—news travels fast in this town. What can you do?"

They shrugged in unison. Everleigh finished the last bite of her granola bar and stood to throw away the wrapper. Her mom grabbed her wrist as she passed. "Are you doing okay?"

Everleigh shrugged again, aiming for nonchalance.

"I'm sure it was very stressful. But I heard you jumped into action. Saved that little boy. I'm so proud of you."

Tears threatening, Everleigh felt a scratchiness climbing up her throat. She clenched her jaw and exhaled. She didn't want to relive the emotional trauma, so she shoved her feelings down.

"Well, I learned it from you, Mom." She dropped a kiss on her mom's head, her brunette hair also pulled into a ponytail today. When Rosalynn released her hand, Everleigh gave her a pat on the shoulder. "I've gotta go. I'll see you tonight."

"Will you? I didn't see you last night. Granted, I went to bed a little early, but you weren't home yet."

"I watched the sunset out at the patch."

"You did? I'll bet it was beautiful."

"It was."

"Crestin watch it with you?"

"No."

"Oh."

"What?"

"Well, how did you get back to town then?"

"Ryker drove me."

"Who's Ryker? Have I heard that name before?"

Dread pulled through Everleigh's insides. Her mom stood up from her seat at the table, so Everleigh started walking toward the front of the house to escape her scrutiny. "Maybe? He's Noah's friend."

"Oh, Noah. How is Noah? I miss him."

Everleigh pretended to watch for Crestin out the front window. "He's fine. And you only knew him for like, three weeks, but you miss him?"

"He's such a nice boy." Seeing the look Everleigh shot over, her mom threw up her hands. "I get it. I do. He wasn't right for you, and you're going off to college . . ."

"Glad you understand." At least all this talk of Noah had sidetracked her mom from asking more about Ryker.

"Will I get to meet Ryker?"

Everleigh sighed. So much for sidetracked. "Crestin's here. Gotta go. Love you."

"Love you too. Maybe I'll see you tonight . . ." Rosalynn called after her, a question in her voice.

Everleigh rushed to the El Camino and dropped into the passenger seat. "It's about time."

"Girl, calm yourself. It's too early in the morning for your dramatics." She narrowed her eyes at her friend.

"But it's never too early to spill some tea. How was The Sunset Experience last night?" Crestin raised his brow and made an exaggerated shoulder roll in her direction.

Her cheeks warmed at the embarrassment of it all. She strategized how to word this so her BFF didn't get wise to her true feelings. "The sunset was absolutely beautiful. The perfect number of clouds, amazing coloring. I could watch sunsets like that every day."

"Annnnnd . . ." he drawled.

"And what?" she asked innocently.

"Girl, you're going to sit there and tell me all about a beautiful sunset and *that's it*?" Crestin sounded offended. And a little doubtful.

Everleigh realized she needed to give him a bit more. "Well, we did talk about my dad. Ryker asked why I avoided him the day before."

"And you told him? Everything?"

"Pretty much, yeah."

"Huh."

"Huh what?"

"You don't tell just anyone anything about you."

He was not wrong. She didn't know how to respond.

"Gurrrrrrl, please."

"Crestin, stop it." The blush from before returned, burning up her cheeks. She couldn't think of Ryker like that. He didn't feel the same.

"I just need to know one teeny tiny thing, and then I'll let it drop." Crestin pulled his eyes from the highway and looked directly at Everleigh. "How good does that tongue taste in your mouth?"

"Oh, my God, Crestin! Stop! We never kissed."

"Not even a little one? I don't believe you. Did he try and you shut him down?"

"No," she replied in a small voice.

"Did *you* try and he shut you down?"

Everleigh could literally die of embarrassment at that very moment. She would not tell another soul about how she'd longed to kiss Ryker, how she'd waited and waited for him to make a move and he never did. So, yeah, you could say he'd shut her down.

"There's nothing there, Crestin. Never will be."

And Crestin laughed and laughed. He laughed until they pulled into the grassy lot of The Sunflower Experience. He finally stopped when he slid his purple visor onto his head, then looked over at her and burst into another fit of giggles.

"I hope you get assigned to the fucking kids' area again today," Everleigh spat as she exited the El Camino in a huff.

# Ryker

He volunteered for the food truck. Typically, Ryker would rather be anywhere other than cooped up inside that hotbox all day long, but with everything that needed to be done to prep the food and the steady stream of visitors, his mind would be too preoccupied to think of her.

He'd slept like crap last night. Kept replaying the evening in his head. Every time he thought about a moment he'd wanted to lean in and kiss Everleigh, he imagined he did. Which was a lot of moments. Which made him think about doing other things with her. Which led to him imagining her lying next to him in his bed, curled around his body as she slept, her bare legs tangled up in his.

He'd finally abandoned the sleep effort around midnight and turned on his Xbox. Played *Fortnite* with strangers for three hours until he was too exhausted to keep his eyes open. Then when his head hit the pillow, he was out, too tired to even dream.

After morning chores, Ryker had gone for a three-mile run, which had cleared his mind a bit. He'd done a few reps on the weight bench before jumping in the shower. Then he'd downed an energy drink before leaving the house to try to stave off a midmorning crash.

Now, when Ryker stepped up into the food truck, he was stopped short by a peal of laughter.

"What's so funny, Crestin?"

A hand waved back and forth between them, communicating that Crestin was unable to talk through his laughter. Ryker was annoyed but chose to ignore him and begin prepping for the day. It was hard though, because the guy wouldn't stop. Even as Ryker moved around him to get into cupboards and grab condiments, Crestin just turned with him, his laugh bouncing off the walls of the small space. Ryker narrowed his eyes at Crestin twice to no avail.

"Can you knock it off already and help?"

Finally, Crestin squeezed the sides of his cheeks between his big hands and got himself under control. The guy was taller than Ryker by a good couple of inches and built like a linebacker. But the contrast between Crestin's style—from the purple visor on his head to his wrists adorned with colorful friendship bracelets to the sparkly HEYDUDEs on his feet—and his stature made him look like a big teddy bear.

"I'm—I'm sorry. Yes, I can help."

"What's so funny, anyway?" It was hard to hold on to any real anger in the presence of a human teddy bear.

"The comedy in which I am a mere bystander. Or maybe it's a tragedy . . ." Crestin placed his finger on his chin as he mused up at the ceiling.

"What are you even talking about?" Ryker walked around him as he set the condiments outside the left window, then the right.

"Boy. Seriously?" Crestin folded his arms across his chest.

Ryker answered with raised eyebrows and rolled his neck around. He needed some assistance with this one.

"You have feelings for her, but you won't do anything about it. And why is that?"

Ryker was stunned into immovable silence.

"What is wrong with you that you can't let someone in?" Crestin pressed, hands on hips.

"What did she tell you?"

"*She* didn't have to tell me anything. *You* are speaking volumes." Crestin held his splayed hand out, circling it around in front of Ryker.

Anger flared in his chest, but it was wholly at himself. How could he be so stupid to let his feelings show? If Crestin had picked up on it, who else had?

But no, he'd kept it locked down. The only person to whom he'd alluded to having feelings for Everleigh was Tyson, and Ryker had never named names. No, Everleigh had to have said something. She had to have read into their interaction last night and assumed Ryker had feelings for her.

Well, he *did*, but he was trying not to.

"I don't know what you think you know, but you don't know anything. There's nothing there. I don't care what she told you." Ryker tried to keep the anger out of his voice, but the look on Crestin's face told him he wasn't very successful.

Thankfully, his dad's voice crackled over the walkie. "Ryker, can you stop by the cutting garden quick and help set up that canopy?"

"Be right there," Ryker responded. He glared at Crestin for a beat before hooking his walkie on his hip and exiting the truck.

When Ryker returned to the food truck fifteen minutes later, Crestin appeared to have dropped the topic, but he had some kind of chip on his shoulder. He only spoke to Ryker if absolutely necessary. Fine by him.

But Crestin's words echoed around in his head: *What is wrong with you that you can't let someone in?*

That wasn't fair. He'd let people in before. He was perfectly capable of letting someone in. If it was the right time. This wasn't the right time. At all. The summer was slipping away fast, and now more than ever he needed to focus on the upcoming year, on meeting Coach's expectations.

Ryker pushed a wave of blankness over his obsessive thoughts and aimed his attention at serving the next visitor in line. And that worked for the next few hours. Until Everleigh appeared in his line. Looking up sweetly from under the curved bill of a pale blue Rustic High ball cap that somehow managed to accent the blue flecks in her hazel eyes.

"What can I get you?" he asked, devoid of any emotion. All business.

"Can I get an order of parm fries, please?"

"That it?"

She nodded.

Ryker placed his full concentration on cooking the fries in the air fryer, watching the timer count down until it beeped. Sprinkling parmesan and seasonings over the fries. Placing a ranch cup in the food boat. He handed it out to her and tried to ignore the electrical current that raced up his hand and made the muscles in his forearm twitch when her fingers brushed against his.

"Thank you," Everleigh said as she smiled.

He quickly looked away from that dimple.

"Ryker, can you grab these?" his father called over from the door, holding a pan of burgers and dogs from the grill. Thankful for an excuse to leave her orbit, Ryker grabbed the pan and put the fresh meat in the roaster, checked for dried or burnt to pitch, and handed the pan back to his dad.

He didn't know why he expected Everleigh to still be standing there, hazel eyes staring up at him, when he returned to the window. She was not. Instead, a young kid standing on his tip toes, fingers clamped on the edge of the outside counter, asked for a blue freezer pop.

⁂

The roll of distant thunder drifted along the wind. Ryker sat at a picnic table, taking a short break, drinking water and watching the ominous clouds build to the west. He knew there was a chance of storms today, but they stayed open as long as they could. Until the lightning got too close for safety, or the rain became heavy enough to turn the paths into muddy messes. By the angry look of that brewing storm spreading across the horizon, they'd be closing the patch soon.

The cool breeze felt nice after a long, hot morning in the food truck. He poured some water on his hand and swiped it around his face and neck, letting the cool air maximize the refreshment of the water on his skin for another minute. Ryker closed his eyes and leaned his head back.

"I think we're going to have to call it, folks. Start closing your stations down," his mom commanded through the walkie. "It's a pretty early day, so if anyone wants some extra hours, we've got some inside farm work we could use help with."

It was nothing new for his mom to offer inside work if the weather closed the patch for half a day or more. She knew that this was the only job some kids had during the summer, so she wanted them to earn the most they could. Few people usually took her up on the offer, though. Most teenagers were happy to get out of work early.

As he stood and walked back to the food truck to help Crestin close it down, the thunder rumbled noticeably louder.

⁕⁕⁕⁕⁕⁕ ⁕⁕⁕⁕⁕⁕

Unsurprisingly, nobody came over to the farm to work. But there was plenty to do, so after walking the horses over to the round indoor pen, Ryker started cleaning stalls. The storm hadn't reached them yet, but the wind blew against the closed barn doors on the western side, rattling the wood with each gust. The sound of an approaching UTV engine carried on the wind around to the eastern side, where the doors remained open. His mom pulled the UTV in and someone hopped out. Okay, so *one* person had come over to work.

He continued shoveling, waiting for them to come and ask for instructions.

"I've never farm-worked before. What do I do?"

At the sound of that voice, Ryker's heart sank and his shoulders drooped. Placing the shovel against the side of the stall, he stepped out.

"You've never done farm work before?"

Everleigh shook her head.

"Then why did you want to come do farm work?"

"Because I've never done it. I'm learning to do a lot of things I've never done before. I'm considering this my Summer of Learning. I am open to all that the summer wants to teach me."

Ryker tried to stifle his groan at the fact that he was going to be spending his afternoon teaching Everleigh how to "farm work."

"You realize you sound like a freaking Instagram post?" he leveled at her.

The corners of her mouth pulled up, and that dimple threatened to show itself.

"Come over here." He tried to ignore it and waved her into the stall, proceeding to show her how to shovel up the manure and dirty straw.

"And this goes here." He walked the shovel over to the wheelbarrow and dumped the contents inside.

"Kind of stinky," she said as she wrinkled her nose.

"Farm work is."

Everleigh nodded in acceptance, then followed Ryker back to the stalls, where he handed her a pair of gloves, a shovel, and a pitchfork and pointed her in the direction of the next stall. Surprisingly, she worked in silence as they moved down the length of the barn, stall after stall. The heavy rain beat a steady percussion on the concrete outside the barn, creating comforting music and the illusion of a safe space away from the now-faint rumbles of the storm.

Once the stalls were properly cleaned, they worked their way back up, adding fresh straw for bedding. He showed her how to pull the straw from the bales, how to spread it around in the stall. She nodded at every direction but remained silent. It was unnerving how much he enjoyed her quiet presence near him.

At one point, the wind picked up and rattled the western doors more vigorously.

"Ryker?"

It was the first time he'd heard her voice in an hour, maybe more.

"Yeah?" He peeked out of a stall.

"How bad is this storm going to get?"

"Not bad, I don't think." He took off his gloves and pulled his phone from his pocket. The local weather app showed another heavier storm cell headed in their direction. But there were no severe warnings on the radar, so he said, "It'll be fine."

Everleigh inhaled a ragged breath and said, "Yeah, okay."

"You okay?"

She nodded, but Ryker could see anxiety clouding her expression. And he wanted to walk over and wrap his arms around her, to provide a safe haven. *Dammit! Stop it!* He gave his head a quick shake and pushed the feeling aside.

Something dark replaced it.

Why did she *really* come here this afternoon? Why, when he was trying so hard to push her away, did she keep pulling him toward her?

He swallowed, licked his bottom lip, and shoved his phone in his pocket. "Can I ask you something?"

Everleigh nodded.

"What did you tell Crestin about last night?"

Her eyes grew wide, then narrowed. "I didn't tell him anything about anything. Why?"

"Sure you did. Just tell me what you said."

"About what?"

"About us." Ryker's voice rose as he pointed his finger back and forth between them.

She turned her head slightly to the side, as if trying to see him from a different angle. "I don't know what he told you, but if you recall, there is nothing to tell. At least from my perspective."

"Well, you told him something, because he thinks we have a thing going on."

Everleigh coughed out a sharp laugh. "That's hilarious."

Ryker wasn't prepared for the stab her words made at his heart. He hadn't imagined the way she'd acted toward him last night. Why was she denying it?

Instead of asking that, he turned hurt into hurt. "Yeah, it is. Like there ever could be anything between us."

"And that's what I told him! Never will be!" The rain was pounding on the roof, on the concrete, all around them now, and Everleigh had to yell to be heard over it. She tugged the gloves off her hands and threw them to the ground.

She marched right up to Ryker, and he was frightened of what she might say next. That she might storm out of here and out of his life. She stood toe-to-toe with him, her face inches from his, irises burning with fire beneath the brim of that ball cap. Her voice trembled as she ended his wait for her next words.

"I don't know how you fooled me into thinking you weren't an asshole, but you did. For one whole day. And boy, do I regret ever opening up to you about anything!"

Ryker spied tears brimming in those hazel eyes, and it ripped at his insides. But this was probably for the best. End it now before anything had a chance to really begin. Because he'd only hurt her. And Everleigh deserved so much better.

Lightning crashed and the wooden barn doors rattled a deafening beat as the wind howled between the cracks, fighting an invisible battle. The heaviest part of the storm was almost upon them.

"God! You're the *worst*!" Her lower lip trembled as she closed the last little space between them, bringing them nose to nose. Everleigh was so angry with him her words shot out like daggers. "I'm trying my best here, and all you have done from day one is make me feel like shit, like I'm not worth the time of day. Like I'm an annoyance you can't wait to be rid of.

If that's true, why did you ask me to watch the sunset yesterday? Out of pity?"

"No—I—"

Ryker didn't know what to say, what to do, to make this right. He knew he should tell her she was absolutely better off steering clear of him. This was the opportunity to turn her away.

At that exact moment, a gust of wind pushed the barn doors wide open. Heavy rain blew in sideways as the doors slammed louder against the barn than the thunder booming after the flashes of lightning. This place was no longer safe from the storm, and torrential rain pelted them in waves, drenching them both, stinging their bare skin with its force.

Ryker rushed over to the door closest to him and started to pull it back away from the wall. To his surprise, Everleigh ran to the other door, a gust of wind whipping her hat clean from her head as she attempted the same. He was getting soaked, could barely see in the deluge unleashed from the sky, but he fought against the wind and pulled at the door until he could switch around to the inside and push it the rest of the way closed. He watched Everleigh struggle to pull her door in the face of the wind, and he looked around to find something to put in front of his door so he could go help her. But she managed to pull it far enough on her own and rolled around it to the inside. She pushed with her back, getting close enough for Ryker to reach out and press it closed beside his door. Holding a hand against the wood, he shifted Everleigh to the right so she was in front of him, still leaning against the doors. He maneuvered his left hand around her until his fingers touched on the latch and turned the lock. He pushed his hands firmly against the wood, hoping to keep out the storm.

Soaking wet, his chest heaving, Ryker realized she was as out of breath as he was, maybe more so.[1] Everleigh slumped against the doors, her chest rising and falling in the same frantic rhythm. Droplets of water fell

---

1. Matt Maeson, "Waltz Right In"

from the strands of his hair onto her face, where they mixed with the rain droplets already on her skin, then trailed down her face and fell to her shirt. He watched every one of them as they migrated to their resting place on her heaving chest.

When her dark-ringed hazel eyes captured his stare, he murmured, "You're not an annoyance. I'm sorry I made you feel that way."

## Everleigh

Those words unlocked something inside. The doubt that he'd cast over her the past few days suddenly melted away. As Ryker stood over her, dripping wet, apologizing, sexy as hell, her chest burned with anticipation, every nerve ending awakened and sending vibrations throughout her body. But he remained a statue, staring into her eyes, hands on the door on either side just above her head.

Everleigh's gaze flickered to something green on his neck. A little wet leaf, plastered to him by the force of the wind and rain. She reached up and gently plucked it from his skin, brushing more fingers than necessary against that place in his neck where his pulse danced a furious beat. The cords of muscles around his throat worked as he swallowed.

She felt herself dying inside with each second that passed without his mouth on hers, and she made a decision she might well regret. Everleigh leaned up and pressed her mouth to Ryker's, hoping to melt the façade from the statue. Grabbing onto his shirt with both hands, she pulled him against her as she teased her tongue against his wet lips, which elicited a moan from him that sent electricity shooting through to her spine.

She was rewarded for her bravery—his arms wrapped around her until there was no space between their bodies, and she reveled in the pressure of his lips fully on hers. Everleigh could feel the terrain of his sculpted abs against her own stomach. Her hands traveled up to his neck, tangling in his hair. His hands slid down her back and gripped her just below her rear. A gasp flew from her when Ryker lifted her, pulling her legs around his waist, pressing her against the barn door. She could feel the wind as it howled between the cracks, the rain pounding angrily on the other side. But she felt safe in this moment, in his arms.

Ryker's lips left hers and trailed warm kisses down one side of her neck and up the other. She sighed, and he swallowed it as he explored her mouth with his tongue. And that tongue did taste so good in her mouth. She pulled at his broad shoulders, needing to be so much closer to his body. In answer, he rolled his hips up into her, causing the old barn wood to scrape against her back where her shirt had ridden up. But all her attention was focused on the throbbing ache his hardness caused between her legs.

Everleigh tugged at the fabric of his shirt, wanting to remove at least one obstacle keeping his skin from hers. He shifted her weight and brought his left hand back, helping her pull the shirt over his head. And before she let him return those luscious lips to hers, she locked her elbows, keeping him at arm's length, her palms on his taut, tan pecs. Her eyes raked over every inch of Ryker's chest, those rippling abs, the trail of dark hair below his navel that disappeared beneath the waistline of his jeans. When her gaze returned to his face, she could see it in his expression—he was pleased that she admired his body. And she did. He was a fine specimen to behold. Pulling him toward her, she kissed her way from the base of his throat, up his neck, and to his ear. His arms wrapped tightly around her waist as he once again rolled his hips up into her, and she took it as a sign that she was doing something right. A soft moan escaped her throat at the delicious pressure he created at the apex of her thighs, and she rolled her own hips in response, savoring the sensation building deep inside her. Ryker brought his hand to her face and brushed the wet strands of hair back from her forehead before guiding her face back to him. He devoured Everleigh's mouth with his own.

Something began vibrating beneath her leg, and she absently thought how strange it was that his hip would be vibrating. A second later, a ringtone sang out above the sound of the thunderstorm. She stilled when he glanced down at his side. Then Ryker quickly untangled her legs and set her on her feet. He hastily pulled the phone from his pocket.

"Shit! Sorry," he said as he grabbed up his shirt and rushed into the tack room, shutting the door behind him. Leaving Everleigh standing, weak and wobbly, leaning against the barn door, chest heaving, as desire still coursed through her veins.

She spent the next several minutes trying to compose herself. Trying to stop thinking about Ryker's body against hers, his mouth on her mouth. Once she could finally think straight, she realized the storm had lessened. The wind no longer howled, and the doors no longer bucked against her back. Out the opening at the other end of the barn, she saw the rain was now a light mist. Hopefully the storms had all passed. Pushing off the old wooden door, she walked to where her ball cap lay in a puddle of water, a muddy mess. She leaned down and picked it up, trying futilely to brush the streaks of mud from the blue fabric before giving up and tossing it onto the nearby workbench.

Ryker had failed to materialize. She decided she might as well finish her job. There were only two stalls left. She placed the straw as he had shown her, then put the shovels and pitchforks against the wall with the other tools. She stole glances at the closed door of the tack room from time to time. Straightened the hand tools on the workbench. When it appeared she had completed all the tasks she could, she dropped onto a straw bale and scanned her social media accounts on her phone. It had been twenty minutes since Ryker left Everleigh wanton, leaning against the barn door, every cell in her body begging for the return of his touch.

The sound of a UTV propelled her to her feet, and she used her phone camera app to check that there were no visible signs of her tryst with Ryker. Other than looking like a wet ragdoll from the rain. She grabbed her dirty hat from the workbench and walked to the eastern opening.

"How goes it here?" Rita asked when she cut the engine.

"Good. Yeah. We got the stalls cleaned and refreshed."

"Excellent! Why are you all wet?"

"Oh." Everleigh gestured over her shoulder. "That last storm blew the doors open. We were standing in the path of the rain, and we got soaked trying to get the doors closed against the wind."

"My goodness! But you accomplished it."

"We did," Everleigh confirmed.

"We . . . Where's Ryker?"

"Um. He got a call. He's been on the phone for a while now." When Rita craned her neck to look for him, Everleigh clarified, "He's in the tack room."

A look of concern colored Rita's features, but she seemed to remember Everleigh standing in her presence, and she quickly shook it off. "I'm sure it's none of my business. Come, let's get you into some dry clothes."

Everleigh glanced at the tack room door one last time, hoping for Ryker to reemerge. But he didn't, so she climbed onto the passenger seat, staring at that door until it was out of sight.

# Chapter 13
# Polaroids from H

**Ryker**

As HE WALKED UP to the house, he assumed Everleigh had gone home for the day. It was for the best. Ryker had let her draw him in again. He'd *wanted* her to draw him in again.

But that phone call was a wake-up call. He'd lost track of the time, forgotten Coach was calling him to talk about the upcoming season, expectations, his performance improvement plan. Coach Sandoval had reminded him of the consequences of being on academic probation and that Ryker was bordering on suspension.

"Never mind the fact that you could no longer play ball with us, son. You wouldn't be able to enroll in classes at that point."

Ryker appreciated Coach putting his faith in him, and he'd said as much. When Coach had asked him if there was anything that could be a distraction to meeting his goals, he'd replied "No" without hesitation.

Everleigh was a fleeting feeling. The very definition of a distraction. And he couldn't let himself, his parents, his coach, or his team down by letting any distractions derail him. Besides, she was going off to college too, and she'd be out of his reach, out of his life.

Ryker felt bad for leading her on, for letting her think he wanted her. Well, he *did* want her. But he couldn't have her, and it wasn't fair for him to let her think otherwise. When he'd walked out of the tack room, he'd planned to apologize. Everleigh really would think he was an asshole after that. Rightly so.

But the barn had been empty. The rain had stopped, sun bathing the concrete at the eastern end. He'd noticed the last two stalls had been finished. The tools were lined up along the wall, straightened on the workbench. Signs that Everleigh had kept busy without him. He'd run a finger along the workbench, below the straight line of tools she'd created, and exhaled heavily. He'd set his mind on spending the next hour straightening up the rest of the barn. When that chore was done, he'd brought the horses back over from the round pen to their stalls.

Now, as Ryker entered the house, the sound of laughter drifted out to the utility room. He kicked off his boots and placed them on the rubber mat by the door. Washed his hands in the utility sink. When he stepped into the kitchen, he froze.

"There you are! Did you get lost out there?" his mom asked through a big, goofy grin.

He shrugged. "There was work to do."

"Always is, isn't there."

Ryker rubbed his hand on the back of his neck and glanced at his mom as he walked over to the refrigerator, opening the door to hide behind. He cracked open an energy drink and took a swig, still standing behind the door.

"I heard you weathered quite the storm out there."

He choked on his drink.

"I made Everleigh come up and get some dry clothes. Maybe you need to go change? I'm making supper soon."

Ryker wiped his mouth with the back of his hand and closed the refrigerator door. His gaze rested on Everleigh for the first time since he'd walked in the door. If he wasn't mistaken, she was wearing his high school state baseball championship T-shirt. He wondered if she was wearing a pair of his shorts as well.

"Her clothes are in the dryer. You don't mind, do you?" his mom asked.

He shrugged again. "It's fine."

"Pork chops."

"Hmm?" His eyebrows lifted.

"Pork chops for supper. And potato salad." His mother looked at Everleigh when she said that, and she smiled in response.

Ryker had not expected Everleigh to be in his house when he came through that door. Nor had he expected to see her in his clothes. Becoming best friends with his mom. His annoyance grew, and he thought about how she was making it a lot easier for him to push her out of his life. She was latching on with both hands, and he was not having it.

"Yeah, I'm meeting Tyson at the track, so I'll warm up leftovers when I get back."

"But Ryker—"

His mom tried to argue as he walked past her and headed down the hallway to his room.

After he changed into his running clothes and shoes, he jogged down the stairs at the front of their split-level house rather than having to walk by them at the breakfast bar again. He figured he'd apologize to Everleigh later.

When his mom wasn't fawning all over her.

# Everleigh

Wow was she an idiot. She'd actually thought he might have feelings for her. Real feelings. But in truth, Ryker was a horny boy reacting to her advances. Everleigh should have known better.

She *did* know better.

She sat on his bed with her freshly laundered clothes in her arms, courtesy of his mother. Rita hadn't just thrown them in the dryer—she'd washed them too, saying she had a load to do anyway as she handed Everleigh an old T-shirt and pair of shorts from Ryker's chest of drawers. So, Everleigh had handed over her wet shirt and shorts and thought how nice it was to spend some time in Ryker's house and get to know his mom after what they'd just unlocked down in that barn during the storm.

She'd thought it was a beginning, not an end.

Everleigh had not been prepared for the cold front that entered the house when Ryker walked into the kitchen. She'd been forced to sit there and burn in her embarrassment at how wrong she had been about him, at how casually he'd acted like she was nothing to him, at how her face had most likely betrayed her and colored a bright shade of red. And her clothes were being held hostage in the dryer, so no matter how much she'd wanted to race out of that house, she couldn't.

Oh, and she didn't have a ride back to town now.

Not wanting to let on that anything weird had happened between them, she'd sat through dinner with Ryker's parents, made small talk, asked questions about the farm, about the sunflower patch, about anything other than Ryker. Although his mom kept wanting to bring him up. How she knew he had talent at his very first T-ball game. How proud she was of him leading his teams to state championships in both baseball and football. How hard he worked on the farm. Too bad Rita's praise was falling flat on Everleigh.

The only good thing about the evening? The potato salad. She'd had seconds. She was lying—she'd had thirds. It was just *so good*.

Before Everleigh had helped Rita clear the table and do dishes, she'd texted Crestin to see if he could come pick her up. Ryker hadn't returned, and it was probably just as well. She didn't really want to be around him anyway. To pick open the scab that had formed as she tried to put what had happened in the barn far behind her as quickly as possible.

As she sighed, her eyes wandered around his bedroom. A corner hutch full of trophies, medals, ribbons. A Breaking Benjamin poster on the wall. A Toby Keith poster. An autographed Chicago Cubs baseball team poster. Long rows of shelves on another wall that held dozens of pristine ball caps, some from sports teams she recognized—baseball and football—and several she didn't. None of them looked like they had ever been worn; not a bill in the lot was broken in. Many of them had stickers still adorning them. She ran her hand along his green and yellow John Deere comforter as her gaze drifted across his personal effects, wondering who the hell was Ryker Martin.

Everleigh pulled his state baseball championship T-shirt over her head. She searched out his name on the list of team members on the back, then neatly folded it and placed it on his bed. She slipped out of his athletic shorts and folded them, placing them on top of the T-shirt. Her still-warm tie-dyed shirt felt heavenly against her skin as she tucked it into her khaki shorts.

Stepping over to the mirror above his chest of drawers, she pulled the ribbon from her messy ponytail, releasing the tangled mass of damp brown hair. She ran her fingers roughly through the knots, knowing she'd be ineffective against the snarls without a proper brush. Smoothing down her locks as best she could, she retied the patterned ribbon, securing her hair back into a ponytail. *Good enough to get me home*, she thought to her reflection.

On the right side of the mirror, the corner of a white envelope shoved between the mirror and wall drew her attention. Everleigh knew she shouldn't, but considering Ryker recently had his hard cock pressed between her thighs, she figured it was okay to invade his privacy a little. She slipped her fingernails behind the envelope and shimmied it out.

*You know how I love my Polaroids. These are for you.* ♥ *H*

Before she could change her mind, Everleigh flipped over the envelope and pulled out the contents: Polaroids, just as promised. Several of them. A beautiful, black-haired girl—more like woman—with piercing light blue eyes had her arm wrapped around Ryker from behind, her chin resting on his shoulder; both were smiling into the camera she held at an angle above them. The next one, a picture of her straddling him on a couch, his hands in the back pockets of her jeans, her voluminous chest nearly spilling out of her low-cut white tank top, both smiling at the camera as she took the photo from the side. The next photo was a duplicate, except in this one, she was running her long, pink tongue up the side of his cheek, and her lens aim was a little off. Everleigh looked a little closer at Ryker's face in this one, at his eyes. He appeared drunk. Very drunk. She glanced back at the previous one, and he seemed drunk in that one too. Sliding past those two again, the next one spiked an unexpected jealousy in her. *H* was once again the photographer, holding the camera up over an obviously naked Ryker in bed, her breasts pressed against his side, her long dark hair spilling over them both. There was nothing inappropriate actually showing in this picture, but it was obvious what they were about to do. Or were doing. Or had just done. The last picture burned Everleigh's retinas, and she dropped the stack onto the dresser with a gasp. *H* full-frontal nude, sitting on the bed, legs folded beneath her and spread wide, hands cupping her breasts. She clearly had not taken it herself. Ryker had to have taken that Polaroid.

"Everleigh, hon, I think your ride is here," Rita's voice called down the hall.

"Uh—I'll be right there," she said as she fumbled to gather the pictures and return them to the envelope, stuffing it behind the mirror, then pulling on the corner to try to return it to the exact position in which she'd found it.

And it hit her—it all made sense. Ryker had a girlfriend back at school. That's why he'd been on the phone so long earlier. His girlfriend had called. And *H* must have some amazing sixth sense to call him at the very moment he was getting hot and heavy with Everleigh in the barn. So of course he felt guilty and had avoided interacting with Everleigh after that. What a jerk.

She left behind all thoughts of Ryker in that room as she rushed out. She told Rita how much she appreciated her hospitality and told Darren she'd see him tomorrow, thanking them for allowing her to earn a couple more hours today with the weather. Then she headed out to Crestin's waiting El Camino.

"Baby girl. Tea," he demanded as she slid into the passenger seat.

"Baby boy, no tea to be spilled." Everleigh shrugged and clicked the seat belt at her hip. She watched the Martin house grow smaller in the side mirror as they drove away, and she told herself she would not keep chasing after a boy who had clearly already been caught by someone else.

# Chapter 14
# Evie

**Everleigh**

Kids' area duty. Could be worse—Everleigh could have kids' area duty with Ryker all day. She tried to take Crestin's lamentations with a grain of salt, knowing how dramatic he was, and vowed to form her own opinion of working a shift in the kids' area. She liked kids. It should be fine.

But by noon, she texted Crestin to inform him that he was right. This specific job was *the worst*. Some parents pulled out their phones as soon as they entered the clearing and acted like Everleigh was there to babysit. Some parents even left their children behind as they set off in search of photo ops where they could pose with the sea of sunflowers, pretending they were twenty-two again with their whole lives ahead of them and not a care in the world. And the parents who did stay with their children? They were helicopters. Following closely behind, not letting a bottom hit the ground, a kernel of corn from the pit enter a mouth, or any other random child potentially bully their own. She'd lost count of the number of mothers who had come up to her and insisted she "take care of that problem child over there." She pretended to hear their concerns, but really, what could she do? She wasn't their mother. And if their mother or father wasn't around, if there wasn't an immediate physical safety concern, she couldn't do anything.

There was one incident that required her actual physical assistance. Two little girls came running up to her, hollering about a boy stuck on the playground equipment. Sure enough, when she arrived on the scene, she found he'd managed to somehow tangle his overalls in a way that held him firmly from behind, mid-air on a trapeze kind of swing.

"How did you manage this?" she asked.

"I don't know," he whimpered. "Please help me! They're laughing at me."

"Oh, poor baby. I'll help you." As Everleigh inspected the twisted fabric around metal, trying to figure out how in the world to disentangle him, she asked, "Are your parents around? Can I call them over to help?"

He burst into tears. "She left me!"

"What?" Everleigh asked through an incredulous laugh.

"She left me," he sobbed.

"Surely, she didn't *leave* you." Then she inquired, "How old are you?"

"Five."

"And what's your name?"

"Bradley."

"Well, Bradley, we're going to get you down from here, and we're going to find your mom, okay?"

"Okay," Bradley whimpered, a little less tearful.

It took her several minutes, but Everleigh figured out how to hold him up to relieve the pressure on the fabric of his overalls while she twisted and turned him enough times to free him from the bar.

"You saved me!" he crooned as he threw his arms around her.

And as if on cue, his mother returned with a girl even younger than Bradley. "Bradley! What did you do?"

"I got stuck," he said, fresh tears falling.

"No worries. He's all better now," Everleigh informed his mom.

"I swear, you take one child to the bathroom and the other manages to get into some sort of trouble or other," Bradley's mom said, exasperated. "Thank you."

By the time her afternoon break rolled around, Everleigh realized she'd had no time to think about Ryker. Not once. She'd been too busy. Nor had she seen him today. Good. She didn't want to waste any more time on him.

She found Crestin, who was at the admissions table, and shared her parm fries with him. A girl named Tara was working with him today. They chatted about nothing really. Everleigh checked in with Mel at the corn pit to see how her day was going on her way back to her post and told her about the Bradley incident.

"Is that what you were doing over there? I wondered what happened. Let's hope for a quiet rest of the day," Mel offered.

"Agreed," Everleigh said as she headed to her designated spot.

Around four o'clock, Darren swung by to see how things were going.

"Good."

"Good. Say, are you feeling okay today?"

Her brow furrowed at the question. "Sure."

"That's good. Ryker said he's come down with something. He's still in bed. I know you worked pretty closely with him in the barn yesterday, so I wanted you to know he's ill. Just in case."

She nodded slowly. "Ah, yeah. Thanks for the heads up. I feel fine right now."

"Great. I'll keep moving along then."

As she watched Darren walking away, Everleigh wondered what bug Ryker could possibly have. The cheater's flu? Asshole-regret-aphylaxis? Ima-douche-itis?

Regardless, she spared no more thoughts for that mercurial boy.

Hard to believe today was day seven. One whole week at the sunflower patch. And the crowds were still arriving in droves to wonder at the blankets of vibrant golden sunflower blossoms stretching as far as the eye could see.

Everleigh was a floater today. She kind of liked being a floater. It allowed her to watch people interacting with one another, with the sunflowers, with the staged photo ops. They were all so happy to be here, amongst the beauty of nature. Well, all of them except the overly tired children who were just ready to go home.

As she walked along the paths, the various things people had left behind on the sunflowers drew her attention time and again—proof they had been here. Anything from bandanas to party hats to actual ball caps placed on top of a stoic flower. Plastic beaded necklaces, candy necklaces, fabric leis. Ribbons, figurines, toy cars. Some visitors carved faces or initials into the disc florets of the sunflowers. It amazed Everleigh how interactive it all was. How it brought adults back to the carefree feelings of childhood.

Lunch break meant another meet-up with Crestin and another boat of heaven with a side of ranch dressing. She'd never get tired of those parm fries.

"I cannot believe we will be at a Chappell Roan concert in one week! Why can't it be today, already?" he pouted.

"Patience, dear Crestin. You know the wait will only make the actual experience that much sweeter."

"I think it would be just as sweet today as it will be in a week," he said matter-of-factly.

She giggled. "We have everything we need for it, right?"

"Sure do. And your aunt is still good with us staying with her?"

Everleigh nodded. She hoped it wouldn't be awkward. It would be the first time seeing her aunt, her father's sister, since he ran off with his new baby mama. Of course, they'd talked on the phone around the holidays, but she hadn't actually spent time with Aunt Bea since they'd moved from Chicago two years ago. Everleigh used to see her all the time. They had lived only blocks away from each other. And Aunt Bea was one of her favorites, so she hoped it would be a nice homecoming.

Who was she kidding? It would be. When she'd texted her aunt to let her know she and her friend were coming to Chicago for a concert and asked if there was any chance they could crash with her, Aunt Bea had immediately called Everleigh, and they'd set all the details. Her aunt had sounded as excited to see her as Everleigh and Crestin were to see Chappell Roan live.

"Did you find a pair of go-go boots yet?"

"Oh yes." Everleigh waggled her eyebrows. "White, platform, with silver sequin designs. They are amazing."

"Ooh, I cannot wait to see them. I'm coming over tonight. Fashion show!" he sang.

Everleigh bobbed her head in agreement as she shoved the last two fries into her mouth. "Back to work. I'll catch up with you later."

❧ ❧

"Everleigh, what is your location?" Darren's voice came over the walkie talkie.

She pressed the button on her walkie and replied, "Just passing the sunflower maze."

"Great. Stay put. I'll be right there."

Curiosity bloomed as she waited. What could he need? Maybe a fill-in at another station? Usually, they just said that over the radio and whoever was requested walked to that station. Maybe Ryker was sicker today and had gone to the doctor, found out he had something contagious, and they had to let her know she'd been exposed? Great, one more reason to resent Ryker. Luckily, Darren arrived quickly on his UTV.

"Hop in, kiddo."

Everleigh did and waited for him to tell her the bad news.

"There's someone here to see you," he said over the sound of the engine.

When Darren noticed the look of confusion on her face, he added, "Your dad said he needed to see you."

*The Bad News* became *The Worst News*.

As they entered the clearing near the front of the patch by the food truck, Everleigh wanted to jump from the UTV and flee as far and as fast as she could. Because the sight of her father sitting at a picnic table, waiting for her, hopeful expression on his traitorous face, set off a wave of anxiety she could not stifle.

Darren pulled up beside the table and cut the engine. "Got your little girl right here," he said to her dad, and she wanted to vomit. "She's one of our best workers. You should be proud."

"Thanks, Darren. Nice to meet you."

"Nice to meet you too, Ted." When Darren realized Everleigh hadn't moved from the passenger seat beside him, a look of concern crossed his features. She wondered if he could see the anxiety and disdain she felt swirling around inside her body in her expression.

Clearly, her dad was going to any length to stalk her, so she might as well get this over with. See what he needed to tell her and then inform him she never wanted to see him again. As she worked her lower lip between her teeth and attempted to tamp down her anxiety, she slowly exited the UTV, thinking he'd better not be here to tell her he was marrying that woman. That could have been said in a voice message. One that Everleigh deleted without listening to it.

Darren, having completed his delivery, drove off. She turned to watch him, wanting to call him back. Her father's timid voice snaked over her shoulder.

"Hey, Evie, how are you?"

"Please don't call me that," she said tightly as she half-turned toward her father.

"You used to love it when I called you that." He shifted uncomfortably at the glare she settled on him. Then he motioned for her to join him at the table. At least he knew better than to stand and try to hug her. His voice took on a nervous timbre and his eyes changed. "Please have a seat?"

Everleigh wanted so badly to spin on her heels and march away. There was nothing he could say to her to change what he'd done, to change the way she felt about him. But that look in his eyes caused the anxiety to outweigh the disdain, and something told her she ought to hear him out. She slid onto the bench across from her father and knotted her hands together in her lap, focusing her gaze on the table rather than him.

"Darren says you're a good employee." When she didn't respond, he continued, "I wouldn't expect anything less from my Evie."

Her eyes flew up to his with a sharp warning, and he cleared his throat, lifting his palms from the table as an apology. Scratching the side of his neck, he said, "Listen. I know I have no right to ask anything of you—"

"You're right. You don't."

"But Evi—Everleigh, I *do* need to ask something of you. And it is quite literally a matter of life and death. And I feel terrible about coming to your work to talk to you, but honey, you haven't responded to any of my messages. I was about to call your mother."

"Don't do that," she scolded. "She doesn't need to be bothered by whatever it is you think is so important."

Again, he lifted his palms from the table, pleading for her grace with a creased forehead, an odd look about him.

"Just spit it out already, would you? I have to get back to work. And it had better not be something ridiculous like an invitation to your wedding." This was the most she'd spoken to her father in a year and a half, and she was unprepared for the heat building in her chest as her anger flared at him.

He choked, and it looked like he was about to sob. His hands flew up to his mouth, and he clamped them tight, as if trying to keep whatever was in there from escaping. Alarm spiked in Everleigh, trumping both the anger and the anxiety. Involuntarily, her hands reached out to him, but she caught herself and instead flattened them on the table in front of her. Before she could collect herself and pull them back, one of his hands shot out and clasped onto hers. He squeezed it so tightly it sent a jag of pain up her arm.

The silent tears tumbling down his cheeks froze her in place. *What is going on?*

"Dad?"

He broke down even more, shoulders heaving, his free hand covering his forehead. After a long moment, he began to compose himself. Wiped the back of his hand over his eyes. He still held her hand in a vice grip.

"Evie, I'm sorry. I'm—" He drew in a ragged breath. "Sorry," he finished on a breathy exhale. His hand ran over his mouth, as if pulling the composure from his face downward. And it seemed to work. He had more control of his voice when he spoke again. "I understand that I hurt you, and I hurt Saralynn, and I broke your trust, and one day I hope to talk through that with you."

Which sounded like torture to Everleigh. But her father's uncharacteristic breakdown kept her in entranced silence.

"Honey, I need to ask the world's biggest favor of you. One I have no right to ask, and I know that." Everleigh had already pulled her free hand to the safety of her lap, but he reached out his other hand and wrapped them both around the one he was holding hostage. Cradled it.

Patted it. He appeared on the verge of tears again. "I was hoping—we were hoping—to catch you here the other day. Hoping you could meet Kyleigh."

She cringed at the sound of his new kid's name.

"She's just a ray of sunshine. The best little girl."

That stung.

"But she's got leukemia, Evie. They've tried everything medically possible to save her. We're at a place now where the only other option to try is a bone marrow transplant."

Any remaining anger melted away, and Everleigh's heart actually ached for that little girl she didn't even know.

"If we can't find a match soon, she'll die." Her dad choked on another sob as he stared deep into her eyes, the ache in his own heart projected across his face.

"I'm so sorry," she said softly.

"Bridget can't donate; she's a hemophiliac. They tested me, but I'm not a close enough match. It wouldn't work. The next best hope is a sibling."

"Does she have a sibling?" Did they have another kid Everleigh knew nothing about?

"She has two," he said slowly, waiting for her to catch up.

Everleigh jerked her hand out of her father's grasp. He couldn't possibly be asking. But his pleading eyes said it all.

"We're just asking you to get tested. That's all. The chance you'll be a match is so small, but baby, there's a *chance*. And that means there's a chance we won't lose our precious Kyleigh. Evie, once you meet her, you'll fall in love with her. She's been through so much in her short time on this earth, but she is amazing."

A wave of nausea washed over Everleigh. She couldn't have heard him right. The man who'd cheated on her mother and started a new family before he abandoned his first family was now asking her to *save the life* of his new child? Of the child he'd replaced her and Saralynn with?

"Is this a joke?" she accused. "Because it feels like a very sick joke."

"I assure you, it is not," her dad responded gently. His hands were flat on the table between them. "I wish I could say it was."

She shook her head, trying to wake herself from this nightmare.

"Everleigh, please. I'm begging you. Think about it. She's on a donor list, but the chances of that coming through in the short time we have are *so* slim. We need you. Kyleigh needs you. Just think about it."

Everleigh stared at her lap. She couldn't make sense of this. What did he expect from her? After everything. Why was this now her burden to bear?

After what felt like an eternity, he stood and stepped beside her, placing a hand on her shoulder. "I will always love you, no matter what." His voice cracked, he squeezed her shoulder, his hand lifted, and he walked away.

And she was shattered.

⁂

Inhaling a deep breath, Everleigh let her head fall backward. The deepening blue of the eastern sky in the distance that transitioned to a pale blue above her was calming. She loved the subtle variations in the blue hues before sunset.

It had taken her a few minutes to process the conversation with her father after he left. To compartmentalize it so she could get through the last couple hours of work. She'd come across Rita just before the end of her shift and asked if she could stay to watch the sunset. Rita had placed a hand on her shoulder, like she knew what had happened earlier with her father, and said of course she could watch the sunset anytime she wanted. Rita also told Everleigh to call her if she needed anything.

Crestin being Crestin wanted to know every detail of her conversation with her dad, but she told him she couldn't get into it now and asked if she could text him later to pick her up. He offered to sit with her. But she needed some time alone. He gave her a big Crestin hug and handed her a blanket from behind his driver's seat before he left.

Everleigh glanced at her phone beside her on the platform in the middle of the sea of sunflowers. Eight o'clock. She'd been sitting here for half an hour, and she hadn't been able to make sense of her tangled thoughts yet. Part of her still believed she was in a nightmare. Her alarm would go off in a few minutes, and she'd wake up, and none of this would have happened.

But when she thought about the fact that it might all be real . . . ?

Suddenly, the platform began to shake, the metal railing clattering and clanking. Heavy footfalls landed on the stairs. Her heart leapt into her throat, and she turned her upper body to see a hand swiftly moving up the railing. She looked away.

"Ryker," she said around a sigh. "Not today."

A glass container slid across the blanket and came to rest at her side. "Not even for potato salad?"

Ryker climbed up the last few steps and moved to the front of the platform on her left, kicking his legs over the edge and folding his arms onto the railing in front of him.

Everleigh's gaze dropped to the container of potato salad. She *was* hungry. And it *was* Rita's recipe. She picked it up and peeled back the lid, inhaling the delicious aroma. "No spoon?"

"Ope." Ryker held up a finger, then reached into his back pocket and produced a spoon.

"Thank you." She took the spoon from his outstretched fingers, careful to touch the barest portion of metal necessary to get a grasp of it.

She devoured the potato salad, watching the sun drift incrementally lower in the western sky, glancing at Ryker once or twice as he lounged over the railing, swinging his feet lazily over the sunflowers below. She didn't dare allow herself to wonder if the potato salad offering had been his mom's idea . . . or his.

"Hey," he said in a leading tone as she licked the spoon clean. She placed it in the dish and secured the lid.

"I really don't think I want to ask what."

He looked over at her. "I wish you would."

Everleigh sighed as she leaned back on the heels of her palms, refusing to grace him with her attention.

After a minute of feeling his gaze upon her while he waited for a response, she sensed him stand and move over to the blanket. He sat down way too close for her liking, but she continued to watch the beauty of the changing horizon.

"I saw your dad today."

"Yeah? Me too," she replied sarcastically. She really didn't want to get into this with him.

"I was working the food truck since Mel had to leave early."

Her head snapped in his direction. "So what you meant to say is you saw *me* and my dad today."

"That's what I meant," Ryker said simply as he shrugged.

She exhaled heavily and shook her head.

"Do you want to talk about it? It looked pretty intense."

Anger flared at his kindness, and Everleigh sat up straight. "You know what was intense? Your tongue down my throat and your hands all over me."

"Whoa."

"Yeah, *whoa*. Good thing your girlfriend called just in time."

"What?" he chuckled.

"You think that's funny, do you?"

"I mean, yeah. What girlfriend?"

"You tell me. Maybe someone whose name begins with an H?"

Ryker's eyes narrowed.

*Crap.* She'd said too much. "I mean, I don't know."

"That phone call was actually my baseball coach. I'd forgotten he planned on calling me that afternoon. I . . . lost track of the time."

*Is that what we're calling what happened between us?* Everleigh wanted to ask. But at this point, she shouldn't care. She glared at the brilliant colors—fuchsia, violet, orange, gold, gray—painting the horizon, pissed that Ryker was ruining this sunset for her.

"I haven't had a girlfriend in a long while, Everleigh. After the last one, I needed a break from relationships. I needed to work on myself."

The images of Ryker and that beautiful, raven-haired, blue-eyed woman in those Polaroids flooded her mind, and she wondered what had happened between them. If she was the one he was referring to. Then she reminded herself she didn't care.

"Hey," he said in a gentle voice, and her gaze shifted from the horizon to his face. "I do want to apologize to you. I acted like an ass after . . . and I'm sorry. You didn't deserve that."

Everleigh didn't know whether to trust him about the girlfriend thing, to trust whether he meant his apology. She didn't know Ryker well enough to know what he might be hiding.

"Tell me something about yourself," she blurted.

"Wh—I'm kinda here to let you talk about *your* thing today. Not to talk about me."

"I'm not ready to talk about my thing. You go first."

When he didn't respond, she pressed, "Tell me what happened in June."

His dark eyebrows shot up and his mouth fell agape. "What do you know about June?"

"We live in a small town, Ryker," she said with a knowing look.

He dragged his hand along his chin, and the sound of stubble scraping against his rough palm crackled in her ears. Finally, he exhaled loudly.

"You really want to know?"

"Do you trust me enough to tell me the truth?"

The sun had dipped below the horizon, and evening was upon them. The last bits of orange and yellow reflected in his amber eyes, revealing the honesty in his answer.

"I do."

Everleigh watched as his expression changed, his jaw tightened.

Ryker took a deep breath. Then he turned to her and, looking her square in the eyes, laid out the truth.

"I'm an alcoholic."

# Chapter 15
# June 12

**Ryker**

THE SUN HAD SET. The dewy evening wrapped around them, kissing their skin with cool moisture. But he could still see the shock on Everleigh's face as she registered his words.

"But I saw you on the river float, always with a beer in your cup holder."

"Yes, but it remained unopened, and it went back in Tyson's cooler at the end of the float."

Of course she was confused. He continued, "I do that sometimes. Hold a beer, have one nearby, just to prove to myself that I can resist it."

Ryker could tell she was still not convinced. It didn't make sense to her, why he would do that. He realized he needed to start at the beginning to help her understand.

"What I'm about to tell you, very few people know about me. Some people have an idea of some of the things, but only my parents, Coach Sandoval, and Tyson know the whole truth."

He summarized the partying during his freshman year before getting into the disaster that was his relationship with Helena, so he could move on to the more important parts. The things he wanted to tell her, the things he really wanted Everleigh to understand. So she'd understand *him.*

"To this day, I can't say why I let it get so out of control. How I got myself under control at the start of last year but couldn't hold on to my sobriety. Maybe it had to do with her, but I can't place any blame on her. My struggle with alcohol lies squarely on my shoulders. It's up to me—no one else.

"And I had done a good job of prioritizing my health, both physical and mental, last summer. But I got cocky, thought I was good. When she wanted to go out and party, I thought I could do it too. If I counted my drinks, I could stop myself before I went too far. But then I forgot to count my drinks. And then I forgot why I needed to count. Next thing I knew, our relationship was imploding. Partly because of who Helena inherently was. But mostly because I got lost along the way. I forgot about what should have been most important in my life: earning my degree, being a successful member of my team.

"So when we broke up, I felt the absence of her more than I thought I would, maybe more than I should have. And that's what I focused on. All the things that were wrong with my life. She was gone, my grades were suffering—again, my mental space was a shitshow. And I turned to the one thing I thought would make it all better. Or at least make me forget the raging dumpster fire that burned around me.

"It started with drinking every day after class, and then it became filling my water jug up with vodka and water every morning, sipping on it all day.

"As you might suspect, my grades suffered even more. My play suffered. I fell from starting first baseman to a third-string benchwarmer. I was lucky I hadn't been kicked off the team yet. I was barreling down a dark tunnel with no light at the end. Yet I kept barreling forward. I numbed my mind day after day. Until the day that, no matter what I did, I couldn't find that numbness I had come to rely on. And *feeling* everything was a fate worse than death."

Ryker glanced over at Everleigh, expecting to see disgust etched all across her face. But she sat with her arms wrapped around her knees, watching him pour out his truth with empathetic eyes.

Suddenly she shifted, slid right up beside him and lifted his right hand onto her lap, cradling it in hers. And that's what gave him the strength to tell her everything about that night.

❧ ☙

## June 12, 2024

"Do you understand what academic probation means, Mr. Martin?" the dean of students asked. Her name was on a plate at the edge of her desk, right in front of him, but the letters blurred and shifted, and he couldn't make it out. He nodded.

"For the avoidance of doubt, let me elaborate. You will be allowed one semester on academic probation. If, by the end of this upcoming semester, you do not show satisfactory improvement in your grade point average, you will be placed on academic suspension. Do you understand what that means?"

He nodded again.

"You will not have access to any financial aid, and you will not be allowed to enroll in any courses at this school. If you wish to continue your academic journey, you will have to obtain sufficient credits at another school, such as a community college, before we will review readmitting you as a student." Her eyes shifted over to Coach Sandoval, who sat in the chair beside him, emitting a dark cloud of disappointment that Ryker felt hovering over him. "It also means you will no longer be eligible to participate in college-sanctioned athletics."

Ryker exhaled a heavy breath but remained emotionless. He knew he should be pleading his case right now, should be promising to heed her warning and to *do better*. But the water jug cradled by his side was nearly empty. He'd poured a heavy hand of vodka in it this morning and only topped it off with water.

"You understand there are thousands of students vying to gain admission to this university each year, correct? I expect not to see you in this office again, Mr. Martin. Agreed?"

He nodded once more. When she gestured toward the closed office door behind them, he stood, cleared his throat, and mumbled a thank you.

Coach Sandoval followed him out of the office. Pulled the door closed behind them. Stepped within an inch of his face. And Ryker knew Coach saw it—he had to see it. But maybe he chose not to?

"Son, you know I am here for you. The entire coaching staff is here for you. Your teammates are here for you. But you don't seem to be here for us. Whatever is going on here?" Coach stepped back and waved his hand up and down in front of Ryker. "*Fix* it."

"Yessir," Ryker said, averting his eyes.

"As it stands now—and I don't want to do this, but you're forcing my hand—you're not traveling with us for the championship games. I can't have your negative headspace infecting the rest of the team. They've already seen you—one of the team leaders—let distractions knock you out of the game. More than once. More than twice. So many times, in fact, that I'm not sure why we reserve a uniform for you. Do you get what I'm trying to tell you?"

Ryker blinked. Nodded. Thought about when he could take another swig from his water jug.

"Goddamn, boy. You have *such* talent, *such* promise." Coach dragged his hand down his cheek. "Whatever you need to do to fix this, you'd better do it. Show us you care about your team."

Ryker's hand twitched at his side as he waited for Coach to be done. He stared forward and blinked. What did he have to contribute to this conversation? He was a fuck-up. He knew it. He accepted it.

Coach stepped up beside him, jabbing his finger into the soft space just below Ryker's shoulder. "There are a dozen other boys who would *kill* for your spot. Would take it tomorrow. You understand that, right?"

"Yessir," he mumbled.

"What was that?"

"Yessir," he said louder.

"Now *fix it*," Coach hissed.

As soon as Coach Sandoval shifted his gaze and brushed past him, Ryker opened his water jug and took a long swig.

⚬⚬⚬⚬⚬ ⚬⚬⚬⚬⚬

"Come on, man![1] One last night before we have to leave for the championship games," Ontario coaxed. "There's a party over on Dubuque Street. We can focus on baseball tomorrow."

Ryker sighed. Tari had no idea he wouldn't be going with them to the championships. Well, they'd all find out soon enough. As they sat in the common area of their floor in the athletic dorms, Ryker took another pull from his water jug. He'd had to refill it when he got back to his room after meeting with Dean What's-Her-Name. He'd wanted to curl up in his bed, sleep for the duration of the day. The duration of the summer.

But Ontario had come barging in, telling him to shower and get ready. "We're about to go out!"

Ryker didn't really want to party, but he figured drinking with others was better than drinking alone. Maybe it would pull him out of this dark abyss he'd fallen into. He vaguely remembered showering.

---

1. Rainbow Kitten Surprise, "It's Called: Freefall"

Vaguely recalled getting dressed. He'd plopped down on the sofa in the common area, his mind buzzing, thinking of the shitstorm he'd created for himself, drinking from his water jug.

"Come on, dude." Tari returned to his side, dressed to go out, pulling a handful of his chin-length braids away from his face and securing them at the back of his head. "Leave that stupid water bottle here. We're gonna put an end to your thirst where we're going!"

Little did Ontario know. But Ryker sat his water bottle on the floor next to the couch and told Tari he needed to hit the can first. He did the old college Puke and Rally. Rinsed his mouth out under the faucet, threw cold water on his face, and headed out to have one last night . . .

Where. He. Didn't. Give. A. Fuck.

Luckily, Tari wanted to grab food along the way. Ryker ordered two cheeseburgers and a large fry hoping it would soak up enough of the alcohol in his system to allow him to keep up with his friend all night. He'd felt better after he puked, but a headache was creeping along the back of his skull.

Ryker parked his car on the street near the house Tari pointed out on South Dubuque Street. He pulled his hand down his face, wondering what the hell he was doing, but also not caring. Time to get wasted. His last fuck had flown away.

Thinking back on it now, the only thing he could clearly recall about that party was the first half an hour. They entered to cheers—several of their teammates were already there. Someone shoved a cold beer into his hand. He shot-gunned it. He found another beer. And a pretty girl by the drink table. She smiled at him. Twenty minutes later, they were fucking in the bathroom. (He left this part out, too ashamed to reveal this much of his depravity to Everleigh.)

He only remembered bits and pieces of the rest of the night. Talking with his friends, listening to them talk about strategy for the upcoming games. Another drink. Or maybe the same drink? A girl grinding on him as they danced. He honestly couldn't say if he followed her to a bedroom or if he'd just imagined it. He was pretty wasted by that time.

And the party lulled, or maybe he'd just had enough and that was why he'd kicked back on the couch. Watched his friends continue to party. Started to go deep inside his head. Like, what the fuck had he done to his life? And why? And how could he pull himself out of it?

The answer was he couldn't. He'd tried over and over again. Since January, he hadn't been able to go more than one day without a drink. Without many drinks. It had become his comfort. His confidence. His crutch. It had stolen so much from him, and yet he worshipped it. Craved it. Desired it above all else. He was losing his scholarships, his spot on the team, his world.

Ryker tried to care. But he didn't. As long as he could have another drink, he would be fine. And what kind of fucking life was that? He was disgusted with himself. He was—

A fuck-up.

A failure.

*Worthless.*

The darkness that had been descending on him since his falling out with Helena fully engulfed him. And he felt . . . empty. He didn't care about anything anymore. Not school. Not baseball. Not his family. Not one damn thing. Well, he cared about vodka.

He must have fallen asleep on the couch, because Tari punched him in the arm and then shook him.

"Ryker, dude. Time to go."

He blinked a few times and forced his eyes open.[2] The party was almost dead. He didn't know what time it was. Didn't care. They stumbled out to his Malibu.

"You good?" Tari asked. Ontario, who was also in no shape to drive.

---

2. The Lumineers, "Salt and the Sea"

"Yeah, bro," Ryker said as his keys slipped from his fingers and clattered on the ground. He bent over to pick them up and hit his head on his car door. Laughed as he rubbed a hand on the flare of pain.

"Dude. What the hell?" Tari chortled as he slid into the passenger seat.

"Put your seatbelt on, fucker," Ryker commanded as he dropped into the driver's seat and started his car.

It could have been two minutes later, or it could have been ten. Ryker had no idea. Time stretched out infinitely and stood still at the same time. All he remembered was punching his foot into the gas and the feeling of flying weightless in the air.

It wasn't until Tari's screams pierced his veil of nothingness that he came to. Water poured into the floorboard of the car, the Iowa River at eye level on his windshield.

"What the fuck! Ryker! What the fuck!"

Ryker pressed his eyelids closed. This was a bad dream, nothing more. But Tari's high-pitched, frantic voice overrode his thoughts, and his eyes flew open. And then relief flooded his body, and his muscles relaxed. This was it. His way out. It would all be over shortly.

He welcomed it.

Now, he wondered if he'd passed out for a moment and only came to again when the sharp slap of Ontario's hand met the side of his cheek. It was mid-June, but the waters of the Iowa River were chilly, swelling around him, over his waist.

"Ryker! We have to get out of here! I can't—it won't!"

Shaking his head to focus, he realized Tari couldn't release his seatbelt for some reason. His own hand was floating on top of the water, and he dragged it below the surface to feel for his seatbelt. He fumbled for a moment, then found the button to release it. The water was up another six inches. He reached over to Tari's seatbelt and tried and tried to release it, but nothing happened. He reached behind and felt for his duffel bag, lodged beneath his seat. Pulled heavily against the water and brought it to the steering wheel, dug around in the side pocket until he found his pocketknife. He began sawing away at the fabric of the belt.

"God, Ryker. Don't let me die here! Don't let me die!"

And if it were possible, Ryker hated himself even more than he did before. He and his teammate, *his friend*, might die here in this river. While he had welcomed it at first, he never wanted such a fate for Tari. And it would be all Ryker's fault. He could be the reason Ontario died tonight.

He worked furiously with the knife, making too little progress with the fabric. Water up to their shoulders now, he had to rely on feel to know if he was accomplishing anything. He heard his friend repeatedly murmuring a low prayer. Tari didn't think Ryker could get them out of this.

The cold river lapped at his neck, and panic ripped through him. Real emotion. He hadn't felt real emotion in so long, it hurt his insides. He cut his finger with the knife, cursed, but knew he *could not* be the reason someone else died. He inhaled deeply and pushed below the surface.

Underwater was a dark abyss. Darker than the raging river and the hovering night around them. But Ryker focused his fragmented mind on his fingers, found the fabric of the seatbelt. He was almost there. He worked with urgency, and the seatbelt finally broke and released Tari.

Ryker resurfaced to see his friend floating against the roof of the car. There was maybe three inches of air in there. "What. Do. We. Do?" Tari choked out.

Suddenly, a thought sprang into his mind about one thing he'd learned in his science course. Once the door was fully submerged, they could open it and get out.

"Hold your breath," Ryker commanded as he sucked in his own breath just before the Iowa River completely submerged the car. As soon as he thought his door was underwater, he yanked on the handle and thrusted his shoulder into it. The door opened, but he knocked the air from his lungs. He pushed to the surface, gasping for air, and hooked his arm around the door frame as he felt the river pulling his body downstream. He reached for Tari with this other hand, hoping his friend was right behind him. There was nothing but water.

Ryker inhaled deeply and pulled himself back into the sinking car. It was so dark, he couldn't see anything. He felt around in the murky water until he touched something. Ontario. He pulled on Tari's arm, dragged him up and out of the car, struggled to move them upward as the surrounding water sucked downward with the car. He broke the surface of the river and flipped to his back, shifting Tari so his face was out of the water. He wasn't moving; he was unconscious. Ryker had to get him to land to save his life. He *could not* have the death of his friend on his conscience.

Spring had brought with it copious amounts of rain, which had all come downstream eventually. The Iowa River was higher than it'd been in years. Flowing more forcefully than Ryker could ever have imagined. And it was so hard swimming with one arm and his muscles shivering with cold. As the dark water lapped at his face, overtook his mouth, he spit it out just as forcefully. And he swam and swam and swam, exhausted in a way he'd never felt before, focused only on the thought of touching the riverbank, of getting Tari to safety.

What seemed like an eternity might have only been a minute or two, but he thanked God when the soft earth met his outstretched hand. He dug his fingers into the loam, pulled them up, up, and out of the rushing water. He hoisted Tari onto the bank and laid him on his side, tried all the tricks he could think of to get that water out of his lungs.

When Ryker glanced out into the river, his car was nowhere to be seen, sinking to the bottom of the dark mass of water. He rolled Tari onto his back and started CPR, begging God to not let his friend die. Promising to do whatever was required of him to just let his friend live. He would gladly trade places if he could.

A splutter and a cough brought tears to Ryker's eyes. He quickly shifted Tari onto his side and breathed a heavy sigh of relief as his friend puked an unbelievable amount of river water onto the grass.

It was only then Ryker admitted to himself that things needed to change.

Before the team left for the championship tournament the next morning, Ryker walked into Coach Sandoval's office and closed the door. He slumped into the seat across from his mentor and broke down, unleashing tears he could no longer hold back. He told his coach what had happened the night before. Told him how frightened he was of himself.

Ryker said in a defeated voice, "I need help."

❧ ☙

## Now

"Coach truly had no idea I had a drinking problem. I'd hid it that well," Ryker confessed as he glanced over at Everleigh. "To his credit, he was very supportive. Told me whatever resources I needed were available to me."

"Was Ontario okay?" she asked with genuine concern.

"He was, thank God. Just rattled by the whole experience. But—"

"But what?"

Ryker scratched his fingernails across his eyebrow. "But even though he says he forgives me for it . . . I can't forgive myself."

A second later, Everleigh scooted beside him, wrapped her arms around his shoulders, and rested her head beside his.

"Ryker. I can't imagine what you've been through."

Her touch surprised him. Why was she comforting him when she should be distancing herself from him, from a disease that controlled his mind and his body if he wasn't vigilant?

But then Ryker realized how Everleigh's warmth brought a feeling of safety. Of support. He slid his arms up around her and accepted her embrace. Dipped his face down into the space between her jaw and her collarbone and inhaled the now familiar scent of vanilla. An unfamiliar feeling of peace washed over him.

"I've never said those words out loud before."

She lifted her head and looked into his eyes with a furrowed brow. Although night had fully fallen around them, he swore he could still see the kaleidoscope of colors in her hazel eyes. "That story?"

"No." Ryker swallowed as he prepared himself to say it again. "That I'm an alcoholic."

When Everleigh pulled away and sat next to him, her leg touching his knee, he expected her to say something about how surprised she was by his actions, how she was upset to learn these terrible things about him. But she simply rested her hands on his leg and waited for him to decide when he was ready to speak again.

He stared out over the field, the chorus of crickets and faraway cries of coyotes the only sounds hovering on the air around them. "I probably should be seeking professional help. Should go to meetings."

"Why don't you?"

He half-shrugged. "Maybe I worry it will make me look weak. Maybe I think I need to do this myself—prove to myself I can. Maybe . . . I'm ashamed, and I don't want anybody trying to make me feel better about it."

"And how are you doing? Going it alone?"

"I'm not gonna lie, it's very hard sometimes. And having something of an obsessive-compulsive tendency, I can get fixated on something, let it control my thoughts before I realize it's happening. I just have to be vigilant. All the time. Manage my tendencies. Keep my mind focused on my priorities. Or find a way to blank everything out and reset my thought process."

"Well, I feel terrible for drinking around you. We all did it, without knowing what you go through to try to protect your sobriety. I'll be more supportive in the future."

Ryker looked down at Everleigh's hand. She didn't seem to realize she was rubbing a circle on his thigh, just above his knee. It wasn't sexual, it was . . . comforting. He lifted his gaze to her face just as she lifted her hand and held out her palm.

"Give me your phone."

"What now?"

"Your phone. I'm going to put my number in it, and whenever you feel like you need someone to talk to, someone to keep you from thinking about drinking or bad things or anything like that, you call me. Text me. Whatever. Day or night." When Ryker didn't immediately pull his phone from his pocket, she continued, "The hardest part is over—you shared the story. You battled through whatever emotions you were feeling and trusted me with this huge burden you carry.

"I know how isolating it can be to feel like you are carrying a burden on your own. How you think it's easier for everyone if you just keep it to yourself and try to get through it. But Ryker, something like this is too important for you to fight alone. You don't have to go it alone."

If it were anyone else, he would brush it off, change the subject. But he found Everleigh's reaction to all he'd just told her . . . surprising. Amazing. And knowing what he knew about himself, there could be a day his resolve shattered, a day so hard he couldn't see his way through. It could be lifesaving to have her on the other end of the line. He unlocked his phone and handed it to her. When Everleigh returned it to him moments later, she said, "Text me."

Ryker began typing her name into his phone. When it populated, a smile tugged at the corners of his mouth. There, beside *Everleigh*, was a sunflower emoji. He cleared his throat.

"Enough about me. Time to talk about your thing. What happened with your dad today?"

She glanced out over the sea of sunflowers as crickets and the occasional frog filled the night air with their songs, but it was too dark to see their beauty now. "I'm not ready to talk about it yet. There's just too much up in here—" she said as she waved her hand around her head—"that I haven't fully processed." Looking back at him, she offered, "Maybe tomorrow?"

"Tomorrow then," he agreed.

But as he walked her to the front of the sunflower patch where Crestin was waiting for her in his El Camino, Ryker couldn't help but wonder—although she said she would be a supportive voice for him—if she wasn't silently running away from the fucking disaster that was Ryker Martin.

# Chapter 16
# Rain Day

**Everleigh**

HER EYELIDS CRACKED OPEN to the muted light that filled her room, gray and gloomy, and she wondered how much of last night she'd dreamt. But recalling Ryker's story, there was no way Everleigh could have conjured something that heartbreakingly awful.

It made sense now, why he'd freaked out on her that day on the river float when he'd dragged her from the water. Likely experiencing PTSD from thinking his friend was going to drown that night in June. From thinking he could have drowned as well.

Everleigh rolled onto her side and picked up her phone. It had dinged, but it wasn't time for her alarm to go off yet. She squeezed her hand over her eyes as she tried to force the sleep from her vision. *Rita.* She'd sent a mass text to the TSE group: *Rain is on the way and forecasted to last the day. We'll be closed today.*

She'd like to say she was bummed, but she wasn't. Her mom should be headed to work soon, and Saralynn would be at the babysitter, so the day would be Everleigh's to finally actually process what her father had told her yesterday. And what the hell she was supposed to do about it.

Her phone dinged again. A message from Crestin: *Thank Gawd! I'm looking forward to a day of bed rot and* Love Island! She chuckled but then blinked at her list of messages. The third one down. When she'd told Ryker to text her last night so she'd have his number.

*Hi.*

Two little letters that held such big meaning. She'd told him to call or text her, day or night, and she'd be there for him.

When Ryker first invaded her sunset time yesterday, she'd been filled with resentment for the way he'd treated her. With the thought that he was a cheating asshole. And it had taken a minute for Everleigh to let those feelings go, to trust that he might be telling her the truth and not just telling her what he wanted her to believe.

Then, surprisingly, he'd apologized for his behavior. Surprised her even further by opening up and trusting her with a glimpse at his struggle, his mistakes, his flaws. Which left her feeling . . . seen. Ryker saw that she was someone he could trust. People always "saw" Everleigh as a good listener, a good friend, a fun friend, an agreeable person. Whatever they saw, it wasn't how she saw herself. Not really. She liked being all those things, but she longed for a deeper relationship with someone. For a connection that made her feel a part of something special. Maybe it was because her father had deserted them, and now she was chasing approval and acceptance, hoping that would be enough to keep people in her life.

The only other person she really felt seen by was Crestin. He got her. She got him. They had that special connection. But there was still a piece missing from that relationship, and she couldn't name it. She didn't know what it was. Just that it was missing.

By the time she and Ryker had descended that platform last night, she'd felt the promise of something bigger between the two of them. Something honest. Something rare. She'd wanted to continue talking with him, but it was getting late, and Crestin was there to pick her up. And she wasn't ready to talk about her dad yet, so their conversation probably would have dwindled anyway. Everleigh typically didn't like to talk about herself, not anything meaningful. She reserved those parts of her for the people she trusted the most. There was power in controlling the information others had about her. In not letting anything out that could be used against her, especially in a small town like Rustic. She'd seen it happen too many times. The gossip mills in Rustic ran 24/7.

Everleigh couldn't help but wonder if Ryker would prove to be one of the few people she trusted the most.

※

Although she thought about going back to sleep for a while, she couldn't. After scrolling through social media for a bit, Everleigh finally threw back her covers and headed to the shower. She started a load of laundry, emptied the dishwasher, rechecked her list against the items she'd already packed for the move to her dorm. It became clear she was trying to occupy herself with anything other than thoughts of her conversation with her dad. She ignored her conscience. Until her phone dinged around 9:30.

*It's tomorrow.*

A smile drew up the corners of her mouth at the text from Ryker. Because he was still thinking about their conversation from last night too.

*It is,* she replied.

*Are you busy?*

*Busy doing anything other than thinking through what I need to.*

*Do you want to talk about it?*

*No.*

Then: *Yes . . .*

Then: *Maybe?*

Which one was it, Everleigh? Did she even know?

*I'll be there in 15,* he quickly responded.

Her phone slipped from her fingers and clattered on the floor. He'd be here. In fifteen minutes. Everleigh rushed to brush out her hair, put on mascara, change out of her joggers and oversized T-shirt and into something more flattering.

When the doorbell rang thirteen minutes later, she inhaled a steadying breath and placed her hand on the doorknob, telling herself to calm down. He was being a friend. Returning the favor of an ear to bend. That was it.

When she opened the door and took in Ryker's muscular frame propped against the side of her porch—sporting his favorite uniform of side-cutout shirt, jeans that hugged him in all the right places, and brown boots—she hoped that was not it.

Ryker looked up from the phone in his hand and smiled. He had an Iowa Hawkeyes jacket slung over one shoulder, wet from his walk through the rain from his truck to the covered porch. His damp hair was sticking to his forehead in places.

"You braved the elements just so I could unload my burden on you? You really are a sweet little boy under it all, aren't you?" she teased.

He chuckled as he pushed off the porch wall. "No one's ever accused me of being sweet." He strode past her into the house, and the scent of his cedarwood cologne filled her senses, sending an unexpected arrow of satisfaction shooting straight through her insides. He removed his boots immediately and hung his jacket on the coat rack to the right of her. Was it weird that she hadn't moved from her spot as she watched him, reveling in his scent assaulting her senses?

"Hawkeye fan?" She checked herself back to reality and pointed to the jacket.

"Lifelong. You?"

"They've grown on me. Come on in." She gestured toward the living room and gave him a wide berth as she moved in that direction. "I feel kind of bad for being happy to have a day off. I realize your parents are losing out on revenue today," she said over her shoulder as Ryker followed her into the living room. She settled on the far end of the couch. He sat on the opposite end.

"They'll be fine. There's plenty to do indoors on a day like this, so I'm sure they're glad to have a day to catch up on other things." He relaxed into the couch, resting his right arm on the back.

Everleigh pulled a leg up under her so she could face him. A long silence blossomed in the space between them. Finally, Ryker said, "I don't know how much you want to tell me. That's completely up to you. But I want you to know I'm here to listen to whatever you want to say."

Unexpectedly, a tear escaped. She swiped at it. "I'm sorry," she mumbled. "I don't know why I'm getting so emotional."

But she did. To say Everleigh had been blindsided by her father yesterday would be a massive understatement. She sucked in a deep breath before she spoke the words out loud for the first time.

"My dad came to see me yesterday . . . to ask me to get tested . . . to see if I can be a bone marrow donor for Kyleigh, his baby with Bridget. It's basically the last-ditch effort to save her from leukemia."

After the initial shock scattered across his features, Ryker looked at her with empathy and sat, patiently waiting for Everleigh to collect herself.

"I didn't think I could hate my dad any more than I already did." She shrugged. "But I feel like . . . he's betraying us all over again. Like we're sitting back in that kitchen, and he's tearing our lives apart *again*."

She pulled her bottom lip between her teeth for a moment, then sighed. "It always comes back to the fact that he made us all feel like we weren't enough for him. Like we would never be what makes him happy.

"I was too young for many years to see it, how he treated my mother. I thought they were the happiest married couple in the world. He'd grab her for no reason and spin her around the kitchen to dance. Show up with an armful of flowers for her just because. They would sit on the couch and laugh loud enough for us to hear in our rooms after we were sent to bed for the night.

"It came on gradually, how he made her feel like she was no longer enough. I started to clue in on the little comments, the backhanded remarks at the end of what sounded like praise. 'This meatloaf is good, Rosalynn . . . almost as good as my mom used to make. Could use just a tad more seasoning, don't you think?' Or, 'You look nice. Are you going to do something with your hair?' When her hair was already curled and she looked fantastic!

"Then his job with the railroad required more and more travel. When he returned, he always seemed distracted. It wouldn't take much for him to get short with her. He would say he had an emergency work call and disappear into the office with his cell phone two, maybe three times a week. His work trips started stretching from one to two weeks at a time. And the weeks he was gone, she was so sad. She tried to hide it when we were around, but I could hear her crying in her room at night, hear her pleading for him to come home soon over the phone. I started to hate him then. He was hurting my mom, and I wondered how a job could be more important than us.

"So, when he said we were relocating to Iowa because of his job, I expressed my objections . . . immediately and *vocally*. Chicago was our home, all our friends were there, and I wanted to graduate with my friends. And he was never around anyway, so why did we have to move with him? Couldn't *he* just move?

"He promised everything would be different when we moved. He would no longer have to travel. He could be at home with us every night. It would be like it used to be. And Mom seemed so happy to have the opportunity to get him back from the road. So, I went along with it, for her. It was nice to see her smiling again.

"We moved so quickly, within three weeks. Dad said he wanted to get us settled before the new school year. I didn't think anything of it. But as soon as the last box was unpacked here, the last curtain hung, he seemed to grow distracted again. This honeymoon period of treating us like we were his world faded in a matter of weeks. He started coming home late a couple times a week, saying he had meetings to get him caught up on the processes and procedures at this new location.

"The night he told Mom he had to start traveling again, she had a meltdown. 'You promised!' she yelled. 'You promised no more travel! We moved here for that very reason!' And he tried to calm her down, told her he had no choice. He'd lose his job if he refused. But she was so mad. Out of her mind with anger. Throwing things at him, breaking dishes. The next day, he left anyway.

"A week later, Saralynn and I came home from my volleyball game, and he was sitting at the table with Mom. She was sobbing. He had a hand on her arm, but the look on his face was not what I expected. He wasn't upset. He wasn't sad. He was . . . relieved. He told us to sit by our mother, so we did. Saralynn scooted her chair so close to me she was almost on my lap. And he told us he had to leave. Saralynn asked, 'When will you be back?' He said, 'I won't.' She burst out crying, hollering at him that it was so unfair. I remember wrapping my arm around her and holding my mother's hand and glaring at him as he broke the hearts of the two most important people to me. As he told us about the woman he'd met—and fallen in love with—he actually *smiled*. Said he felt terrible for it, but he had no choice. *No choice*." Everleigh looked at Ryker with incredulous eyes. She chewed on the inside of her mouth before continuing. "He moved out the next day.

"My hatred for my father grew with everything that came out over the next few weeks. I overheard my mom talking on speakerphone with my Aunt Bea, his sister, late one night. Mom was in her room, and it was late, so she assumed we were in bed. She asked Aunt Bea if she'd had any idea he was having an affair. Aunt Bea said no, but he always did have a wandering eye. My mother agreed but said she never thought he would physically cheat. Aunt Bea asked if he'd admitted to any other affairs. Six over the years, I heard her say. *Six.* Aunt Bea was just as upset at what her brother had done to our family.

"I started hearing rumors that my dad had moved in with a young woman in the next town. I heard rumors he'd promised to marry her. I tried to ignore them, because with each new story I heard, I hated him more. And then he showed up to my volleyball game. Parents' night. With *her.* An enormously *pregnant* her. And flaunted her in front of my mother, my teammates, my friends. I was so embarrassed. And my mother looked like she wanted to die. After they announced the parents between matches, she hugged me and apologized, said she had to go. I understood. I wanted to run away from the sight of him too.

"That man destroyed my mother. Turned her into a lifeless, depressed shell of a woman for well over a year. He crushed my sister. Left her feeling abandoned, unloved." Everleigh stared out the window, watching the steady rainfall collect in puddles on the sidewalk.

"And you?" Ryker asked hoarsely.

She gave a sarcastic little laugh. "I'm sure that's something a high-priced therapist can help me unpack."

"You don't know how it made you feel, or you don't want to talk about how it made you feel?"

Her eyes narrowed as she brought them back to his. "Are you charging me for this session?"

The corner of his mouth ticked up.

Everleigh worried her lower lip between her teeth, then confessed, "It made me hate him. And then feel guilty for hating him. Because he's my dad. And he's still trying to reach out and have a relationship with Saralynn and me. Saralynn talks to him on the phone now and again. But I can't do it. I can't forgive him. For *so many years,* we were like an afterthought to him. An inconvenience. And now, when it's convenient for him, he comes back into my life and asks *this* of me?"

"I wouldn't say it's convenient, Everleigh. Seems kind of important."

She leveled a hard glare at Ryker for not taking her side. "Why is this on *me*, though? He's asking too much. He threw us away when he didn't want us, and now—now when he *needs* me—?" Her voice broke, and she squeezed her lips with her hand, looking out the window. She whispered, "When he needs me to save his new little girl . . . ?"

She drew in a ragged breath. "Wow, that sounds terrible. I'm a horrible person."

Ryker leaned forward and placed his hand on her knee, the warmth burning through her jeans to her skin. "No, you aren't. You've been through something. Undoubtedly, your dad is a shit. You are allowed to feel whatever it is you need to feel as you process this."

Throwing a grateful glance at him, Everleigh wiped at the tears forming in her eyes, then propelled herself up from the couch, walking a few steps around the living room, a nervous energy dancing in her muscles. She hadn't allowed herself to think about the specifics of what her father had done to them for so long. Hadn't wanted to give him the power over her by acknowledging the hurt he'd inflicted on them. It had been so much easier to push it all down, pretend she'd awakened one day and her dad simply no longer lived here.

Everleigh blew out a long breath and shook her head to clear out the anxiety. Letting her gaze travel back to Ryker, she said, "Thank you, for letting me vent. I haven't said anything to my mom—can't say anything to her. After all he put her through, and now she's finally getting back on her feet again, I can't bring this up to her. She would relive all that pain of the past, and she just doesn't need to know."

"Are you going to get tested then?"

Flinging her hands into the air, she shrugged, a fresh wave of tears threatening. Ryker lifted his tall frame from the couch and walked over to Everleigh. It was his turn to offer comfort with a hug. He folded his strong arms around her, and she literally felt the stress evaporate as his hands curled around her sides. She tried not to think about how his embrace tugged a feeling from her mind.

*Safety.*

"I just don't know what to do," she whispered into his shoulder, trying not to breathe in the scent of him. After a long moment, she pulled away, grabbed a tissue, and dabbed at her eyes. "I probably won't even be a match, and I'm freaking out over nothing."

"And what if you are?"

She looked at him with honesty and confessed, "I'll probably hate my dad even more."

He was quiet for a moment, letting her pull herself together. Everleigh couldn't believe she'd just spilled her guts to Ryker—told him her deepest secrets, her harshest feelings. And he was here for her. A safe presence intent only on supporting her.

His head tilted to the right; he scratched his upper left arm, just above his tattoo, with his right hand.

"What?" she asked.

"You know what always helps me when I need to clear my head?"

# Chapter 17
# Fastballs and Parm Fries

**Ryker**

"Okay, if you remember nothing else, remember this: That ball is coming at you at ninety miles per hour. Whatever you do, do not lean forward, fall forward, or walk forward into the line of fire while the machine's on. Got it?"

A look of sheer terror spread across Everleigh's features. "Ninety miles per hour? Are you trying to kill me?"

Ryker laughed. "You've really never been to a batting cage before?"

She shook her head, and her baseball helmet waggled from side to side. It was a little big, but it served its purpose. He pointed to a spot behind him.

"Okay, you can watch this round. Go on the other side of the fence so I don't have to worry about a foul ball hitting you."

She obeyed and stood just to the right of him, so she had a good vantage point.

"Don't put your fingers on the fence. You don't want a stray ball to break one."

"You mean you don't hit every pitch?" she teased.

"Just watch me," he instructed, fighting a smile as he moved into his stance, adjusting his helmet with one hand, then swinging his bat forward four times in his ritual. The first ball came screaming at him. He swung, making contact with a loud crack. The ball sailed up into the net.

"Holy cow!" she chirped excitedly, and he let the smile pull across his face this time as he watched for the next pitch.

Another low ball, another satisfying crack of the bat. Eight more pitches flew at him, and he connected with them all, hitting foul twice. One pop-flied straight upward off the bat, while the other glanced off the bat and shot backward, hitting the fence in front of Everleigh. She squealed and jumped, then laughed, which drew a laugh from him too.

"Are you ready to try?" Ryker asked after the machine shut off. She appeared doubtful. "Come on." He waved her in.

Everleigh moved slowly up to him, gingerly taking the bat from his outstretched hand. "Ninety miles per hour?" she hedged.

"I can turn it down for you. How about seventy?"

"Does it go lower than that?"

He chuckled as he set the machine to fifty miles per hour. Surely she could handle that. "Let me see your stance," Ryker said as he returned to her.

A smirk split across his face.

"What? What's wrong with my stance?"

"You're never going to hit a ball standing like that. You've really never played softball? T-ball?"

Everleigh shook her head, the corner of her mouth twisting.

"Okay, let's do this."[1] Moving in front of her, he lifted the bat up with her fingers still curled around it. Ryker took her right hand and placed it higher on the neck of the bat. He took her left hand and placed it near her right, noticing that her chipped purple fingernail polish had been replaced with a fresh coat of glittery pink. "You see where your hands are

---

1. AWOLNATION, "Panoramic View"

positioned? That's where you want to start. You may need to choke up on the bat or down, depending on how your swing looks."

"How will I know that?"

"I'll tell you. Now, show me your stance again." Everleigh pulled the bat up to rest on her shoulder. "That's how you're going to stand? Did you see how I was standing?"

She shifted her weight and held the bat out behind her. His eyebrows shot up. He was going to have to be a little more hands-on.

"Okay, let me help you. Now, let's get you in the right position."

Ryker walked around behind Everleigh, placed his hands on her hips, and moved her forward a step and to her left a step, lining her up near the path of the pitching machine. He applied pressure to her hips with his fingers as he said, "Loosen your hips. Keep your knees a little bent and your hips loose so you can shift your body in one fluid motion." He reached around and wrapped his hands over hers. "Hold the bat right about here. See that?" She glanced to her right and nodded. Ryker released her hands and lifted her elbow with this palm. "Elbow up. Now swing."

She chopped the bat through the air. *Oh boy.*

"Let's try this. Put your bat back up. Good. Now," he brought his arms around Everleigh and wrapped his hands over hers again, then fit his hips to her backside. "You're going to roll your wrists as you move the bat from the back to the front. Like this." He guided her arms around, showed her what her wrists should look like as they moved in front of her, and extended his arms with hers, holding the bat out in its final position. "You see how level we kept it? And you should end as if pointing straight ahead."

"But it looked like you were swinging up and down and all around."

Ryker nodded. "Once you get more practice, you can adjust your swing to modify the direction you want the ball to go after you hit it."

"You can do that?"

"Yep. We're starting with the basics, so level swing."

"Okay."

"You ready?"

"No, but go ahead."

He chuckled under his breath and turned the machine on. "Watch for the light. That means the ball is coming."

The first ball shot out and Everleigh jumped backward. "Yikes! Yikes!"

"What's the matter?"

"That's so fast!"

"It's really not. Get back in there. Not too close."

She set her stance, and this time when the ball came, she at least stayed in there.

"You gonna swing?"

"This time. This time for sure." When the pitch shot out, Everleigh did swing. But late.

"Try to track the ball as soon as it leaves the machine and start your swing before it gets to you. Better! Try again. Foul ball, nice!" Ryker clapped at her progress over two more pitches. She hit another foul ball, but straighter than the first. Finally, on the seventh pitch, she hit the ball forward, a grounder.

"Whoo!" she yelled.

"Nice! Do it again."

Everleigh made good contact again on the eighth, and by the ninth and final pitches, she seemed to have figured it out. She lifted her arms into the air, holding the bat high. "I did it!"

"You did it," he agreed around a laugh. Ryker was fully unprepared for her to throw her arms around his neck and pull him into a tight hug, but after the initial surprise subsided, he wrapped his arms around her too. She was so happy about her accomplishment, which made him happy. Everleigh pulled away, and he immediately felt the absence of her warmth.

"Let's do it again! What other pointers do you have for me?"

They spent the next hour taking turns, him narrating his adjustments with each pitch to make the ball go in the direction he wanted. Then he instructed her on using her front leg for leverage, changing her grip on the bat to hit differently, modifying the way she swung to direct the ball. He couldn't remember the last time he'd had this much fun at the batting cage. Usually, he was in a foul mood and trying to slug away his frustrations. And she seemed to be in much lighter spirits since this morning.

When Everleigh finally appeared to be losing gas, Ryker took the bat from her and lifted the too-big helmet off her head. "You hungry?"

"Starved. This really is a workout."

"It is. Let's go."

They stopped at a local bar and grill, and although it had an extensive menu, her eyes lit up when she noticed parmesan fries under the appetizers heading. "I'll take an order of parm fries. With a side of ranch, please," she told the waitress.

"You really like those fries, huh?" Ryker drawled after the waitress left their table.

"Oh, I love them. I could eat them every day. I kind of do right now," she reflected.

They ran out of small talk when they were halfway done eating, and Ryker thought of asking Everleigh something he was curious about. But he also didn't want to upset her. Honestly, he could continue to sit in this comfortable silence with her and be just fine.

But it was nagging at him. And now that he was thinking about it, he couldn't stop. He wiped his mouth with his napkin and decided to go for it.

"Can I ask you something?"

"Yes."

"And don't get mad at me, okay? Because I'm not trying to make you mad or upset or anything like that."

"Okay?"

"If you take away the circumstances behind how Kyleigh came to be, and you heard she needed a bone marrow transplant to save her life, and you might be a match, would you still refuse to get tested?"

✥✥✥✥✥ ✥✥✥✥✥

## Everleigh

His words cut her deep. And anger immediately flowed from that wound. "Ryker, that's not fair. You're making me out to be a monster."

"No, now—*no*." He held up his hand. "You know I don't mean that. Think of it this way. Let's say Marla has a baby—"

"She's too old to have a baby now."

"—and sweet Marla Junior is dying, and the only way to save her is to find a bone marrow match."

"Highly unlikely that would be happening to two local babies at once."

"Anyone can get tested to see if they match. Would you get tested?"

Everleigh sat with her arms folded across her chest, glaring at him. Why was he doing this? Ryker knew how terrible she felt as it was.

"I'm only challenging you because I think you want to do something other than what you're letting yourself do."

"What does that even mean? You know I haven't decided one way or the other yet."

She continued to glower at him, and he watched her with a look on his face. Like he knew what she was going to do before she knew what she was going to do—he was just waiting for her to say the words. It was unnerving.

But Ryker was one hundred percent right. If you removed the fact that Kyleigh was her father's child, she wouldn't hesitate to see if she could help save that baby's life. Could Everleigh set all the betrayal aside, though? Could she reward her father for being a wretched man to the family he'd had first?

"I don't know," she muttered just loud enough for Ryker to hear.

The only words exchanged on the drive home were when she asked if she could change the radio station, and he responded yes. Everleigh stared out the side window at the streams of rain trickling along the glass. He'd be dropping her off soon.

Things had gotten awkward at lunch after they'd been getting along so well. He'd listened to her vent this morning without judgment. He'd taken her to the batting cage to work out her frustrations. He'd taught her to actually hit a fast pitch. He'd wrapped his arms around her during that lesson, and rather than make her nervous and tense, the physical contact had relaxed her.

But then Ryker had questioned her judgment. And that's where their conversation had ended. Yet she felt like their conversations had just begun. She wanted to continue to talk through this decision with him. He had good insight. Everleigh knew he wasn't trying to upset her. She knew she needed to figure out how to move out of this juvenile mindset when it came to anything concerning her father. But she wasn't sure how to overcome it.

She turned her head and let it rest on the headrest, settling her eyes on Ryker as he drove. Over these recent days, she'd experienced a roller coaster of emotions as she'd gotten to know him. She felt maybe he had too.

But Everleigh couldn't be wrong that there was definitely something between them. A trust. An honesty.

Feelings?

Something was growing within her.[2] Fast. From the moment he'd opened up to her last night, it was like everything had shifted for them. A mutual respect had started to build. An appreciation for what they each had been through and how they could help one another navigate the rough waters. If Everleigh knew only one thing, it was that she was going to grab onto this opportunity with both hands and see where it would take them.

Ryker parked the truck in her driveway. Just like the last time they'd been in these very same seats, she felt the space expanding between them. The quiet pattering of raindrops on the roof of the truck was comforting. The water-soaked windows provided the illusion of privacy as they sat and gazed into one another's eyes. Neither seemed ready to give up the other's presence.

"Thank you for today," Everleigh said softly. "I really appreciate your insight, Ryker. And your support. And your batting lessons." A smile crept along her mouth.

He smiled in return. "Merely paying back what your friendship provided for me last night."

Her smile faltered. *Friendship?*

Anxiety rose in her chest at that comment, and she knew she could not let this moment slip away without showing him she truly wanted to be more than friends. So much more.

Everleigh released her seatbelt and looked at her house.

"I'll see you tomorrow?" he said.

If she wasn't mistaken, there was a touch of regret in that phrase, which solidified her resolve. She climbed across to his seat and slid onto his lap, straddling him. Ryker's eyes widened with surprise, but she didn't pause to ask permission. She placed her hands on either side of

---

2. Amber Run, "I Found"

his face as she kissed him—open mouth, tongue searching for his. And Ryker delivered. His hot breath and his tongue wrapped up with her own in answer, his arms snaking around her, pulling her against him.

Everleigh drew her hands up into his thick hair and pulled away to look into his shining amber eyes. Seeing her desire mirrored there, she crashed her mouth back into his, moving her hands down around his neck, his shoulders, pulling him, pulling him toward her. She heard the click of his seatbelt, and she allowed enough space between them for him to shimmy the belt away. And then it felt as though there was no barrier between them. He was holding her tighter than she'd ever been held before, and her body sang in response. Ryker withdrew his mouth. At first she worried he was pulling away, but then his lips found her neck, and he kissed and licked his way up to her ear. And she was not prepared for the electric waves that shot down her body. She gasped as he sucked.

She returned the favor by lifting his jaw and kissing his neck along his collarbone. Teasing him all the way up to his jawline, swiping her tongue around his ear. His soft sigh emboldened her, and Everleigh slid her hands into the openings of his side-cutout shirt. How she loved that he wore these shirts. Running her hands along his sides, she reveled in the muscular landscape. The strength beneath her fingertips . . .

Ryker's hands touched the skin of her back, and a shudder tripped up her spine. Those strong, rough hands glided up to her shoulders and pressed her into him, their mouths returning to one another. Everleigh rocked her hips forward, and his hands slid down, clutching her around the waist. Need raced through her blood like a wildfire.

Her phone rang.

She ignored it.

It rang again.

They both glanced over at it. *Mom.* Everleigh reached over and snatched it up, still breathing heavily. She said "Hello?" in a wobbly voice, then covered her mouth with her hand as she tried to regulate her breathing. But Ryker was breathing so heavily, she worried her mom could hear it through the phone. She moved her hand to his open mouth and held it closed. His darkened gaze seared into her.

"What?" she asked her mom, trying to make sense of what she'd heard.

"Saralynn fell at the babysitter's apparently. She's cut pretty badly. I'm almost half an hour away, you know. Can you take her to urgent care? I can meet you there. She'll probably need stitches."

"Yeah. Yeah, I'll go right now."

"Are you okay? You sound out of breath."

"I'm fine. Yeah." Everleigh's eyes widened at Ryker.

"Okay. Good. I'll see you in a bit."

"Yep."

Ryker peeled her fingers away from his mouth before she even ended the call. "What is it?"

"My sister's hurt. I've got to take her to urgent care. Mom's going to meet us there."

"Oh. Do you want me to drive you?"

"No!"

He was taken aback by her forcefulness.

"I mean, no thank you. I can't have you anywhere near me after this." Everleigh moved her hand in a circle between them.

"Wha—?"

She quickly slid back to the passenger seat and ran her hands down her face. "I won't be able to focus on anything if you are within fifty feet of me." She leaned over once more and grabbed Ryker by the chin, kissed his lips, and jumped out of the truck.

⁂

Everleigh allowed poor Saralynn to squeeze her hand as tightly as she wanted, even though she felt her bones scraping together. It was a big cut on her little sister's leg, jagged, with skin flapping when Everleigh pulled the wash rag away to check it. She almost puked as she saw the outer layer of Saralynn's skin separate from her soft tissue. And the blood! She quickly pressed the rag back down and asked Heather, the babysitter, for a dishtowel so she could tie the rag in place to transport her sister to urgent care.

Luckily, they didn't have to wait long. Maybe it was the blood-soaked rag that pushed them up in line. Maybe it was the fact that Saralynn was small for a nine-year-old, so they thought she was younger. Whatever it was, they only had to wait about five minutes before they were called back, Everleigh pushing Saralynn in a wheelchair. That seemed to be what finally got Saralynn to calm down a bit and stop crying—the fact that she got to ride in a wheelchair.

As they injected localized anesthetic around the wound, Sarahlynn let out the highest-pitched screams Everleigh had ever heard. Saralynn continued to squeeze her hand as if her life depended on it. Everleigh understood—it was a very scary situation to start with, and then you brought in huge needles, several sharp objects, and something that looked like a fishing line. And her mom wasn't here. Saralynn moaned over and over that she wanted her mommy, sniffled with her eyes shut tight. Moments like this was when it really sucked that Rosalynn had to commute to the north side of Cedar Rapids—twenty-five minutes from their home—to find a high-paying job to support their family. Her mom really should be the one here soothing poor, frightened Saralynn.

Everleigh looked away as soon as the nurse pulled the skin flap back to clean the wound. She focused instead on the pink polish she'd painted on Saralynn's fingers the other night when she'd repainted her own nails. Her sister's polish was already chipping in the corners. The skin around her fingertips was stark white compared to the pink polish as she clutched Everleigh's hand. Dropping a kiss on her sister's hand, she thought about ways she could distract Saralynn from the frightening experience.

"Hey, did you decide when you want Mom to bring you to the sunflower patch? There're only a few days left of the season. And the flowers are all blooming near peak right now."

"No," she whimpered with eyes screwed closed. "I want Bailey to come with. Mom says she has to call her mom to ask."

"I'll remind Mom tonight."

"Okay," Saralynn said weakly. "And we get to bring a flower home, right?"

"Yes, everybody gets one."

"What if I'm too little to reach the one I want?"

Everleigh chuckled softly. "Then you come find me, and I'll help you get it. You have to be able to get the flower you love the most, right?"

Saralynn nodded, and the paper table cover crackled and crinkled beneath her. There was a soft knock on the door, and a doctor entered, followed by their mother. "Look who I found, Miss Saralynn," he said.

She opened one eye, then the tears flowed again as soon as she realized Mom was here.

"Mommy!"

"Hey, baby, how are you doing? I'm so sorry I couldn't be here sooner." Her mom came to the table and placed one hand on Saralynn's good leg and one on Everleigh's shoulder.

"It's okay," her sister responded in a small voice.

Her mother mouthed a thank-you to Everleigh before turning her attention to the doctor, who was explaining the severity of the injury and what they were going to do to fix it. He gestured to the nurse cleaning the wound, saying something about debriding or something, to lessen the chance of infection. He studied the cut for a moment, then said it would take about twenty-five, maybe thirty stitches. He claimed she'd lucked out and didn't hit any major blood vessels or nerves. Everleigh raised her eyebrows at that, because she'd thought for sure her sister would need a blood transfusion with all the blood that had poured out of her.

Her mom turned to Everleigh. "Do you want to take a break? Wait for us out front? I can take it from here."

Her first instinct was to say she was fine staying, but Saralynn released her hand and grabbed their mother's, so she decided she could get out of the way. The worst of the traumatic incident was over; her sister would be fine. She relinquished her chair to her mom and patted her sister on the knee.

"You got this. See you out there."

Saralynn nodded.

The nurse had finished cleaning the wound and was now typing notes into the computer while the doctor prepped for stitches. "Ah, Jarah, can you get me 4-0 suture instead?"

"Sure." The nurse headed for the door, and Everleigh followed her out into the hallway.

A compulsive thought entered her mind, and she had to get it out. This was the opportunity, right?

"Excuse me?"

Jarah turned around. "Yes?"

"Can I ask you just one quick question? By the way, thanks for being so great with my sister."

"Sure, and you're welcome. She's a cutie."

"I have a friend . . . who might need to get tested to see if she's a match for a bone marrow transplant. Do you know what that testing involves?"

"Of course. It's a blood test, so a needle is involved, and they take enough tubes of blood to do the appropriate testing, probably four to five. And maybe a cheek swab for further testing."

"That's it?" Everleigh asked, trying to control her surprise.

Jarah nodded. "That's it. But you should encourage your friend to read up on the full donation procedure, so she knows all that's involved if she is, in fact, a match."

Everleigh nodded. "I will. Thank you."

As she walked out to the waiting room, Ryker's words echoed in her mind.

* * *

# Ryker

*How is your sister?*

As Ryker lay on his bed that evening, that seemed the safest text to send. He'd started typing a text to Everleigh five different times since she'd straddled him and driven him crazy with her mouth before jumping out of the truck, leaving him wanting more.

Ryker was trying to be a friend—he really was. She'd listened to his shit yesterday; he'd wanted to repay the favor today. But as the day had gone on, and they'd had fun together at the batting cage, he'd be lying if he said his mind hadn't drifted back to the barn, back to when he'd wrapped her legs around his waist and thrilled at the way she looked at him, like she wanted to possess him.

That was before she'd known his secret. As cathartic as it had felt to share it with her, to let the darkest parts of himself out into the light, he'd honestly worried it would cause Everleigh to distance herself from the shitshow that was Ryker Martin.

So when he'd texted her this morning, purely with the offer of friendship, he'd been surprised she'd responded so quickly. And when he'd stepped from the porch across her threshold, his thoughts had only been on helping her talk through the thing with her dad. Even as he'd hugged her in her living room, his sole intention had been comforting his hurting friend. He knew a relationship with any girl at this point would derail his progress, distract his focus from what he needed to be working on. But having a friend he could trust and look to for support? Those were few and far between.

How easily they'd gotten on at the batting cage had been a bit unexpected. She'd been fun, lighthearted, and open to his coaching. Then that second hug—the one after Everleigh had finished her batting rep, ecstatic at her accomplishment—had triggered his feels.

Ryker had battled it as they sat through a lunch that turned awkward too fast. He'd become nervous, worried about what she thought, how she felt. About him. Could she put aside the way he'd treated her before to allow him a space in her heart?

On the silent ride home, Ryker had reminded himself that it was not what he wanted or needed right now. He'd set his resolve to only offer himself as a friend.

Then she'd shown him why that wasn't a possibility. Sitting in that truck in her driveway, in a dry bubble, safe from the rain surrounding them . . . her touch, her taste, had fiercely consumed him. And she'd set up camp once again in that space in his mind. The space that allowed him to fixate on everything that was perfect about Everleigh Wilson.

*She'll be okay. 28 stitches! She's currently enjoying a large bowl of ice cream while watching her favorite Disney movie with her leg propped up on three pillows.*

*Poor kid*, he replied.

*Honestly, it was almost as scary as when she gets a bee sting. So much blood. And the gash itself? It was almost 3 inches total. Somehow fell into their glass coffee table and it shattered. She's lucky that was the only cut she got. A bunch of small scrapes, but those will all be fine.*

He wanted to call Everleigh. To hear her voice tell him all of this. He wanted to suggest he come over, and she could share everything in person.

*I'm exhausted after the stress of it all,* she continued.

Never mind. Ryker thought for a moment about an appropriate response. Finally, he settled on, *Understandable. Get some rest.*

*Thank you.*

He dropped his phone onto his chest. Readjusted his head on his pillow. Wondered if she regretted coming on to him today.

A succession of messages pinged his phone. He quickly lifted it.

*And Ryker?*

*Thanks again for today.*

*It helped me more than you know.*

He smiled. Thought for a long moment. But the only thing he could think to respond was, *Any time.*

# Chapter 18
# A Long Night Ahead of Us

## Everleigh

"You pretty little liar!"

"Crestin! I'm *not* a liar," Everleigh protested. "I mean, maybe I was lying to myself . . ."

She finished plaiting her hair into a braid in the car as he backed out of her driveway. Because she was running late today. Because all the trauma caused by Saralynn's incident kept her from sleeping well last night.

Partly true.

The rest of the story? After her text chat with Ryker, she couldn't stop thinking about him. And that kiss. And how his touch had burned into her when he ran his hands up the bare skin of her back.

*Was he thinking about it too?*

"Girl. 'Never will be.' That's what you said. Like, five days ago. I have so many questions."

Everleigh was beginning to regret telling Crestin about the kiss with Ryker yesterday. She'd blurted it out to him when she'd dropped into the passenger seat in the El Camino, hoping for some clarity from her best friend. He always shot straight with her, even if the truth might hurt her feelings. And if it would hurt her, he delivered the news as gently as a virtual hug. So far, she hadn't gleaned any advice from him, and now he had more questions.

"I know I said that. I truly believed it at the time," she defended herself as she tied her white, patterned hair ribbon around her head and secured it at the base of her neck below her braid. "But I think there may be something there."

"I'm sure you want me to say DNA—"

"DNA?"

"Did Not Anticipate. It's a new phrase I'm trying out," he said with a dismissive wave of his hand. "Anyway, I'm sure you want me to say DNA, but I *totally* Aed."

"What do you mean?" She narrowed her eyes at his smug profile.

"How am I the only one who saw this coming?" He threw his hands up and rolled his head in her direction. "Evs, the sexual tension has been *palpable* between the two of you. The Will-They-Won't-They of the summer."

A scoff burst from her. "Save the drama for New York, Crestin. I'm still not sure They Will." Everleigh looked out the side window as they pulled into the parking lot of The Sunflower Experience. She spoke more softly, "I'm not sure they *should*."

"Um, wait a minute. Dish!" Crestin parked and quickly shifted in his seat to face her. "What did you find out? Did he tell you what happened in June?"

She'd said too much. She should have known Crestin was still on his sleuthing mission to find out what Ryker had done to get kicked off the baseball team. But, being wrapped up in her own drama, she'd forgotten. Everleigh wasn't about to betray Ryker's confidence, even to her best friend. It wasn't her story to tell. So she sidestepped.

"I do know that whatever he's dealing with, he's working very hard on personal growth this summer. I admire him for that."

Crestin's eyes squinted into slits as he settled his visor onto his head, and she could tell he was about to call her out.

"Time for work," she said hurriedly and popped out of the car.

Admissions table again. Which meant Everleigh wouldn't see Ryker all day unless he came over to give breaks, which probably wouldn't happen since there were two of them at the table under the canopy today. She checked her phone for the tenth time in two hours. She didn't know why she expected him to message her. What did they have to talk about that they hadn't already discussed?

The kiss, for one.

Maybe she was hoping he'd bring it up, so she knew it meant something to him too. Maybe she was hoping he wouldn't so she could have some more time to sort through her potential feelings for him.

She was hoping he did. Bring it up, that is.

The stream of visitors was steady, people not wanting to miss the opportunity for perfect sunflower sea photos ahead of the end of the blooming season. Eric, her working partner today, took his morning break around ten. Everleigh checked her phone again. When Eric returned, she set off on her break and refilled her water bottle. Looked at her phone. Finally, she decided to just do it. Just message him. She was a big girl. She could start the conversation. If he didn't feel the same way, she could respect that. But she was going crazy not knowing.

She began with something basic: *Skipping work? I haven't seen you wandering around.*

She stared at the screen for several agonizing seconds, wondering if he would respond. She let out a breath she hadn't realized she'd been holding when the three dots appeared.

*LOL. Helping out in the kids' area. Full house today.*

A smile crept across her face. He'd answered pretty quickly. She thought for a moment, then typed, *I won't keep you from babysitting then. What time are you taking lunch?*

Another quick response: *Noon. You?*

*Meet you at the food truck.* She included a winky face emoji.

*See you there.* Smiling emoji. Then a second message: *With parm fries.*

Her smile was a full-on grin now. And her stomach was teeming with butterflies. Noon couldn't come fast enough.

## Ryker

He'd thought about messaging her all morning. But what would he say? And then, right after he'd pulled two little boys who were scrapping on the jumping pillow apart, his phone dinged. As soon as he'd seen *Everleigh* with the sunflower emoji after her name, a grin had swept over his mouth.

Now, as Ryker sat at the picnic table by the food truck with a boat of parm fries on the table beside him, he watched her walking toward him in her tie-dyed shirt, khaki shorts, and miles of tan legs. And he thought about her fingernails scraping up his skin yesterday with tantalizing pressure.

"For me?" she asked as she sat next to him.

"Hot and fresh."

Everleigh smiled, and his eyes settled on that dimple.

"Did they have ranch?" she asked. Ryker lifted his hand above the table and deposited a small cup of ranch in front of her. She laughed as she peeled the lid from the container. "I've taught you well."

Chuckling, his gaze didn't leave her mouth, hoping she'd turn her head toward him again so he could see that dimple. He wished she'd sat across from him now, so he could stare at her kaleidoscope eyes as well.

"So, I was wondering . . ." Ryker started. He was rewarded with eye contact. "Would you like to watch the sunset with me this evening?"

"I'll do you one better," Everleigh said after swallowing a fry, setting her phone on the table and tapping on it. She slid it in front of him and pointed at the screen. "The weather app says there's a meteor shower tonight. Prime viewing is between 10:30 p.m. and 1:00 a.m."

Ryker glanced down at the phone and then up at Everleigh. "Sounds like we have a long night ahead of us."

Ryker sat in her driveway, waiting for her to appear on the porch. When he'd asked Everleigh to watch the sunset this evening, he'd been hoping for a chance to talk, to see if there really was something forming between them. When she'd mentioned the meteor shower, he'd felt a surge of anticipation, knowing she was extending the time they'd be spending together. She wouldn't be doing that if she wasn't into him, right? Everleigh didn't honestly just want to watch a meteor shower, did she?

When she'd told him she wanted to go home and shower and change after work and asked if he would pick her up before sunset, it had suddenly felt like a date. An official date. Nervousness had begun to grow in his gut, and as he'd stood, freshly showered and shaven with his towel around his waist in front of his dresser, he'd cared about what he wore for the very first time. Cared about what he looked like. For her. Ryker had rethought his clothing choices three times. Settled on a new pair of dark jeans and a tan, button-up, sleeveless denim shirt that showed off one of his favorite features: his biceps. He'd tucked it in, untucked it, tucked it in again. Top two buttons open. Then he'd pulled on his dark brown cowboy boots and put on an extra splash of cologne.

As he glanced at the clock on the truck dash, the front door opened, drawing his gaze once again to that porch. Everleigh stepped out. And his heart skipped a beat. Her long brown hair fell around her shoulders in loose curls, held back from her face with a white ribbon. She was sporting a denim jacket that stopped just above her waist and drew attention to how her floral dress curved around her hips. She nearly skipped down the sidewalk in strappy sandals with a smile on her face like she was happy to see him. And she was gorgeous.

Everleigh opened the truck door and climbed in, saying in a breathy voice, "I'm so excited for tonight! Mom says this meteor shower only comes along every fifty years. And it's supposed to be a heavy shower."

"A heavy one, huh?" was all Ryker could muster as he stared at her, mesmerized by her casual beauty. She was wearing a touch of makeup, a little mascara, and the combination made her hazel eyes vibrant, enhancing the dark ring around the color. Or maybe it was the excitement dancing in those hazels at the impending astronomical showcase. When she looked away to put on her seatbelt, Ryker blinked, bringing himself to his senses. This was going to be one long night if Everleigh really only did care about the meteors.

The drive out to the sunflower patch was awkwardly silent. She made a little small talk, asked how his day went, told him how her day went. But he didn't dare look at her, because if he did, he might just whip the truck over to the side of the road and pull her onto his lap. And what if that wasn't what she wanted? What if she'd only agreed to hang out with him tonight as friends? There'd been no mention of the kiss since it happened. And the longer it took for it to come up in conversation, the more Ryker feared she wanted to keep their relationship platonic. Which would be okay, he guessed. She had proven she would be a good friend to him. He could see himself maintaining a friendship with Everleigh long past this summer job at The Sunflower Experience. Messaging with her from time to time to talk about life. It would be easy to be Everleigh's friend when she wasn't sitting so close beside him, looking like a model and smelling like vanilla.

He parked the truck in the driveway at the back of his house, and they moved to the UTV. Ryker started the engine; Everleigh scooped her hair into one hand to keep it from blowing everywhere. The roar of the engine made it hard to converse on the drive over to the platform of choice, so they didn't.

He cut the engine and allowed his gaze to settle on her for the first time since she'd bounced up into the truck. She was running her hands through her hair, fluffing her brunette curls, scattering her vanilla scent into the air.

"What?" she said, a smile tugging at her mouth.

Ryker shook his head as his eyes wandered to the dimple in her right cheek. He hopped out of the UTV and lifted a blanket from the back, along with a cooler of drinks. He hadn't known what she'd want, so he'd packed bottles of water, juice, and soda. He motioned to the steps of the platform, and as he followed her up, he took in the sway of her hips from side to side beneath her dress. A warmth unfurled through his body. At the top, Everleigh turned around and reached for the blanket. Setting the cooler down, he handed her one end. They situated it and then themselves on the platform, legs dangling over the front edge.

"You came prepared." She nodded at the cooler.

"I did." Ryker scooted it closer. "I wasn't sure what you would like, so it's packed pretty full."

"Do you have water in there?"

"I do." He retrieved a cold bottle of water, shook the ice pieces off, and handed it to her. He grabbed a bottle for himself.

"Thank you." Everleigh took a sip, then set the bottle aside. She leaned back on her palms and sighed. "I think this may be a sunset fail."

Ryker's heart dropped at her comment. "How so?"

"No clouds in the sky for the light to play with. The colors will still be pretty as the evening blues take over the yellow, but it won't be as spectacular as I was hoping."

He studied her profile. The glow of the setting sun made her skin radiant, and he wanted to reach out and run the backs of his fingers along her golden cheek. "No clouds probably bode well for meteor-shower-viewing later."

"True," Everleigh agreed as she brought her gaze to his. Ryker watched her eyes dip down and back up. "You look nice tonight."

"As do you," he said, his voice a bit hoarse.

"I wasn't sure . . . what to expect when I was getting ready, so I decided to show my hand and let the cards fall where they may."

There went Ryker's nerves again. This was more-than-friends talk. This was we-might-be-making-out-before-the-night-is-over talk. And he was here for it.

"I'd say you have a winning hand," Ryker drawled with a slow smile. If he wasn't mistaken, a blush crept up Everleigh's cheeks as she looked to the west.

The sunset came and went rather quickly, as they'd spent time getting ready after their shifts rather than heading straight to the platform. The crickets and cicadas added their usual accompaniment to the summer evening as the last yellow slice of the sun disappeared beneath the horizon, leaving orange bleeding into pink bleeding into light purple, aquamarine, and deep blue. Stars were becoming visible above them, glimmering to life one by one. As he dropped his gaze from the dark blue sea above, he noticed her pink-polished fingertips less than an inch from his own work-worn hand. He could move his hand slightly and brush his fingers across hers. He did. When he looked up, she'd turned her head toward him, resting her chin on her shoulder.

"Ryker, what are you most afraid of?"

*Whoa.*

He thought for a long moment, letting his fingers rest on top of hers. "I would say . . ." He swallowed the lump that formed in his throat at the question. "Losing control of myself. Because if that happens, I don't know if I can get it back."

"What do you think would make you lose control?"

Clearing his throat, he sat up straight as he watched the orange and pink fade, overtaken by nightfall. He rubbed a hand on the side of his face.

"Truthfully?"

"Yes, I always prefer truth."

Ryker looked squarely at Everleigh and admitted, "You."

## Everleigh

He'd punched her in the chest. Figuratively, of course, but it hurt the same as if he'd balled up his fist and physically slammed it into her. Ryker believed she could ruin everything for him. That was the last thing Everleigh would ever want. But at the same time, the yearning in her heart for him swelled even more. What if she *could* actually help him remain in control? Be the support she'd offered to him the other night?

He must have seen how her face fell at his comment; Ryker rushed to soften the blow. "I mean, there are a lot of things that could make that happen, I guess. Failing at school, not getting back on my team, maybe even something ridiculously simple that I can't even think of because it's too silly to give it a thought now."

Everleigh's head bobbed, as if she understood. But her mind was stuck on the fact that the one thing she wanted most could be the one thing he needed least. For his mental health. For his journey to recovery.

She sat up straight as well, taking a drink of water. Then, she looked at him again. "What do you do? On a daily basis to maintain control?"

"Focus is the biggest thing. Focus on the things that are important to me. The farm, my workouts, baseball strategizing. Doing the things I know will make my parents proud of me again."

"Ryker, you don't think they were ever not proud of you, do you?" Her voice was gentle yet censuring as she placed her hand on his leg.

He let out a bitter laugh. "I know they weren't. How could they be? You know the story. How could any parent be proud of a child who's screwed up his life so royally?"

Everleigh chewed on her lip as she wondered what she could say to make him feel better, as she regretted asking the question that led him to feel this way. She pulled her legs up, crossing them as she turned to face him, and arranged her dress over her knees. She lifted Ryker's hand into hers and rested them on her lap.

"Even if they weren't, it's easy to see they are so proud of you now. Of the strides you've made in your recovery."

"Yeah, I don't know . . ."

"I do." She squeezed his hand and dipped her head to capture his gaze. "The way they talk about you, the way they look at you. They are proud parents."

Ryker scoffed, but she could see a tiny upturn at the corners of his mouth. Rubbing her hand over his, she looked at the veins that trailed over the top of his strong hand, raised reminders of the hard work it had seen.

"You know what I'm most afraid of?"

"What?" His eyes softened, and Everleigh wished it was lighter outside so she could take in the full force of his handsome features.

Sighing, she studied his hand again, a safe place to focus her attention. "I'm afraid I'll decide to help Kyleigh, and she'll die anyway, and my dad will hate me." Her heart constricted at the confession, causing her shoulders to curve inward at the pain. A tear escaped from her eye, falling on top of Ryker's cradled hand. She hastily swiped it away with her thumb.

Suddenly scooped into his strong embrace, a swirl of emotions unleashed inside her. After a moment, she circled her hands around him. She'd had no intention of letting this out, but now that it was, the admission ripped at her heart. Another tear fell, and another, and Everleigh thought past the ache in her mind to how she needed to get herself under control. This wasn't meant to be about her. It was meant to be about getting to know Ryker. As his hand slid gently up her back and curled around her neck, she felt safety, comfort in his embrace. And it gave her the strength to pull herself together.

## Ryker

It was after ten o'clock. The night had taken an unexpected turn—for both of them, he thought—when their conversation got a bit too real. On the one hand, he felt the bond with Everleigh grow as they shared their deepest fears. On the other, he could feel her uncertainty growing at his confession that she could be his undoing if he wasn't careful. Ryker hadn't shared that to make her feel like she was a problem for him; he'd done it to let her know how much power she had over him, if she chose to exercise that power. Now he was afraid she would not.

Their conversation on the platform gradually shifted to their most embarrassing moments this summer, then to their most embarrassing moments in high school, then to general playful banter. They were getting along so well, as well as they had yesterday in the batting cage, and it was easy to think life could always be this simple. With her. Yet he could feel her holding back. Sitting just outside his reach after she'd pulled away from his hug.

Everleigh's stomach growled during one of the few lulls in their conversation, and she laughed, saying she must not have eaten enough at supper. He suggested they pop over to his house and rummage through the refrigerator. They could be back before the meteor shower began. She agreed.

As they tiptoed into the house, she excused herself to use the bathroom, and Ryker went to the fridge to scope out the multitude of covered containers of his mother's cooking. The fourth container held the jackpot: Oreo fluff. He set the glass container on the breakfast bar and pulled out two spoons from the silverware drawer.

Everleigh gasped as she came up beside him. "Is that what I think it is?"

He nodded and handed her a spoon.

"I haven't had this in forever," she gushed in a low voice, remembering his sleeping parents.

They giggled as they took turns scooping spoonfuls out of the bowl, and Ryker felt like a kid. Then Everleigh tapped her full spoon on his nose, leaving a dollop of fluff on the end before placing the spoon in her mouth. Shocked, he froze, crossing his eyes down at the blob of dessert before lifting them and leveling a hard glare at her.

She apologized profusely, as quietly as she could, fighting her laughter all the while. Her shoulders shook and she trembled, and he didn't know whether it was from suppressing her laughter or fear of his retaliation. He slowly wiped the fluff from his nose with his forefinger as he debated his next move. Like a viper, he struck forward, lunging at her with an outstretched finger. She yelped but swept gracefully backward before spinning and darting away from him, grabbing at the island countertop for purchase. He chased her around the breakfast bar with his fluff-covered finger tracing her every move, threatening to smear it all over her face.

After a couple of rounds, he gave up following her and shifted his body quickly, coming at her in the opposite direction, catching her around the corner and wrapping his arm around her while holding what dessert was left on his finger inches from her face. She was laughing hysterically, trying to keep her voice down, wriggling beneath his grasp.

"I'm sorry! I'm sorry!" Everleigh pleaded in a loud whisper as she composed herself, a whine entering her voice.

"Do unto me only what you want done unto you, no?"

Her head shook in disagreement while errant giggles continued to erupt from her chest. "I'm sorry."

Ryker moved his finger closer to her cheek, right over her dimple, and prepared to smear the fluff on her, but decided instead on mercy as she murmured "No-no-no" and squirmed against his body, trying to peel herself out of the cage of his arm. Reluctantly—he quite enjoyed this playful side of Everleigh—Ryker released her and licked his finger, holding up his clean hands for her inspection. Everleigh stepped forward, laced her fingers in his, and squeezed their hands together.

"Thank you," she said, gratitude in her expression.

And he was consumed with the desire to pull her body against his and kiss her. To drag one hand into her brown curls while the other splayed along her lower back, drawing their bodies flush. But too quickly Everleigh released his hands and returned to her spoon by the Oreo fluff bowl, dipping it in and eating as if she hadn't just felt the earth shudder beneath them as well. She glanced at Ryker with concern, and he realized he hadn't moved since she'd dropped his hands.

Recovering, he cleared his throat. "Ready to head back out?"

She nodded, scooped up one last bite of fluff, and rinsed their spoons in the sink while he covered the container and returned it to the fridge.

"Tell your mom that was the best Oreo fluff I've ever tasted," she said as they headed back into the night.

On the drive to the patch, Everleigh realized for the first time that there was a radio in the UTV.[1] She asked if she could turn it on, and he nodded. Classic rock swelled from the speakers, and Ryker thought his dad must have been the last one to use the radio.

"Aerosmith!" she exclaimed, turning up the volume.

"Angel"—a song from the late eighties, maybe?

"You know Aerosmith?" he asked incredulously.

"They're one of my mom's favorite bands. She's been to, like, five concerts. Plays them all the time when cooking or cleaning the house or whatever." Everleigh began to sing along. She knew all the lyrics.

Ryker drove them back to the jumping pillow this time, thinking it would give them the best (and most comfortable) vantage point for watching the meteor show. When he shifted the gear to park, he didn't immediately cut the engine. Instead, he grabbed Everleigh by the hand and pulled her out his side of the UTV, causing her to stop singing mid-lyric.

"What are you doing?" she asked as he turned to face her.

"Showing my hand." Ryker drew her into him, placing his hand on her lower back and lifting her hand with his right. Then he danced her around in the headlights of the UTV, twirling her to the right, to the left, and back into his chest. He watched as her dress flared around with each circle, laughed when she giggled. When she sang the chorus, held tightly against him, he sang along, dipping her at the end, anticipating the taste of her mouth when he kissed her. As he lowered his face toward hers, his eyelids began to lower as well.

---

1. Aerosmith, "Angel"

Then Everleigh gasped, sending his eyes flying open. After a split second of confusion, Ryker realized she was looking over his shoulder, up at the sky.

"It's started!"

Blanket spread out in the middle of the jumping pillow, Ryker lay with his hands stacked behind his head. He pulled his left knee up, adjusting his position. Lying beside him, Everleigh's head nested in the crook of his shoulder, her hair tickling his bare underarm. Her right arm was slung across her body, absently tracing circles on the right side of his abdomen. He wondered if the cells of her body were as jittery as his were where their bodies touched.

The meteor shower was amazing, falling stars by the handful streaking above every few minutes. But he found his gaze landing on Everleigh more than the sky. Watching her chest rise and fall with each breath. Watching her delicate finger circle over his shirt. Watching her eyelashes flutter every time she blinked. Ryker ached to pull her into his arms, to kiss her. But she was enraptured by the meteor show, and he wanted her to have this moment. The shower would end in an hour or so, and he could pick up where they'd left off at the end of their dance. The waiting only built the anticipation and coaxed more and more of his cells into a jittery high.

Suddenly, she shifted her head to look up at him. "Did you see that? Three of them right together?"

"Yeah," he lied.

Everleigh rolled onto her elbows and rested her chin in her palm. "Do you think I'm the biggest nerd for getting so excited over shooting stars?"

"I do not," he chuckled.

It was dark, but Ryker thought her eyes narrowed at him. "I don't," he reiterated. "It *is* pretty amazing."

She released a contented sigh and situated herself on her backside, held up by her crooked elbows perpendicular to him. Her curls spilled down her back onto his stomach as she trained her eyes on the sky. Ryker traced her profile with his eyes, all the way down her curved neck, past her collarbone, down to her chest rising and falling. She lowered herself, resting her head on his stomach, folding her arms across her midsection.

"I could never see anything like this in Chicago—not this clearly. Too many lights everywhere."

She turned her head toward him and continued. "Honestly? I'm still a little afraid of the dark. I wouldn't be able to do this if you weren't here with me." She brought her right hand up and placed it on his left cheek. "You bring me strength."

When Everleigh smiled, he pulled his right hand from behind his head and touched that dimple with this fingertip, a gentle caress. Which caused it to disappear. Sadly, Ryker had been the one to make it disappear. But then she was moving toward him, leaning above him with both hands cupping his cheeks. Her breaths quickening, her eyes boring directly into his, his breathing stopped. Her gaze dipped to his lips, then returned to his stare, holding him hostage as desire burned through his body. What happened next was completely up to Everleigh.

She grazed her soft lips in the barest touch over his, and it was all Ryker could do not to lift his head and crash his mouth into hers, to drag her on top of him. He wondered if she could feel his heart racing in his chest as she relaxed onto him, her mouth still hovering over his. Everleigh closed her eyes, but he didn't, *couldn't*. He needed to see her, proof of what was happening between them. He breathed in as she breathed out, and finally she dropped her warm lips onto his, gently at first, then more firmly. Her tongue slid along his lips, and he opened his mouth for her. It was only then that he curled his hands around her, slipping them beneath her denim jacket, pulling her closer. Ryker let his eyelids fall closed and reveled in the feeling of her tongue dancing around his.

Everleigh drifted away, and he immediately felt the absence of her warmth. But then he was rewarded with the full weight of her body settling on top of him. He lifted his hips while hugging her against him, and her answering sigh was the sweetest sound he'd ever heard. She kissed his mouth, trailing her fingers down his cheeks. She moved one hand into his hair and brought the other to his shoulder, sliding it down along his arm, wrapping her fingers around his biceps as her lips worked their way across his jawline and over to his neck. His breath hitched when she hit a particularly sensitive spot, and he leaned up as he tangled his hands in her dress, grasping at each side until he could feel her soft skin against his rough hands. Ryker slid those hands up her legs and squeezed her ass, pressing her into his aching need.

She returned her mouth to his, her kisses more urgent, dancing her lips down his chin, down his neck, around his collarbone, over his chest. She arched her back and sank her hips into him. A groan rumbled in his throat. Everleigh looked up at him, captured his gaze, and smiled. He placed his hand under her chin and guided her face back to him, tracing his tongue over her dimple, kissing it, then meeting her lips with his own. He circled his hand behind her head, tangling his fingers in her curls along the way. She began to rock her hips over him, and it drove Ryker wild. He pressed his hand into her lower back and moved his mouth from hers, sucked and licked her neck all the way to her ear, where he teased her earlobe with this tongue. A soft whimper escaped her, and he raked his teeth along her skin. Her mouth beside his ear, she whispered a breathless, "Do you have a condom?"

In a split second, he wrapped his left arm around her and rolled, taking her place on top, while simultaneously pulling his wallet from his back pocket in one fluid motion. He opened it with one hand and snagged a foil wrapper out with his teeth.

Still breathless, Everleigh giggled. She yanked at his shirt, freeing it from his jeans. As she fumbled, trying to unhook the button, Ryker helped, but he needed her lips on his again. So their mouths never separated as he unzipped his jeans and put on the condom and she worked at the buttons on his shirt.

Her delicate fingers on his skin sent a shiver up his spine as she ran her hands up his abs, his chest, and along his shoulders, hooking them around his collar and pushing his shirt down his back.[2] He reached behind and pulled it the rest of the way off, tossing it to the side. Before Ryker could bring himself down on top of her, she locked her elbows, holding him at arm's length, reminiscent of their tryst in the barn. He again watched her eyes roam over his body and again thrilled at the desire he could see burning in them, even in the dark. As her bare feet slid up his calves—somehow she'd already lost her sandals—her chest seemed to be rising up toward him. Everleigh flicked her tongue along her bottom lip before bringing that lip between her teeth. Ryker couldn't wait another second—he pushed down on her arms so he could wrap himself around her, feel her body against his. With his fly open, he thrust his hips forward between her legs, only the fabric of her dress and her underwear standing between him and paradise.

Ryker felt Everleigh's chest heaving beneath him, and as much as he wanted this moment to last for her, he feared he might not in the face of her perfect body, her whimpers, her soft moans. He lifted off of her, tore his boots from his feet, and pushed his jeans and briefs from his legs. She followed suit and tossed her jacket aside, moved to lift her dress over her head.

"No," Ryker's husky voice commanded as he hovered above her. Everleigh looked at him, confused. He placed his hands over hers. "Let me." She released the fabric and allowed him to lift the dress over her

---

2. Zach Bryan, "Sun to Me"

arms before she lay down beneath him. As he moved between her legs, he took a moment to admire the view. Her dark, lacy bra holding in her breasts, her matching lacy thong. He dipped down and licked a circle around her navel, peppered kisses all the way up between her breasts. Her fingernails dragged along the skin of his back with perfect pressure. He reached behind her and unhooked her bra, pulled it away from her, and tossed it to the side. His eyes flickered to hers, and he saw the moment. The one where the girl wondered if her body was acceptable.

"You're so beautiful," he breathed. A smile tugged at the corners of her lips, and Ryker kissed that smile away before turning his attention to her breasts, licking and teasing each one as her fingers knotted in his hair. Her hips pressed up against his, her legs curling around him, her center rubbing delicious friction against his hard length.

He moved his mouth down her body; her hands remained in his hair. He kissed along the lacy line of her thong that brushed her stomach as he slipped his fingers beneath the fabric. Slowly peeling the delicate material down her hips, kissing the inside of her upper thigh as he went, grazing his nose across her sensitive skin as he moved to the other thigh. Everleigh's hips lifted, and he dug his fingers into her thighs, eliciting a gasp from her. He slid her fragile-looking underwear down, down, and off, pausing to cradle her leg and lick and kiss the skin behind her right knee, just as he'd once imagined doing. Then Ryker raked his hands up her thighs, her hips, her stomach, her breasts, feeling her softness writhing beneath his rough hands. He curled his fingers around her shoulders as he locked onto her gaze.

Everleigh battled against his weight as she tried to pull herself up to his body, but she was helpless against his strength. When she whimpered and began to shift her hips beneath him, trying to coax him to continue, he was finally able to break the trance of her beauty. Ryker slid his hands behind her shoulders, resting one hand between her shoulder blades and cradling the other at the base of her head. Her hands sank into the soft skin of his ass as she silently communicated her need. He obeyed, plunging into her. The thought of possessing Everleigh drove the desire in his blood to a boiling point.

She moaned as he thrust in farther and farther with each movement of his hips, her fingernails scraping up his back. The tightness of her walls surrounding his cock nearly drove him over the edge. She fit around him perfectly. He crushed his mouth on hers, maybe too hard, but she seemed to like it, kissing him just as fervently.

Ryker pulled his left hand from behind her and wrapped his arm beneath her leg, lifting it as he pushed deeper inside her, burying himself to the hilt. Her shoulders arched, pressing her taut breasts into his chest, flesh against delicate flesh. He moved his mouth down her throat, sucking at the side of her neck as he quickened his rhythm. Everleigh's hand slid into his hair and closed into a fist, tugging hard. But he loved it, and he responded by bucking harder and faster into her. He brought his mouth back to hers and wrapped his tongue around her moan, breathing it into his lungs. He could feel his orgasm building, building, and cascading over the edge, and Ryker growled out a curse as he released into her when she lifted her hips off the blanket and gasped and moaned one last time.

Holding him like she would never let go.

He didn't release Everleigh from his grip, didn't remove the pressure against her center. Partly because he didn't want to. Partly because she rocked her hips into him a few more times as her spasms slowed against his cock, and she let out a long sigh, the kind you release when falling into blissful contentment. His face beside hers, Ryker turned his head and brushed his nose up and down her cheek. The soft laugh that escaped her brought a smile to his face.

Eventually, she relaxed her arms around him. He pulled out of her but didn't loosen his embrace, afraid that if he let her go, he'd wake up from this dream. She trailed her fingernails gently up and down his back, tripping a shiver along his spine. He finally released her right leg and brought his hand up behind her shoulder, where he dropped a kiss. She curled that leg around him, a contented sound rumbling in her chest.

She nudged his cheek with her shoulder. He leaned up on his elbow and stared down at her. That dimple in her smile.

"Wow," Everleigh said.

"Wow," Ryker repeated with a chuckle. He reached over and grabbed the corner of the blanket, pulling it over them as he rolled onto his back and tucked her into his side.

She traced a finger along the upper arm he had draped across her, as if she knew the exact landscape of skin his tattoo covered. It was soothing, and he felt his breathing fall into the same slow rhythm as hers.

And they fell asleep watching the stars fall across the black sky.

## Everleigh

"We can't stay here all night," Ryker whispered into her ear.

Her eyelids fluttered, but she couldn't make out anything. The dark, cool night wrapped around them. Everleigh felt him move away from her, and she didn't like it. Lifting onto her elbows, her eyes adjusted, and she spied him walking gently around the jumping pillow, retrieving their clothes. She noticed her hair ribbon on the blanket beside her and tucked it into her jacket pocket. Ryker handed over her dress and undergarments. She dropped onto her back, sad that their night had to end so soon. Such a sound, comforting sleep had held her, snuggled in the cage of his arms and legs. Everleigh hooked her bra and lifted the straps over her shoulders as she watched Ryker don his clothes.

When they were both dressed, he picked up the blanket, threw it over his arm and reached for her hand. She followed him to the UTV. When Ryker joined her in the front seat, she wrapped her hands around his arm and curled into his shoulder, closing her eyes.

Everleigh awoke to him gently placing her in his bed, pulling the covers up to her shoulders. She expected him to join her, longed for him to so she could settle into his strong embrace once more, but he didn't. Her eyes drooped closed.

She forced them open when she recognized the sound of the shower running. Sitting up in his bed, she ran her hand through her hair, let it drop to her chest, ran it down to her waist. Still feeling the afterglow of him inside of her, she craved it again. Everleigh pushed the covers off and peeled the denim jacket from her shoulders, tossing it onto his dresser as she opened the door to his bathroom.

Steam immediately gathered on her bare shoulders, neck, and face. The mirror was fogged over with it. Her eyes were drawn to Ryker's outline through the frosted shower glass, and she moved toward him as if heeding a force she could not fight. Wrapping her fingers around the handle, she pulled the door open.

Surprise was the first emotion to cross his features, followed quickly by a darkening of his eyes. A glint shining in those amber irises.

"Can I join you?" Everleigh asked, her gaze roaming greedily over his muscular, naked body, appreciating a full view for the first time. His dark hair was swept back on his head. Water droplets peppered his face and trailed tiny waterfalls down the sharp planes of his cheekbones, falling to his spectacularly cut chest, down the ridges of his abs, catching in the dark path of hair that ran from below his navel to—

Her insides tightened sharply, but his outstretched hand suddenly obscured her view. She blinked then placed her hand in his dripping wet palm, her mind already caught up in what bliss awaited her in that shower.

"You might want to . . ." The smirk on his face brought her back to her senses. She was still dressed.

Wanting to tease him as his beautifully bare, dripping wet body teased her, she locked her eyes on his, tugging in the inner corners the slightest bit as she aimed her most sultry stare at Ryker. She slowly pulled her dress over her head and dropped it on the floor at her feet. Took her sweet time unhooking her bra and letting it slide down her arms. Finally, shimmied her lacy thong down her hips and stepped out, one foot at a time. Placing her hand in his strong grasp, she stepped up into the hot water.

Broad hands roamed from her shoulders all the way to her hips before he tugged her into him.[3] Everleigh reached up and ran her hands through her hair, wetting it in the shower, enjoying the feeling of the water and his fingers dancing in tandem on her skin. His hands glided from her hips up and around her heavy breasts and intertwined with her fingers in her hair, all while he moved his mouth along her neck and collarbone. She released a sigh, enjoying the sensations he awakened within her.

Ryker reached for the shampoo bottle on the corner shelf and squeezed a dollop onto his palm, moving so close she could feel his length stretching out between her legs, long and strong. He rubbed his hands together then massaged the shampoo into her scalp, working his hands around her head, down the back of her neck, around her shoulders to her throat, along her collarbone, down her breasts, where his hands lingered, his fingers teased.

Everleigh moaned under his expert touch and moved closer to him, so his cock was firmly between her legs. She swayed back and forth over him as the water washed the suds from her hair and skin, enjoying the fullness of him sliding along her most sensitive areas. Ryker kissed her, sliding his tongue along her bottom lip, possessing her mouth, and she melted in his arms. As his hands moved around her waist, circling around her,

---

3. Chappell Roan, "Bad for You"

she gasped when he spun her around. But then as his hands explored her stomach, her breasts, her upper thighs, she lifted her arms and linked her fingers behind his neck, letting him know she was a canvas on which he could create a masterpiece.

He fit his body to hers from behind and nipped and sucked on her neck as he continued to explore her with his hands. Those hands drifted lower between her legs and pressed against her thighs until she separated them. One hand slipped between her legs, a finger tracing gentle orbits around the apex of her thighs. She gasped and squeezed her hands tighter against his neck. Ryker grazed his hand over her breasts, teasing each one in turn, and closed his teeth around her earlobe, tugging and drawing another gasp from Everleigh. He chuckled, a low vibration that traveled through her body as well, and he moved his hand to her interlaced fingers, sliding between them, releasing her grip, and placing his hand on her shoulder as he guided her forward.

Flattening her palms on the shower wall, she arched her back and curled into his fingers between her legs, the unbelievable sensations unfurling and tightening in a battling dance. He brushed her wet hair to her left side and kissed her neck, her shoulder, and between her shoulders as he continued to tease her clit with his thumb and slid two of his fingers inside her. She moaned again. How could Ryker work such magic on her body?

Everleigh felt herself starting to shudder as his fingers moved expertly against every swollen nerve ending, her insides spasming. She leaned into her palms, pressing her body back into his, seeking the rush of pleasure just around the corner. But he pulled his hands away from her and she whimpered. Immediately, his hands firmly grasped her hips and Ryker tipped them forward, thrusting himself between her legs. And she inhaled sharply with such satisfaction, because his thick, hard cock hit all the right spots on the way in. Hot water streamed over her shoulders, down her back, and yet she shivered with anticipation.

As Ryker wrapped his left arm around her waist to keep her in place when he started to move, his right hand teased her peaked nipples before finding the sweet spot between her legs once more. Everleigh had never known someone else's touch could burn her skin and send electrical currents throughout her body like this. Ryker matched the rhythm of his finger on her clit to his rhythm between her legs, and she nearly lost her mind with the sensations building deep within her, threatening to shatter her from the inside out. Her fingers curled against the shower wall and if it weren't for Ryker's strong arm sealing their flesh together, she knew she'd have fallen boneless to the floor, with every cell in her body singing.

"Fuck! Oh, fuck!" Ryker moaned against her shoulder, and Everleigh reveled in the sound of him coming undone around her, gasping and spitting water while holding her so tightly. She spiraled, finding the promised pleasure from moments before, triggering fireworks in her mind, searing euphoria throughout her body. She gasped as she pushed herself into him, even as her legs trembled beneath her.

Suddenly, Ryker stepped away as he pulled out of her, but then he hugged her firmly against him, a hand cupping her breast, as he pressed himself against her lower back, finishing his release. She vaguely felt his forehead against the nape of her neck, but his finger never stopped its rapid motion over her sensitive bundle of nerves, so she barely noticed the absence of him inside her. She moaned with pleasure, her breath hitching as her insides clenched and shuddered a second time, her vision going dark along the edges. His hand ceased moving, and he pressed it against her swollen clit as she leaned, breathless, against him, her head resting on his shoulder. As Everleigh basked in a long, heavenly moment of ecstasy, Ryker spun her around and backed her into the shower wall, wrapping his arms around her and kissing her so sweetly.

Everleigh was higher than she'd ever been, and she couldn't imagine coming down from these great heights. She rested her hands on his shoulders and accepted his kisses and his nuzzles against her neck, fearing if she tried to move anytime soon, her legs would collapse beneath her.

When the water turned cool, Ryker lifted his head from her shoulder and pushed her wet hair back on her forehead, kissing between her eyebrows, the tip of her nose, her chin, her lips. He reached over and shut off the water.

Opening the shower door, he leaned around to grab a towel without taking his eyes off hers. He handed it to Everleigh, then reached for one for himself. He ran the towel over his head, leaving a mess of brown hair in all directions, and then wrapped it around his waist. Stepping out, he helped her out of the shower.

Working the towel around in her hair, she tried to sop up most of the water. She wiped her face, wrapped the towel around herself and tucked the corner under her arm. Ryker lifted a hand and ran his thumb over her dimple. She hadn't realized she was smiling. Her smile grew into a heady grin.

Ryker slipped his hand around hers and led her into the bedroom. He dug in his dresser and offered up a T-shirt for her to wear. The same high school state baseball championship shirt she'd worn before. Everleigh wondered if he realized that, but she didn't say anything. This might be her new favorite shirt. She pulled it over her shoulders as he stepped into a pair of boxer briefs, and she followed him to his bed. He helped her into the bed, then stared at her for a moment as he held the sheets up in his outstretched hand.

"What?" Everleigh asked with a self-conscious smile.

Ryker grinned in return. "Nothing." He climbed in, wrapped his strong arms around her, and pulled her into him. She fell asleep with her body still humming along to his song.

Everleigh awoke disoriented, being jostled about.

"Shh. It's okay. I have to do chores. Go back to sleep."

Ryker. He was brushing the hair from her face.

Her eyes cracked open enough to see him pulling on his jeans and a cutout shirt as he sat on the edge of his bed. But his bed was so comfortable and warm, she drifted off quickly.

Cool hands sliding up her ribcage forced her eyelids open. Everleigh was on her back, the covers pulled away. A shiver racked her body. Rough fingers closed around her breasts, and her muscles tensed. She looked down. Ryker had returned. Where had he gone again? He was propped on his elbows above her, rolling his T-shirt up her body and kissing his way up her goose-pimpled skin. As he slid the fabric over her breasts, he grazed her nipples with his thumbs, teasing her.

"Ryker," she groaned. *It's too early for this.*

He had the shirt bunched at her shoulders as he smiled up at her. "Do you hear that?" he murmured.

"I'm sleeping. Hear what?"

"It's raining cats and dogs outside. So you don't have to go anywhere." Ryker continued to kiss his way around her midsection.

Everleigh only realized she'd never put on her underwear last night when his fingers touched the sensitive skin at the apex of her thighs. An electrical current traveled through her body. Her back arched involuntarily, and Ryker responded by sliding his hands up her sides and pulling the shirt over her head, tossing it on the floor beside the bed. She let her arms fall onto his shoulders, and he kissed her as possessively as he had last night. And she thrilled at the sensation.

When his mouth moved away, she wanted to bring his face back up to hers, but his lips circled around first one peaked nipple and then the other, and his fingers continued to dance between her legs. And then Ryker left her body completely and her eyes flew open, searching for him. She watched him pull his shirt over his head and toss it to the side. Then he scooped her legs into his arms and smirked up at her, his face hovering between her thighs, his dark hair falling over his brow in a tousled mess.

"What are you doing?" Everleigh asked as she fought a smile.

His face disappeared, and she had to grip the bedsheets for dear life. She pressed her heels into the bed as Ryker teased her higher and higher with his tongue. Her hand flew to her chest, dragging against her breast as he held on firmly to her hips, and she knew she was on the verge of ecstasy.

Just when she thought she could go no further, Ryker curled two fingers into her and hit *that spot*. Everleigh screamed out. His hand darted swiftly from her hip and clamped over her mouth, but he didn't stop owning her body, and she exploded from the inside out, shuddering all the way back down.

Ryker crawled over top of her, reached into his nightstand to grab a condom, and tore it open with his teeth. Moments later, he slid into her wetness, pressing himself into her vibrating body. It was only then that he removed his hand from her mouth and replaced it with his lips, kissing her tenderly as she continued to freefall beneath him. Everleigh couldn't take any more. She'd disintegrate, rupture into a million little pieces.

She was weak in his arms, but Ryker stared into her eyes like he knew where he was taking them and she'd better hold on. She lifted her hands, placing them on his bulging biceps. She couldn't lift her legs but discovered she didn't want to. The friction he created between her thighs felt better if she straightened them and tilted her hips up, so he filled her entirely and rubbed in all the right places.

Everleigh tightened her grip on Ryker, lifted her mouth to his, and accepted every hungry swipe of his tongue, every possessive movement of his lips over hers. He broke the kiss, nipped at her lower lip, and pressed his forehead into her own. And they came together, gazes locked, bodies trembling, grunting softly, clutching onto one another.

# Chapter 19
# Big Green Tractor

**Everleigh**

A SOFT KNOCK AT the door startled her awake. Everleigh's eyes flew open, and she felt Ryker sit up in bed, felt the sheets drift up over her bare back. She was sprawled out on her stomach next to him, facing the wall, but she was certain she was still buck naked.

"Ryker, oh—I'm sorry."

Rita.

Everleigh wanted to die as she clamped her eyes shut. She pretended to sleep, trying to maintain even breathing.

"Ah, so the rain's moved off, and the ground is drying out quickly. We're going to call everyone in to open at noon, okay?"

"Yeah, okay," he replied in a gruff voice.

"Okay," Rita repeated. "There's, um . . . breakfast out in the microwave, if you're interested."

Maybe he nodded, but the door closed, and Everleigh heard a loud exhale issue from Ryker. She turned her head to find him sitting up, bedsheet pulled tightly around his waist. His gaze met hers, and they shared a conspiratorial grin.

He dropped a kiss on her shoulder. "Dammit. I was hoping we wouldn't have to leave this bed today. Wanna shower with me?"

She smiled at his devilish smirk, but said, "I don't think I can. I'm not sure my legs will support me today."

He chuckled in response.

"What time is it?" Everleigh asked.

"Eleven."

"*Eleven?*" she balked as she rolled onto her side to fully face him. "Do you have time to take me home so I can grab my shirt?"

"I've got you," he responded.

As Ryker strode over to his closet, she leaned up on her elbow, holding the sheet against her chest while admiring his tight bare ass. Damn was he buff. A muscular masterpiece. He returned with a staff shirt in hand. "Wait, it still has sleeves," she drawled as she held it up. "I'm impressed."

The corners of his mouth twisted upward as she caught him fighting a smile.

He lent her a pair of athletic shorts as well, and she was good to go. When Ryker headed into his bathroom to shower, she spotted an empty grocery bag in his desk chair and put her dress and jacket in it. Noticing his state championship shirt on the floor next to his bed, she shoved that into the bag too.

Everleigh remembered Crestin would be heading to her house to pick her up soon, so she pulled out her phone to text him. Two missed calls and three texts from her mother.

*Where are you?*

*Are you alive?*

*I know you're an adult, but I'm losing my mind.*

Everleigh quickly responded, *I'm sorry! I lost track of time with the meteor shower, and I overslept. I'm heading to work now.*

She started to message Crestin when a text from her mom came through: *But where are you?*

Not wanting to get into that now, she ignored it and typed the message to Crestin. *You don't have to pick me up today. See you at work.*

Her phone dinged almost instantly with a response from him. *GIRRRRRRRRRL.*

She ignored that too and focused on braiding her hair in the mirror over Ryker's dresser. Lacking a hair tie, she used her white, patterned ribbon to secure it at the bottom.

When Ryker reemerged from the bathroom, she asked, "Can I use your toothbrush?"

He looked askance at her and made a face.

"Do you remember where your mouth was this morning? You really think it's that bad for me to use your toothbrush?"

He appeared thoughtful for a moment, then said, "Good point. Have at it."

## Ryker

He'd assumed his parents would be over at the sunflower patch already. But when he led Everleigh to the kitchen, he was surprised to see them both still at the dining table. He noticed their eyes immediately home in on his hand wrapped around hers.

"Morning," Ryker said as he released Everleigh's hand and moved his to her lower back, leading her over to the breakfast bar. "You said there's food in the microwave?"

"Ah, yeah," his mom said. "Good morning, Everleigh. Nice to see you."

He couldn't tell if she was being genuine, and the tiny hairs on the back of his neck stood up.

"Good morning," Everleigh replied in her sweet voice. "Good morning, Mr. Martin."

"It's Darren—you know that," his dad said as he looked up from the papers spread out across the table.

"Sorry. Good morning, Darren," Everleigh repeated sheepishly.

Ryker brought over the reheated plate of eggs and sausage and set it in front of her. He pulled out two forks from the silverware drawer, and he was reminded of the Oreo fluff debacle from last night.

"Why are you grinning?" Everleigh murmured.

"Am I?" he asked as he took a bite of sausage.

"You are."

Ryker shrugged.

⁂

Everleigh had food truck duty today with Crestin. Since they were opening late, they had to hurry to get the lunchtime food prepped. Ryker vowed to return at her afternoon break at three o'clock before he jumped on the UTV and began his rounds checking out the stations around the sunflower patch.

He came across his dad near the back of the forty acres where a fence was broken. "That wasn't that way last week, was it?" Ryker asked.

"Pretty certain it wasn't. But it is now. We'll have to get it fixed tonight."

Ryker nodded and returned to the UTV.

"Say, son?" The tone of his dad's voice gave him pause. "What's, ah, going on with that Wilson girl?"

His dad had always called Everleigh by her first name and always acted like he liked her, so Ryker was unsure why the sudden formality. He shrugged. "We're hanging out for a bit."

His dad's stare bored into him. "That it?"

Ryker didn't know how to respond. His dad continued, "Just because you're doing so well. And you're about to go back to school. And if I'm not mistaken, she's going off to school too, right?"

Ryker nodded.

"Okay, well." His dad looked off into the distance before bringing his attention back to Ryker. "Just make sure you're making the best decisions for yourself. For your health, right? For your future."

Ryker turned the key to start the engine and met his father's stare. "Yeah. Of course."

His dad nodded. Ryker drove away, hating the fact that his father was echoing the same worries that had been kicking around inside his brain for over two days.

Three o'clock came quickly, and he raced to the food truck in the UTV, not wanting to keep her waiting.[1] When he arrived, Everleigh was just stepping through the door, talking to Crestin over her shoulder. Ryker wondered if she'd said anything to her best friend about them. Not that it mattered. Did it?

A smile lit up her features as he pulled up beside her, and he couldn't wait to kiss that dimple. She hopped into the passenger seat and grabbed onto the handlebar above her head as he pressed the gas to the floor. There was no time to waste. They had fifteen minutes before he had to deliver her back to the food truck door.

When Ryker parked in the driveway behind his house, he met her in front of the UTV and wrapped his hand around hers. As he led Everleigh up the deck stairs and into the house, she asked, "More Oreo fluff?"

---

1. Matt Hansen, "Chemicals"

He spun her around in the utility room and walked her backward into his mom's washing machine. "You can have all the fluff you want after this," he said, his lips already on hers.

Ryker lifted her on top of the washing machine, and her ankles hooked together behind him as her hands slid into his hair and she brought her lips to his. He pulled her hips toward him and pressed his already aching need into her. There wasn't enough time to do this right, in the respectful way he would rather Everleigh experience everything at his hands. But with the way she pulled him toward her and sank her teeth into his lower lip, he thought maybe she wouldn't mind a quick and dirty encounter. He bit back and laughed at the startled gasp that escaped her chest. Maybe he'd bit just a little too hard.

He tugged the borrowed athletic shorts and her lacy thong down to her knees, unzipped his jeans, and quickly put on a condom. As she kissed his neck, he thrust into her, her ass making a squeaking sound across the metal top of the washing machine as he pulled her against him. Everleigh wrapped her arm around his shoulders, arched her back, lifted her chest into his. He could feel her trying to push the shorts down her legs so she could wrap them around him, so Ryker reached down and helped free her legs. Locking her ankles around his waist, she grabbed at his shoulders like she couldn't get him close enough. He suckled her neck as she panted by his ear.

Suddenly, he realized this wasn't right. This wasn't the way he would ever want her to feel as he was worshipping her body. They'd feel disconnected and likely unfulfilled after. He'd been here before, even if she hadn't, and he knew what she would feel five minutes from now.

Ryker grabbed the nape of her neck and lifted her away, forcing her hazel eyes to connect with his. As he kissed Everleigh gently on the mouth, he adjusted his hips to a slow rhythm, moving deliberately in and out, reaching up into her. The confusion in her eyes melted swiftly into trust as she allowed him to lead them through this. Her hands moved under his shirt, and she dragged her fingertips up his back to his shoulders, sending shivers along his spine with her touch.

He held fast to her gaze, only breaking it to drop kisses on her deliciously full lips, her chin, the phantom dimple on her cheek. As he felt it building, desire pooling at the base of his spine, he pulled her tightly to him, pressing his forehead to hers, staring into her eyes. This time, when she locked her legs behind him, he knew it was because she was almost there too. Ryker dug his fingers into the soft skin of her ass as he increased his rhythm, pushed as far as he could up into her, reveling in the tight walls that encircled his cock. Breathy whimpers escaped her throat over and over and over again, pulling that desire taut within him, edging him closer and closer to oblivion.

"Ryker," she whispered on a gasp as those hazel eyes reached into his very soul. He captured Everleigh's mouth in his and danced his tongue around hers as they spiraled apart and together, their eyes never breaking contact.

Her chest heaving against him, he dropped his head onto her shoulder, hugging her close. Feeling like he could never get her as close to him as he needed.

***

## Everleigh

Crestin wouldn't let it go. He refused to just drop her off after work. Followed her into her house and up to her room.

"But *cariño*, my burglar alarms have been going off for twenty-four hours! Simply Safe says you are *not* safe!"

Everleigh spun around to face him, holding her hands out to get him to lower his voice. "*My mom is downstairs, Crestin!*" she said in the loudest whisper she could muster.

"Does Mama Rosalynn know where you were last night?" he demanded with a hand on his hip and eyebrows ten feet high, clearly not picking up on her *keep it down* cues.

"I'll tell her, yes. I haven't had the chance to yet," she muttered in a less convincing voice than she'd intended.

"Lies," he sang.

She glared at him.

"Chica, you know I am *here for you*. And I am worried *for you*. This is all so fast, and it could end just as fast."

Everleigh was hurt Crestin thought her relationship with Ryker could end quickly. Yes, it had been a whirlwind over the past three days, but she was happier than she'd ever been in her life. And she truly felt Ryker was just as into her as she was him. Never mind what he did to her body, he made her feel safe. Important. Loved.

"Isn't Ryker your friend?" Everleigh threw back at him.

"Yes, but he's still a man. With a dumb dick. I am worried he's only thinking with that dumb dick and not with his much smarter brain."

She rolled her eyes. "Do you realize what you are saying about *me*?"

"Baby girl," Crestin soothed as he clasped his hands around her wrists. "I will allow that the lure of the Adonis Ryker is great. He is a man amongst men. A specimen to behold. And sidebar, good for you for tasting that rainbow. But you still need to guard your heart around someone like him. He's messy." Crestin pulled a face as he waved his hands in the air. "And you deserve a clean house."

Everleigh sighed as she processed what her best friend was telling her. She determined the best way to placate him was to agree. "I hear you. And thank you for your input. You have no idea how much you mean to me, Crestin."

His hands clasped together over his heart. "Same, Evs. Same."

Ten minutes later, she waved goodbye to him as he backed the El Camino out of her driveway. She knew her mom was in the kitchen but decided she would tackle that conversation another day, so she trotted back up to her room.

Her phone vibrated as she hit the top stair, and she pulled it out of her pocket.

*Can I pick u up?*

Everleigh smiled.

# Ryker

After work and farm chores, he'd hurried through a shower and driven over the speed limit on the way to town to pick her up.[2] Suddenly, Ryker couldn't get enough of her, couldn't stop thinking about her, kept wishing Everleigh was there beside him so he could talk with her.

A light drizzle had moved in that was supposed to last the evening, so after she ran to the truck, they drove around the county on gravel roads, singing along to 90s country songs and talking about everything completely unimportant. He now knew she still had the Bratz doll collection she'd received for her ninth birthday, and she used to have a phobia of mismatched socks. It nearly drove her crazy when the fad swept her school where *everyone* was wearing mismatched socks *on purpose.* Ryker told her about every heifer he'd shown at the state fair throughout his 4-H and FFA careers, and which ones he'd earned a

---

2. New West, "Those Eyes"

ribbon with. He even remembered the exact place he'd won with each one.

In any town they went through with a car dealership, he drove slowly around the lot and they window shopped as best they could with water droplets clinging to the side windows of the truck. Everleigh would point out a nice truck. He would check the price on the tag hanging from the rearview mirror. Sometimes he'd put the Dodge in park, roll down the window, and study the vehicle, looking for rust, seeing if the mileage was written on the tag. Other times, he'd say "Too rich for my blood" and move on to the next. He noticed Everleigh was drawn to the trucks, maybe because she assumed that's what he'd want. She'd only ever seen him in a truck this summer. Truth was, he'd be fine with any kind of vehicle as long as it was all-wheel drive, rust-free, had low enough mileage, and was dependable. But he had a few days before moving to campus to get it figured out.

Ryker pulled into a local restaurant with a drive-through and bought them barbecue sandwiches. Sitting in a school parking lot as they ate, they returned to the discussion of their most embarrassing moments, this time going all the way back to elementary school.

An amazing thing happened—the clouds rolled to the east, taking the rain with them, as dusk fell upon the land. When their conversation hit a lull as he drove along a gravel road that would eventually lead them to the Martin farm, he glanced over to find Everleigh watching him. Staring at him with those dancing hazel eyes. Ryker turned the truck on the last corner of the home stretch, and as they neared his home, she suddenly said, "Can we go back to the sunflower patch?"

Of course, he obliged.

Parking in the grassy lot near the entrance, he knew he could have driven as far into the patch as she wanted to go. But he felt like maybe the walk was what she wanted right now. Exiting the truck, he met her at the hood, fingers reaching out and lacing with hers.

They meandered the empty paths of the sunflower patch, now slightly muddy thanks to the light rain, but she didn't seem to care that her HEYDUDEs were getting ruined, likely beyond all restoration. She just continued to chatter about this and that, and he reveled in the warmth of her fingers linked between his. The skip in her step as she read aloud the factoids written on placards affixed to posts that were scattered at intervals along the path. How she would turn to him from time to time with wonder in her eyes, thinking they seemed entirely unbelievable.

"An average sunflower has one thousand seeds? Really?" When he nodded, he felt a tug on his arm, pulling him backward as she abruptly stopped to examine the disk of the nearest sunflower. "Huh," Everleigh said after a long moment. Then she led them forward on the path once again.

"The scientific name of a sunflower is helianthus." Ryker couldn't help but give her hand a squeeze as she pronounced the word perfectly.

"The larger false flower is actually made up of many tiny flowers, or florets, in an attempt to attract pollinators," she read as she squinted at a sign a few feet up the path from them. Everleigh immediately turned to Ryker. "That lying, cheating flower! I can never think of the sunflower the same way again!"

"What?" he said on a laugh.

She looked up at him earnestly. "This is saying the sunflower is out and out lying about what it really is! It's lying about itself to trick pollinators to come to it. That's . . . that's just not right."

"It's a flower," Ryker said as his brows furrowed.

"It's a liar is what it is," she corrected. "Honesty at all times. That's my motto."

His brows lifted. "At all times?"

"Of course. There's no reason for untruths. Especially not if you're a flower."

A smirk crawled up the lines of his mouth. "Not even if that sunflower has doubts about itself? Is worried it isn't the best flower for that pollinator? Is worried it will disappoint that little bee or butterfly?"

"If its nectar is as sweet as its beauty promises, how could it possibly disappoint a bee or butterfly?" She mused as she reached out and rubbed her finger and thumb along the golden petals of a flower.

Ryker suddenly felt as if they were no longer talking about the sunflowers.

He was brought back to the moment when she read, "Sunflowers are heliotropes. While they are young, their flower heads track the movement of the sun. At night, the flowers reorient themselves to the east, awaiting the warmth of the rising sun." Everleigh sighed, "Isn't that just so romantic?"

His eyebrows quirked in response. "Romantic how?"

The look she shot him made him immediately regret asking. Her lips pursed as she said, "Romantic in that this beautiful flower will always look toward the thing that makes it most happy." She settled her chin on his shoulder, her fingers still intertwined with his, her dark-rimmed hazel eyes dimmed in the dusk falling around them. They turned the corner near the middle of the patch, and her sudden gasp startled him.

"Ooo! Will you take my picture on the big green tractor before it gets too dark?" She shoved her phone into Ryker's hands before he knew what was happening. The next moment, she was skipping the last steps to the tractor they had out here as a photo op, brown half-barrels overflowing with colorful flowers around the large back tires. Tires that stood nearly as tall as Everleigh. Clambering up the step to the padded seat, she efficiently swiped her hand to remove any stray water droplets that remained before depositing herself with a smile plastered across her face.

He couldn't help the chuckle that shook his chest at her child-like excitement. As he lifted her phone, he asked, "You're really this excited about an old tractor?"

"Ryker. Stop," she reprimanded as she settled in the seat and placed her hands on the steering wheel, dropping a shoulder and giving him her most glowing smile. Popping that dimple in her cheek. When he stared at her beauty rather than snapping the picture, she must have taken it as him disapproving of her exuberance, for she rushed out, "What? I've never been on a real tractor before. City girl, remember?" She lifted her right hand from the wheel and swiveled her wrist to point toward herself.

He laughed again at her genuine nature shining through, making his shoulders dip and his head droop with a shake. The things that amazed her amazed him. He lifted her phone once again and snapped several photos as she posed for him.

"You ever drive one of these?" Everleigh asked as she ran her hands around the black coated steering wheel. He was amused at how wowed she seemed to be by this big old hunk of metal.

"I can operate any piece of equipment on this farm," he purred as he climbed up to return her phone. He curled one hand around the back of the seat and the other around the steering wheel right beside hers, ascending onto the top tractor step.

One of her eyebrows hitched upward and her mouth curled as she asked, "Any? Even this beast?"

Little did she know this "beast" was one of the smaller tractors they owned. An old John Deere 730 workhorse relegated to photo ops at the patch rather than day-to-day farm chores. He let a short laugh escape through his nose before he locked eyes with her and nodded. He couldn't deny the pure joy that rippled up his insides when she squealed and clapped her hands together.

"Eeee!" she cheered. "Can you take me for a ride? Like, a real ride on a real tractor?"

Barely containing his grin, Ryker pulled himself up and slid behind her as she stood, taking his place on the seat of the tractor. He drew her down onto his lap, reached around both sides of her, and engaged the electric start by feel alone. He knew this tractor like the back of his hand. Everleigh vibrated with excitement, which fed into Ryker's own excitement, as he revved the engine, delighting in her squeal of elation when the tractor sputtered and chugged a loud rhythm, awaiting a command from its operator.

"Hold tight," he told her as he switched on the headlights, then gripped the wheel with his left hand, leaving the right to maneuver the gears. Admittedly, there wasn't much for her to grab on to. Her grip closed around the outside of his legs, just above his knees. When the tractor lurched forward, popping and rattling in acceleration, her scream pierced the late evening air. He moved his hand from the steering wheel, wrapping it around her waist, using his other hand to alternate from the wheel to the gears when he needed to shift. Her hands clasped around the arm Ryker had secured around her waist, and he instinctively held her tighter, tucked his chin over her shoulder.

Everleigh's long waves blew across his face, but he didn't care. He rather liked it. Liked the way she settled into his chest, the way her hands loosened their grip on his arm and became a mere warm presence on his skin. Liked the way she sighed and rested her head on his shoulder as he rounded another corner of the path along the backside of the sunflower patch.

Fuck, he'd drive this tractor around this patch all night just to feel this feeling weaving itself around him. Just to think that Everleigh saw him as that perfect sunflower that she'd spend all her time hovering around and making magic with. But he knew someday she'd wise up to his trickery and realize he'd been lying to her all along. There was nothing beautiful, nothing sweet, about him.

He made two laps around the back half of the forty-acre sunflower fields before he figured he'd better park the tractor or risk running it out of diesel fuel. Reluctantly, he pulled near the spot where the tractor belonged, backing in perfectly beside the barrels of plants so they would flank the huge black rubber and yellow metal rear tires.

Everleigh had seemed to melt into him at some point, becoming one with his body so that every turn, every bounce in the tractor seat had them moving as one being. Of course, his arm had remained wrapped around her waist this whole time, but her hands had also remained rested around his forearm. Her warmth radiated up his arm even as the chill in the night air sank around them. He brought the tractor to a stop, flicked off the headlights, killed the engine, and curled himself around her.

Darkness surrounded them now, the crescent moon barely a thought in the sky tonight. Crickets chirped on the gentle breeze. Lightning bugs lent their rhythmic glow to the muted scenery, seeming to levitate from the sea of sunflower stalks. Ryker tightened his embrace and placed a soft kiss on her neck. When Everleigh remained motionless on his lap, he wondered if she'd fallen asleep on him during the ride. He let his left hand travel up her body, over her breast, her collarbone, the column of her neck, and he brought his hand to rest on her cheek, fingers laced on either side of her ear. Pulling her closer to him, he buried his face in her neck and inhaled her decadent vanilla scent. He'd never get used to her alluring fragrance, her silky-soft skin. The sunshine she radiated on him even in the dark of night.

To his surprise, Everleigh shifted in his lap, lifting away from him. His hands futilely tried to grasp her to him, to keep her near, but she stood, hands reaching out to the steering wheel to help her up. She turned herself on the narrow column that ran from the seat to the engine, one muddy HEYDUDE maneuvering around the other. All he could do was hold his arms out in a halo, there to grab her if she, God forbid, lost her footing and slipped.

He worried she was doing just that, tripping over her feet, when he realized she was reaching down and removing her shoes, one by one, a hand holding tightly to his thigh at all times. Then she leaned beside him and placed her DUDEs on the fender over the tire.

Her warmth quickly returned to him as Everleigh lifted first one knee and then the other, straddling Ryker on the padded seat of that old green tractor. Arms falling to his shoulders, hands lifting upward and carding into his hair just above the nape of his neck. His eyes drifted closed in sheer pleasure for just one moment before he released a breath and lifted his gaze to hers. And then she crashed her mouth down upon his.

## Everleigh

Was there nothing this man couldn't do? He continued to surprise her in the best ways—most recently by gifting her with her first ride on a real tractor. Not that she'd ever before thought a tractor ride was on her bucket list. But as she'd walked around the sunflower patch day after day and her gaze fell upon this big green tractor time and again, she began to wonder what it would be like to ride on something so big and intimidating. She was certain not just anyone could drive a tractor; she knew she'd never be able to.

And tonight, Ryker had driven her around these fields of flowers like a professional. Driving this loudly chugging metal machine one-handed while he kept her safely tucked into him. She loved the feel of being in his strong embrace, loved watching the muscles work beneath the skin of his arm as he shifted gears and turned the steering wheel. Loved the cedarwood smell of him wafting up to her nose as she leaned her head on his shoulder. She realized with a pang that she didn't want these days and nights with Ryker to end. She didn't want to lose what they had begun to build when The Sunflower Experience ended. When they faced veering paths into different futures.

So Everleigh decided to make the most of the time she knew they had together, hoping it was enough to keep Ryker hers even when they were apart. When he parked the tractor in its spot and shut off the engine, her mind whirred with ideas of what she could do to make him see their future as clearly as she did. As his hand trailed up her body and his warmth curled around her jawline, fingers lacing into her hair, she hoped showing him how well they fit together was enough to do just that.

As she settled herself on his lap, hands sliding up into his hair, she thought how amazing it was that Ryker Martin was here with her now. That he'd deigned to even give her the time of day, considering the way their summer had started off. How had she gotten so lucky to be the one he was choosing to spend his time with, the one he was choosing to give his perfect kisses to, the one he was letting into his world?

He seemed to inhale her scent as she looked down at him, and when he released that breath in a sigh and brought his eyes to hers, her body took over and her mind shoved out any thought past Ryker being hers in this moment. How she craved to have him inside her, quenching the ache growing deep within. She crashed her mouth down to his, taking his lower lip into her mouth and dragging her teeth along it. The groan she elicited from Ryker sent a shiver down her own spine, and she wrapped her arms around his shoulders as she tried to pull him even closer to her. His tongue found hers as he deepened the kiss, and she reveled in the warm intrusion filling her mouth.

Everleigh was wild for Ryker, flames of desire curling low in her stomach, licking up her spine. Every touch of his rough hands on her thighs, her evening-cooled arms, her cheeks, her waist as his hands slid up under her shirt, fueled those flames. She rocked into his hips, searching for friction as she continued to dance her mouth on his.

"Ryker," she moaned as his hands palmed her ass cheeks, squeezing deliciously as he lifted his hips into her. He, apparently, was wild for her too. She could feel him, hard and firm beneath the fly of his jeans.

Trailing kisses along his jaw, down the column of his neck, and back up to his ear, she snaked one hand back into his hair and brought the other between them so she could start undoing the buttons of his sleeveless shirt. God, how she loved that he wore this kind of shirt, showcasing the cut of his muscled arms, the dip between his collarbones, the enticing tan at the top of his chest.

"Have you ever had sex on a tractor before?" she whispered into his ear before nipping at his earlobe.

"I have not," he replied in a low, husky voice.

"This will be a first for us both then." Everleigh smiled conspiratorially as she stared into his darkened eyes. She ran her tongue slowly over her bottom lip, thinking maybe it was time to slow things down a bit. Draw this first out into an unforgettable moment. She unbuttoned the last button on his shirt and brushed the fabric to his sides, running her hands down the length of his chest, feeling every ripple of muscle contract beneath her fingertips. When her hands pushed back up his skin to his chest, palms grazing over his hardened nipples, Ryker's hands squeezed her buttocks again as he inhaled a sharp breath.

Everleigh dropped her mouth to Ryker's skin and began kissing and licking her way from his collarbone to his pecs, giving equal attention to both, before sliding her tongue up, up the column of his neck, along his jawline and back to his ear, where the soft noises that escaped him told her this was quite a sensitive spot. She responded by running her tongue along the shell of his ear. Then she sucked his earlobe into her mouth and grazed her teeth along it before she began licking and sucking the soft skin below his ear.

Ryker moaned then leaned back, and both his hands came to rest on her cheeks. He pulled her mouth to his in a kiss so thorough, so possessive, Everleigh's toes curled in anticipation of what was to come. She ran her finger along the waistband of his jeans, feeling his muscles tighten at her touch. Unfastening the button and unzipping his pants, she never broke the kiss. She palmed his hard length, curling her fingers around him through the fabric of his briefs. Teasing her tongue against his as her hand teased his cock.

Ryker was the one to break the kiss, tipping his forehead into hers as his breath came out in ragged bursts. His hands splayed on the skin just above her waist. He dragged them up her back and made quick work of unfastening her bra, sliding the straps down through her shirt sleeves so she could pull her hands free. She released her grip on his length for only the second it took to free herself from the bra, then focused her attention on freeing him from his constricting black briefs. Ryker lifted his hips just enough for her to slide them and his jeans down to his thighs. He seemed reluctant to put much space between their bodies, and she was grateful for it. She wanted him wrapped as tightly around her as she could get him.

For now, she settled for stroking his cock from root to tip, watching the pleasure she brought him transform his features.[3] Everleigh ran her free hand along his forehead, brushing back the dark hair that had fallen over it, as she stared into his unfocused eyes. She gasped when his calloused hands squeezed around her breasts, and her hand involuntarily squeezed his cock harder at the base, which elicited a groan from the back of Ryker's throat.

"I can't wait to get inside you," he growled as he rolled her nipples between his fingers. "Don't make me wait too long." The pinch he gave her peaked buds caused her hips to buck against him, and her hand abandoned his length in favor of her center rubbing up against his hardness.

---

3. Noah Kahan, "Everywhere, Everything"

"Condom," she demanded as her hand wrapped around his waist, pulling him flush against her rocking hips. His fingers were still teasing her nipples, sending waves of pleasure through her, causing the ache between her legs to throb an insistent beat. Everleigh needed Ryker inside her as badly as he wanted to be there.

He stopped his torturous punishment of her breasts and moved to grab his wallet from the pocket of his jeans, which were now beneath him, pinned to the seat. Everleigh took the opportunity to push up from the seat and shimmy out of her shorts and underwear, careful not to knock into anything that might trip her and send her toppling from the tractor to the ground in the small space between the steering column, the gears, and the seat. That would absolutely ruin this moment and make it unforgettable in the worst way possible.

By the time she laid her discarded clothes on the fender opposite her muddy shoes, Ryker had secured the condom on his length and was pulling her back onto him. To her dismay, he didn't immediately place her on his cock. Rather, he pulled her against him with one hand as he slid to the edge of the seat. The other dove between them, his fingers gliding along her, from opening to clit. She shuddered at the pleasure shooting through her sensitive nerves.

"So wet for me," Ryker murmured before he claimed her mouth in a hungry kiss.

Everleigh simultaneously melted into his kiss and arched her back to allow his fingers better access to her throbbing core. Her hands curled around his shoulders to steady herself as she moved against his exploring touch. He circled her clit once, twice, three times, until she thought she might explode right on his hand. "Ryker, please," she begged, aching for him to fill her when she did find her release.

In a swift movement, Ryker lifted her hips and notched himself at her entrance. A slow moan worked its way up her throat as he brought her down inch by delicious inch, the glorious pressure of him pushing against her walls triggering every nerve ending along the way.

"Fuck, you're so perfect," Ryker groaned into her collarbone as he sheathed himself fully inside her. And then he kissed his way up her neck, over her chin, to her lips, his arms wrapping her in a tight cage, holding her to him in this moment of adjustment. In this one moment where Ryker felt like everything to Everleigh, and she hoped he felt the same about her.

Then he broke the kiss, and his hands slid down to her hips, where he began to set the rhythm. She matched him thrust for thrust. It was a lazy, heady cadence at first, where his eyes roamed over her face and down her shirt. Suddenly, a look of irritation crossed his features.

"No, no, no." He shook his head. "This won't do."

In the next moment, his hands rucked up her shirt, pushing the fabric up to her shoulders. She quickly lifted her arms to assist him. Then she brought her hands down to his chest, thinking it only fair he should be shirtless too. Craving skin-on-skin connection, she pushed his shirt off his shoulders. He shook out of it and added them both to her stack of discarded clothing on the fender.

Everleigh pressed her body into his carved chest, wrapping her arms around his neck and moving again over his length while dancing her lips on his. The feel of her hardened nipples brushing over his taut pecs was decadent. She'd never had the pleasure of grinding against such a firm, sculpted body before, and she could safely say she'd never grow tired of this feeling. Ryker's fingers dug into her hips as he quickened their pace and drove his tongue punishingly into her mouth.

Needing Ryker deeper inside her, Everleigh leaned backward, placing her palms on the steering wheel behind her and arching her back. As she swiveled her hips forward, she not only created friction on her clit but had the added benefit of rubbing his cock on that sacred, sensitive spot inside her. She let her head fall back at the pleasure. And suddenly,

Ryker's hand was gliding over her stomach, circling her breast. Teasing her nipple. In the next moment, his mouth latched on to her other nipple, sucking, licking, teasing.

The pleasure building within her grew to a fever pitch, and she pulled one hand from the steering wheel behind her and threw it over Ryker's shoulder, anchoring him to her as she swiveled and thrust again and again. His hips met hers again and again. His mouth and his fingers continued their dance, and she felt herself splintering. Ecstasy exploded within her core, shot through the recesses of her mind with a blinding light that enveloped her on this dark night, triggering the muscles of her inner walls to spasm.

"Fuck! Ev—Aaah!" Ryker shouted as he wrapped both arms around Everleigh's waist, spearing himself up into her and riding out his own orgasm. The friction of his body against hers kept her clit tingling in gratification long after her orgasm faded. Ryker thrust once more into her and pulled her tightly to him, dropping his face in the crook of her neck.

After a long moment, their heavy breathing the only sound around them, he spoke with gravel in his voice, "God, that was amazing."

Everleigh let out a little laugh as she pulled his face up to hers. "Best tractor sex I've ever had, that's for sure." She dropped a kiss on his lips and remained at his mouth while her arms snaked around his neck again, eyes staring deeply into his.

Ryker chuckled and traced his knuckles along her cheek. "I'll admit, tractor sex was not on my bingo card for tonight."

"No? Maybe you should find a more exciting stack of bingo cards to choose from."

His eyebrows shot up at that. Everleigh smirked as she lifted off his lap and dug through the clothes for her undergarments. She felt the satisfaction of achieving her goal tonight: giving Ryker an unforgettable memory of her.

And hopefully keeping him intrigued enough to want to see what other memories they could make. Together.

# Chapter 20
# Chores

**Ryker**

THEY FELL INTO A tangle of arms and legs and ecstasy in his bedroom less than thirty minutes later. Of course, one time with Everleigh wasn't nearly enough to slake his thirst for her. If anything, every orgasm she triggered in him made him crave another. And another.

This was becoming a vicious cycle.

An obsession?

Ryker pushed the thought from his mind. He wasn't *obsessed* with Everleigh. Just thoroughly enjoying everything she was willing to share with him. From now until the end of the summer, he'd take whatever she would give.

As they lay together in the late hours of the night, Everleigh tucked against him in a way that made this bed feel like home, her finger traced along his tattoo again. He sensed she wanted to ask him about it, and finally the silence broke with her words.

"What does your tattoo mean to you?"

He swallowed as an unexpected emotion tugged at him at her phrasing. He'd become accustomed to people asking what his design was, out of slight curiosity or when comparing ink. But he couldn't remember a time someone had asked what it *meant* to him. Clearing the catch from his voice, he explained, "I wanted something to always remind me of the most important things in my life."

He thought about the design he'd asked the tattoo artist to create: a diamond shape made of green cornstalks on the bottom two sides and wooden Slugger bats on the top sides, the necks of the bats crisscrossing at the peak. The bats and cornstalks formed the borders of a lighter green infield, with a white baseball with red laces in the very middle. A black "M" for his last name marked the center of that baseball. Each word of the phrase "PLAY HARD WORK HARDER" was inked along the outside of the diamond shape.

"Hmmm," she hummed against his chest as he told her about each piece. "Seems very fitting. Combining your roots on the farm with your love of the game. Do you think you could choose one over the other if you had to?"

Ryker's head pulled back at the question. He'd never imagined a reason he'd have to choose. "I hope I never have to. They're both woven deep in my fabric. Losing either one would be devastating."

Memories of when he thought he might lose his spot on the baseball team twisted his insides. Thinking it might truly happen had pushed him to make the drastic changes he needed to reset his mental health. But even with the threat of losing baseball, he'd still known he had the farm, his family, to fall back on. His parents might have vowed to kick him out had he not changed for the better, but deep down, he knew they would never bar him from this place in the long run. It was too much a point of pride that they ran this farm together. Darren and Rita would find a way to help him, even if he couldn't help himself, and he knew they would all emerge on the other side a stronger family unit.

As Everleigh snuggled more closely into him and wrapped her arm around his midsection, his resolve set once again to ensure nothing came between those two things his tattoo was meant to always remind him of: the family farm and baseball.

Her next words vibrated against his chest. "When did you decide to get it?"

A smile laced Ryker's voice at the memory. "Team-building exercise."

"What?" Her head snapped up to look at him, incredulous. "Seriously? The team decided to get tattoos for a team-building exercise?"

He nodded. "It's tradition."

Her narrowed eyes clearly held doubt. "Tattoos are a tradition?"

"No, the team-building is. Every year, just before the start of the season, the incoming freshmen get to put ideas into a pot for the captains to draw from. The best idea wins." His smile widened remembering that the tattoo idea was his that year. It had earned him points with nearly everyone on the team.

"Tattoos was the best idea you all could come up with?" She remained skeptical.

"Hey," he chided, "you seem to like my tattoo."

"I do," she allowed. "I just can't imagine a whole team of ball players excited to mutilate their bodies."

"You don't think you'd ever get a tattoo?"

She thought for a moment. "I don't know. It would have to mean something very important to me, like yours does to you. And I'd have to be okay with having it on my body for the rest of my life."

"You definitely have to be okay with the part about it being there for the rest of your life."

"What were some of the other team-building ideas?"

"Well, let's see, that year someone suggested ice fishing at Lake Macbride. Very few of us wanted to spend a day huddled up cold on the ice in tiny shacks. Another idea was a craft beer and painting class—that was quickly thrown out. Last year, the winning suggestion was a day trip to the ski mountain up north."

"That sounds like fun."

"It was, yeah. Until our catcher sprained his ankle when he wiped out on the slopes and consequently missed the first two games of the season. Coach was pissed. Said all sports ideas had to be coach-approved. Gave us a list of such approved ideas: batting practice, infielding drills, playing catch—"

"Sounds like a day of practice," she interrupted.

"Exactly. Oh—and there was one other on that list. Pickleball."

"Pickleball!" She snorted a laugh. "We played that in gym class. It was . . . kinda fun."

"*Kinda fun* is an overstatement."

She laughed again, and he rolled out from beneath her, circled his arms around her, and began teasing his teeth along the sensitive skin of her neck. "I can think of something more than kinda fun," he murmured at the base of her ear. And his pulse jumped when her laughter ceased and her hazel eyes locked on his with a burning intensity that mirrored his own.

⁂

Yesterday, when she'd come running out of her house to the truck with a bag slung over her shoulder, he'd known Everleigh planned on staying the night. He'd beamed on the inside.

Now, he tapped the screen on his phone, figuring he only had about twenty more minutes of this quiet content with her. Then it was time to rise and shine and start farm chores. He wrapped his arms around her delicate frame and pulled her into his side.

Ryker had awakened ten minutes ago and briefly thought about waking Everleigh with kisses and teasing caresses, but she looked like an angel there on the pillow, her dark hair falling over the side of her face, spilling over her shoulder. He wanted to watch her breathe softly, watch her eyelids flutter as she dreamt. He wondered what she was dreaming about. If she was dreaming about them, just as he'd dreamt about them last night.

She stirred. Ryker gathered her closer to him, placing a kiss on her forehead. She moaned softly, cleared her throat, blinked her eyes open. Her gaze settled on him and a smile tugged at her mouth—a smile he returned.

"What time is it?" Everleigh asked in a sleepy voice.

"5:15."

She groaned. "Why are you awake?"

"Chores."

"Oh," she said in a thick voice as her eyelids drooped closed again. Then, just as he thought she was about to drift back to sleep she asked, "Can I help?"

## Everleigh

She could not believe how much she loved farm chores. She told Ryker as much as she scattered feed for the chickens.

"You just wait then," he said with a sarcastic laugh.

"Why? What?"

He shook his head. "We'll get there. Right after this."

The smirk that had taken up residence on his face made Everleigh nervous, worried they'd be scooping poop next. Luckily, Ryker had found a spare pair of his mom's boots for her to wear, so if she stepped in anything gross, she wouldn't be ruining the shoes she had to wear all day. Well, ruining more than the mud that already caked the bottom halves of her DUDEs after walking around the sunflower patch yesterday evening. Mud, she could handle. Animal defecation, not so much.

He led her into the chicken coop, telling her it was time to collect eggs. She clapped her hands in anticipation. "Yay! I've always wanted to collect eggs."

He shot a dubious look at her.

"Okay, maybe not *always*. But I do think this is so cool."

Ryker chuckled softly and opened the caged door, gesturing for her to enter. He followed her in and secured the door tightly behind them. "So, these shelves here? This is where you'll find the eggs." He handed her a wire mesh basket. "Put them in here. Gently, so they don't crack."

Everleigh nodded and began her search for eggs. "There's one!" she said excitedly as she placed it in the basket. "And another one!"

He smiled, but he was not smiling at her. She followed his gaze.

"A rooster!" she exclaimed. Then her smile fell flat. "Why is it looking at me like that?"

The rooster, she noticed as it strutted toward them, was much bigger than she'd thought, and its large eye seemed to ask, *Why are you in my coop?* And if it were possible for a rooster to look angry, this one definitely did. Suddenly, it released a deafening crow and furiously flapped its wings. Then it bolted into a dead sprint. *Right at her.*

Everleigh screamed and ran around Ryker, nearly dropping the basket of eggs. The rooster followed, cawing and flapping and scaring the crap out of her.

"Ryker! What is it doing?"

He chortled as he watched her spinning and dancing around, trying to stay out of the path of the monster's huge beak. It lunged at her, jumped and flapped.

"*Help me*, Ryker!"

Ryker laughed harder but finally grabbed a spray bottle from a nearby shelf and started spraying the rooster with a steady stream of water. The rooster retreated, but then another rooster made an appearance in the same vicinity.

"How many are there?" she hollered, anxiety lacing her voice.

"Just two. Don't worry. I'll hold them off while you finish gathering the eggs." Ryker nodded his head toward the shelves and stood between her and the roosters, still chuckling.

"You knew that would happen, didn't you!" Everleigh accused in her best hurt tone. "You're so mean. You and your roosters both!" She rushed to grab the remaining eggs and marched to the door. Stepping outside to safety, she breathed a sigh of relief. Then yelped when strong arms scooped around her and lifted her from behind. Ryker kissed her cheek.

"You nearly gave me an anxiety attack."

"I'm sorry," he murmured into her neck. "Honestly, I hate those roosters."

She broke free from his embrace and spun around. "So you *did* know they would attack me! How can I trust you ever again?" she chastised. He laughed as he wrapped his arms around her and kissed her mouth. "Careful—the eggs!" Everleigh dissolved into a fit of giggles when he didn't let her go and continued to kiss all over her face.

The last of the chores completed, they headed to the house with the basket of eggs. She removed Rita's boots in the utility room, and her eyes settled on the washing machine in the corner. She bit her lower lip as she remembered their tryst yesterday afternoon.

Ryker led the way into the kitchen; his parents were sitting at the table drinking coffee.

"Breakfast is in the microwave if you're hungry," Rita offered. When she looked up from her magazine, she smiled. "Well, good morning, Everleigh. Ryker putting you to work already?"

Everleigh nodded. "Where would you like the eggs?"

"Just there on the counter by the sink, please. Thank you."

Ryker pulled a dish out of the microwave and placed two pieces of French toast and sausage links on two plates. Everleigh followed as he carried the plates to the table, and they dug in.

"Only a couple days left of blooming season, it seems," Darren said as he looked up from his phone.

"Your farm report tell you that?" Ryker gestured his fork at the phone.

"Mother Nature did." Darren cleared his throat and appeared to settle a pointed look on his son. "Which means a lot of work tearing everything down for the season. It would be nice to have some help, if you can spare the time."

Ryker nodded as he chewed but didn't meet his dad's stare. A long, awkward moment later, Rita reached out and patted Darren's hand. "I'm sure he knows, dear."

And Everleigh suddenly felt like an intruder in their house.

⚶⚶⚶⚶ ⚶⚶⚶⚶

"Umm . . . does your dad not like me?" she asked after Ryker pulled up to the cutting garden. He killed the engine on the UTV, and Everleigh exited and walked around to his side.

"Of course he likes you. Why would you ask that?"

"That just felt like a really pointed comment at breakfast. I want to make sure it's okay that I'm around, that I'm trying to help."

"It's nothing you've done, believe me. All passive aggressive comments were solely for my benefit." Ryker reached out and took her hand in his. "Darren gets this way sometimes. When he thinks I'm not heeding his directives, he gets butthurt."

"Are you . . . meaning to not heed his directives?" Everleigh asked as she stepped closer to the UTV and leaned into his leg, wrapping both her hands around his.

"Of course I'm not *meaning* to," Ryker replied hastily. When she waited patiently, he continued, "He just has to understand that, even though I'm trying to make up for the shit I pulled before, it doesn't mean he owns every minute of my day."

She opened her mouth to ask a follow-up question, but he turned the key in the ignition and the engine roared to life. "I'll be back around later," he said.

As Ryker drove away, she noticed Mel coming around the corner. "Rita says we might be done tomorrow," she called as she neared the table.

Everleigh nodded. "I heard that too."

"I'm kind of bummed. I mean, we had a pretty good season this year. I hate when it's over. I feel like I'm in a mystical utopia all day for a couple of weeks, and then I have to go back to the drab real world. The Sunflower Experience withdrawal is real."

Everleigh worried her lip between her teeth as she thought about Mel's words. What would her life be like after The Sunflower Experience? She believed as long as she and Ryker could keep their romance going strong, it would be like taking the Experience with her every day.

❧ ❧

"Evie!" Saralynn called as she limped up to the cutting table with their mom and her friend, Bailey, on either side of her, holding hands. Saralynn was the only person Everleigh tolerated calling her Evie—only because she'd done it her whole life, and Everleigh didn't have the heart to tell her little sister why she no longer liked the nickname.

"Hey, guys!" Everleigh said. "You made it!"

"We made it," her mom agreed. "And Saralynn here has been a trooper as we trekked around the paths."

"My leg started to hurt a while ago, but I'm not missing out on this! And I just *have* to get my sunflower."

"Of course you do." Everleigh grabbed two small shears from the table and handed one to each girl, providing instructions on how to safely hold and use them. "Mom will help you."

"What happened to your sister?" Mel asked, nodding at her bandaged leg as the three walked into the cutting garden.

"She had an accident at the babysitter's. Saralynn—zero. Glass coffee table—one."

Mel took a deep breath in through her teeth. "Ow."

"Very ow. I nearly fainted when I saw the wound. There's a reason I'm not going to medical school."

Saralynn came limping back with Bailey still holding her hand. It was sweet that her friend was being so supportive, making sure she had someone to lean on.

"Look at the flowers we picked out! We found the very biggest blooms in the whole patch."

"You sure did," Everleigh confirmed. "Now, place your stems in that bucket of water so they can take a nice long drink, and then we'll wrap them up for the ride home."

Saralynn chattered with Bailey for a moment while they held the stems in the water. When she handed her flower to Everleigh to wrap in plastic, she gasped as she remembered something. "Evie, I almost forgot! Dad came to see me last night!"

Everleigh's eyes darted to her mother, who responded with a curt nod.

"Oh, he did?" she asked Saralynn.

"He did! He said he heard about my accident and just had to come over and make sure I was all right. And . . ." She waved her hands excitedly in the air. "Guess what?"

"What?" Everleigh asked cautiously.

"He brought me a big, stuffed, rainbow-colored penguin! It's so cute!"

"He did?" Everleigh narrowed her eyes, glancing at her mom again. If this was true, it was completely out of character for her father. Last summer, when Saralynn had surgery to remove her tonsils, their dad had called—two days after the fact. And he'd promised to come see her and bring her a big bouquet of get-well balloons. Saralynn had been so excited. First at the promise of seeing her dad in person for the first time in months. Second, that he would be bringing her a present. Four days later, when he still hadn't shown up, Everleigh went to the party supply store and spent her whole week's paycheck on a huge balloon bouquet to make it up to her sister, who'd been crushed by the thought of her father forgetting about his promise.

Mel wrapped Bailey's stem in plastic, and the girls wandered over to a stack of straw bales around the corner as Saralynn lamented her aching leg. Everleigh called to Ryker over her walkie to see if he would be willing to drive a disabled little sister to the front of the patch.

"Oh, bless you, child," her mother said. "I was worried I was going to have to start carrying her, and I don't think my back could take it."

"He should be here in a minute."

"Say," her mom said, with a definite leading tone. "Your dad did mention that he'd hoped to talk with you about something. But he wouldn't say what."

Everleigh blanched. Had he really used Saralynn's accident as an excuse to show up at her house and hound her about the whole testing thing?

"He's not going to say he's marrying that woman, is he?" her mom asked with an edge to her voice.

Everleigh spoke around the lump that had formed in her throat, "Ah, I'm not sure . . . what he would need to talk with me about. Probably nothing. I'll message him."

"Not that I care. She can have him. He looked absolutely disheveled when he showed up. Almost gaunt. The whole thing was kind of weird.

But Saralynn was so happy to see him, so . . . whatever." Her mother shrugged her shoulder and brushed her hair behind it.

The lump in Everleigh's throat expanded. Could Kyleigh possibly be getting worse so quickly? She'd hoped for more time to sort through what the right choice would be for her. But she hadn't had time to really think about it with her mind solidly on Ryker over the past few days.

Speaking of, his UTV rounded the corner. He shut it down in front of them and leapt from the seat. "Where's our special guest?"

"She's right around the corner." Everleigh pointed in the direction the girls had disappeared moments before.

His eyebrows lifted. "Your sister has been marching around this acreage with her battle wound? Impressive." He headed down the path to the right.

"Who. Is. That?"

Everleigh blushed under her mom's inquiring smirk.

"Is that the boy you've deserted us for? What's-his-name?"

"Ryker."

"Ryker, huh? Is this a real thing?" she murmured as he reappeared carrying Saralynn in his arms.

Saralynn was clearly loving the attention, her arms wrapped around his neck, yammering about something. Bailey followed behind, holding their sunflowers. He set her sister gently in the back seat and directed Bailey to the other side. Helped them both with their seatbelts.

Spinning on his heel, he stepped forward and extended his hand. "Ms. Wilson, I'm Ryker Martin. Nice to meet you."

Her mother glanced at Everleigh as she accepted his handshake. "You can call me Rosalynn. Nice to meet you as well."

"Are we ready to ride?" he asked.

"I believe we are." As her mom walked in front of Everleigh, she paused and asked in a hushed tone. "Will we see you tonight? Or will you be . . . otherwise occupied?"

"Mom! *Stop*." She pushed her mother away.

Everleigh waved at them as Ryker started the UTV and drove away.

But why had her mom asked if this was a real thing?

# Chapter 21
# Was Any of It Real?

**Ryker**

HE WENT ONE STEP further and delivered Rosalynn, Saralynn, and her friend to their car in the parking lot. Ryker carried Saralynn around and carefully placed her in her seat. He pointed at her bandage and said how impressed he was with her toughness. When he noticed Bailey standing behind him clutching the flowers, he asked which one was Saralynn's, passed it along to her, and then carried Bailey around to the other side of the car and placed her in her seat as well. She grinned and giggled the whole time. Rosalynn thanked him again for the ride and the help with the girls.

It was what she didn't say that bothered him.

Before Rosalynn opened her door, she audibly inhaled and turned toward him. Ryker was halfway seated in the UTV. He stood.

"I'm glad I got the chance to meet you." She eyed him for a moment. "She can be very private, Everleigh. Holds things closely to herself, and I feel at times I don't even know what's happening in my own daughter's life." She shook her head. "Just know that if she's choosing you to be part of her world, there's a reason." Rosalynn opened her mouth to say something else as an unreadable expression colored her features, but then she clamped it shut. "Thanks again."

As Ryker sat in the UTV and watched Everleigh's mother drive away, he felt the unmistakable pang of guilt take root in his chest. The longer he sat there and replayed the perfection of the last few days with Everleigh—pictured her smile, that dimple, her sweet sighs—the more that guilt permeated his muscles. The more he tried to look ahead to what their future could be, the more it wrapped around his bones.

He'd gotten so lost in discovering her, knowing her, possessing her, borrowing a little of her positive light to heal his soul, that he'd failed to see the diverging paths they were heading toward. This little world they'd built for themselves was in a bubble. In less than a week, Ryker would return to school. Return to the grind of classes, practices, keeping his mental focus sharp.

Hits of Everleigh made him high. She was a drug that laced herself through his veins. She was becoming an addiction. Even now, when they were apart, thoughts of her scent, her laugh, her body were constantly assaulting his mind. He'd thought it was the thrill of the late-summer fling, but somehow she'd become something that possessed him. And how far would he crash without her?

*"If she's choosing you to be part of her world, there's a reason."*

That phrase hit him hard. It meant Everleigh wasn't the kind of girl who thoughtlessly gave herself to just anyone. She took care in selecting someone she thought worthy of her attention, of her trust. Rosalynn wanted to—but didn't—ask Ryker if he was worthy of her daughter.

And he was not worthy.

⬥⬥⬥ ⬥⬥⬥

Ryker spent the rest of the day warring with himself. One minute thinking there could be a way he wouldn't have to give Everleigh up. He could learn not to fixate so singularly, to allow his mind to properly prioritize and distribute his attention to everything important . . .

couldn't he? The next minute, he was reminding himself that he had to leave all distractions behind. It was a girl who had sent him spiraling out of control last time.

Now every step forward felt mired down as he walked through the sunflower patch at the end of the shift, heading to the platform where he was to meet Everleigh for their date to watch the sunset. He could have driven the UTV, but that would have brought him that much quicker to her, to what he knew he needed to do.

No, Ryker needed the extra time to prepare.

Rounding the corner, he found her sitting on their platform, legs dangling over the front, arms folded on the railing. He swallowed hard, then propelled his feet forward. Climbing the steps had never felt this difficult. And that guilt? It crushed his chest when she turned to him, a brilliant smile popping his favorite dimple into her cheek.

"There you are! I saved you a spot." Everleigh patted the platform beside her. "Tonight's going to be a good one. Look at all the wispy clouds along the skyline."

Ryker followed her gaze to the western horizon—which was admittedly setting up for a beautiful sunset—and ruminated on the wonder that was Everleigh. How she took delight in things like sunsets and meteor showers. Her quiet observations that brought a quality to their conversations he rarely found with others. The fact that she was so unaware of her physical beauty that her personality shone even more. The fact that she only showed her true self to a very select few. A reminder that he was not worthy of her sunlight. And it would be a travesty if he snuffed out that light with his darkness.

But when he returned his stare to her still-smiling face, he longed to tempt fate. A voice echoed from Ryker's chest up into the back of his brain, saying she might be able to make him worthy. And how long would that take? For his growth under her encouragement to make him the man Everleigh deserved to have by her side?

He sat. She drew up her legs, tucking them to the side and leaning into him. Automatically, he wrapped his arm around her. Inhaled her vanilla scent. Closed his eyes as he kissed her temple.

"We really might be done tomorrow?" she asked.

Ryker coughed, then recovered. Was she thinking the same thing he was?

Everleigh pulled away, concern coloring her features. "Are you okay?"

He cleared his throat and swallowed. "Yeah."

She eyed him for a moment before she spoke again. "Mel said your mom told her tomorrow will likely be the last day for the season."

*Oh.*

"Sounds that way."

"Should we . . . set a date for tomorrow's sunset?" She smiled, leaned in, and brought her warm, full lips to his. Ryker's thoughts became an impossible jumble as Everleigh brushed her mouth softly around his lips, teasing him with her tongue. Her hand slid up his thigh, then pressed against his hardening length as she moved to the waist of his jeans and hooked a finger behind the button.

Ryker wanted to grab her onto his lap and fuck his confusion away. He wanted to push her in another direction and tell her all the reasons why she should leave tomorrow and never look back.

As if she sensed his hesitation, Everleigh's lips stilled. Her eyelids lifted, exposing the dark-ringed hazels he dreamt about so often. She moved her mouth to his ear and whispered, "Shouldn't we make the most of the time we have left together?"

And when her tongue slid around the shell of his ear and she pulled his earlobe between her teeth, Ryker could no longer think straight, let alone restrain his urges. She'd basically just confirmed that this thing between them was going to end in short order, and she was clearly wanting to take advantage of the waning days. A weight lifted from his conscience, and he dragged her on top of him as he lay back on the platform.

A giggle erupted from her chest, and he reached up, pressing his thumb into her dimple for what might be the last time. She cupped her hand around his, turned her face, and placed a sensual kiss on his palm. He slipped his hand behind her neck and pulled her mouth down to his. Adjusting her hips, she pressed herself against him, and Ryker could hear her breathing escalating as their tongues intertwined. He traveled his hand from her leg to her hip and guided her motion, encouraging that delicious friction. Everleigh sighed a soft moan, arching her back. He lifted his head to kiss and suck on her neck, causing her moan to lengthen and increase in tenor, quickening her rocking motion.

Honestly, if she wanted to climax on top of him this way, Ryker wouldn't object. Because he was enjoying watching her come undone with the colors of the fading day as her backdrop. It seemed every time they had sex, Everleigh let herself go a little more. Stepped further and further out of her head and her comfort zone. Explored what made her feel good. He liked being a part of her self-exploration.

Everleigh brought her forehead down to Ryker's, latched onto his gaze, and lingered. Her lips just grazed his, and she stopped moving. He pressed his hand into her hip, encouraging her to continue. She didn't, instead closing her teeth around his bottom lip and gently tugging on it as the corners of her mouth twitched upward. He stopped breathing when the ache in his groin shot heavy need throughout his body. God, she was literally breathtaking as she hovered above him, holding all the power in her heated stare.

As she released his lip, a challenge surged into that stare, and she whispered, "I think maybe I'll make you earn this one." Her palms flattened on the platform on either side of his head, and Everleigh dragged her body down him and back up with a look of excitement on her face, then jumped to her feet. She bent over, planting one last kiss on his lips before stepping over him and racing down the steps. Leaving him aching for her touch. Ryker groaned and craned his neck to spy which direction she went.

Carefully standing and adjusting himself in his jeans, he caught a glimpse of her running toward the back of the acreage. He leapt down the stairs three at a time and took off to the left down a different path, but he knew he was faster and he'd be able to cut her off.

The thrill of the chase enhanced the sensations Everleigh had unlocked in his body, and he became lightheaded as his breathing became more labored. Thoughts of what dirty things he'd do to her when he got his hands on her again flooded his mind. Or even what he'd let her do to him if she wanted to be on top again.

The sound of her laughter carried to him on the wind as he neared the clearing by the corn pit. She'd probably stopped, trying to figure out which way to go next. Ryker cut into the sunflowers so he'd have the element of surprise when he came upon her.

A smile pulled his cheeks as he spotted Everleigh, just feet away, scanning the paths. She'd made it too easy. He sprang out of the dense patch and wrapped his arms around her. A scream ripped up her throat, the sound quickly dissolving into laughter. Ryker spun her in his embrace, holding her arms behind her back, his hungry mouth going immediately for her neck, then her ear. Her laugh became breathy, curling into a high, tiny squeak before she searched for his mouth with her own. He rewarded her with a long, deep kiss. Somehow, she maneuvered her arms free and tugged at his shirt, pulling it the rest of the way from his jeans, sliding her hands up his skin, making him wish all her perfect skin was against his. Everleigh's fingers worked up to his shoulders and through his collar, settling on his neck. He pressed his hips into her, dying to lay her down right here on the hard ground.

She stopped kissing him and drew his gaze to hers. Maintaining eye contact, Everleigh slid her hands down his body, teasing her fingertips along every ridge and muscle until she gathered the hem of his shirt in her hands and slowly lifted it higher and higher, until Ryker had to release her hips and raise his arms to allow her to pull it over his head. He quickly brought his hands back down to claim her again, but his view was immediately obscured by the T-shirt she'd just flung at his face!

Her breath caught loudly in her chest before he heard her take off running. Ryker flung the T-shirt aside and followed on her heels, dipping into the sunflower patch again to try and cut her off. The wide leaves and prickly stems stung his bare skin as he catapulted himself through the stalks. He darted out into the path where he expected her to be, but Everleigh wasn't there. The sound of her feet on the ground and the rustling of the towering plants drew his attention farther to the left. She had the same idea. He continued running down the path, thinking she would pop out from the patch at any moment.

But she didn't. He halted and listened. The only sound was the wind twisting the leaves of the plants against one another. And then her faint laugh. By the sunflower maze. Ryker raced toward it, and when he entered the mouth, he called out, "A fatal mistake! I don't think you realize how well I know this maze!"

A yelp arose from the right side. He moved in that direction. There was a chance Everleigh could outmaneuver him in here. He knew the maze like the back of his hand, and there were two places where she could circle around him and back out to safety. If she picked her path correctly. But the odds were in Ryker's favor.

His heart galloped with anticipation. Would she let him catch her this time? Or was she enjoying the cat-and-mouse game as much as he was? A mirthful sound worked up his chest at the thought of laying his hands on her again. He turned a corner to a dead end, half expecting her to be there. She was not.

"I thought you knew this maze so well!" Everleigh's chiding voice called out to him.

One path, maybe two away? He picked up his pace, but with stealth. Ryker could hear her footfalls. He was so close.

And then nothing. No sound of her feet, no soft laughter. Only the wind, the buzz of a bee, the check and chit calls of a red-winged blackbird.

Ryker froze, listened, and then he knew. Of course. He doubled back, took a left, then a right, and . . .

There she was. Sitting atop a pyramid of straw bales at the center of the maze, pots of colorful flowers spaced around it at intervals. A reward photo op for the visitors who successfully made it to the middle. Everleigh was leaning back on her palms, her right leg bent with her heel on the straw bale, her left leg dangling lazily. Like she didn't just run through a sunflower patch and a maze.

Ryker straightened as he slowed to a prowl. He had her cornered. As he approached, the glint in her eyes told him that was what she wanted. She was acting cool, but her chest was heaving, just like his own. Raking his gaze up and down her body, he let a crooked smile pull on his face. Everleigh smiled devilishly in return. His fingers twitched, aching to dance across her soft skin again.

"I thought you'd never find me." She let her leg drop slightly to the side, an invitation, and immediately all he wanted was to be deep between those thighs.

Ryker stepped up to her, staring into those dark-ringed hazels, waiting for the moment. She thought this was her victory, but really, it was going to be all his. Drawing a lazy path along his lower lip with his tongue, he let his dark gaze bore into her. When her smile faded, he could read her thoughts. She was wondering why he wasn't touching her yet. Wondering if she could make him touch her before she had to reach out and touch him.

Her lip twitched. Her breathing escalated. He held firm.

Finally—after another torturous moment where desire thoroughly heated his blood and he began to question his restraint—Everleigh kicked her heel off the straw bale and hooked her leg around his waist, pulling him toward her. She sat up and brought her palms to rest on Ryker's bare chest, tracing her fingertips over his hardened nipples.

The anticipation was delicious, but it was time to act. He wrapped his hands around the back of her head, tangling his fingers in her disheveled braid, and crashed his mouth down onto hers, swallowing the gasp that escaped her. As their mouths devoured one another, he could feel her curling her limbs around him, pulling herself closer and closer. Ryker moved his mouth to her throat; she sighed that sweet sigh. He smiled against her skin and kissed a trail down and along her collarbone.

Everleigh laughed softly. "Ahhh . . . I love this."

He smirked as he straightened and looked down at her. "You love what?"

Placing her hands on either side of his face, she stroked her thumbs along his cheeks. "Everything." Her expression turned wistful. "I love the connection we're building."

Ryker chuckled. "You love what I do to your body." He slid his hands under her shirt and caressed her nipples over her lacy bralette, turning them peaked and needy.

Her breath caught in her throat, and then she grinned. "Of course there's that. But I'm excited to see what's next for us," Everleigh said with unfocused eyes as she leaned up to kiss him.

But then she stopped.

"What is it, Ryker?"

She must have noticed the change in his expression.

Suddenly, the truths he'd uncovered came crashing back, invading his thoughts.[1] And he had to get it out. "It's not real," Ryker said, barely above a whisper. Absently, his hands dropped to his sides.

"What does that mean?" Confusion swept across Everleigh's face. She reached her hand out and trailed her fingers along his forearm. When he didn't answer, she said, "It feels pretty real to me."

He closed his eyes, shaking his head. Earlier? When she'd said they should make the most of the time they had left? She hadn't meant it in the way he'd thought. And Ryker was a fool for not seeing more clearly. He leveled his stare at her, letting the clarity flow through and out of him.

"Everleigh, we were both in a place that allowed us to be open to the experience. And it's been a great one, but—"

She choked out a bitter laugh. "Is that all I am to you? An *experience*?"

❧ ❦

# Everleigh

When Ryker didn't respond, she had her answer. He opened his mouth like he was going to say something, but no words materialized.

Everleigh pushed past him then, furious that she'd thought he might be different from the boy he'd first presented himself to be. That she had *believed* he was different.

She was even more furious with herself for falling for his act. As she marched into the maze, trembling with outrage, anger clouding her vision, she walked five feet in before spinning on her heel. No, he was *not* getting off that easy.

---

1. Seafret, "Atlantis"

Stomping back into the center clearing, her finger pointed at him, Everleigh accused, "You made me trust you, Ryker! You made me believe I was important to you, that you cared for me!"

He stood stock-still as she stepped up to him and spat, "Was any of it real?" Then she answered her own question, "No, of course not. We've already covered that, haven't we?"

Tears threatened, and the fact she might cry in front of this asshole pushed her to another level of fury. "I can't believe I let my guard down with you," she said, but it came out barely above a whisper. "I cannot believe I trusted you with . . . so much of me." Hot tears spilled down her cheeks, and she swiped them away. "So much you didn't deserve."

"You're right," Ryker replied simply. He tensed, as if he expected her to start yelling at him again, but Everleigh stood unmoving, a far-off look blurring her vision, her jaw clenched. One more tear tumbled down her face, and she didn't bother to wipe it.

After a long moment, Ryker asked, as if he cared, "What are you thinking?"

His words pulled Everleigh from her trance, and although she continued to stare over his shoulder, she answered, "I'm thinking that I'm standing in the most beautiful place on Earth with the worst person on Earth."

A harsh laugh ripped from her throat when she brought her eyes to his. "I mean," Everleigh said as she discovered a truth about herself, "I realize now that I was the one who chased you, who craved your attention, who pushed you into something you didn't want. But you didn't have to let me catch you. You could have shut me down if I was asking for more than you were willing to give. But . . . you took advantage of my moments of weakness, didn't you?"

His jawline ticked and he shrugged. *Ryker shrugged.*

Everleigh bit the inside of her mouth hard as she searched for the man she thought she'd found in his eyes. But they were glassy. Hollow. "And not in my wildest dreams did I think you were capable of killing what we had so quickly."

Suddenly, the memory of a dream—a nightmare—from just a few days ago came screaming back to her. The one where Ryker turned away from her as she lay dying on the platform in the middle of the sunflower patch. Walked away as Everleigh took her last breaths, as she reached out for him. "Or maybe I always did," she whispered, haunted.

She ran her hand over her eyes to quell the tears. She was done crying over Ryker Martin. She folded her arms across her chest, allowing him one last opportunity to speak, to say something that made sense after the days of heaven and the memories of happiness had been stripped away from her. His silence made her scoff.

"What else should I have expected?"

Everleigh spun on her heel and rushed to get away from him. She told herself she wouldn't shed any more tears, yet here they came. At least he wouldn't see her cry over him. Over the broken promise of love she'd felt him giving to her. She couldn't have been wrong—Ryker *had* been giving himself to her. Bit by bit, moment by special moment.

But just like that, it had all disappeared.

The echo of her name carried through the maze, and Everleigh started to run, afraid she wasn't just imagining it. If Ryker was coming after her, she wouldn't let him catch her.

He'd had his chance, and he'd blown it.

# Chapter 22
# What We Left Behind

## Everleigh

STANDING AT THE BACK door of the Martins' home, chest heaving, she knocked again.[1] Her bag was in there, and she wanted no reason to have to see Ryker again. Everleigh probably could have gone right in and grabbed it, considering she'd spent the past two nights here, but that felt wrong now.

She texted Crestin as she waited, commanding him to come get her *now*.

Rita slid open the glass door with a smile. "Everleigh!" Her smile fell, taking in Everleigh's agitated state. "What is it, hon?"

"Sorry. I just need to get my bag."

Rita's gaze flickered to the UTV in the driveway, her confusion apparent.

"I, ah, drove that over. I hope you don't mind."

She put her arm around Everleigh's shoulders and guided her into the house. "Of course, of course. Come on in."

Luckily, Rita allowed her to walk down the hallway to Ryker's bedroom alone to gather her things. Everleigh was a compulsive organizer, so everything was already packed neatly in her bag, sitting on

---

1. flora cash, "You're Somebody Else"

his dresser. She looped the straps over her shoulder and caught sight of her frightfully red eyes in her reflection in the mirror. Rubbing her fingers over her eyelids, she exhaled heavily. She pulled her hands through her messy braid, and the next thing that caught her eye was the corner of that stupid envelope sticking out between the wall and the mirror.

Everleigh should have known better. The signs had been there.

"You okay, honey?" Rita's soft voice startled her when she leaned against the doorframe.

Everleigh put on a stoic face. "I will be, yes."

As she walked toward the door, Rita met her halfway and placed her hands on Everleigh's arms and rubbed them in a soothing fashion. "Will you allow me to apologize for him? He's been working on himself, but it would appear he's not working hard enough."

Everleigh gave her head a quick shake. His mother was about to make her cry again, and she didn't want to cry anymore. "That's not necessary. It was a misunderstanding. I misunderstood. I know that now."

Rita's expression of pity was exactly what Everleigh didn't want to see. She moved past Ryker's mom toward the door. "Crestin is coming to get me. I think he might be out waiting."

"Okay, hon. You let me know if there's anything I can do."

Everleigh tried to offer a smile as she left the room. Once she was safely in the hallway, she rushed to the front of the house and out the door before Ryker materialized.

Crestin must have sped all the way here, because he whipped into the front driveway as Everleigh was descending the steps. When she opened the passenger door of the El Camino, she caught the moment the golden sun dipped all the way below the horizon. Everleigh stood for a moment, watching it disappearing, feeling her heart sink with it.

It was Monday, August 12. The last day of The Sunflower Experience. Everleigh donned her tie-dyed staff T-shirt for the last time. She plaited her hair in a French braid. Tied her white patterned ribbon around it to keep it under control. Then she stared at her reflection in the mirror. Her eyes were puffy. As much as she'd never wanted to cry over that boy again, she had. Half the night.

She was still so mad she'd allowed herself to be the fool. Dabbing concealer under her eyes and sprucing her lashes up with some mascara, she decided on a bit of blush to draw attention away from her red eyes. Then she applied her SPF lip balm.

*You are in control of you*, she reminded herself. *Now, control yourself. No matter what.*

Crestin texted to let her know he was out front. She dashed down the stairs and grabbed a plastic container from the kitchen counter. When she slid into the front seat and buckled, she turned to him and froze. The expression on his face was part incredulous, part angrily annoyed.

"What?"

"Girl. You made your famous chocolate-chocolate cookies last night?"

Everleigh shrugged. "I promised Rita a replacement batch of cookies. I didn't think I would get another chance to deliver on my promise."

"Open up that container right now." When she didn't move, Crestin leveled an impatient glare at her. Realizing he would not leave her driveway if she didn't relent, she pulled back the lid. He reached over and took out two cookies. She frowned at him as she closed the lid. Handing a cookie over to her, he commanded, "Eat up, *cariño*. Less chance that asshole will get to taste any of your delicious treats."

As Crestin drove away, they each ate their cookie in silence. Somehow, it was not a satisfying rebellion.

# Ryker

The last day at The Sunflower Experience was normally his favorite. The day to say farewell to the teenage girls who spent more time on their phones than actually working. By this day, he was sick and tired of picking up their slack. And thoroughly annoyed.

But this year was different. In more ways than one. Miraculously, most of the workers this year were decent. Some were even hard-working. The weather had allowed more good days than usual, creating more revenue for the farm. His parents were thrilled.

And then there was the unexpected Everleigh of it all. A pain in Ryker's ass in the beginning, she'd started to grow on him.

And then she'd become everything to him.

And now she was nothing to him.

As he made his rounds throughout the day, Ryker quickly figured out Everleigh was a floater. At first, he tried to avoid her, to give her space. When he spied her walking down a path in front of him, he diverted to another path. When he heard her laughter as he came up to an intersection in the field—and he could tell she was talking with Crestin, who was also a floater—he turned around and walked the other way. Not without noting the fact that she was laughing without a care. As if she hadn't convinced him just last night that he'd crushed her world.

Ryker decided he would no longer feel bad for any "wrongdoing" Everleigh wanted to place on him in their very short-lived fling.

For being a Monday, it was very busy, with everyone trying to get in before they closed for the season. As the six o'clock hour approached, he did one last loop around the perimeter of the patch. Most visitors had come and gone, just a few stragglers remaining.

As Ryker turned the corner of a path, he froze then stepped behind the cover of the tall sunflower plants. For there, twenty feet ahead of him, were Crestin and Everleigh again. He thought about turning on his heel and walking away, but he also realized this might be the last opportunity he had to see her. To figure out . . . what? If she was okay without him? If she was really that unaffected by their parting?

"Okay, Evs, what are you leaving behind?" Crestin asked.

"What do you mean?"

"Well, you've seen all the souvenirs visitors leave behind on the sunflowers, right? To show they've been here?"

"Yeah, I have."

"Well, now it's our turn. We have to leave our mark."

"I don't know, Crestin. Do I *want* to leave a reminder that I've been here?"

Ryker couldn't see their expressions, but he imagined Crestin giving her a look like only Crestin could.

"Girl. First of all, it's a tradition, and you don't disrespect tradition. And second of all, yes! You want to tell the world Everleigh. Was. Here!" He put special emphasis on the last three words.

After a beat, she asked, "What are you leaving behind?"

"My favorite visor," he stated. "It's going right here. How about you, love?"

She sighed loudly.

Then a moment later: "There you go, girl." Crestin approved. "Let's head up front."

Ryker dipped into the patch of plants and rustled his way to the spot where they'd been standing, concealing himself as they walked past him on the path. When he reached the spot, he remained under cover of the flowers. Sitting atop the big blossom of a tall sunflower was Crestin's purple visor. There, tied around the thick stem of the blossom next to it, was the white patterned ribbon Everleigh always wore in her hair, the sunlight gleaming off the shiny silver border.

Ryker reached his hand out and slid the ribbon between his fingertips.

## Everleigh

"Girl! We are going to the concert of a lifetime tomorrow. Snap out of it!"[2]

Everleigh rolled onto her back and threw her covers down to her waist. Why had she ever told Crestin where the spare key to her house was located?

"I'm sleeping!" she lamented.

"No, you're currently talking to me," he corrected.

She growled as her hands flew up over her face. "I would *much* rather be sleeping."

"Ouch. You're a nasty cat lady. Give me my sweet Everleigh back! Where did she go?" he called toward her feet as he lifted her comforter. "Evs, are you in there? Say 'Pink Pony Club' if you're in there!"

"Oh my God, Crestin!" She kicked her legs in protest, sat up, and snatched the blanket from his hand. Collapsing back onto her bed with a huff, she pulled the covers up to her armpits. He placed a hand on his hip and leveled a look at her. Rolling her eyes, she groaned, "Is this what love feels like? Because if so, I never want to experience it again."

Everleigh had spent the last sixteen hours in bed, still feeling sorry for herself, not wanting to get out and face the world. She hadn't seen

---

2. Matt Hansen, "lesson learned"

Ryker at all yesterday. Not even his shadow. Not that she'd *wanted* to, but there'd been the tiniest hope that he would come to his senses. Realize how wrong he'd been and how he couldn't live without her after all. He'd come up to her and tell her that whatever it took, they'd make it work. And after she made him feel sufficiently bad, she would take him back, making him promise to never treat her poorly again.

But that hadn't happened. And although she'd dreamt of several such scenarios overnight, when she'd woken up this morning, she'd known in her heart none of them would ever transpire. She and Ryker were done. *Done* done. And she felt worse than the day before . . . and the day before that.

Crestin wrung his hands together. "Aww, my baby girl's first heartbreak. In your next era, you can be the Heartbreaker. But—you must get out of bed first. Come, come! Time for some retail therapy." He ripped the covers unceremoniously from her bed. "Let's go to Marla's!"

An hour later, Everleigh was wandering around the racks at Fashionably Rustic with Crestin. It had taken an hour for her to prepare herself to leave the house. No, she hadn't showered. Yes, she had run a brush through her hair. She had brushed her teeth—wait, had she? Maybe? She'd absently stared at the clothes she still had hanging in her closet (most were packed away already), finally settling on a pair of gray joggers and a navy V-neck T-shirt. Despite Crestin's severe disapproval, this was what she'd left the house wearing. And what she'd gone to the town square wearing. And what she'd stepped into a boutique wearing. No one could say anything to hurt her worse than she already felt. Fashion police or otherwise.

She mostly followed Crestin around as he jumped from rack to rack, commenting yea or nay to the items he pulled out and held up to his body.

Near the back of the store, about fifteen minutes into their shopping trip, Crestin spun around to her with wide eyes and a wicked grin. "Evs, do you have your outfit complete for tomorrow?"

"Yeah. I think so."

He jerked his hand out from the rack and held a hanger up between them. She narrowed her eyes. Yes. Yes, this was something. Everleigh reached out and took the fabric in her hands.

"Well, try it on," he urged.

So she did.

***

## Ryker

"Are you good, man?"

"Yeah," Ryker chuckled. "Why wouldn't I be?"

"You know. I've just heard some things. Small town and all."

Ryker gave Tyson a look. "Never believe anything you hear . . ."

"And only half of what you see," Tyson finished with a smirk. "Just know that I'm always here for you, okay? No matter what. We're brothers, you and me. And don't be a stranger."

Ryker set the last box into the back of his truck. *His* truck. He'd bought it yesterday. After finishing teardown at the sunflower patch around three o'clock, he'd still had time to run to the dealership in the neighboring town and execute a purchase agreement for an older model Dodge Dakota. No rust, low mileage, good deal. He'd spent almost all his summer earnings on it, but he felt good about the purchase.

"And you might want to stop in to see Noah before you skip town. He's pretty upset with you."

A scoff shot from Ryker's throat. But he knew he'd go see his friend to smooth things over. Lord only knew what Noah had heard from the Rustic rumor mill.

"Tyson, man, I appreciate you." Ryker reached out and grabbed his friend's hand, giving it a firm shake. "Don't you be a stranger, either. Goes both ways."

"I hear you." Tyson hopped into his car and waved as he reversed a wide arc in the back drive then drove away. His friend wasn't scheduled to move into his dorm for a couple more days, but Ryker appreciated him coming out to say goodbye. With their schedules and sports, it could be next summer before they laid eyes on each other again.

The sound of the sliding door closing drew Ryker's attention. His mom and dad descended the stairs from the deck. She extended her arms before she even hit the bottom step. "My baby boy."

He accepted her hug. "I'm almost twenty-one, Mom."

"But you'll always be my baby." She pulled back but left her arms around his shoulders. "You'll call if you need anything?"

He nodded.

"*Any*thing."

"Yes, Mom," he said around a chuckle.

"And you continue to focus on you and your recovery, and you'll be just fine," his dad inserted.

Ryker nodded.

As he moved toward the driver's side door, his mom walked with him, her arm still around his shoulder.

"I just have to say this," she sighed, turning him so he had to look her in the face. "I don't know what happened between you two, and maybe I'm completely off base here, but I don't think I am."

He swallowed under her scrutinizing stare.

"Ryker. I know you need to keep working on you. You do. But don't mistake the people who come into your life to help you as hindrances. Right?"

He got it. She liked Everleigh. Everyone liked Everleigh.

His mother continued, "It may seem difficult, to fix yourself and let someone in to see your struggles." She reached toward his father, who stepped forward and accepted her hand. A gesture that felt odd to observe. She returned her gaze to Ryker. "But you need to figure it out. In order to truly be happy. Please . . . please think about seeing a professional, okay? You don't realize it now, but you will appreciate it when you see their wisdom in action in your life."

God, he felt so uncomfortable right now. His mother, thankfully, quit talking and pulled him into a tight embrace. "I love you, Ryker."

"Love you," he murmured before he stepped away.

And then his dad came at him. A big man-hug, complete with hand claps on his back. Ryker tried to contain his laughter. "Okay, Dad. Love you, too."

As he pulled out of the driveway, his parents waving goodbye, he knew he had it better than most. He just needed to figure out how to appreciate it enough to keep his life on track for them. For himself.

❧ ☙

The bell rang and clattered against the door, announcing his entrance. He nodded to Mrs. Koeppen at the register.

"Ryker, how are you? Haven't seen you in a while."

"I'm well, thank you. And you?"

"Oh, just dandy. Thanks for asking. Although with the price of lumber, we may just go out of business, you know. But how about this weather we're having? A real hot and humid spell. Of course, it always is during State Fair time. And don't get me started on the first week of school. It's as if the devil knows all those little angels will be trying to study and learn, and he just cranks that heat up. Right?" She finally took a breath and chuckled, a mannerism Ryker had come to expect from Noah's mom.

"I hear ya," he agreed. Then, before she could start on another rant, he quickly added, "Noah working today?"

"Oh, sure. Sure. He's back in the gardening section, stocking shelves."

"Good to see you. Tell Mr. Koeppen I said hi," he said as he headed to the back of the store.

"Will do. You take care now," she called after him.

Six rows down, Ryker turned to the left and spied Noah leaning over, stacking flowerpots. He moved quietly beside him.

"Noah!"

"Argh!" Noah jumped and spun. His shoulders crumpled inward as he exhaled. "*Fuck*, Ryker."

"Hey."

Noah's expression flashed annoyance. "Hey."

Ryker chewed on the inside of his lip as he thought about how to approach this. He understood that his friend was probably upset that he'd gotten further with Everleigh than Noah had. But it wasn't like it was a competition. "So, I'm heading back to campus."

"Good. I mean . . . see ya at break, maybe?"

"Maybe," Ryker confirmed. "Listen . . ." But the right words didn't come.

Noah held up his hands. "Nah, man. Really? Is this the runner-up condolence speech? I don't want any part of that."

Ryker pulled his hand down his chin. "Like, should I be apologizing? What? You tell me, friend."

"Friend. That's just it. *Friend*. I really liked her, man. Like, *really* liked her. And you just swooped in and took her. That's cold."

Ryker didn't feel that was a fair assessment. Everleigh had ended things with Noah before he'd stepped into the picture. Well, as long as you didn't count the night at his Independence Day party. You *couldn't* count that. She'd been drunk and hadn't known what she was doing. And he could have taken advantage of that, but he hadn't. He shook his head to flush out the memory.

"First of all, it wasn't like that—"

"It wasn't like that?" Noah parroted with a shocked look on his face.

"No, it wasn't. Look, I feel terrible that you feel some type of way about all this, but you have to know nothing happened between us until last week."

"*Last week*?" The shock grew, if possible. And there was a measure of distrust mixed in there, too.

"You don't believe me?"

Noah shrugged his arms out from his sides.

"Well, you don't have to believe me. But it's true. And it was nothing really, so there's that."

"But did you kiss her?"

Ryker bit down on his tongue, knowing Noah had never made it that far with Everleigh and not wanting to rub it in his face.

"Did you . . . hook up with her?" Noah pressed.

Ryker was annoyed. He shouldn't have to answer any of this. But Noah was his friend. Had been for years. As such, Ryker didn't want to hurt his pride.

"It was really nothing, man. I'm leaving for school. She's leaving for school. It was nothing."

"So, nothing really happened?" Noah sought affirmation.

Shaking his head, Ryker shoved his guilty conscience down, justifying that it was for Noah's own good. Relief flashed across his friend's face, and maybe even a tinge of . . . hope?

Well past ready to move on from the topic of Everleigh, Ryker said, "Okay, so . . . I've gotta hit the road. Move-in day and all."

"Right, right. Did I tell you I'm taking Kirkwood classes this year?"

"Nah, man. Good for you."

"Yeah. Business management. So I can take over the store someday."

"Nice. Well . . . we'll both be college students this year, huh? I'm proud of you." Ryker threw a playful punch into his friend's shoulder.

"So, when will you be back? Any idea?"

"Ah, yeah. Not sure. Maybe winter break? Maybe summer? I have a lot of work to do, practice and whatnot. So, we'll see. But keep in touch, Noah."

"Yeah, you too." They shook hands, and Ryker walked out thinking maybe he should encourage Noah to go after Everleigh again. She deserved a nice guy like him.

A nice, uncomplicated, upstanding guy like Noah Koeppen was what every girl deserved over a messy, complicated fuckup like Ryker.

# Chapter 23
# When We Don't Let Our Emotions Blind Us

## Everleigh

Somehow, she'd powered through it. She'd wallowed for a couple of days, then shifted her focus back to Hot Girl Summer (as Crestin called it). This was a summer about feeling like herself and living her best life. And it was time Everleigh got back to that.

Today was Chappell Roan Concert Day. A very appropriate day to reset and live in the moment. She'd taken her time curling her hair, applying a heavier hand with her makeup, rubbing glitter lotion on her shoulders and chest, making sure her concert outfit was just right.

When she descended the stairs and went to the kitchen to grab a bottle of water for the road, she found her mom at the table with the laptop. It took only two seconds for Everleigh to realize her mom was on The Rustic Sunflower Experience website, looking at the pictures the professional photographer had captured of them during their visit. Everleigh paused and watched over her mom's shoulder as she clicked through the photos.

There was one of her mom, Saralynn, and Bailey standing on a platform overlooking the sunflowers. The next one featured the girls holding hands as Bailey pointed down from the platform at a flower with a party hat on it.

"Oh, I just love the friendship those two have," her mom said over her shoulder at Everleigh.

"Bailey does seem like a very good friend to Saralynn. I love that she has someone like that."

"Bailey is her Crestin, don't you think?"

Everleigh nodded. "Every girl needs a friend like Crestin."

Her mom continued through the photos. There was one of Everleigh kneeling by the water bucket with the girls as they held their flowers in the water. Another one of the two girls walking hand in hand with their freshly cut sunflowers, and a couple of them chatting and smiling on the straw bales around the corner from where Everleigh and her mom had stood.

"These pictures are so good. The photographer really captured the moments, didn't he?"

"He did," Everleigh agreed.

"I might have to print some of these off, hang them on the wall."

The next picture made Everleigh's stomach constrict. It was Ryker, kneeling in front of the girls, and they were laughing at something he'd said. Then the next picture was Ryker laughing at something Saralynn had said. In the following one, Saralynn had her arms around his neck after he'd lifted her from the straw bale, Bailey looking up at them both with a happy grin on her face as she held both flowers in her little hands. The photographer had followed them all the way to the UTV. How had Everleigh not noticed him that day? The next few pictures were of Ryker carrying Saralynn to the UTV and setting her in it. What pained Everleigh the most was the expressions on her sister and her mom's faces. Smiling at him as he interacted so sweetly with the girls. The joy, the trust, the love Everleigh had for Ryker was written all over her features. She had to look away.

Stepping over to the refrigerator and grabbing a water, she lingered until she was sure her mom had looked at all the photos. When her mom looked up at her, Everleigh knew her face told the whole story.

"Oh, honey. Do you want to talk about it?"

She bit her lip to keep from crying, which would ruin her makeup. She shook her head.

Her mom tilted her head to the side and waited patiently.

"It's just . . . I feel like I did it again. I told myself I was going to trust my instincts and not end up in another situation that was wrong for me, like I did with Noah. And my instincts told me Ryker was bad news. But once we opened up to one another, it really felt right. Like I'd found something I didn't even know I'd been missing. Like he felt the same way too."

Her mom nodded with understanding. "It's tough. Sometimes our emotions blind us to what our instincts are trying to tell us."

That hit Everleigh in the chest, because she knew her mom might be speaking from experience. "So how do I make sure I'm not blinded in the future?"

A frown drew her mom's mouth downward. "My dear child, if I knew the answer to that, we might have lived a very different life over the past few years. But what I do know," she said as she leaned forward in her chair, "is what has helped me recently, and that's trying to set aside the emotions I'm feeling. Trying to look at the situation rationally and ask myself if what's happening makes sense. Logically. Then I know I'm not letting my emotions tell me a story that's not true."

"And that works?"

"It's helped me in a couple of different ways this year."

"Wait a minute—are you saying you are putting yourself back out there? Like dating?"

Her mother tried to keep her smile contained. "Nothing official yet. But there is one gentleman I've been talking to lately, and I think there might be something there."

"Wow, Mom. That's great. I'm happy for you."

"But—we aren't meant to be talking about me, are we?"

Everleigh sighed. "I don't really want to talk about me though. It still hurts too much."

Her mom came over and pulled her into an embrace. "It may hurt for a while too. And that's okay. It means you felt something real. Just give yourself the time and the grace to work through your feelings and learn from the experience, right?"

Everleigh nodded against her mom's shoulder.

"By the way, do you maybe want to grab a sweater to wear over this?"

A laugh bubbled up her throat as her mom tugged at the thin strap of her tank top. "It's a concert, Mom. Not church. It'll be fine."

Rosalynn looked at her dubiously but said no more.

By the time Crestin arrived to pick her up, Everleigh was ready to compartmentalize the hurt for another day and let his pure enthusiasm be contagious. Her own excitement grew simply because of how excited her best friend was. Crestin would make certain this was a night to remember.

⁂

They listened to a Chappell Roan playlist the entire three-and-a-half-hour drive to the Aragon Ballroom in Chicago. They took selfies for ten whole minutes outside the concert venue. Everleigh was starting to feel like herself amongst the gathering crowd of fans who had come to this show with no judgement, no ill will toward one another, no self-consciousness. She'd worried a bit about her outfit as they'd left Rustic, but here she felt . . . part of the scene.

They ate overpriced cheeseburgers from the food vendor, bought Chappell Roan concert tees, and hurried to get to the front of the general admission area near the stage. Everleigh held her white, rainbow-maned pony up as she sang her heart out to "My Kink is Karma" and "Casual." And at the end of the night, after a very satisfactory encore, they drove to her Aunt Bea's house to crash.

Her aunt was so gracious, allowing them to ramble into her house at 11:30 on a Wednesday night. She showed them their rooms, making sure they had water bottles and knew where the bathrooms were. After changing into her pajamas and brushing her teeth, Everleigh curled into bed with Crestin and wrapped her arm around him.

"You really are my favorite human, Crestin. Thank you for sharing this experience with me."

"Girl, same. I was in *absolute heaven* tonight. And—" he grinned "—I got three different contact infos."

"You go, girl," Everleigh said approvingly as she hugged him close. "Can I just stay here tonight?"

He kissed her forehead and tucked her into him. "You'd better not go anywhere."

❧ ☙

Everleigh awoke in the morning to find Crestin gone. She didn't hear the shower, so she trudged downstairs. To her surprise, he and Aunt Bea were in a deep conversation about something or other when she entered the kitchen.

"There she is!" Aunt Bea exclaimed. She pulled Everleigh into a big hug. "Oh, how I've missed my Evie. Come, have some breakfast."

Everleigh joined Crestin at the table and looked at the spread of fruit and Danishes and . . . bacon! She loaded up a plate. Aunt Bea brought over a glass of orange juice and placed it in front of her, then settled in at the table.

"Crestin said you had a splendid time last night."

"We did."

"Crestin also said you can bring me with you when you go visit him in New York City."

"He did, did he?" Everleigh shot him a look.

"Girl, how you never shared this lovely Mama Bea with me, I'll never understand. But now that we are such good friends, you absolutely *cannot* come visit me without her."

"Crestin, you two literally just met."

"What?" He shrugged. "She's my spirit animal. Did you know she crochets purple bucket hats?"

Everleigh chuckled around the strawberry in her mouth. "I did know she is quite the accomplished crocheter."

"And you're not leaving here without bucket hats," Aunt Bea stated.

"Okay, thank you," Everleigh allowed as she took a bite of cheese Danish.

"Ladies, please excuse me while I go shower." Crestin hopped up from the table and skipped upstairs.

"I absolutely adore him," Aunt Bea said.

"As do I."

After an unusually awkward moment of Aunt Bea watching her eat, her aunt finally broke the silence. "And how are you doing, my dear? I feel as though it's been forever since I've seen you."

"I'm doing well. Moving to campus in a few days. Which will be such a change, but I'm ready for it."

"Good. And how is little Saralynn?"

"Oh, we just had a scare with her. She almost tore half her leg off. She got into a tiffle with a glass coffee table, and she ended up with a huge gash in her leg, and there was blood everywhere, and the wound itself was disgusting."

"My poor baby! Is she okay?"

"Yes, she will be. No nerve damage, thank goodness. No surgery needed. Just a lot of stitches."

"Oh, well that's good." Everleigh sensed her aunt watching her again, and she couldn't shake the feeling it meant she wanted to say something uncomfortable. And then she did. "So, I hear you've learned about little Kyleigh's predicament."

Everleigh bristled, but she wanted to allow her aunt some grace, so she replied, "I have, yeah."

"And? Has your father told you how dire the situation is?"

"I mean . . . I guess he has. He came to ask if I would get tested to see if I could donate my bone marrow."

"I got tested," Aunt Bea said quickly, as if trying to say that it was no big deal.

But it was a big deal to Everleigh. A very big deal. Because of all the implications.

"I'm not a match, of course, but I had to try. For that precious little girl, I had to try."

Everleigh stopped eating, swallowing around the lump forming in her throat, and began pushing the fruit around on her plate. She couldn't even process the thoughts zipping around her mind at this moment. She felt betrayed that her aunt was championing her dad's new family. Felt terrible that even her aunt had no problem getting tested to see if she could save a life. She hated her father for putting her in this position. She wished she could save Kyleigh's life as easily as they all made it sound.

"Have you . . . gotten tested yet?" Aunt Bea asked tentatively as she reached her hand out and gave Everleigh's wrist a gentle squeeze.

"I mean . . . not yet."

"But you're going to."

The expectation in her aunt's voice stabbed at Everleigh. "Ah . . ."

She remembered her Aunt Bea was an adult she'd once trusted with her every secret. Everleigh used to love sitting on her lap while her aunt read The Berenstain Bears books to her. She used to run to Aunt Bea when the neighborhood boys wouldn't let her play street hockey with them. Everleigh knew she could trust her now. So she said, "I think I want to, but I'm also scared to."

"Whyever would you be scared? It's a very simple blood test."

"It's not that." Her voice came out small.

"Oh, honey, what is it?"

Everleigh released the secret she'd only told one other person on Earth.

"What if I'm a match, and she dies anyway? Dad will hate me for not saving his precious new baby."

Everleigh couldn't control the flood of tears that broke free. So many tears her vision blurred. Then she felt her aunt's embrace wrap around her—a feeling she'd longed for but hadn't experienced in so long.

"Shh . . . shh, my darling. Your father could never hate you. No one could ever hate you for trying. And that's all they are asking. That we try. To give Kyleigh the same chance at a life that we've all had."

"But—" Everleigh choked out.

"What is it?" her aunt asked tenderly as she returned to her seat and placed her hand over Everleigh's.

"I'm still trying to wrap my head around what he did to my mother. To me and to Saralynn all those years. How he's living a new life with a new family and just . . . discarded us. And now he expects me to be the savior to his brand-new little girl? I just—I can't even—"

Another sob choked her.

"But Everleigh, baby? Listen to me. It's not about your father or the wrong he's done. Lord knows he's done plenty. It's not even about you. Or your mother. And although you've all felt the trauma of his failures, you don't deserve anything bad to happen to you, right?"

Everleigh let that sink in, and she nodded her agreement.

"Right. Neither does this poor little girl deserve what's happening to her. Even though her father has caused so much hurt to others. Do you see what I'm getting at?"

Everleigh did. And in her heart, at this very moment, she recognized that she'd always known. Ever since Ryker had challenged her to be impartial. She'd just needed to get past her trauma to see the reality of the situation.

"And I know you are such a strong girl. You've weathered this storm so well. I hear from your mother what a lovely young woman you've become. Thoughtful, kind, generous . . ."

Everleigh swallowed and wiped the tears from her eyes.

Her aunt hugged her once more. "Ultimately, it's your choice. It's your body. Just know that no one will hate you for trying. And Everleigh?" Aunt Bea sat back abruptly in her chair and bored into her with hazel eyes that reminded her of her father's. "If you decide to get tested, and if you are a match, and if you donate? It doesn't mean you have to forgive your father for anything. These are two very separate things, okay? You can one hundred percent keep your feelings about the person he's been in your life separate from your feelings about helping Kyleigh. Do you understand what I'm saying?" she asked as she screwed her lips to the side.

Everleigh nodded. "I do."

⚘ ⚘

As Crestin drove the last fifty miles home—purple crocheted bucket hat from Aunt Bea atop his mess of brown hair—Everleigh stared out the side window at the never-ending fields of corn and soybeans. She couldn't help but think how the past four days had been the most exhausting of her life. Everleigh had absolutely loved her road trip and the concert with Crestin. But damn. This week had taken it out of her.

Lounging in the passenger seat, her own brown waves flowing beneath the bottom of a baby blue bucket hat, she turned her head in his direction. "Hey? Can we make a pit stop?"

Thirty minutes later, she was knocking on the door, her stomach in knots. She glanced over her shoulder at Crestin sitting in the El Camino. Thoughts of spinning around and heading back to the car battled to the surface. This was a dumb idea. No one knew she was coming.

Just as she began to turn, the front door opened with a snick. And she stopped breathing.

"Oh! My God! Everleigh! Come in!"

And she was pulled down into a crushing embrace. She hadn't realized how short this woman was.

"Come in!" she continued to coo as she took Everleigh's hand and dragged her into the foyer. "Your father is in the living room. He's going to be *so* happy to see you!"

As Everleigh let Bridget lead her into the room, she couldn't help but notice her wiping tears from her cheeks with her free hand. It choked Everleigh up as well.

# Chapter 24

# Fake It Till You Make It

**Everleigh**

MOVE-IN DAY HAD OFFICIALLY arrived. Crestin was flying out to New York tomorrow, so he volunteered his services to help Everleigh and her mom today. Since she was moving into a dorm, she didn't have a lot of furniture. In fact, most of her stuff fit in her car's back seat and her mom's SUV, but it was nice to have Crestin's strong arms to help carry the heavier items—like her dorm fridge—up the four floors to her room. Saralynn tried to help with the lighter things, although she began limping and making a production over her stitched leg as soon as they were in the presence of sympathetic eyes throughout the hallways.

"Baby girl, you sure you don't want to come to the Big Apple with me? I am certain Broadway will snatch you up in no time with these skills," Crestin teased Saralynn.

"What's a Big Apple?"

"The greatest city in the world: New York City," he announced in a grand voice.

"Oh," she said, and her expression became more confused. "Do they have a lot of big apples there?"

A laugh belted from Crestin's belly. "My dear child, I actually do not know. But I will send you a postcard as soon as I get there and tell you if they do."

Saralynn jumped up and down, forgetting all about her injury. "A postcard! Mom—a postcard!"

Their mom nodded. "Won't that be a treat?"

Everleigh unlocked her assigned dorm room, and they filed in.

"Oh! You're here already."

"Hi." Her new roommate waved. "Got here early this morning. I hope you don't mind I took the right side?"

"No, that's fine." Everleigh dropped her armful of belongings onto the bed to the left, wiped her hands on her shorts, then held out her hand. "I'm Everleigh. Nice to meet you in person."

"Abhayankari Singh. Nice to meet you as well. And you all," she said as she looked over the rest of the entourage. She quickly added, "My name is a mouthful, I know. Most people just call me Kari."

"Okay. Kari it is."

"What is your field of study, Kari?" Rosalynn asked as she set a box on the desk by Everleigh's bed.

"Pharmaceutical, I think." Her shoulders pulled up into a shrug. "Or maybe something else in the medical field. Or I might actually rebel against my parents and get an art history degree. I love art."

"Those all sound very interesting," Everleigh's mom replied.

"What about you?" Abhayankari asked Everleigh.

"Political science."

"Law school?"

"Maybe." Everleigh shrugged. "I haven't fully decided on a career path yet."

"And I'm Crestin, by the way," he said as he stepped forward and pulled Kari's slight hand into his large hands. "I am the best friend, so . . . just letting you know that position is already filled. Don't be trying to steal my bestie from me."

Kari released a surprised chuckle. "Oh, okay. Got it. Nice to meet you, Crestin the Bestin."

His left hand flew to his chest as he gasped, "D.N.A. I *love* that. Girl, respect."

Kari's deep brown eyes flickered to Everleigh, who waved a hand and mouthed that she would explain later.

Four more trips, and they had the last of her possessions deposited in the room. Everleigh doled out hugs, allowing her mom to squeeze her extra-long when she heard sniffles over her shoulder. Her mother again told Kari it was nice to meet her and told Everleigh to call if she needed anything, day or night, as she exited the room.

Everleigh closed the door and surveyed the mountain of stuff she now had to put away and organize. Good thing she loved to organize.

"They seem really nice," Kari mused.

"Thank you. I'm really lucky to have them."

"My parents had to work today, so I had to move in all by myself. Restaurants never take a day off, you know."

"Oh, I wish I would have known that. We could have coordinated an earlier time to help you." Everleigh noticed for the first time as she glanced around Kari's side of the room how sparse her roommate's possessions were.

"Didn't take me long."

Everleigh nodded and let her gaze rest on her mountain again.

"Do you want any help?"

"Oh, no. That's fine. I actually really love unpacking and organizing things. If my major doesn't work out, I can always go into business as an organizer."

"I'm glad you said that, because I hate organizing. I like a tidy space, but I don't go much beyond that." Kari sat on the edge of her bed. "Say, there's a freshman mixer tonight. Would you want to go with me? I'm not really one for socializing, but I'm trying to be better, so I thought this might be a good chance to test it out. See if I can push myself out of my comfort zone."

"Sure. But I'll warn you, I'm kind of the same. I tend to keep to myself in a crowd of strangers. We might spend the whole night hovering in a corner if you leave it up to me."

"Oh boy," Kari sighed lightheartedly. "Well, we'll just have to push one another this year, right?"

✺✺✺✺✺ ✺✺✺✺✺

The first full week of school had drawn to an end. Everleigh would like to say she'd thoroughly enjoyed it, but everything felt kind of muted. Like looking through a grayscale filter. She and Kari had gone to the freshman mixer Sunday evening, and they hadn't had much of an opportunity to hide in the corner. There'd been student ambassadors everywhere, pulling people together into conversations, handing out little prizes, pushing people to play the games they'd set up around the grassy area. Everleigh had found herself separated from Kari at one point. She wasn't sure how it had happened. And then she'd found herself surrounded by three boys who came from the same high school in western Iowa. They'd kept trying to draw her into conversation, but she'd kept her answers short and sweet and deflected any chance she could. After about fifteen minutes, they'd lost interest and moved on. Then she'd gone on a mission to find Kari but got pulled into a game of Spikeball (which she was terrible at but actually had fun trying to play). She'd finally found Kari talking with a small group out of the way of the student ambassadors and settled in with them.

Classes were fine.[1] Everleigh had a little anxiety about how much harder it would be than high school. How much more homework and study time would be required. Most of her classes were gen eds, but one was in her major: Introduction to American Politics. She was excited

---

1. Taylor Swift, "Fortnight (feat. Post Malone)"

to be learning something for her major already. And the professor had mentioned a couple of student clubs they could join and meet up with other students with similar majors and share insights, find extra learning opportunities. She'd gone to the first meeting of a club on Wednesday evening, and she'd really liked it. Although there was a disproportionate number of males to females, and she found herself surrounded by boys once again.

She just didn't have the energy to deal with attention from boys. (Even though, as she appraised her reflection in the mirror now, one could also argue she was thirsty for their attention.) It was Saturday evening, and she and Kari were heading off-campus to grab a bite at a restaurant Kari said had food like her parents' restaurant. Everleigh wore her hair in loose curls nowadays. She almost cut bangs earlier this week but chickened out at the last minute and opted instead for a center part, which allowed her waves to frame her face. Since Iowa would only be warm for a short time longer before the fall chill swept in, she'd been wearing shorts, skorts, and skirts. She loved a good V-neck, whether it be a blouse or a tee, and those had been her tops of choice this week. For this evening, she'd selected a navy V-neck, long-sleeve blouse and khaki skort. Birkenstock sandals completed the look.

Everleigh had always worn light makeup, and that hadn't changed. Well, maybe she applied a heavier coat of mascara and reapplied lip gloss more often. But these things she did for herself. Not anyone else. Her self-esteem had taken a huge hit two weeks ago, and after she allowed herself a sufficient amount of wallowing, Everleigh told herself she had to shake it off. She had to take back control of her emotions and her life. And the best way to do that was to look like you felt great. And smile often. Fake it till you make it.

That mantra had allowed her to get through her days, but sitting alone in her room most evenings (Kari had found a club and an intramural volleyball team to participate in) gave her far too much time to analyze the stupid things she'd said and the stupid things she'd done this summer.

Yesterday, she'd had enough moping and decided to check out the recreation center. She'd seen online it had a pool with open swim and multiple diving boards, including platforms. Packing her swimsuit and towel into a bag, she'd headed that way. Once she was suited up and standing at the edge of the platform, Everleigh had felt a calm, comfort blanketing her mind. She'd fallen into her process, thinking through the dive in her mind, breathing, executing. She'd kept the first few dives basic. She was a little rusty. Then she'd progressively increased her difficulty until she was performing competition dives almost on muscle memory alone.

Clearing her mind and focusing on the mechanics of her positions had been freeing. Relaxing. Until the dive that had pushed Everleigh out of the pool, afraid of the thoughts she'd let creep in. That last dive—a forward one-and-a-half somersault with two twists. She'd executed it well, entering the water with little splash. But as she'd sprung up automatically from the bottom of the pool, she'd done something unexplainable. She'd rolled onto her back and let the weight of her body drag her slowly down. Closed her eyes. Waited for Ryker's strong arm to wrap around her and pull her to safety, as he'd done once before. When Everleigh had felt her toes scrape the concrete, her heels touch the bottom, she'd longed for it—for him—until she'd realized she would have to save herself. Her eyes had flown open, and she'd propelled herself swiftly to the surface, gasping for air when she broke above. She'd gathered herself, then swam to the edge of the pool and immediately headed to the locker room.

"Ready for some delicious Indian food?" Kari broke into her reverie as she entered the room.

Everleigh blinked and breathed out at her reflection. "Yes! Let's go!"

Another week and a half of school flew by, and she was finally finding her rhythm. Three classes on Mondays, Wednesdays, and Fridays. Two classes on Tuesdays and Thursdays. Club meetings on Wednesday evenings. Everleigh went to the rec center to dive several afternoons a week between her last class and dinner, spending half an hour to an hour on the platforms (depending on how busy it was) and losing herself in her mind. In a good way. A *productive* way.

She'd made some friends. From her classes, from the club, through the social activities designed to bring students together on their floor and in their building. Kari was still her preferred partner in crime. There was a boy though who she thought could become a good friend. She had no capacity for anything beyond friendship with him, and she tried to make that very clear anytime their conversation took on even a hint of non-platonic talk. He seemed to be cool with it.

She hadn't made it to the home football game last weekend, but she was hoping to this weekend. The big rivalry game was on their turf this year. Everleigh might see if her mom and Saralynn wanted to come for the day and go with her, thinking she could get some extra tickets.

One bad thing about college? The wait to use the washing machines and dryers. It was 9:30 on a Tuesday night, and she was still waiting on her loads to finish in the dryer. At least it gave her almost three hours of uninterrupted time to complete assigned reading and work on writing papers.

Well, not necessarily uninterrupted. Rita Martin sent out a link to the TSE group text. The professional photographer had put together a little montage of staff pictures for the season. At first, Everleigh's heart leapt at the sight of a text in the TSE group; it brought her right back to those long, hot August days in the sunflower patch. But her thumb hovered over the link. Did she want to see those photos? What if there were pictures of Ryker in there? Anxiety gripped her chest as she dropped her thumb on the screen.

Holding her eyes shut tight, Everleigh had to work up the courage to open them. At the count of three, she finally did. She swiped through several pictures without breathing. All very safe. Staff manning the stations. Her and Crestin in the food truck. Mel and her handing visitors their wrapped cut sunflowers. Some outtakes of them trying to get a decent group staff photo (taken on the day Ryker was "sick").

Just when she relaxed and allowed herself to take some joy in the shots of herself and her co-workers having a great time working TSE, a knife stabbed directly into her heart. For the next picture was one she'd dreaded seeing. Ryker, walking beside Everleigh down a path. Her head tossed back in carefree laughter, a smile on his face as he beamed at her. He was reaching toward her in this shot. In the next one, his arms were snaking around her, pulling her into an embrace. Her eyes snagged on his expression, displayed clearly in these pictures.

Suddenly, she was sick to her stomach. How had the photographer captured these photos without them knowing? Would they have acted differently if they had known he was lurking there with his camera? Well, of course they would have. But the fact that they hadn't known they were being watched made the photos seem even more real. Everleigh swiped back to the first picture and analyzed Ryker's expression. Then did the same with the second. She blinked as she realized he'd lied to her. He'd felt something . . . and it was written all over his face. The connection they'd shared had been real.

*So why had he broken her heart?*

Shaking her head, she knew she couldn't live in that space. What was done was done, and she'd moved on. She swiped out of the link without looking at any more pictures.

Fortunately, the dryer cycle was complete, and she loaded her clothes into her basket and headed back to her room. As she pushed through her door, she glanced at Kari's empty side of the room, then walked over and deposited her basket onto her bed. Kari must still be at volleyball. Everleigh hurriedly folded her clothes, thinking how tiresome it was waiting in that hot laundry room and how she just might go to bed early tonight.

She hung her skirts and blouses in her closet. Matched her socks. Folded her T-shirts. She took a stack of shirts over to her dresser and pulled out the second drawer. As she was about to plop them inside, something caught her eye. Something she'd forgotten she'd packed. Setting the stack on top of the dresser, she reached into the drawer and ran her fingers along the shirt. She lifted it out and set it next to the stack of clean shirts, then placed the stack in its spot in the drawer. Next, she traveled down the hall to the community bathroom to remove her makeup, wash her face, and brush her teeth.

Everleigh returned to the room, put her caddy in her closet, stripped down, and headed over to the dresser. She lifted the shirt, slid it on, adjusted the shoulders, and fluffed her hair out of the collar. Before climbing into bed, she paused in front of the full-length mirror. The reflection of Ryker's state baseball championship T-shirt did something to her insides that she couldn't explain. She ran her hand down the front, smoothing the fabric, trying not to think about the last time she'd worn his shirt.

Everleigh climbed under the covers and fell right to sleep.

# Chapter 25
# This Can't Be Happening

**Ryker**

RYKER SAT IN HIS usual spot on one of the couches in the common area on his dorm floor. He had taken to sitting out here most afternoons and evenings. Well, just about any time he wasn't in class, at practice, or at the gym. He'd discovered that the feeling of isolation swiftly crept over him when he sat alone in his room. But if he was alone in the common area—well, then he wasn't alone, not really. People regularly ambled through the halls, and if teammates saw him in here, they often dropped their backpacks, sat on the couches or chairs around him, and chatted for a few minutes.

Three full weeks ago, he'd moved in. And it was great how quickly he'd felt at home again in the athletic dorm. Friends and teammates were in constant supply. Ontario Henry had moved in a day after Ryker, and he couldn't explain how relieved he'd felt when Tari had pulled him into a hug and said how glad he was to see Ryker giving it another go. His friend had promised to go to the gym with him, to be there for him, whatever he needed. And he had been. They went to the gym most days together, alternating weightlifting routines and getting in at least a two-mile-run every morning at the rec center.

Ryker wished he could say he felt as good about his academics. He had been scared to death he wasn't going to measure up once he attended the first days of each new course. Heavy into his major studies, this semester was promising to be his toughest yet. After several class sessions, he was already worried he was going to have to seek out the help of tutors to get him through this year. His buddy, Parker O'Hara—a sophomore and likely starting third baseman in the upcoming season—had promised to help him with his economics class. Ryker wasn't sure why Parker was the best choice for academic help, other than he did seem pretty smart. So, he'd told him he would keep the offer in mind if needed.

The one area Ryker flat out lied to himself about? [1] That he was emotionally grounded. That he was stable enough to make appropriate decisions for his mental health. But he was a damn good liar. So good, in fact, he kept finding himself in bad situations. Ones that were bad for him, anyway. And somehow, he justified his actions away.

The first Friday after the athletes had moved in, he and a bunch of the guys hung out in the common area, some of them drinking, several of them not. Ryne had held his phone in the air and hollered out, "You're welcome, gentlemen! Guess who just got the volleyball girls to agree to come hang out?" Which had been met with a chorus of disbelief, hoots, and hollers. "Yessir, yessir! A whole bunch of 'em are on their way," Ryne confirmed.

And it had been fun . . . for a while. Several of the girls had taken turns chatting Ryker up. But the conversations had all fallen flat, and as more and more of the group started drinking, the less he'd felt like interacting with any of them. Not really wanting to be alone, though, he'd pulled his phone out of his pocket and scrolled through social media. It had become an absent-minded time-filler until he'd come across something on Instagram that made him pause. And feel like he'd taken a punch to the gut.

---

1. TALK, "Run Away to Mars"

There, beaming up at him from his phone screen, was Everleigh with Crestin at the Chappell Roan concert. It was a selfie, mostly just their faces. They were holding up those silly toy horses. Crestin had a pink cowboy hat on. Everleigh's hair was curled, crowned with a sparkling tiara. Ryker had found himself routing to her Instagram page, hungry for more. And he'd been rewarded with several pictures of them before and at the concert. He'd stared at one picture in particular until the image was burned into his memory bank to access at any time: Everleigh, posing for the camera, her brown curls cascading around her shoulders—bare shoulders. She wore a white crocheted tank top that barely covered her, with two strings that tied behind her neck. It was shorter than a midriff and appeared almost backless from the angle of her pose. She wore a pink miniskirt, the toy horse held between her legs, and completely rocked a pair of white, sequined go-go boots. The color scheme made her tan skin glow, and she appeared to be almost shimmering on her shoulder, cheeks, and chest.

Without thinking, he'd taken a screenshot. Then promptly deleted all his social media apps. He wouldn't be able to handle her dimple assaulting his eyes every time he checked his socials. She'd bounced back like she'd recognized she was so much better off now. And that stabbed like a knife in Ryker's chest.

Realizing he'd had enough of the impromptu party, he'd sneaked out of the common area without attracting any notice and headed to his room. As he'd unlocked the door, a soft hand had touched his arm.

"Where are you going so soon?" she'd asked. *What was her name. Miranda?* "Mind if I join you?"

"Ah, I was just going to turn in, actually."

"But it's early. And it's Friday. Do you have anything to drink in there?" She'd sounded like she'd had plenty to drink already.

"Nope. I don't drink."

"Ohhhh," she'd drawled, sounding surprised at first, then maybe a little turned on? Her chest had rubbed against him as she leaned forward and pushed his door all the way open. Then she'd slipped past him. He'd puffed out a breath but followed her in.

What's-Her-Name had sat on his bed. Ryker had stood by the door, arms folded across his chest.

"You don't remember me, do you?" she'd asked, smiling demurely.

Should he have?

"Last spring? Spring Break Fest, the first Saturday of break. We partied all day together, remember? Were on the same beer pong team all afternoon." She'd laughed as she lounged on his bed. "We spent a little time right here."

He'd felt kind of bad, because he didn't remember her. Well, bits of the beer pong, maybe. Ryker hadn't wanted her to feel used, so he'd lied and laughed along with her, if unconvincingly.

"Yeah, we did, didn't we?"

She'd lifted off the bed and come over to him. Started unbuttoning his jeans. "How about a repeat? I quite enjoyed myself the last time."

He'd wanted to tell her no. But her hands were already working their magic on him through the fabric of his briefs, and in his mind was etched that photo of Everleigh. Closing his eyes, he'd let her kiss his neck. When she'd dropped to her knees, he'd kept his eyes closed as he tangled his hands in her blonde hair. As Ryker neared climax, he'd made the mistake of looking down and been pulled back to the reality of straight blonde, not wavy brunette hair. He'd pushed her away, but she hadn't taken the hint. *Maybe Miranda* had grabbed his hand and drawn him over to the bed, pulling off her shirt as she climbed atop his covers. Unhooked her bra. Peeled off her pants. And then she'd retrieved a condom from the pocket of her pants, and Ryker had stood there while she unrolled it on his length. But when she'd put her lips on his, he'd spun her around and set her on her feet facing away from him, adjusting her stance and leaning her forward as he thrust inside her, closing his eyes again. She'd cried out as she braced herself on his bed and met his hips with her own again and again and again, until he could hear her whimpering and feel her reach out and dig her fingernails into his ass. She'd let out a long moan as she arched her back and pushed herself into him, and he was finally able to release his frustration. She'd collapsed onto his bed with a satisfied sigh, and he'd leaned over her, gasping for breath. Only then did Ryker open his eyes.

Then there was the first week of class—Thursday, maybe? The same cute girl who had sat by him during lecture on Tuesday found a spot by him again, striking up a conversation this time. When she'd suggested they go for a drink on Friday, he'd told her he wasn't looking to date anybody at the moment. With a devilish smile, she'd said she wasn't asking to date anybody. After that class, she'd led Ryker to a gender-neutral bathroom down the hall, and they'd fucked so hard against the bathroom door that when they exited, several bystanders stared at them with disapproving glares. She'd grabbed his hand as they walked out of the building and written her phone number on it with a pen. He'd washed it off when he got back to his dorm, but not before Parker caught up to him as he walked across campus. Of course, Parker had noticed it and asked him about it. The less Ryker said, the more Parker—rightly so—assumed it was about a girl.

He justified his actions because *they* had come on to *him*. Same with the third girl he'd met while they were all tailgating before the home football game this past weekend. It wasn't like Ryker was replacing alcohol with sex, because he didn't need it all the time. He didn't seek it out. But he didn't turn it away if it found him.

Never mind the fact that he felt hollow on the inside after each encounter. And that he felt more and more jealous of Ontario as he talked about his girlfriend from home who was coming up to see him next weekend. And of Parker as he talked about this "beautiful freshman girl" he was trying to work up the nerve to ask out.

Once again, Ryker reminded himself he didn't want the distractions of a girlfriend. That it was, in fact, the last thing he needed.

Parker, Tari, and José dropped onto the couch and chairs around the coffee table in the commons area. José, a junior from Puerto Rico, leaned forward, pretending to read the textbook in front of Ryker upside down. "What're you doing, bro?"

Ryker lifted an eyebrow. "Studying."

José nodded and nodded and nodded.

"What, guys?" Ryker said in an exasperated voice, all eyes seemingly on him.

"I mean, nothing," Parker said. "It's just, José here turns twenty-one this weekend. And you know it won't be a party unless you're there, right? You bring the party."

Ryker laughed, somewhat bitterly, and his gaze settled on Tari. The one person who should understand why he could no longer *bring the party*.

"I mean, it's okay," José said with his hands up in the air. "You don't want to celebrate with me? It's okay."

"Shit," Ryker countered. "You know it's not that, man."

"No?"

"Nah, man. I really need to focus this semester, right? You know what I'm saying, Tari."

At that, his friend finally piped up. "I get it, bro. You do you. We get it, right guys?" Tari looked to José and Parker, trying to encourage support.

"Come on, man. It's one night," Parker still insisted.

But Ryker knew what one night could lead to. He shrugged noncommittally.

"Okay!" José slapped his hands in a rumbling beat on the coffee table between them. "Okay, you know what this means?"

Ryker looked at him with raised brows.

"You better be back on that field as our first baseman, right? No excuses, bitch!"

The side of Ryker's mouth hitched upward, and he shook his head slowly, breathed deeply. "Yeah, no excuses, bitch."

"Aaaagh, Ryker!" Ontario jumped up and clasped Ryker's right hand as he threw an arm around him. "You got this, bro."

Ryker nodded as Tari dropped back onto the chair.

Parker turned his attention to José. "Where is this party, anyway? Did you get that figured out yet?"

"Not yet. Got some ideas."

"Dude, you've only got a couple days to get it straight," Tari said.

José bobbed his head. "I got you, Tari. Don't worry."

"Listen." Parker shifted forward in his seat. "I'm thinking of inviting this girl I've been talking to, so as soon as you know, let me know. Okay?"

"I got you," José reiterated.

"It's just . . ." Parker continued. "She's a tough nut to crack, and I've tried just about everything I can think of. Walking her home after our club meetings? She declines. Asking her to coffee to talk about the political landscape? She declines. I've noticed her at the gym, and she did allow me to walk her back to her dorm a couple of times from there, but man . . . even that was a tough sell. I just think, if I can get her in a social situation, where she can see how fun I am? Maybe she'll look at me in a different light."

Ontario held his hands up in front of him and said, "Parker, bro, it sounds like you might be borderline stalking. Maybe she's not the girl for you."

Parker sighed heavily. "I don't know, man. Maybe? It's just—you ever find a girl who doesn't know how beautiful she is, doesn't realize how hard we guys are trying to get her to even notice us? Like, a group of us? And we all walk away feeling decimated at her lack of interest in any one of us? And then you learn more about her, and everything you discover makes you want her more? Like how unbelievably perfect she is? And she doesn't give *two shits* about the fact that you worship the ground on which she walks?"

Sounded a lot like a girl Ryker had recently known. But he turned his attention back to his notes on economics. This was not a conversation he wanted to be a part of.

"Oh, dude, good luck to you, Parker," Tari laughed.

⚘

The very next day, Ryker's world was turned upside down. As he sat in his usual spot in the common area working on homework, he tried to block out Ontario, Jackson, Ryne, and Kepler as they babbled about José's twenty-first birthday party this weekend. He still didn't care about it. Didn't want to be involved.

Parker came sprinting down the hallway and popped his head in. "Listen! Listen. Remember the girl I was talking about yesterday?"

Tari thought for a moment then nodded. The other guys squinted at him. Ryker ignored him.

"Anyway, she's here. I told her I had notes from a class she's taking this year, and she agreed to come over and get them."

Ryker narrowed his eyes, grudgingly pulled into the conversation. "But do you have the notes?"

"Yeah, of course I do." Parker waved his hand dismissively. "That's not a worry. I always keep my notes. The big deal is that she agreed to come over and get the notes! She's on her way here now! And I might die."

Tall, muscular, formidable Parker suddenly appeared small and ill as he pulled at the collar of his shirt, swallowing hard.

The group barked out laughter, deprecating jokes, whistles. Ryker tried to focus again on his homework.

"You guys don't understand. When I bring her in here . . . you'll get it. You'll see." Parker disappeared from the room.

The guys waved their hands dismissively at him as they laughed and continued to make fun. Again, Ryker tried to concentrate on his work. He might have to retreat to his room to get some quiet time.

Moments later, Parker reappeared, but Ryker barely noticed. He tried to block out the introduction of the guys to her. He might have heard his name, but he didn't look up. It was only when he heard Parker say her name he lifted his eyes from the pages of the textbook and really paid attention.

*This can't be happening*, played on repeat in his mind. She was not standing in front of him at this very moment, waving her hand around the circle of boys sitting in the common area.

And yet . . . she was.

Everleigh's gaze tracked around the room. If she recognized Ryker in this group of boys, she didn't show it. Other than the fact that her eyes stopped a beat on his before moving on to the next guy. And at that moment? When her dark-ringed hazels locked on his? His heart quit beating.

He blinked again and again, trying to make sense of all this. And then she was gone, taking her dimpled smile with her. Ryker watched through the windows separating the common area from the corridor, seeing that Parker had his hand on Everleigh's lower back, escorting her down the hall to his room.

Every cell of Ryker's body wanted to follow her down that hall. And yet he knew he could not. Instead, he slammed his textbook closed, bringing an abrupt cease to the group's chatter about how hot Parker's girl was. Amid the raised-eyebrow stares that focused on him, he quickly stood and headed for the stairs. He *could not* be in the same building as her. Knowing she was so close, yet so far away. He pushed forcefully through the front door out onto campus and stalked away from the building.

Ryker didn't understand what he'd just witnessed. How was she here? How could Everleigh be *here*?

Walking a long circle around the block, the implications of her being on the same campus assaulted his brain. How had they never talked about the fact that she would be attending the University of Iowa this fall? They'd talked about him going back to school. They'd talked about her going off to school. Yet they'd *never* talked about the schools they were each attending.

And . . . would it have changed anything? Damn straight it would have. If he'd known she'd be on the same campus? Well within his reach? Every day?

And yet, it couldn't change anything. He still knew he needed to focus on his recovery. On his academics. He couldn't let her be a distraction for him. Because she totally would be. Every day.

Ryker walked for what felt like hours, trying to clear his mind, but the sun shifted too slowly in the sky for it to have been that long. He set his steps in the direction of his dorm. As he neared the concrete stairs to the entryway of his building, he froze in his tracks.

Everleigh was pushing through the glass door, descending the steps with a stack of papers in hand. Her brunette hair falling in loose waves over her shoulders, a black, long-sleeve wrap shirt hugging her body, her tan legs going for miles between her ripped jean shorts and her brown sandals. He hoped she'd keep her gaze diverted as she walked past him and he'd go unnoticed. But as Everleigh hit the bottom step, she looked up, and her eyes locked on his stare.

Ryker saw the moment of hesitation in her stride, observed her recovery, held his breath as she continued like she would walk right past. But at the last moment, she changed direction, marching right up to him. Blinking as she leveled her hazel gaze on his. And he wanted to disappear under her scrutinizing glare.

She inhaled, exhaled. "Ryker."

And his heart soared at the sound of his name in Everleigh's sweet voice. "How, in everything we talked about, did we never talk about what school we were going to this fall?" he asked.

Her mouth twitched at the corner. Finally, she said, "Would it have made a difference?"

He swallowed. How did she always cut right to the truth? Ryker dropped his gaze to the ground between them. Her stare continued to burn into him, even as he refused to look up, feeling so small in her presence. And yet . . . he noticed his hand reaching out toward her wrist. She was mere inches from him. If he could just touch her, he'd know this whole thing was real and not just a horrible nightmare.

As if Everleigh sensed his intent, she took a step backward. "It's a big campus," she commented. "I'm sure I can give you your desired space. I'm sorry if I bothered you today."

She took two more steps backward and Ryker followed, instinctively. "Everleigh, wait."

She stopped moving, and he was now standing over her, looking down into her kaleidoscope irises. Just weeks before, when he'd stood this close to her, her breathing had become labored, her hands reaching out to touch him as if some mysterious magnetic force hovered between the two of them.

Now? Now, he saw the set in her jaw, the resolve in her brow. Everleigh was completely unaffected by his closeness. Ryker wanted to graze his fingers along her arm, down her neck, to make her smile so he could place his fingertip over that dimple. But that seemed impossible now, after everything.

Lifting her hand, she brushed away a lock of hair that had blown across her face, sending a waft of her vanilla scent into the air, invading his senses. As her hand dropped, Ryker caught it, holding it between them. The desire to touch more than her hand burned within him.

With a curious expression, he tapped his finger on the colorful silicone bracelet around her wrist. "Fight with Kyleigh?" he read aloud.

Everleigh pulled her lower lip between her teeth, as if trying to decide if she would confide in him. He noticed she allowed her hand to remain in his. Inhaling deeply, slowly dragging her lip free, she said, "Bridget's co-workers had these made up. To raise money for the medical bills and everything." She looked everywhere but at Ryker.

He sensed that was not all she wanted to say, so he waited patiently for her to continue.

"And . . ." She finally looked at him again. "I . . . got tested. And I'm a match. I'll go in a couple weeks to do the donation procedure. Kyleigh's undergoing a conditioning regimen until then."

Ryker's eyes went wide at this news. Everleigh had actually done it. And pride surged through his chest at her selfless action. "Wow. That's really a big deal."

"I—" She glanced away, like she wasn't sure she wanted to continue, but then returned her gaze to his and said, "I kept coming back to something you said. That if I took away the circumstances of the situation, what would I do? And I believe this is the right thing to do."

Ryker couldn't deny how good it felt to hear her say that. How good it felt to know he had made a positive impact.

But how quickly that feeling disappeared when Everleigh pulled her hand from his. And he had to ask: "So are you with Parker now?"

Her expression flashed annoyance. "I'm not sure how that's your business. But no, I'm not with anyone right now. I'm here to focus on myself and my future. That's what I intend to do."

Relief flooded through him at her words, followed quickly by a wave of anxiety at the thought of Single Everleigh walking around the same campus he did every day. Could he maintain an orbit far enough away from her to keep her off his mind?

"Ryker," she said as she closed the space between them, redrawing his attention to her. Everleigh took a breath, swallowed, then opened her mouth again to speak. "I'm still trying to reconcile the man who showed up for me when I truly needed someone, who fulfilled my every desire, anticipated my every need . . . with the boy from before and at the end of our 'experience.'" She gestured air quotes as she threw his phrase back at him.

He couldn't offer any explanation that would make her feel any better about his behavior. So Ryker asked, "And your determination?"

Her eyes narrowed, as if trying to read his mind.[2] Good luck with that. *He* didn't even know what to make of his thoughts most of the time. Finally, she responded, "Inconclusive."

Everleigh stepped away and continued, "Perhaps that's something you yourself need to make the determination on."

She offered him a smile, but without a trace of her dimple.

And Ryker was annoyed. Because he'd do anything to see that dimple again.

That magnetic pull made him reach out for her as she turned to go. She was too far away, though. He let his hand drop to his side.

Several feet away, side-stepping, Everleigh leveled her gaze on him once more as she called over her shoulder, "I guess I'll be seeing you around, Ryker."

---

2. Birdy, "Surrender"

That night, he lay awake in bed, overthinking the events of the afternoon. In one moment, he could see a clear path forward. In the next, all roads led to disaster. Ryker rolled onto his side, pulled the drawer of his nightstand open, and lifted out the one piece of Everleigh he'd refused to let go. As he wrapped the chevron-patterned white ribbon around his fingers, he wished it still smelled of her vanilla fragrance. And he wished he had an answer about what to do.

The next morning, he fit in a solo three-mile run, a lifting session, and a shower all before breakfast. By nine o'clock, he stepped into Coach Sandoval's office and sat in the chair across from him. By 9:30, he was shaking Coach's hand, a renewed resolve settling in his bones. He took the paper from Coach and exited into the bright September morning sun. By ten o'clock, he was leaving the Student Health Center with a couple of pamphlets and an appointment reminder card for Monday with a therapist.

Ryker checked his smartwatch. He had twenty minutes to get over to the Iowa Memorial Union. He could make it.

Once there, after he stopped and bought a bottle of water from the food court, he was surprised at how calm he felt. Though he'd fully expected to be anxious at what he was about to do, the opposite seemed to be true. Maybe thanks to how helpful everyone had been today, maybe because deep down he knew this was what he should have done all along. He'd wasted so much time trying to prove a point that only really mattered to him.

Walking into the designated room, he was caught off guard by the group gathered there. Because they all looked just like him. Typical college students.

"Welcome. We're about to get started." A young woman who seemed barely older than the group members leaned against a table, gesturing to an open chair. "This your first time?"

He nodded as he took an empty seat in the circle of chairs.

"Great. Glad to have you. Would you like to introduce yourself?"

Ryker slid his eyes around the group of people who could be his classmates, his teammates, his friends. Inhaling a deep breath and wiping his hands down his jeans, he sat forward and said, "Hi. My name is Ryker. And I'm an alcoholic."

# Dying to know what happens next?

Read on for scenes from
*After the Sunflower Experience*

# Never Met a Girl Like You

## Parker

As he wove his way through the students on the sidewalks between his dorm and hers, the butterflies started kicking up their incessant fluttering.[1] He rushed through the entryway and onto the elevator, pressing the number four. By the time the elevator doors opened on the second and third floors to let people on, he regretted not just taking the stairs. He checked his hair one last time using the camera app on his phone, then shoved it into his pocket when a loud ding announced his arrival on the fourth floor. Excusing his way past the several people now between him and the door, he exited the elevator. Inhaled a deep breath. Exhaled to settle his nerves.

Parker O'Hara had always been kind of nervous around girls, but not one he'd met in his entire nineteen years made him as self-conscious and unsure of himself as Everleigh Wilson did. To make matters worse, she'd barely given him the time of day when they first met in the Political Science Club that gathered every Wednesday evening in Schaeffer Hall. From the first moment he laid eyes on her, he was in awe of her beauty. Even more in awe that she had no idea how pretty she was and seemed completely oblivious to the fact that all the straight men in that room

---

1. Edwyn Collins, "A Girl Like You"

were shooting their shot at her. She had some sort of impenetrable barrier around herself, an air of disinterest that only fueled the desire Parker had to know more about her. Like where did she come from? What would make her lips break into a full grin? Coax a laugh to escape her throat? And what did those full pink lips taste like?

He'd made sure to get a seat next to her at the table when that first meeting was called to order. Then in the span of ten minutes, he'd collected several facts about Everleigh Wilson. One: She smelled deliciously like vanilla. Two: Her shimmery brown hair framed her face and her beautiful hazel eyes as it fell in soft waves well past her shoulders. Three: Her soft, lilting voice did not have an accent of any kind, so she was likely from the Midwest, like him. Four: She had a habit of twirling her pen around the graceful fingers of her right hand, showing off pale blue fingernail polish that sparkled in the light. Five: She preferred to listen and observe rather than speak out and lead the group conversations. He wondered if that was because she was shy or because she was always gathering information to use down the road at a time that suited her needs. The latter would make her an excellent attorney one day if that was the case.

Six: He had to figure out what would draw her to notice him.

When the group dismissed at the end of the meeting, he'd tried as nonchalantly as he could to suggest he walk her to her dorm, for safety reasons. She'd politely declined. He'd followed up with an offer to grab coffee one morning between classes; he could give her advice about the poli sci program. She'd seemed to give it a brief thought—but politely declined again. As he'd watched her walk out the door of the meeting room—her short skirt swaying around her thighs, her long, tan legs picture perfect—it was all he could do not to run after her with some excuse to get her attention. But part of him had known that would only drive her further away. She was closed off for a reason, and he would have to bide his time to figure out why and crack that impenetrable façade.

Parker had tried to walk her home from Poli Sci Club again the next week. She'd replied, "I'm good, thank you." He'd once again offered to grab coffee with her, suggesting they could continue the discussions started during the meeting. She'd responded that she was super busy this week, maybe some other time. Which had given him a huge amount of hope. *Maybe some other time* wasn't an outright no.

And then Parker couldn't believe his luck when, as he was heading out of the rec center after a workout the very next afternoon, he'd spotted Everleigh climbing up the ladder and exiting the indoor pool through the glass walls between the main track area and the pool. First of all, that girl in a one-piece swimsuit was a sight to behold. Her straight shoulders gave her a poised presence, her body curving in all the right places. Curiosity had pulled him toward the glass partition as she turned to her left and headed in the direction of the diving platforms. He'd watched her climb the nearest platform, one tall enough it would make him think twice about diving from its height. But she'd gracefully walked to the edge of the platform, turned her body around, and positioned the balls of her feet on the lip of the surface. Her shoulders had lifted and lowered as he assumed she was taking a deep breath, and then a second later, she'd bent her knees and propelled herself airborne with ease, twisting and somersaulting all the way until just before the water's surface, where she'd straightened her body into a perfect line and entered with barely a splash.

Parker was certain his jaw had fallen to the floor, and he'd lifted his hand to close his mouth and dragged his fingers down his chin as he processed what he'd just seen. Everleigh was more amazing than he'd thought. In addition to all the other incredible things about her, she could dive like an Olympic athlete. What else could this girl do?

As her hands had emerged from the water and clasped around the metal bars of the ladder, Parker had known he couldn't let her catch him staring at her, drooling over her. He'd ducked over to a bench nearby that faced the track but would allow him to watch her from time to time over his shoulder. He wasn't trying to be a creeper, but his thirst to know everything about her was almost consuming him. She'd only performed three more dives—all spectacular in his layman's opinion—before she headed to the locker room. And he'd decided to take the chance that maybe today was the day she'd allow an actual conversation to occur between the two of them.

When Everleigh pushed through the glass door from the pool area, he'd leapt from his seat on the bench and hurried over, coming up alongside her and acting like he was simply heading in the same direction. He'd done an exaggerated doubletake and turned toward her, furrowing his brow.

"Everleigh? Right?"

Her head had swiveled toward him at the sound of her name, and she'd slowed her step. A look of recognition had swept across her face, and Parker had been thoroughly pleased there was no trace of annoyance or disdain in her features. That was good. That was really good.

"Yeah," she'd said, offering a little smile. "Parker, is it?"

He'd nodded, trying to keep his insides calm as they started rioting at the sound of his name tumbling from her lips. This was his opportunity, and he couldn't mess it up. His mind racing, he'd pulled out a thought and went with it. "Crazy running into you here. I just got done with a baseball workout. You?"

If he wasn't mistaken, she'd seemed to hesitate a step, so he'd slowed as well. Her brow lowered, she'd responded, "You play baseball?"

"I do. Second year actually. You like baseball?"

"Um, I've never really been into it, no."

*Dammit.* He'd cursed himself for giving her something to not like about him so soon. He'd thought for sure she'd be impressed he was a college athlete. It took a lot of hard work and dedication to keep up with his schoolwork and clubs as well as his lifting and practice schedule, even in the off season. That showed his drive and organizational skills. But it fell flat on her, so he'd tried something else to salvage the conversation before she had a chance to excuse herself.

"You came from the pool. Are you a swimmer?"

"Not part of the team, if that's what you mean," she'd said as she ran her hand through her damp hair, pushing it over her shoulder. "I come here to dive some afternoons."

"Diving?" he'd asked, as if he hadn't just watched her for the last fifteen minutes.

She'd nodded but didn't expand.

"But not part of the diving team?"

She'd shaken her head. "I used to dive competitively. I didn't realize how much I missed it until I found out anyone could use the pool and the platforms, so I decided to have a go at it."

Parker had wanted to tell her how amazing a diver she was, but that would let on that he'd been creeping. Not a good foot to start off a relationship. Instead, he'd said, "I'm sure it's a great way to stay in shape."

"Sure, but that's not why I do it."

"It's not?"

She'd shaken her head again. "I like how it calms my mind. Helps me reset from the stress of classes and . . . whatever."

"Nice. Hopefully class isn't too stressful yet. The year's just started."

"Oh, yeah. Not bad. Well, that first week kind of was, trying to find my buildings, the classrooms, worrying about what college classes would really be like." She'd looked up at Parker, almost as if seeing him for the first time. "Can I ask you something?"

"Sure. Anything." He'd cursed himself again for sounding way too enthusiastic. Thankfully, she hadn't seemed to notice.

"When did you feel comfortable on campus? Like you weren't a stranger in a strange land?"

"Huh," he'd said as he thought about her question. "I think I was always comfortable on campus. Maybe because I was part of a team, and we moved in ahead of everyone else. It was like having a big group of brothers to show me the ropes."

When he'd seen her brow still furrowed, he'd felt like he had the opening he'd been hoping for. He once again tried to be as nonchalant as he could muster. "You know, if you ever have any questions about classes or campus, or anything really, you can ask me. I've been through the grind for a year. Full of knowledge." He'd lifted his hand and pointed at his face, giving her a goofy grin, which brought a real smile to her face. And he'd noticed for the first time she had a dimple in her right cheek. He'd also noticed that they'd walked for two blocks already together. "If you want, I can walk you to your dorm and answer any questions you have."

"Oh, you don't have to do that," she'd replied in a rush. "I don't want you to go out of your way."

"What dorm do you live in?"

"Hillcrest."

"That's right beside Petersen, actually. Not a big deal."

She'd seemed to accept that, which made a supreme happiness bloom inside Parker. He was stretching out his time with her. As they'd crossed the bridge over the Iowa River to the western side of campus, he'd pressed his luck. "We could stop at the dining hall on the way, if you aren't doing anything. I'm kinda hungry after that workout."

She'd seemed to bristle at that, and he realized he'd gone too far too fast. Before he could walk it back, she'd said, "That's okay. I have a lot of homework actually, so . . ."

"Oh, yeah. I get it. No worries." He'd caught himself before he tacked on *Maybe another time*. That would have been too presumptuous.

To his relief, she'd still allowed him to walk her to the front entrance of Hillcrest. She'd seemed comfortable enough to ask him questions about campus, about the law building, about how sophomore year classes compared to freshman year. By the time they'd said their goodbyes, he'd felt like her walls were coming down just the tiniest bit. He'd felt like he'd succeeded in getting Everleigh to trust him the slightest bit more. But at the same time, he recognized how monumental a task it would be to get her to open all the way up to him.

And yes, he may have sought her out at the rec center every day after that, hoping to find her on the diving platforms so he could "chance" running into her again and offer to walk her home. He did luck out once, on the following Monday, crossing paths with her as she exited the building. To his delight, she'd seemed pleased to see him. It had been easier to get her talking that time. Honestly, she seemed to do more listening than talking, but she'd let him ramble on without seeming annoyed with him.

During Poli Sci Club on Wednesday, he noticed she'd opened up more during the discussions, welcoming more side conversations with Parker about some of the topics. This time, when he'd asked to walk her to her dorm, she hadn't hesitated before saying yes. On the sixteen-minute walk from Schaeffer Hall to Hillcrest, the conversation had flowed easily. When he'd offered to give her his notes from the Intro to American Politics class she was taking this year, she'd seemed to jump at the offer. When he'd asked her to grab coffee with him the next morning, she'd drawn a line by saying, somewhat mysteriously, "I don't think that's a good idea." Her tone kept him from inquiring further.

The best part of getting her to swing by his dorm to get the class notes hadn't been the fact he'd gotten to show off his hot crush to his teammates. It was that Everleigh had actually spent a solid hour hanging out in his room. The first five minutes had been awkward. He'd sensed she regretted coming over, catching her looking at his closed door multiple times, almost as if looking beyond it to what was on the other side. After he'd handed her the stack of notes though, he'd managed to draw her out, and he'd watched her settle in somewhat. Gradually, she'd allowed him to pepper her with more personal questions than they had touched on so far. He found out about her mother, Rosalynn, and her little sister, Saralynn. But when he asked about her father, she'd said simply, "He doesn't live with us." Then she'd turned the tables and asked him about his family, his hometown, his thoughts about being on a collegiate baseball team. By the time she said she needed to head out, they'd both been sitting on his bed, a foot or so apart. Her body language had been relaxed, open. So, he'd once again decided to press his luck.

"A group of us are tailgating on Saturday ahead of the game. Would you want to join? I could introduce you to a bunch of my friends. There'll be games and drinks, and it's always a great time. Have you been tailgating before?"

"I have not," she'd hedged. "I was going to ask my mom and sister to come to the game with me. With it being the big rivalry game against Iowa State, I thought they would really enjoy it."

Parker had nodded, stuffing down his disappointment.

"But I haven't talked to them yet, so I don't know if they can." Everleigh had pulled her lower lip between her teeth, and Parker wanted to reach over and tug that lip out with his thumb. "Who all will be tailgating?"

There was something in the squint of her eyes that had raised a question in his mind, but he couldn't put a finger on what he was seeing, so he'd ignored it. "Pretty much the entire squad tailgates together. A team-building activity, if you will."

"Is tailgating a coach-approved form of team building?" she'd asked dubiously, almost as if she knew Coach Sandoval's strict rules on the subject.

Parker had shrugged. "I mean, we don't log *all* our activities with our coaches. But hey, they tell us to spend as much time as we can together. Solidify our bonds. All that B.S." The smirk he flashed had drawn a smile from Everleigh, popping that cute dimple into her cheek. Every muscle in his body pulled toward her. His mind had been overtaken with thoughts of tasting her lips, slipping his tongue between them. He'd felt himself moving in slow motion.

Suddenly, she'd jumped up from his bed. Cleared her throat while pushing her hair behind her ear. "I'd better get going. Thanks for the notes. I really appreciate it." She'd held up the papers as she backed toward his door. Parker had lifted from the bed and followed her, angry with himself for being an idiot and scaring her away so soon. How much damage had he done to her trust in that brief moment he'd lost his senses?

"Anytime," he'd said as he caught up to Everleigh, reaching around her to open the door. He noticed she angled her body slightly away from him and felt her walls reconstructing. "Ah, listen . . ." He'd placed his hand on the edge of the door as he held it open and leaned his upper body into it. His mind was a scramble, trying to come up with something—anything—to salvage this situation.

She'd spoken up immediately, lifting a hand between them. "I'll let you know if I can tailgate. If my family can't come, I think it would be fun. And it would be good for me to make more friends. Would you mind if I invited my roommate, Kari?"

"Kari?"

"Abhayankari. She goes by Kari."

Parker had nodded. "Sure, invite anyone you want." *If more people make you feel more comfortable coming to the tailgate, bring everyone.*

"Okay. I'll let you know."

"Here. Let me put my number in your phone." At her startled expression, he'd reassured her, "So you can text me to let me know."

A noticeable blush had crept up her cheeks as she said a hasty "Of course" while handing over her phone. He'd quickly typed in his contact info, trying hard not to let his eyes wander with curiosity over what other apps she had on her phone's home page. But he still noticed the standard social media apps, email, music. She had a large tile at the top that showed photos, and his eyes had stuck on the photo of Everleigh, gorgeous as hell, scantily clad next to a cute, rather large guy with a pink cowboy hat on his head. The desire to ask her about the picture had swelled within him, barely contained.

She must have noticed his eyes lingering, and she'd pulled the phone from his palm. Lifting the papers in her hand once more, she'd said, "Thanks again."

As she turned to leave, it had taken everything in his power to remain stock-still against his door. He'd wanted to walk her out. He'd wanted to ask her to eat at the dining hall with him this evening. But he'd known he needed to give her space or she might just keep walking away and never come back. Someone had hurt her—possibly that guy in the photo—and she hadn't gotten over it yet. He'd have to tread very lightly when it came to Everleigh Wilson.

Hard as it was, Parker had vowed to give her that space. Even though he'd noticed her diving at the rec center on Friday, he'd stifled his craving to wait for her after his workout, to walk her home, and he'd left while she was still on the diving platform.

And it had paid off. Friday night at 9:36 p.m., his phone had dinged. The text message bubble read Unknown. He'd quickly swiped into it.

*Hey, it's Everleigh. Can I still RSVP myself and Kari to tailgate tomorrow?*

*Absolutely!* He'd typed, then promptly deleted the message. Instead, he sent: *Sure.*

*Great! What time and where?*

*It's an afternoon kickoff, so we'll start tailgating by 11. I'll swing by to pick you up just before that. What's your room number?*

Three dots chased each other in a bubble for what felt like forever. Was it too much to suggest he'd pick her up? Did she think he meant it to be a date? Was she worried about giving him her room number? What was taking so long for her to answer?

The message had finally materialized, and he'd let out the breath he hadn't realized he'd been holding. She'd responded, *414. See you then.*

Parker had pumped his fist into the air and Ontario, Ryker, and José had stopped their conversation and stared at him.

"You good, man?" Ontario asked.

"I. Am. Fantastic!" The grin plastered across Parker's face was still there when he woke up the next morning.

Now, as he stood in front of Room 414, he took one last steadying breath before he knocked on Everleigh's door. He couldn't let on how excited he was to be hanging out with her today. In his mind, this was monumental. They'd be spending all day together, and with any luck, when he extended the invitation to José's birthday party this evening, she'd accept and they would spend all night together as well. Getting to know one another on a deeper level than the surface questions she'd allowed him to ask so far. He could hardly wait to know Everleigh so much better. He was certain she would continue to amaze him the more he learned about her.

He reached a hand up and knocked. After a moment, the door swung open and Parker was met with the most beautiful smile in the entire world, complete with a tiny dimple of joy.

# I Guess I'll Be Seeing You Around

## Everleigh

Introductions made, Everleigh, Kari, and Parker started the walk over to the place where his group was tailgating. Across from Kinnick Stadium was a row of houses converted into student apartments. Parker informed them that one such old brick house had a very large side yard where cars packed in as many rows as they could fit, tables of food were shared, and cornhole and all manner of drinking games were played ahead of football kickoff. That's where they were headed.

As they walked, Everleigh tried to focus on the conversation Parker was leading, but she often found her mind wandering as she let Kari do more of the talking with him. Everleigh's stomach had been twisting and turning all morning in anticipation of what the day would bring.

First of all, she sensed Parker wasn't picking up on the *I-Just-Want-to-Be-Friends* vibe she'd been trying to convey. He'd proven to be a good friend to her, giving her valuable campus and class information, making her transition to campus life a little easier. He was very easy to talk with. But there was an underlying tension in his mannerisms, his aura. She might have been off base, but she'd thought he was leaning in to kiss her the other day as they sat on his bed, so she'd quickly leapt up to put a stop to any kind of awkward situation. As much as she'd thought this tailgating event would help push her to meet more people, make more friends, she worried it might send the wrong signals to Parker. Like that she wanted to be more than friends with him. Which she did not.

It had taken her fifteen minutes to text him last night that she and Kari wanted to come along today. She'd kept rewriting her message. Trying to word it in a way that sounded completely platonic. In a way he couldn't read any subtext into. But his expression when she'd opened the door to him a few minutes earlier told her he'd still found subtext. She'd dropped her smile quickly, replacing it with a more neutral expression. She'd have to be very cognizant of her behavior toward him today to ensure everything communicated *Just Friends*.

Secondly, and maybe more importantly, she was concerned Ryker would be among the teammates at this tailgating event. Short of coming right out and asking Parker, she'd asked in general who would be there, and he'd said, "Pretty much the entire squad."

Once the initial shock of unexpectedly coming face to face with Ryker Martin on Thursday afternoon had subsided, the stab of pain at his rejection had flared again in her chest. To say it was an absolute gut punch to see him sitting there, ignoring her presence, would be an understatement. But then, after he'd heard her name, she'd seen one pure moment of emotion on his face as his eyes snapped up from his textbook. She'd averted her eyes just as quickly, not wanting to allow him the satisfaction of catching her watching him. So, she'd swept her gaze around the group as she waved hello and forced her eyes to move away from his when he captured her stare, her heart squeezing in her chest.

But then she'd found herself looking beyond the closed door of Parker's room as they sat and talked, wondering what Ryker was doing at that moment. Was he telling his friends he knew her? Was he thinking about her at all? Or had his mind shifted back to his studies as soon as she'd left the room, effectively leaving her in his past? As much as she didn't want to care, when she'd left Parker's room an hour later, she'd found her head turning toward the wall of windows in the common room, her gaze searching for Ryker sitting in the same spot on the couch with his textbook. Wondering if she could catch his eye as she passed, if she could read something in his returning stare.

Not that she even knew what she'd hoped to find there. He'd made it clear that after The Sunflower Experience ended, they ended. So why was she torturing herself by caring what he might think of seeing her now? To her relief, the spot Ryker had filled on the couch was empty. She'd allowed herself to relax just a bit, to push thoughts of him out of her mind. But one nagging thought had remained: The fact that Ryker had been in the very dorm beside hers this whole time. That he had most likely been eating in the same dining hall she had, every day. And somehow, their paths had not crossed before that moment.

Descending the steps down to the main floor, she'd exited through the front doors into the warm September air. Everleigh had inhaled a cleansing breath and lifted her head to let the sunlight soak into her skin. She'd dropped her attention to the steps, lifting her head again once she hit the last one.

That's when she'd seen him. Standing mere feet away, a look she couldn't interpret sweeping across his face. Her body had nearly jolted to a complete halt at the impact of his tall, muscular frame standing before her, hands shoved into his pockets. His brooding gaze snagged hers and held it hostage until she forced herself to look away, in the direction she intended to walk. She'd taken several steps in that direction, trying to block him out of her mind, to ignore the riot of emotions he'd stirred within her. But suddenly, her feet had betrayed her and turned toward him. Much to her dismay, she'd craved some kind of closure to allow her to move past the heartbreak, the feelings of betrayal and abandonment after he had offered her a glimpse of love in a safe space. She'd needed some answers on how his feelings for her disappeared quicker than they'd appeared. Which might then help her to understand how she could have let him so far deep into her psyche when her instincts had warned her off from the beginning.

Once again, it came back to the whole debacle being her own damn fault. Maybe that's what Everleigh hated most about it—that she couldn't blame Ryker for anything.

She was proud of herself for keeping her cool during their exchange.[1] Keeping her anger and frustration and disappointment hidden under the surface of her words. And had she imagined it? The way his body had still seemed to pull toward hers? She'd felt overcome with dizziness as he stepped closer until he was nearly standing over her. As Everleigh's heart slammed against her chest, she'd tightened her jaw and squared her shoulders, forcing an armor around herself, keeping the onslaught of his cedarwood scent and dark, intense gaze from reaching the cozy part of her mind she used to reserve only for him. When the breeze lifted a lock of hair across her face, she'd reached up and secured it behind her ear. And as her hand had fallen to her side, Ryker had captured it midair in his strong, workworn hand. A hand that used to tease amazing feelings from the depths of her body. Her thoughts had jumbled as she struggled to keep her composure with his touch burning into her skin and his eyes brooding on hers. She'd had to tear her gaze away to keep from melting into him. How embarrassing that would have been, knowing he no longer wanted her in that way! But when he'd asked her about Kyleigh, she couldn't help but tell him about taking the bone marrow match test and about being a match. Because it was Ryker who had helped her see the right answer in that situation: that she did want to try to help save her little half-sister's life from the terminal leukemia if she could. She'd wanted to give Ryker the credit he was due.

---

1. Gracie Abrams, "Friend"

She'd pulled her hand from his grasp at that point, because she'd suddenly felt the need to put a lot of distance between herself and Ryker's perfect body. His elation at her confession had swept an endearing expression across his face, which made her even more confused at the emotions stirring inside her. But the next words out of his mouth had stripped all those emotions down to anger.

"So are you with Parker now?"

He'd actually asked her that. Number one—why would he think she was "with Parker"? And number two—what business was it of his if she was? Ryker had given up all rights to that kind of information weeks ago. She'd told him as much. Told him her sole focus was on her studies and her future, which was the truth. But why did a little voice at the back of her mind whisper that Ryker just might prove that statement a lie?

Everleigh didn't need mind games distracting her from her goals here at the University of Iowa . . . but when he was standing in front of her once again, she'd realized she did want to know something. She wanted to know which version of Ryker was the real one. Would he be honest with her if she asked? Thinking about the professional pictures that captured their intimate moments at TSE, the unfiltered expression on his face in those photos, she'd wondered—was he capable of being honest with himself?

So in a moment of strength, she'd stepped up to him, leveling a cool look into his amber eyes as she said, "I'm still trying to reconcile the man who showed up for me when I truly needed someone, who fulfilled my every desire, anticipated my every need . . . with the boy from before and at the end of our 'experience.'" She'd gestured air quotes as she threw his phrase back at him.

He'd proven he couldn't be honest with either of them when he gave a nonanswer: "And your determination?"

As she tried to read him, it'd felt as though he might be as confused as she was about his behavior. But why wouldn't he just say so? At the same time, she recognized the last thing she needed was for him to say anything that might confuse her, might trick her mind into pining for him again. So she'd returned his nonanswer with her own: "Inconclusive." Then decided it was time to leave Ryker behind for good. It was clear her attempt at closure was going to be fruitless.

Everleigh had started to walk away, then turned to throw one last dig at him. "Perhaps that's something you yourself need to make the determination on." A thrill of victory had surged through her at the look that flashed across his face as his jaw dropped the slightest bit. She'd gotten to him. Several feet away, in the emotional high of putting him in his place, Everleigh had side-stepped so she could level her gaze at him one last time, calling out over her shoulder, "I guess I'll be seeing you around, Ryker."

Now, as she realized that parting shot was more accurate than she'd anticipated, her mind was on overdrive about how any interaction between them could go. Or would he simply avoid her? As they walked past the front of the brick house and into the side yard where everyone was gathered—music blaring, the delicious smells of grilled food and crockpot sides wafting on the air, the faint sounds of cans cracking open at intervals amongst the laughter and din—she saw she wouldn't have to wait long to find out.

The group Parker led them to was centered around Ryker himself. He was pointing around the circle, calling out names. "Ryne, you're with Tari. Kepler, you're with Jackson." He caught sight of Parker as he joined the group and said, "Perfect. Parker you're with—" His voice faltered as his gaze fell on Everleigh. He swallowed. A hint of satisfaction that her presence had flustered him blossomed within her.

Clearing his throat, Ryker recovered and asked, "You girls want to play cornhole?"

"Definitely," Kari spoke up before Everleigh had a chance to politely decline. She knew she'd come here today to make new friends, but she would rather have Parker at her side introducing her to people than have to make awkward small talk as she made a fool of herself trying to play cornhole (a game she was *not* good at).

"Great," Ryker chirped, then his eyebrows shifted a fraction as if an idea had come to him. "You'll be on my team . . . what's your name?"

"Kari."

"Kari?"

"That's it," she confirmed.

"Got it." He then pointed at Everleigh and said, "That means you're partners with Parker." Who drew her attention when he let out a cheer of approval and beamed at her. Then she heard, "What's your name?" come from Ryker's mouth.

Head snapping in his direction, she wanted to scoff at his gall, at the tiny smirk pulling at the corner of his mouth. But she realized she didn't really want people to know their history either, so she played along.

"Everleigh."

"Emily?" he asked as he craned his neck as if to hear her better.

She cleared her throat in annoyance and stared daggers into him as she repeated, "*Everleigh.*"

"Got it. Ellie, you're on this end of the boards with me." He motioned to the first set of cornhole boards beside them before he pointed to the other end. "Parker, you and Kari get the opposite end."

# "Friends"

## Ryker

EVERY CELL OF RYKER'S body was vibrating.[1] The steady sound of small, square bags filled with dried corn kernels hitting wooden boards in the grassy area between the rows of vehicles filled the space around him, and all he could think about was what to say to Everleigh. He was surprised she'd followed his lead and acted like she didn't know him, like this summer had never happened. He'd expected her to call him out in front of his friends, which he probably deserved. He'd been admittedly relieved when it didn't happen. He didn't know if it was because she'd forgiven him for being such an ass, if she was willing to give him another chance, or if she truly wanted to act like she'd never met him.

On Thursday night, Ryker had wondered how quickly he would run into Everleigh on campus again, especially when he'd watched her walk away from him and seen her turn left at the end of the block toward Hillcrest Hall. The dorm *right next to his*. The dorm where he often ate his meals. The thought of her in such close proximity sent zings of hope through his chest. Likely a very far-fetched hope, given the fact she'd said with conviction she wasn't looking for a relationship with anyone.

---

1. Eliza & The Delusionals, "Pull Apart Heart"

Ryker thought Parker must not know Everleigh didn't want a boyfriend right now. That or he did but was choosing to go after her anyway. Ryker could see it in the way Parker's gaze was always on Everleigh today. The way he squeezed her shoulders and wished her good luck before moving to the opposite board with Kari. Parker definitely wanted to be more than friends. And suddenly Ryker worried Everleigh might have only told him she wasn't into Parker because she didn't want him to know. Ryker completely understood if she wanted him to keep his nose out of her business after the way things had ended between them. But that didn't mean he would respect her wishes on that front.

"Are you sure there's nothing between you and Parker? I see the way he's been watching you," Ryker threw out of the side of his mouth, pretending to focus on the board across the way.

She paused as she was about to toss a bag, her right hand outstretched. She looked at the ground, shook her head, then stood upright. "Stop trying to distract me."

As Everleigh moved into her form again, Ryker allowed her to toss the bag over to the other board. It fell right on the lip of the board, resting on the ground. "That one doesn't count," he pointed out.

She glared at him as he tossed his first bag. It entered the hole without even touching the sides. "I know that, thank you. I do know how to play cornhole." She pulled her arm back and tossed her second bag into the air. It sailed past the board and landed near Kari's feet. "I just suck at it."

Ryker tossed his second bag. It landed in the middle of the board and had enough momentum to slide up and into the hole. He suppressed a laugh when Everleigh cursed under her breath.

She prepared to throw her third bag. "You should take a step forward," he suggested. She ignored him and sent her bag through the air. It hit right beside the first bag. When she stood upright, he caught her glancing at him from the corner of her eye.

"Watch me," he said as he tossed a bag into the air with a perfect arc. It hit the back of the hole and dropped in. He straightened and smiled, lifting his palms in the air. "Just like that."

"Oh my God," she scoffed as she folded her arms across her chest. "I do *not* need any lessons of any kind from you. Best believe."

Ryker quirked a brow. "If I recall, my lessons have taught you quite well in the past."

She opened her mouth to retort, but Parker's voice interrupted. "What's the hold up, guys?"

She tore her icy glare from Ryker and waved a hand in the air. "Nothing! Sorry!" she called in response. Yet he noticed her take one small step forward before she tossed her last bag across. And it landed solidly on the board, just inches below the hole.

"See?" he said triumphantly. "Nice job."

"Shut up," she muttered.

As Kari and Parker alternated throwing bags back, Everleigh kept her attention wholly on the board, doing her damnedest to ignore Ryker's presence. He made it difficult by loudly cheering every time Kari landed a bag on the board. When Parker sank his third bag in the hole, Everleigh cheered, almost obstinately. When Parker's fourth bag slid forcefully up the board and knocked Kari's bag to the ground while remaining on the board, Everleigh called over to him, "Nice!" Parker beamed in return.

"Good thing you have a partner who can carry you," Ryker teased.

"I'd say I have a great partner, you are correct," she confirmed. "What's the score?"

"Fourteen to sixteen."

"Who has sixteen?" she asked, a knowing hint in her voice.

"Your team."

"That's right."

Ryker watched her position herself one step ahead of where she'd thrown her last toss. The bag sailed through the air, landing on the corner of the hole, one end drooping in but balancing on the board.

"Darn it," she cursed under her breath.

"Still not a bad toss." Ryker sent his bag across the space, and it pushed Everleigh's bag into the hole, following in right after.

"Oh!" she said excitedly. "My first bag in the hole!"

"You're welcome," he said as he fought a smile.

"I mean, I know it cancels out, but still." She shrugged and moved into position to throw again. Just the slightest bit farther forward than the last time. This time her bag went right into the hole.

"Oh! Yay!" she cheered, throwing her arms up into the air.

"Nice! Do it again!" Parker yelled.

Ryker didn't fight his smile this time, and the distraction caused him to toss his bag clear over the board onto the ground behind.

Everleigh's next throw landed at the mouth of the hole but didn't go in. Ryker sent a bag that sailed over the top of hers and entered the hole, once again without touching the sides. Her next bag landed behind the first, pushing it incrementally forward, but not into the hole.

"Argh!" she growled.

Ryker set a lower arc to his last throw. His bag landed behind her two with enough momentum to push them both in to score, leaving his sitting at the mouth of the hole.

"Why thank you, sir," she drawled as she turned and gave him a smug look.

"That's five points for you."

"Which makes twenty-one!" Her mouth broke into a grin, and that dimple he coveted showed itself.

"Good game," he said with a sincere smile, holding out his hand. Her stare rested on it for a moment before she reached out and shook it. The electrical current that shot up his arm made his heart skip a beat, and he wanted to pull her by the hand into him, wanted to wrap his arms around her so badly his chest ached. He wondered if she could see it in his eyes, because she abruptly dropped his hand and moved away, stepping toward Parker as he came over to celebrate. Parker high fived Everleigh and wrapped her in the embrace Ryker wished he'd had. But if he wasn't mistaken, she stiffened in Parker's arms and pushed away after only a second or two.

"Nice game." Kari gave Everleigh high five too. "You really did well there at the end."

"Won the round for us!" Parker gushed.

Everleigh blushed, and her eyes darted over to Ryker. Was she going to acknowledge that his coaching helped her?

"Yeah, dumb luck."

Guess not.

"Who are we playing next?" Parker asked.

"Um, looks like Ryne and Tari are walking this way. Why don't you two take their spot with Kepler and Jackson." As Ryker watched Everleigh depart, he felt the weight of her disregard heavy on his soul.

"Let's win this one, right?" Kari said as she reached out to fist bump Ryker, pulling his attention back. "We've got this."

"We've got this!" he echoed. "Tari, you're going down!"

"Oh, you think so?" Ontario said archly as he took his position beside Ryker. "We won the last round by ten."

"Pshaw, pshaw." Ryker scoffed, then called out, "Start the domination, Kari!"

They played two more rounds of cornhole before taking a break to eat, and Ryker definitely did not dominate in either of those games. He found himself sneaking glances at Everleigh any time a cheer erupted from her. She had taken his pointers and she, in fact, was now dominating. Sticking bag after bag safely onto the board or even into the hole. He didn't care that she never gave him credit for his assistance.

Not in the slightest. He was just happy to see her so damn happy. Happy and laughing and gorgeous in her tight, black V-neck shirt with a gold, bejeweled Hawkeye logo across her chest. Today, she wore a white skort that made her tan legs stand out in contrast. Her hair was in two French braids reminiscent of their sunflower patch days, although rather than tie her white, patterned ribbon around her hair to keep it from escaping, she had several wavy, brown tendrils framing the sides of her face. *Not that she could have tied the white ribbon in her hair even if she'd wanted to,* he thought. She'd tied that ribbon to a sunflower stalk in the patch next to Crestin's purple visor on the last day of work before they'd left the field for the final time. And she probably thought that's where it had stayed.

Ryker and Kari managed to win the last game, thanks only to Kari's stellar performance. After he walked over to congratulate her, he turned to find Ontario looking at him with concern.

"What?" he chuckled as he went over to his friend. "You good, Tari?"

"*I'm* good," Tari responded. "The question is, are *you* good?"

Ryker pulled his head back in surprise. "Yeah. Why do you ask?"

"You seem . . . distracted, like your head's a million miles away."

The corner of his mouth lifted as he tried to reassure his friend. "Nah, man. I'm good."

But Tari continued to assess him. "I know there's a lot of drinking going on today," he said as he gestured around the crowd. "If you're lost in your head, you can talk to me, right? I'm here for you. Whatever you need. We gotta make sure to stay on the positive road you've been traveling. You've really come a long way, bro."

"Thanks, man," Ryker said, and he meant it. Tari was a big reason he'd made the strides he had. He'd been a constant cheerleader lately.

"Okay. I know you're going to meetings now, but you can still rely on me if you need anything. Anything at all."

"I appreciate you," Ryker said as he clapped a hand on his friend's back. Of course he'd told Ontario he'd started going to AA yesterday, as soon as he'd run into him after the meeting. He'd wanted to tell *someone*. To make it feel real. And to have someone to hold him accountable to going every week.

"All right. Shall we get some grub before the guys eat it all?"

Ryker nodded and followed Tari over to the food tables. He filled his plate with barbeque meatballs, party potatoes, mac and cheese, and smoked weenies. He skipped the vegetable tray but grabbed a bottle of water and started toward his chair. He stopped when he noticed Kari, Parker, and Everleigh sitting right beside it. He felt that familiar pull tugging him into her orbit and wanted nothing more than to obey her siren call and sit right beside her. But he thought better of it.

And then Parker placed a hand on Everleigh's knee, and Ryker changed his mind.

"Heard you're the reigning champs," Ryker congratulated them as he sat in his chair next to her. "Well done."

He glanced over just in time to see her unceremoniously lift Parker's hand from her leg, and he smiled on the inside. She kept her focus on the plate in her lap but said, "Thank you."

"Hey, I'm gonna hit the john. Need anything while I'm up?" Parker asked Everleigh as he stood. She shook her head in response.

Watching Parker leave, Ryker couldn't resist pointing out his role in their wins to her. "I think moving your stance up made all the difference."

She shrugged. "Maybe."

"Maybe," he choked out around a laugh.

She eyed him but said nothing.

"Okay." He lifted his hands in surrender. "If that's how you want to play it."

"Are you forever going to take credit for everything I accomplish in life?" she asked in exasperation.

"If I give you advice, and you take it, and it causes an improvement, then yes. It's called coaching." Even he heard the smile in his voice.

"Okay, Coach. Whatever."

"But all credit goes to you for taking my advice and leveling up your skills. That was all you."

"Oh, you don't want to take credit for my abilities as well? Shocking."

He chuckled under his breath. She crumpled her napkin and tossed it onto her plate before turning in her seat and settling her dark-ringed hazel stare on him. And his heart skipped a beat just as the smirk pulled higher on his cheeks. Their gazes locked, the tilt of her chin seeming to dare him to look away first. Of course, he wouldn't do that.

She was the one to finally break, facing her head forward and muttering, "Still so infuriating."

And he couldn't help but chuckle again. God, it felt good to get under her skin. Reminded him of old times. Back when he was hoping to somehow gain her affection while still trying to bar her from his thoughts. And once he had gained her affection, how wonderful it had—

"I can't do this," Everleigh said, abruptly facing him.

His smile dropped, his brow furrowing in worry. Had he offended her that quickly? He was only playing.

"Ryker, I'm sorry. I don't want to be mean."

Oh, *she* was apologizing to *him*? He opened his mouth to protest, to tell her he was the one sorry for goading her, but she spoke again before he could.

"Listen. Clearly, we're going to be seeing more of each other than probably either of us anticipated. And I don't want to have animosity hanging between us. It's not worth the stress. So can we be friends? Like, really friends?"

He blinked as he processed her words. He wanted to tell her he wanted to be more than friends. Wanted to say how stupid he'd been for treating her the way he had. But even as she said those words, he could hear the underlying hesitation in her voice. He could see the distance between them in her body language, the set of her shoulders as she leaned away from him, the way her arms folded over her chest.

While Ryker remained committed to his vow to take the necessary steps to gain full control over his mental health before trying to renew a relationship with Everleigh, the itch to start building that bridge between them gnawed at his mind relentlessly. It had since he'd first seen her two days ago. Even as he'd sat through his first AA meeting yesterday morning, his thoughts kept returning to the day he could tell her all he had accomplished to become the man she needed him to be. That day wouldn't be today. She was still closed off to him; it was too early for him to show his hand.

He nodded and forced the word across his lips. "Friends."

Parker returned then, sank into his chair, and leaned forward, placing a hand on Everleigh's arm as he said, "Ready to head into the stadium and watch Iowa crush Iowa State?"

And Ryker was annoyed. As he stared hard at Parker's fingers touching her soft, tan skin, his insides burned, an argument against the lie he'd just told.

He could never be "friends" with Everleigh again.

# Everleigh's Famous Chocolate-chocolate Cookies

The recipe for the cookies Ryker Martin lost his mind over is as follows:

3/4 cup granulated sugar

3/4 cup packed light brown sugar

1 cup stick unsalted butter, softened

1 large egg

1 teaspoon vanilla extract

2 1/4 cups all-purpose flour

1 teaspoon baking soda

1/4 teaspoon salt

1 cup milk chocolate chips

1 cup semisweet chocolate chunks

Heat oven to 375°F. Mix sugars, butter, egg, and vanilla extract in a large bowl. Stir in flour, baking soda, and salt until dough is stiff. Stir in chocolate chips and chocolate chunks. Drop dough by rounded tablespoonfuls 2-3 inches apart on a cookie sheet lined with parchment paper or a baking stone. Bake 8-10 minutes or until light brown (center will be soft). Allow to cool slightly before removing from cookie sheet and fully cooling on a wire rack. Store in an airtight container. (Do NOT let Ryker anywhere near these delicious treats, or unfair cookie abuse may result!)

# Acknowledgements

The fact that I'm publishing a second book – in as many years – I can't fathom it! Thank you to everyone who has supported me on this journey to realize my dreams. My family: from my husband and kids and immediate family to my extended family to my friends that are my family. All of you have made this journey so much sweeter!

I owe a great debt to my faithful Beta Readers who read this story in its early stages and provided such valuable feedback – Dulcie, Cass, Cailie, Amy, Kippen. And my mom (yes – my mom read it. I warned her in advance of all the spice. She swore she could handle it. I marked the pages of the manuscript with color coded tabs so she knew the places to skip over if she felt they were too spicy. I'm still waiting for the day the bill shows up for her therapy.). If you liked the Big Green Tractor chapter, you can thank Amy for that one. She told me she wanted more sunflower patch and more spice. I hope I delivered on both counts.

Thank you to everyone who agreed to ARC read for me as well. You will never know how grateful I am for your time and trust in my story!

Once again, this book would not be nearly as well presented had it not been for my amazing editor, Sarah Purdy, at The Write Place. Such a wonderful and reliable working partner!

And once again, a huge thank you goes out to you, my Dear Reader. For going on yet another journey with me. I hope to see you *After the Sunflower Experience*. I know you won't be disappointed in the outcome!